Memo

From: Marsha

To: Shayla

The first episode is in the can! Will do final edit after last episode, of course, but this is probably pretty close to what the final cut will look like. Good intro of contestants, and Camilla looks good. It looks like this show might actually work! Thanks for all your hard work. I hope seeing the finished product changes your mind about doing a reality show. It's going to be fun! I promise!

Love,
Marsha

THE GIRL NEXT DOOR

THE GIRL
NEXT DOOR

Roberta Gayle

Gayle

THE GIRL NEXT DOOR

An Arabesque novel

ISBN 1-58314-602-4

www.kimanipress.com

Printed in U.S.A.

Chapter 1

For a change, everything seemed to be going smoothly. As the assistant producer on the new reality show *Lady's Choice,* Shayla was responsible for hundreds of the details that went into the creation of the show she was currently viewing on videotape. She watched the drama unfold on the television screen in front of her with a critical eye, but there was nothing wrong with the opening montage of the premier episode of the matchmaking program that she had affectionately dubbed *Stud Muffins.* Shayla thought the show's title, *Lady's Choice,* lacked something. It was so obvious. She supposed that lack of subtlety was precisely what had caused the executives at AAT to buy it. But since the show had gone into production, she had continued to suggest alternative titles for it, all of which were rejected as quickly as *Stud Muffins* had been. She supposed she could understand why her bosses hadn't liked *He's Gotta Have It,* given its postfeminist connotations, and

Swains might not have the necessary zing to pull in younger viewers, but she really thought they should have given *Super-sexy Studs* or *The Dreamy Dozen* a try with the test audience.

The cameos and photos that made up the opening montage disappeared from the TV screen, and the star of the show, Camilla Lyons, was introduced by the host to the television-viewing audience. That audience consisted of Shayla and her sister, Deanna, who were watching the final cut of the first episode on videotape. As the beefcake parade began, Deanna leaned forward slightly on the couch to watch the show's host introduce the twelve men whom Shayla's bosses at GoGo Girls Productions cast as candidates to try to seduce a soap opera star on national television. Two-thousand-odd men had submitted videotapes in the hope they would be chosen. And Shayla was hoping that women all over the country were as entranced by the contestants as her sister seemed to be. She noticed that Dee seemed particularly fixated on bachelor number five, Charlie Thompson. The computer salesman, Shayla had to admit, was the most gorgeous man in the world.

"You and I both know she won't choose him," Deanna said, referring to number five. "Camilla couldn't stand being with a man who's prettier than she is."

Shayla glanced at her older sister and repressed the urge to say, "You should know." She planned to make it through this one evening without bickering, even if she had to bite off her tongue. "Uh-huh," she mumbled. She was not going to ruin this unexpected visit by defending Camilla from her sister's catty remarks.

Dee had appeared on her doorstep the night before, without warning. So far they were getting along better than they had in years. In fact, Shayla didn't remember feeling this close to her famous sister since Deanna's teen pop star career had taken off when she was a freshman in high school. Shayla had no idea why Dee had shown up at her door all of a sudden. Before she appeared on the cover of *Teen Magazine,* the sisters had been the best of friends—or at least that was what Shayla had always thought. The three-year difference in their ages had only served to make her feel grateful that Dee included her in her circle of older, cooler, sophisticated friends. Back then, she enjoyed being around her sister, even if her role was to fetch snacks from the kitchen or to stand watch outside the bathroom while the older girls experimented with her mother's make-up. At thirteen, Shayla had worshipped her big sister and was grateful for every bit of attention Dee deigned to bestow upon her.

As Deanna's fame grew, Shayla found herself one of a crowd of equally devoted admirers, and she began to wonder if Big Sister might have been taking advantage of her adulation. Perhaps it was seeing how Dee treated her new followers, or maybe it was plain old sibling rivalry, but once it occurred to her that her idol might not be the paragon of kindness and generosity she had once thought, she couldn't seem to shake the idea. The threads of doubt grew quickly until all she could see were her golden, gorgeous sister's imperfections.

They slowly drifted apart as Deanna's singing career took off. She moved to New York at eighteen, and the sisters' very different lifestyles kept them from spending much time together after that. Deanna was ambitious and worked hard, and Shayla was too busy with high school and then college to try and repair the relationship with her sister. By the time she realized she might have lost something of value, they were living in two completely different worlds, and Shay didn't know how to bridge the gap between them. She was determined, now, almost ten years later, to make the most of this opportunity, to spend some time alone together getting to know each other again.

Deanna seemed to have the same idea. The cell phone, which was usually glued to her ear when she came home for her fleeting holiday visits, had been turned off since she'd arrived. Shay didn't think she'd even checked her messages. Dee said she needed a rest after a manic few months. It appeared that the little two-bedroom house in Baltimore that Shayla had bought a couple of years before was the perfect hideout. The night before, they had ordered Thai food and had talked until one in the morning. Dee said she hadn't felt so relaxed in months.

They reminisced about the good times they had together growing up in Detroit, Michigan. They shared their amazement at the recent changes in their formerly staid, predictable parents' lives. Dad was working more hours now as a security consultant than he had before he retired from the police force. Mom had lost forty pounds and lived in the pool at the YWCA these days. She taught CPR and ran the youth health program, which, since she'd been a nurse for over thirty years, would not have been surprising except that she always said she hated her teaching duties at the hospital. She insisted she just didn't have the temperament to teach. When Shayla finally went to bed that night, she was surrounded by a pleasant haze that was equal parts nostalgia for the past and hope for the future.

When she woke up on Saturday morning to the smell of coffee brewing, she felt a sense of deep satisfaction as she thought of the weekend ahead. Dee fell in happily with the plans she proposed for the day, and that afternoon and evening, the easy camaraderie that began on Friday night continued. She took her sister on a tour of her favorite spots in D.C. Shay had gotten to know the city well when she attended Howard University, and after she earned her degree in communications, she decided to stay in Washington. Five years later, she felt like a native. She took Dee to a couple of the tourist sites, such as the African American Museum, and to some less touristy spots, such as the Skipper's Pier overlooking Chesapeake Bay.

Over the famous Maryland crab cakes at Skipper's, Dee told Shay about the rigors of being an actress, and Shay educated Dee about the pleasures and pitfalls of producing a reality TV show. Deanna had actually seemed excited when Shayla offered to show her the videotape of the premier episode. Now, sitting on the couch twenty-four hours after her sister's arrival, Shay was torn between her desire to boast about the work she'd done and her urge to defend it.

Shayla didn't know that her sister and Camilla Lyons were rivals until she had mentioned that Camilla was starring on her show. "That bitch," Dee said, shaking her head in disapproval. To Shay's relief, she didn't say anything more about it. Shayla didn't want to know what kind of bad blood there was between the two women. No matter what Dee had against Cami, Shayla knew there was no way she could defend the soap opera star without seeming to take sides against her own flesh and blood. She told Dee that she had nothing to do with the casting for the program, neatly sidestepping the issue of whether or not she agreed with Dee's opinion of the actress. She didn't bother to mention that she had actually forged a decent working relationship with the show's petulant star, probably, in part, because she credited her success to growing up in a house with a budding celebrity in the next bedroom.

Shayla spoke Cami's language. She knew what was important to her, and she understood how difficult it was to be a successful entertainer. Most people thought celebrities lived untroubled lives. But Shayla had spent her formative years listening to her sister whine about how celebs were people, too, and how they had the same problems that everyone else had; so the actress's complaints, for the most part, were familiar to her. She understood the catch-22 that a successful artist was caught in—working hard at their craft, trying to build a fan base, and being dependent on those same fans for their continued success, but at the mercy of those who exploited them and their work. More important, she knew exactly how to make Cami feel as if she wasn't alone.

Since Cami's vain, self-indulgent behavior didn't bother Shayla the way it did others on the set, she tried to smooth things over with her coworkers as best she could. Acting as the soap star's buffer on the show wasn't difficult for her, and it won her the undying gratitude of the director and the crew, who found it insulting to be treated like servants when they were professionals who actually spent their days trying to make Camilla Lyons look and sound like the most desirable woman in America. The relationship between Shayla and the leading lady did not go unnoticed by the powerful figures who ran the production, either, and they left the star's care and management in her hands. She didn't dare mention her budding friendship with Cami Lyons to her sister, though. Nor did she plan to mention to Camilla that Deanna Jones was her sister, now that she knew there was something between them.

Deanna leaned forward again, peering more intently at the screen. "Who's he?" she asked, whistling between her teeth in appreciation of contestant number three. Shay glanced at the television and almost groaned out loud. Of course, the contestant Deanna found so interesting was Michael Grant, the most irritating guy on the set. He asked who everyone was and what their jobs were. And while he was good at getting answers by making friends with the technicians and the staff, she found it odd, and a little disconcerting, to see how quickly people were taken in by him. They saw him as their ally, but in her opinion, he didn't have any authority to do anything for them. He was just one of twelve bachelors, supposedly looking for a wife—he was not on the production staff. She didn't know why he seemed to generate such trust.

Dee watched, rapt, as he introduced himself to Camilla. Shayla listened, again, as he deviated from the lines they'd rehearsed over and over. It still irked her that he'd refused at the taping to say the lines as they had been scripted. She had to admit, seeing the finished product, that his intro seemed more natural and genuine than most of the other men. He was handsome, of course, just as all of the other contestants were, but he wasn't drop-dead gorgeous like Charlie Thompson, or buff, bold, and brash like Jordan Freeman, the professional athlete. There was just something about him that seemed to appeal to a wide range of women. His square, strong jaw and deep coffee-colored eyes were his best features, but it was his self-assurance and quiet, masculine presence that seemed to command attention and respect.

Michael wore his usual half-smile, the one that said he didn't give a damn about this contest, the television cameras, or what the audience thought of him. He didn't actually smirk but, to her, his attitude was plain to see. For some reason, his arrogance didn't seem to annoy anyone except her. In fact, her bosses—Lita and Marsha, the show's producers—acted like teenagers around him. They treated all the other contestants either like male strippers or like bratty little boys. But when they spoke of, or to, Michael, their behavior reminded Shayla of high school freshmen fluttering around a handsome senior—even though Lita must have been at least twenty years older than Michael, and Marsha was almost a decade older than Lita. They shared coy, secret little smiles whenever he was anywhere in the vicinity.

It was bad enough that the two women Shayla respected most seemed to find this man so irresistible, it was even worse that Cami, too, was drawn to his questionable charm. Shayla didn't share their fascination. She had never been interested in that type. She preferred men like Lance, the veterinarian, who was sweet and idealistic and didn't have a dishonest bone in his body. Or even Luther, the youngest bachelor, who—despite his boyish exuberance—was obviously in way over his head competing with this group of well-established, self-assured, confident men.

Lita and Marsha had chosen an eclectic group for Camilla Lyons to choose from, and Michael was the only one who had the nerve to pretend he didn't care whether or not he won the competition. Even the arrogant restaurateur, Claude Foster, and the insufferable investment banker, James Hardy, were not conceited enough to play hard-to-get with the unattainable beauty whose affection they were all competing to win. There was no point in Michael pretending he wasn't thrilled to be in Camilla's presence. Why else would he have submitted his application?

"Michael Grant and Jordan Freeman are definitely the two most interesting specimens so far," Deanna proclaimed as the credits filled the screen at the end of episode one. Jordan didn't lack for ego, either, Shayla realized, wondering if that was part of the attraction for her sister.

"The troublemaker and the jock, that figures," she muttered under her breath, quickly jumping up and heading into the kitchen for more snacks when Deanna asked, "What?"

"More baby carrots?" she yelled over the counter that separated the kitchen from the living room where Deanna sat.

"Have you got any of those low-fat chips?" Dee asked.

"Sorry, no," Shayla answered, looking in the refrigerator for a snack that would satisfy both her and her sister. There wasn't much to choose from. Her schedule had been so hectic lately that she had been grabbing quick dinners on her way home from work. She didn't even have the makings for a salad in her crisper. "All I've got is leftover takeout," she called out.

Deanna came around the island and stood beside her, looking into the refrigerator at the pathetic collection of plastic takeout dishes and white cardboard containers that occupied Shayla's refrigerator. "That looks good," she said, pointing at a transparent container. "What is it, lasagna?"

"Yeah." Shayla picked up the dish and gestured toward the microwave. "It's only a couple of days old, so it's still good. Want me to heat it up for you?"

Deanna visibly wavered, but then shook her head. "Have you got any capellini? I can make my famous low-fat pasta primavera."

"At least you're not one of those no–carb people," Shayla replied, shaking her head as she brought out the package of pasta noodles.

A drop of olive oil, some thin-sliced baby carrots, and a sprinkle of garlic powder later, Deanna served up two dishes of angel-hair pasta.

"Not bad," Shayla complimented her after taking a bite.

"Thanks. I'm not very domestic, but there's not a lot you can do to ruin spaghetti."

"I know," Shayla agreed. "That's my staple dish." *There!* she thought. *That's one thing we have in common, anyway.* It was not, however, a great conversation starter. She cast about for another topic and finally came up with, "Have you talked to Mom and Dad?"

"I called them a couple of weeks ago," Deanna answered. "They sounded good. As usual."

"They're great," Shayla said in assent. That pretty much exhausted that topic.

They had talked for hours on Friday night and throughout the day today, and it had been fun. She didn't know where this sudden strained silence came from. Had they really run out of things to say to each other already? Was their past all they could discuss? Or was she just so unused to spending time with her sister that she had actually forgotten how to do it?

Shayla ducked her head as she shoveled another bite into her mouth; then she watched Deanna neatly twirl a few strands of the thin pasta around her fork and then daintily carry it to her ruby-red lips. She had forgotten how utterly feminine her sister was and how butch she always felt around her in comparison. Shay was four inches taller than her sister and was a size ten to Deanna's petite size four. But it wasn't just the difference in their bulk that made Shay feel so oversized and awkward around her dainty sister. Shay barely found time to put mascara on her long eyelashes or to highlight her dark orbs with any shadow, whereas Dee's eyebrows were always perfectly plucked in a delicate arch above her almond-shaped eyes and long, black-tipped lashes. Dee had a thin, delicate nose, of the type her grandmother's generation called a "good" nose, and a perfect oval face. Although they had almost the exact same golden café au lait skin, Dee's bronzer made her cheeks glow, and the high cheekbones that they shared looked exotic on her and seemed severe on Shay.

When Dee had shown up at her doorway, Shayla was surprised, taken aback even, but she hadn't realized until this moment—as her mind skipped back in time to the days when she'd always felt so overshadowed by her famous older sister—how completely she had lost touch with her. She didn't have a clue what interested Dee beyond the music world. Shay wondered if Dee, too, felt like she had nothing left to say, now that they had brought each other up-to-date on their respective lives. "So…" she said tentatively, wondering if it would be lame to ask her own sister if she'd read any good books lately.

"So how do you like working with Camilla?" Dee asked. The question was voiced in a light enough tone, but her wry half-smile told Shayla it was a question with only one right answer.

Shayla couldn't give it. If she told Deanna that she found Camilla a challenge to work with, as her sister clearly anticipated, she'd only be telling half the truth. The whole truth was that she did derive some satisfaction from working with the woman. Partly because she was good at it, and partly because Cami was not without charm. Shay couldn't say she really liked the actress, though. Camilla Lyons was a vain, petty, self-involved woman. She was not someone Shay would have befriended if work hadn't made the move an expedient one. She considered trying to explain her feelings to her sister, but Shay knew Dee wasn't interested in hearing the real response to her question. In fact, Shay was certain that if she told the truth, it would make Dee defensive.

Honesty was out of the question here. But Shayla couldn't bear to lie, either. She was good at her job, and even to protect her big sister's feelings, she couldn't completely sacrifice her pride. "At least there's only one of her," she answered finally. "The guys are a real handful. Twelve different men, all with sizable egos, make for a lot of baby-sitting."

There. Deanna could infer whatever she wanted about the

competition, and Shay had not had to lie. The men truly were making her job difficult. As assistant producer, Shay had to try and keep the entire cast happy, not just the show's temperamental star. It was no small task. The boys, as she and most of the crew called them, were an energetic lot. "Speaking of men…" Dee's open-ended question hung in the air, too vague to be taken as any kind of personal attack on Shay, and yet it hit a nerve.

"I wasn't." She tried to keep the annoyance out of her voice. "I was talking about work," Shay retorted.

"You know what they say about all work and no play," she said, shrugging.

"Dee, it's my job. It's not *all* I do."

"So what about outside of the job? Met any interesting men lately?" her sister asked.

Outside work, Shay didn't have the time or the energy to think about men, let alone try to hook up with one. "Nah," she said, offhand. "What about you?" she asked, expecting the usual litany.

Being a famous pop star, Dee usually had a string of men trailing after her, including rich men who expected her to roll over and beg for their attention and sharks from the music industry who treated the talent, especially women who looked like Dee, like so many pieces of meat and then dangled lucrative contracts in front of them as if the women were no more than high-priced whores. To her surprise, however, Dee was silent. It was the first time in Shay's memory that Dee hadn't had a lengthy and amusing response to the question.

"No," she finally answered. "Not really."

"No?" Shay said in disbelief. "No men at all?"

"Ever since Leon and I broke up last year, I just haven't felt like getting back into the dating thing." Leon had been

Dee's not-really-husband-material boyfriend for the last three or four years; he had even been invited to their parents' for Christmas a couple of years before. Shay had never thought of them as a real couple. He reminded Shay of Dee's best friend from high school, Al, who borrowed her older sister's make-up more often than Shay did and who liked to shop for designer clothes with the girls. These days he was a small-time designer with a shop in San Francisco. Deanna occasionally wore his clothes to social events to get him some exposure. Leon wasn't all that much like Al, really. He was straight, for one thing, and not at all effeminate. He didn't share Dee or Al's interest in high fashion, either. He was a professional photographer who agreed to shoot some celebrities every once in a while when Dee got on his case or when he wanted to make a quick buck to subsidize his more artistic work.

The reason, she supposed, that she equated Leon with Al was because both men were the only two who had ever treated her sister as if she was a regular woman rather than some unattainable goddess. They both talked to her and teased her and genuinely seemed to like her—flaws and all—and neither one let her get away with any of her don't-hate-me-because-I'm-a-famous-rock-star crap.

Shayla knew there had been some kind of argument the previous year when Dee refused to appear at some charity event Leon had promised she'd attend, but she had assumed that would have blown over by now. Shayla couldn't think of any response to the news of their breakup. She never realized they'd really been together. "Leon, huh?" she said, trying to adjust to this new view of their relationship.

"I don't know. Maybe I'm just burned-out," Dee offered.

Shay's jaw dropped. "Burned-out? You?" she echoed stupidly. "That's impossible." When it came to dating, Dee was a champion. She never lacked for an escort, partly because of her exotic beauty, but largely because she had no qualms at all about asking men out. Though she said it happened, Shayla had yet to see anyone refuse her. Dee would approach anyone: tall, short, handsome, rich, whatever. No matter what a man did for a living, or how successfully he did it, Dee did not perceive herself—ever!—as lacking the necessary qualities to intrigue or entice him. The few rejections she said she'd received had never fazed her or given her a moment's pause. She saw herself as a woman any man should be honored to go out with—whether he was a scholar, a mogul, or a male model. Shayla wished she had a tenth of her sister's self-confidence with men. How could she be burned-out? It was all so effortless for her.

"Mechanical failure might be a better way to put it," Dee elaborated. "My heart needs a little recharging."

"Wow!" Shay shook her head wonderingly. "I never thought of you as—"

"As what?" Dee asked, stiffening.

"As needing anything when it came to guys. You've always been so on top of all that."

"Yeah," she responded, relaxing, "I guess that's what everyone thinks about me. But I get tired of being the woman they want me to be. You know, always having to be careful that I look like I'm a pop star. That's why I miss Leon, I guess. I never had to worry about what I did or said in front of him. He didn't care about any of that surface stuff."

For a moment, Shay felt as if she was seeing her sister in a new light. She hadn't thought they had anything in common other than their parentage, but Dee suddenly reminded her of her other girlfriends: normal, down-to-earth, working women, who spent most of their time trying to figure out who they were and what their bosses wanted and whether they should get married and have kids. "Have you talked to him?" she asked, wondering if Leon knew how her sister felt.

"That ass? No way. He flaked on me for no good reason. I wouldn't talk to him if he begged me on his hands and knees."

"Oh." So much for missing him, she guessed. "Has he called?"

"No idea." Dee shrugged. "I changed my cell phone number."

"Oh," Shay said again. "Well, that's good then, I guess."

"Yup," her big sister said. "Good riddance."

Memo

FROM THE DESK OF LITA TOLLIVER

TO: Marsha James, Shayla Tennison

Lost my ID again, so I left the office door unlocked.

   If you go into the office over the weekend, don't lock it, okay? I'll get a new pass on Monday afternoon.

Lita

Chapter 2

He made no sound, and in the low light, Michael didn't even cast a shadow. Clad in unrelieved black, he crept down the carpeted passageway, hugging the wall. When he reached the correct door, he automatically tried the doorknob with one hand while he reached into his pocket for his lock-picking tools with the other. He didn't expect the knob to turn or the door to open and silently beckon him into the dark office beyond. "Unlocked, of course," he muttered scornfully under his breath, though he probably could have shouted it. The security in this place was a joke. "Why'd I ever think they might actually lock the doors?" he asked himself, shaking his head. Of course, if they had a decent system in place, he never would have been hired. The thought didn't stop him from letting out a quiet huff of annoyance at the fact that he'd been able to get into the building completely undetected.

Michael entered the darkened room slowly, directing the

thin beam of his flashlight down at the floor in front of him. He was more worried about bumping into something than about alerting the guards on duty to his presence. It had been a snap to get into the studio, just as it had been a simple task to sneak out of the hotel—despite all the cameras that were focused on him and the other contestants day and night. All he had had to do was pretend he was going with the others to the hotel's hot tub and then duck out of the changing room through the service exit. The camera crew wasn't responsible for knowing who was where. No one would count heads. If anyone even noticed he wasn't there, they'd assume he was back in his room—where they relied on a small motion sensor to turn on the automated camera, rather than keeping any kind of record. He had warned the producers that they were relying too heavily on the honor system to control the contestants' movements, but they had downplayed his concerns.

In this case, he supposed he should be glad that they hadn't listened to him, since he couldn't have made this little midnight foray to their studio offices if they had, but he couldn't help but find it annoying that they wouldn't heed the advice that they paid him for.

The room he was in was small, obviously a working space. In the darkness, he couldn't see the posters and pictures that adorned the walls, but he'd seen the decor before—a lower-level studio exec's version of a suitable atmosphere for her position as assistant producer with a small television production company. Shayla Tennison, the woman who occupied this office, was extremely self-conscious about her professional image. She was probably a nice, down-to-earth girl outside of work, but she was very much aware of the impression she created in the office, and she spent a good bit of energy on projecting a dignified, knowledgeable image. Someone,

somewhere, had made her very self-conscious about her
behavior. It was his job to read people, and it hadn't been hard
to peg her. He'd bet a week's paycheck that she was naturally
inclined to be friendly, warm, a little self-deprecating perhaps.
She was fighting it. In his experience, people who worked that
hard to appear a certain way—in Shayla's case, cool, calm,
and in control—were usually convinced that those were the
qualities they most lacked.

He didn't have time at the moment, though, to search the
office for clues to Ms. Tennison's psyche. It was her desk that
he was interested in on this visit. It was one of those large, in-
elegant slabs with a functional black veneer, probably from
Staples or Office Depot. The young assistant producer had left
papers, books, file folders, and video cassettes piled high on
her desktop, but his goal was the computer that took up about
half of the desk's expanse. He would leave the papers and the
file cabinets lined up against the wall for later—after he'd
accessed the computer files. He was pretty sure that the documents he was looking for would be contained in the computer's hard drive.

Michael set to work quickly and efficiently. GoGo Girls
Productions's logo came up on the computer as soon as he
touched the mouse. Shayla hadn't even taken the simple precaution of turning her computer off when she left for the
night; it had just been in sleep mode, waiting for him to come
and retrieve the files. Now he was sure it wouldn't take him
long to find the documents he needed. The people he was after
were not criminal masterminds: He doubted they had even
bothered to try and cover their tracks. These women were
amateurs, trying to play in the big leagues, and tonight he
planned to get the evidence he needed to prove it.

He read through the files on the computer: text documents,

e-mails; he even checked the bookkeeping functions for internal memoranda, but Michael didn't find what he was looking for. There was one moment when he found a more heavily guarded file that required a password to open; he grew hopeful, but it turned out to be a glitch. When he accessed "Current Projects," he found it contained only Web links to sites such as Victoria's Secret and *Modern Photography* magazine. Apparently, Shayla Tennison did her shopping on-line. Another dead end. Michael moved on. He was certain that, if he was right, the files he needed would have been generated right here, if not at this terminal, then at one of the others connected to the small company's internal network.

When the owners of GoGo Girls had hired his firm to handle security for their latest production, it had seemed like a pretty straightforward job: a few background checks, a little surveillance, nothing out of the ordinary. They had received some threatening messages about the star of their show. Typically, they were from some freak professing his undying love for Camilla Lyons and promising that he would like to meet with her in the near future.

Michael and his partner, Darren, had disagreed with their clients about using a plant inside the production company. Ultimately, they were persuaded and installed one of their men at GoGo as a computer consultant. Their guy, Josh, sniffed around for a couple of days as requested, but he found nothing suspicious on the premises.

Michael had been ready to report to the women producing *Lady's Choice* that they had nothing to worry about when Josh was suddenly put out of commission by a car accident. Even then, neither Michael nor Darren were particularly concerned. Accidents happened. It was only when they spoke to Josh in the hospital after his surgery and he told them that the car that hit him seemed to be deliberately trying to run him down that they started to wonder whether his assignment at GoGo Girls had anything to do with the collision. It didn't seem very likely, but since they couldn't rule it out, Michael allowed himself to be cast as bachelor number three on the reality show. Taping was about to begin, and it was the only cover that would allow him access to everyone involved with the television show.

Darren would have been happy to take the assignment, but he'd been stuck in a wheelchair since the Gulf War. Michael's suggestion that a paraplegic war hero would be a unique entry in a matchmaking show was not given serious consideration by the program's producers. It was a shame, since Darren probably would have gotten a kick out of the whole thing. Michael, on the other hand, planned to get himself eliminated as soon as possible. Investigating an organization from the inside was nothing new—but Michael had never felt as uncomfortable doing undercover work in his life before. Being a contestant on a reality show was even more humiliating than he had anticipated.

He probably would have quit if it hadn't been for the two letters that had arrived after he agreed to the job. He couldn't turn his back on the clients when they were still receiving threats that forced the show's producers to hire 24/7 Security in the first place. Darren hadn't been able to trace either the letters or the telephone calls. The letters had no distinguishing characteristics and were printed on a popular brand of inkjet paper. The recordings of the phone calls contained a muffled male voice with no background noise to identify or even place him. Once on the show, Michael had begun to think that the whole thing was a setup, some kind of publicity stunt by someone working at GoGo Girls. He'd gotten a sense of the kind of commitment felt by those who were involved in this strange business, and he could envision most, if not all, of these people happily agreeing to do just about anything in order to make their television program a success.

No matter how hard he tried to relate to these folks, he just couldn't understand why anyone would choose to make their living making a television show. In his line of work, the stakes were life and death. He protected people. Making *Lady's Choice* seemed like a big waste of time. The reality show did not serve a single useful purpose. His partner, Darren, said it entertained people and that was enough of a reason for doing it, but Michael couldn't help feeling that it was all a huge waste of time and money. Talented, intelligent people spent incredibly long hours on an endeavor that was ultimately pointless. In his opinion, reality TV pandered to the worst aspects of human nature. However, he had found that the producers, their staff, and the crew, especially Camilla and his fellow bachelors, were all desperate to make the show a success. And success, for all of them, was measured strictly by the numbers. All of them spent an inordinate amount of energy worrying about how many viewers would tune into the program once a week and watch the people on-screen embarrass themselves. Michael just didn't get it. He did, however, get that this ridiculous ambition was shared by every single person with a stake in this production, which made them all suspects. They were all candidates for the role of the stalker whom he had been employed to identify and expose.

After two weeks playing the role of a desperate bachelor, he was no closer to finding out who the culprit was. If someone on the inside was the psycho sending those threats, then he—or she—was a very good actor. On the other hand, if someone on the inside was running a scam, then everything fit. That was why he was here, prowling around Shayla's office at two in the morning, trying to find proof of his theory.

There was only one problem with his hypothesis, one question that continued to nag at him: Why had someone tried to hurt, or kill, Joshua Davis? That didn't fit his theory of an inside job.

On the other hand, if there was a nutcase currently stalking the star of the show, how had he or she known that Josh was a plant? No one except the show's two producers even knew that they'd hired a security consultant. It wasn't as if Josh had discovered anything during his investigation, so it was hard to imagine that a stalker would have felt threatened by him. It was a paradox. If he'd been run down because of his assignment on this show, then someone had to know who he really was; but if someone connected to the program was just trying to create a stalker as a publicity stunt, then they wouldn't have wanted to injure Josh, even if they did figure out who he was.

Michael was almost convinced that the ambush was just a coincidence. Neither he nor Darren were willing to proceed according to that assumption, however. They had never failed a client—never even came up short, according to the glowing references they'd received—and they weren't about to start now. They wouldn't close this case until they found out who these threats were coming from and whether that person was responsible for Josh's broken leg. Michael could find nothing on the computer, so he moved on to Shayla's paper files. He wasn't ready to concede yet. If he could find something, anything, that proved that this whole stalker story was a publicity stunt, he could leave the show without any twinges of conscience. That was enough to keep him searching all night. Even if he was starting to think his theory might just be wishful thinking. He opened the file cabinet with a sigh.

This assignment had seemed so simple at the start. The beauty queen star of the show had received a few scary fan letters and a couple of calls, and the producers wanted to be sure she was protected, at least as long as she was working for them. They felt responsible, they claimed, for the unwelcome attention Camilla Lyons was suddenly being subjected to. They had, after all, been the ones to cast her as the star actress who could not find a mate. It hadn't been Camilla's idea to dangle herself in front of her male fans like some tasty tidbit. Marsha James and Lita Tolliver were the ones who had come up with the plan. It had been their idea to encourage ordinary guys to think that a celebrity might fall in love with one of them—including the psycho who was threatening her.

Michael had to agree that this situation wasn't really of the soap actress's making. Camilla wasn't one of those unattainable beauties who regretted that her career had put her out of reach of most men she met. She liked it. It had only been the allure of her starring on her own television show that induced her to take the role. She thought it would boost her acting career. If she was in danger because of the role, the producers were indeed responsible, just as they said. Marsha and Lita cast their net wide when they'd gone searching for the heroine of their fairy tale, and they had been thrilled when they caught Camilla. She was perfect for the part. They didn't have to worry about her getting her heart broken. The actress was a perfectly charming woman, but she was tough as nails. She could handle the pressure that was inherent in being the object of twelve men's focused efforts to win her. In fact, she took it in stride, since she had always been sought after. Throughout her adult life, she had been the object of men's fantasies. She and this television role were a perfect fit.

Michael, on the other hand, was accustomed to keeping a

low profile. In his line of work, the object was usually *not* to draw attention to himself—24/7 Security guarded the celebs; they didn't party with them. When it came to the lives of the rich and powerful, Michael was content working in the background. He felt more comfortable here, creeping around in this dark disorganized office, than he had felt since this assignment began. Shayla Tennison's workspace might be a chaotic mess, but at least he felt like he knew where he was and what he was doing. His search had a purpose, a clearly defined goal. He wasn't making a fool of himself in front of the television crew or trying to remember to stay in character in front of the hidden cameras. He was an investigator, looking for the answer to a mystery.

Michael had been surprised when he first came into this room, because Shayla had been so cool and professional, so careful to appear on top of everything in the studio. He supposed he had just assumed her office would reflect that side of her personality. It didn't. It hinted at something uncontrolled, even rebellious, beneath that calm, collected exterior. He had already figured out that her uptight, superefficient personality was a cover, but he hadn't expected her other side to be so…messy. It was then that it struck him that the production company itself might be making the threats against the star of their show. They had a good motive. Something like this, if it leaked to the media, would definitely make it into the news—free publicity. It might only get a brief mention in the *Washington Post*, but the tabloids would love the story.

And even if the news never leaked out or was announced, there would always be rumors. He knew. He had already heard some rumblings. Michael didn't want to believe Shayla was mixed up in something that shady, but she was exceedingly loyal to her bosses. If those two piranhas asked her for her help, he couldn't see her refusing them. She might even be helping them without knowing it. She was smart, but she was also blind when it came to her bosses. She clearly admired them, and he'd seen that they completely took advantage of it, while Shayla didn't seem to notice at all.

Whatever Shayla's part was in the scheme, Michael was determined to get to the bottom of it. He hoped she wasn't too involved, but he would have no sympathy for her if it turned out that she was. She was a big girl.

If the two women who had hired him were trying to pull some kind of publicity stunt and were using him and his company to do it, neither his sympathy for Shayla, nor for anyone else caught up in the hoax, would prevent him from exposing all of them. Michael spent the next three hours going through every file, on paper and in the computer, before he finally admitted defeat. He found nothing to indicate that the threatening letters or the phone calls had originated within the production company. He left, exhausted and a little less certain that hiring him as Camilla's bodyguard was just a bid for publicity. It might still be some kind of a stunt, but he couldn't think of anywhere else to look to confirm his suspicions.

At 5:00 a.m., he snuck back into the hotel where he and the other eleven contestants were being lodged by GoGo Girls, resigned to the fact that he was going to have to continue playing the role of idiot for a while longer. He hated it, more than he hated the three-week stakeout in the rented van that smelled like liverwurst. Every day, as the next round of fawning and flattery began again, his nerves grew thinner. The inane antics of the other men and their star's little temper tantrums didn't really affect him, but pretending to care about this competition was embarrassing. Shayla Tennison was annoyed that he didn't fall all over himself like the others, but he was equally frustrated that he had to pretend to be interested in winning this ridiculous contest at all.

There were two messages waiting for Michael when he let himself into his room. The first was from Jared Appleton, a carpenter and the only contestant who did not have a college degree. He was absolutely determined to have fun doing the show. "Hey, Mikey, a group of us are going down to the hotel bar at eleven. Join us if you want a little extra camera time." Jared was a good guy at the heart of a small cadre, and he had decided to form a sort of support group for the bachelors as they underwent the process of being selected or rejected each week by their soap-opera prize. The carpenter didn't believe he stood any chance of winning, because of his blue-collar background, but he was determined to make the most of every opportunity he was given to impress Camilla. Michael liked him, but he didn't want or need any extra time in front of the cameras, which were everywhere as it was. He particularly didn't need to spend any more time socializing with this crew, either. He was glad he'd missed that call.

He wished he'd been in the room to receive the second call, however. The message was left by Darren. "Michael, how's it going? I've checked out all the phone numbers you gave me but didn't find anything. If the ladies made the calls themselves, there's no record of it that I can find. We're not talking about criminals here. You need to take this investigation in a new direction that might actually lead you somewhere." He chuckled softly into the tape recorder, and Michael wished he was here, laughing with him instead of at him. This case was giving Darren way too many chances to make fun of his partner. Michael caught sight of his own sour expression in the mirror, and he shook his head ruefully as Darren continued. "Hey, man, I'm behind you, whichever way you decide to go. You're the lead on this case, you're on the scene." The supportive words were belied by the snide tone, but Michael knew Darren had his back. They'd been partners for almost ten years and friends for even longer while in the service. No matter how crazy this assignment might make him, Michael knew his partner was just messing with him.

He started to undress, going into the bathroom to change into his pajamas in private. In a few hours, he had to be at breakfast with the rest of the bachelors. He needed to get some rest. He came out of the bathroom with his clothes draped over his arm, hiding the gun he held in his hand. He slid the nine millimeter between a couple of pairs of jeans in the dresser, careful to keep his body between the drawer and the camera mounted in the ceiling. He got into bed thinking that he would kill to be alone, without that camera filming him. Never one to spend much time wishing for the impossible, Michael sighed. Tomorrow was going to be another long, long day.

From: Marsha James
To: Lita Tolliver
Bc:
Cc:
Subject: Security
Lita,
Michael is NOT HAPPY about you losing your key, and he
wants EVERYONE to lock all of their office doors whenever
they leave. He says we have no computer security, either,
and anyone could find out where Camilla is at any time of
day just by reading through our interoffice stuff on-line. He
suggests we use passwords and stuff more.
So I'm writing an e-mail to everyone about locking their
doors and carrying their ID and using their passwords. I
hope they do it.
Marsh
P.S. I'm forwarding a message from Shayla, who is freaked
out because he's always talking to the staff. Do you want
to get back to her? What are you going to say?

Original message sent
From: Shayla Tennison
To: Marsha James
Bc:
Cc:
Subject: Michael Grant
Marsha,
Michael Grant's bedroom camera was activated at two in
the morning, and I think he was coming in from some-
where. The other cameras didn't catch him leaving the

hotel, though. Should we ask him about this? I think there's something up with this guy. He keeps disappearing when we're shooting, too.
Shayla

Chapter 3

Shayla awakened on Monday morning from a dreamless sleep and lay in bed for a second, feeling completely relaxed. Usually the start of the workweek caused her to tense up, and before she'd even fully awakened, it seemed her mind would be on overdrive, cataloguing all of the possible disasters that could occur during the next eight to twelve hours. Today, however, memories of the weekend she had just spent with her sister ran behind her eyelids like a montage of scenes from a chick flick: brunch with Deanna at the Rose Garden in D.C., touring the small but beautiful African American Museum, and finally sitting on the steps of the Lincoln Memorial on Sunday afternoon with large cappuccinos from Starbucks, languidly chatting about work and Dee's ambitions. She lay there savoring the peaceful, contented feeling for a moment; then she bounded out of bed with more energy than she'd felt since *Lady's Choice* had been declared a go by AAT network.

She and her sister were finally becoming friends again, real friends. After twenty years, the cool, distant relationship between them had been replaced by the kind of close familial bond she'd always dreamed of. Nothing could get her down today, Shay thought.

When she arrived at work, she found the usual mayhem, but it couldn't dampen her spirits.

"Shay, camera two is acting up again," the electrician reported as she walked into reception.

"Call Phil," she ordered, without even breaking stride. If she let Sam corner her, she knew she'd have to listen to a twenty-minute lecture on how keeping the old camera in repair cost more than buying a new one. She'd explained to him, repeatedly, that her company had no authority over the network's purchasing practices and that he needed to talk to someone with AAT about buying new equipment, but he kept coming back to her. She supposed he just needed someone to listen to him gripe, but she wasn't in the mood to deal with him this morning.

"The princess says her blush is the wrong color," came a second complaint as Shay walked down the hall to her office. Camilla liked to use her own brand of cosmetics, saying no one else made the right colors. That meant the studio couldn't order her stuff from their regular supplier. Every time Cami needed a new mascara, it was an emergency.

Typical. She'd been at work less than ten minutes and was already dealing with her second crisis of the day. Luckily, Shay had an easy fix for this one.

"Follow me," she told the make-up woman who had brought the matter to her attention. Shay kept a secret stash of the essential cosmetics in her desk drawer, just in case. Ever since the first time the soap star had thrown a hissy fit over her make-up, Shayla had been expecting this. After the need for eyeliner had held up shooting for nearly half a day, her boss had authorized her to make any cosmetic purchases she wanted wherever she wanted. Shayla had bought a complete backup supply. *No problem,* she thought. *I'm way ahead of you, Princess.*

Shayla smiled cheerfully at the cosmetician as she led the way into her office. She reached into her desk drawer and produced the precious blush with a flourish. "Here you go."

The other woman gave her a tight-lipped smile and trundled off.

She handled a host of other small problems as they arose during the morning, and not one of them made her feel like reverting to her usual tense, anxious state. In fact, she felt amazingly on top of things. Nor was she the only one in the studio who was in good spirits. Everyone was feeling jazzed after the recent viewing of the premier episode. The test audience had responded positively to the show, and there was already some good buzz on the radio and on the streets. It gave everyone in the *Lady's Choice* office, and everyone else who worked on the set, a little boost.

While Marsha and Lita spent the morning reporting the success of the test screening to the network executives, Shayla checked in with the editors. They were pleased with the footage that had been shot over the weekend at the hotel of the men bonding with one another and with Camilla. As the assistant producer, Shayla was the one who got to deliver the good news to her bosses. "They're cutting together the best stuff, and it will be ready for you to look at by three this afternoon," she reported to Marsha's answering machine.

This week they were filming the first three rounds of dates and eliminating some of the contestants, but the prospect of being rejected didn't appear to faze any of the competitors. They were all buzzed about filming the next few segments. Even those of the twelve who were not all that confident about the impression they had made on the actress thus far were still hopeful they would survive the first few rounds of the game. Shayla supposed it was human nature, or maybe it was just a guy thing, but all twelve were enjoying themselves and had high hopes about the upcoming dates. Stranger, to her, than their optimism was the fact that all of the contestants were quite pleased with the videotape of the premier. Although they hadn't seen it, they'd heard the buzz, and that was all they needed to know, apparently. She couldn't imagine why they weren't more worried, since some of them had made complete fools of themselves on the first show, but she was happy that they were happy. It made her job easier.

She even managed a smile for Michael Grant when she stopped by the set to pick up the time sheets. He looked surprised, but he smiled back, which made her feel a little guilty about the way she'd been treating him. It wasn't his fault that he was full of questions or that he couldn't seem to stay where he was told. He had never been on television before; it was only natural that he was curious. He probably wasn't used to being told where to stand, and he definitely didn't seem like the type who was used to waiting around to have his picture taken. She decided, then and there, to forge a new and better relationship with the man she had come to think of as her nemesis; when he came over to where she was standing, waiting for the technicians to give her the paperwork, she said, "Hi," rather than ignoring him as had become her habit.

"Hi, yourself," he replied. "You're in a good mood."

"I am, huh?" He was so full of himself, she'd have thought

it would take a lot more than a friendly greeting to get his attention.

"Yes, there's something different about you today," he said quizzically.

"Oh, really?" Shayla said, feeling her eyebrows rise of their own accord and knowing her skeptical tone matched her facial expression. She had never been any good at disguising her feelings; everything she thought was reflected in her face. Every boy and man she ever dated could read her like a book. It put her at a distinct disadvantage. She'd always wished she could be more like her big sister. Men never knew what Deanna thought of them, which made them scramble about trying to please her. Now that they were growing closer, Shayla decided she would ask her sister for a few tips on how she did it. It might help a lot in a situation like this one if she could appear all cool and collected when faced with a man like Michael Grant, who was so self-possessed. Nothing she said seemed to get through to him, and, frankly, he intimidated her a little.

When Tim came back with the paperwork, she took it and turned to leave, but Michael stopped her. "Wait," he ordered.

"Yes?" she asked.

"Whatcha doing this weekend?"

"Not much," she answered. "See ya later." She thought that would be the end of it, but he fell into step beside her as she started toward the door.

"Come on. If you tell me what put you in such a good mood for a change, I'll tell you what the guys are saying about you in the changing room."

"That's all right; I don't think I want to know," Shay said cordially but firmly.

"You might," he said, not at all discouraged. He accompanied her all the way back to her office, where he leaned casually against the door frame, arms crossed in front of his chest, looking for all the world as if he was her friend rather than a constant thorn in her side.

Former thorn, she reminded herself, and tried to sound as if she was really interested as she asked, "So, how was your weekend?"

"You've seen the footage, I'm sure," he answered. Shay nodded. It was her job to check on the editors' work with the film. She had seen some of the weekend highlights already. "Mine wasn't as good as yours, I bet." She shrugged. "What did you do, get lucky?"

Shayla's smile slipped a little. "They probably need you back on the set," she commented, looking pointedly at her watch. Like the others, he was supposed to stay within the view of the cameras as much as possible.

"They won't miss me. They've got their hands full with the others," he replied.

"They're going to be discussing upcoming events. Don't you want to know what's going to happen next?" she queried, wishing he would take the hint and leave her alone.

"Whatever happens, happens," he answered. "I've seen enough of these shows to have a pretty good idea. Some of us will be chosen to spend time with Camilla either as a group or alone, and then she'll get rid of one of us."

"Two," Shayla informed him. "Two of you will be leaving this week."

"There's nothing I can do about that," he said nonchalantly.

Shayla was not all that surprised. She believed he honestly didn't care. Which left her wondering, again, why he auditioned to be on the show.

"This is much more interesting than standing around waiting for Camilla to come out of her suite," he said.

"Interrogating me about my personal life is your idea of a good time?"

"When people behave out of character, I get curious," Michael said, sounding almost apologetic. "I was just wondering why the change?"

Shayla sighed. He was always asking her stupid questions—about the shoot, the set, the company, the show. This was the first time he'd gotten personal. Submitting to yet another interrogation was definitely not a part of her job description. "Nothing's changed," she replied. "You'd better get back."

"Just tell me this," he stalled. "What's he like?"

Typical. All guys seemed to think a woman couldn't be happy unless a man was involved somehow.

"He?" she echoed, as if she didn't get his inference.

"New boyfriend?" he asked.

"You guys have ruined me for other men."

"Ah, give me something. I'm stuck here all day, every day with these jokers, talking about whether Camilla smells like apples or vanilla. Tell me what's going on in the outside world. Anything."

"Read a newspaper," she suggested.

"Not allowed, remember?" he reminded her. "Your rules."

The contestants were told not to read the newspaper because sometimes there were press releases about them or the show that the producers didn't want them to know about until they were told or until the competition was over.

"They're not my rules."

"So tell me the latest. Nothing about the show. Just tell me what happened to make you smile."

"Why is my weekend so important to you?"

"Usually you're wound up so tight, I worry that your head is gonna explode. But today you're different. Relaxed."

"Not *that* different," she protested.

"Yes, you are," he stated emphatically. "You've been here almost twenty minutes and you haven't subjected a single person to one of your lectures."

Shayla was about to say she didn't lecture, that she just did her job and expected other people to do theirs, and if they didn't, she tried to help, but she realized that that might sound a bit like a lecture. "I—!" she began, then snapped her mouth shut. She took a deep breath and started again. "I'm very busy right now. We've got a long shooting schedule today, and I don't have time to stand here talking about my many flaws."

"Just tell me what put you in such a good mood," he persisted. "I'm dying of curiosity."

"Nothing happened. I'm not in a good mood," Shayla replied. Adding silently, *Not anymore.* He had ruined it. She didn't even think he meant to do it. It was just the way he was. It was sad. They were two grown-up, reasonably intelligent people who couldn't exchange two words without bickering like children. "Now, I have to get back to work. So if you don't mind…"

Michael could see that she was not going to tell him anything. He was generally pretty good at getting people to talk to him, but he had obviously offended her. He knew he'd crossed the line with that crack about her lecturing, but he just hadn't been able to resist. She had obviously disliked him on sight, and she had never appreciated his little suggestions concerning security, yet she had smiled at him this morning—almost as if she really meant it. What had inspired this sudden change? Had she somehow found out that he had searched her office? If she had, he would have thought she'd be less friendly toward him, not more. In fact, he was sure she would have him kicked off the show.

He wasn't able to resist the urge to push a little and see if he could find out what had caused the change in her. "I'm sorry. I can't go until you answer the question," he insisted. He didn't expect her to go on the offensive.

"What's with you?" she asked. "What are you doing here?"

He was surprised by her timing, but Michael had been expecting *someone* to ask the question for days. He was pretty good at undercover work, but he was no actor. He knew someone was eventually going to catch on to the fact that he didn't care about this stupid competition and wonder why he had ever entered it. This was as good a time as ever to try out the cover story he and Darren had come up with. "It was a bet," he answered smoothly. "A friend of mine bet me I could get on the show."

"Bet you wouldn't, you mean?"

"No, I bet I wouldn't be chosen, he bet I would. I didn't think I'd make it through the selection process."

"That explains a lot," Shayla said, nodding. "So you never wanted to marry a star?"

"No," he confessed, smiling. "I'm not saying I have anything against it. No man in his right mind would turn down a date with a woman like Camilla Lyons. She's beautiful, and she's bright, too. But trying to seduce a woman on national television is a lot like trying to guard a seven-foot b-ball player. Even if you catch him, you can't stop him. It's virtually impossible, and you're almost guaranteed to end up on your ass."

"By being rejected on national television, for example?"

"Yeah. That's a perfect example."

"So why do all this? Why not just quit? Or is this all part of the bet?"

"No more bet. I just figured as long as I was here, anyway, I might as well go for it."

"Go for it?" Shayla repeated. "This is a person we're talking about here, *not* a basketball game. You don't want to take this sports analogy too far."

"Impossible," he said, grinning. "There's no such thing as taking a sports analogy too far. But you can mix 'em up. For example, being on this show is a lot like big-game fishing. No one laughs at you for falling on your butt if you do it while you're trying to catch the mako."

"Mako?"

"It's a shark."

"Now you're dating a big fish?"

"I don't want to *date* the fish," he said wryly. "I just want to land it."

"So what's so great about catching a mako?" she asked.

He smiled condescendingly at her. "It's dangerous. They've been known to bite even after they're dead."

"I see," Shayla said, clearly just as confused as ever. "Danger turns you on."

That got rid of the smile. "Danger doesn't turn me on. I'm not a comic book character." She looked like she would have liked to argue the point, but Michael went on before she had the chance. "Pitting yourself against nature, head-to-head, that's a challenge. It's exciting. And winning is always good. Don't you like to win?"

"It depends on what I'm winning," she responded. "Not sharks, I don't."

"Camilla is not a shark," he explained. "She's...she's a rare, exotic creature." He liked the sound of that. It made the whole thing sound sort of noble, or at least just a little less like he was a jerk.

"Ah," she said. "Now I understand. She's gorgeous. You could have just said that to begin with, you know."

"Okay, fine. So now I told you my secret. Why don't you tell me yours?" he asked.

"I don't have any secrets. My sister came to visit—that's why I was in such a good mood."

"Your sister? That's it? So why didn't you just tell me that in the first place?" Michael asked.

"Because it's none of your business," Shayla answered.

"That's true," he said. "I'm sorry. I guess I'm going a little stir-crazy, stuck in that hotel."

"Well, tonight's your chance to get out and do something a little different," she offered. Her tone was softer than it had been. He still didn't know why she had smiled at him that morning, but it felt like he'd made some progress. Maybe she really had just been in a good mood. Whatever the reason for her change of heart, perhaps he hadn't totally wasted the last twenty minutes. He might have gotten her to lower her defenses a little. He could only hope that would be useful to him in the future, in his investigation. At the moment, he couldn't trust anyone employed by GoGo Girls, but whether the production company was just pulling some kind of a stunt or not, he could use an ally who was an insider. If Ms. Tennison ended up being his liaison with the producers, he could live with that.

After the incident with Michael, Shay remained slightly on edge for the rest of the morning. She caught herself lecturing crew members on two separate occasions, which didn't improve her mood. A better woman might have thanked the man for making her aware of an annoying and unattractive tendency to make long speeches to people who were hoping for short answers to their questions, but Shay clung to her resentment like a drowning woman clinging to a lifeboat. She didn't need any insights into her character from Michael Grant. He was obnoxious enough in person; she didn't want to hear his voice in her head.

She'd known plenty of bigger jerks. He wasn't even the worst of the dozen men on the show. The investment banker, James Hardy, was more arrogant and more condescending, and yet she managed to maintain a relatively cordial relationship with that jackass. Only Michael had managed to get under her skin. She didn't know why. Luckily, she didn't have time to dwell on the question. When she told Michael that she had a lot of work to do, it wasn't simply an excuse to get rid of him. It was the truth. She had to plan the six outings that were supposed to occur during the week, and she had to make them work.

Whether people tuned in to the show because they'd gotten hooked on these kinds of shows, or because they were looking for an alternative to the earlier versions, *Lady's Choice* would be measured against the major networks' versions of the concept, such as *Who Wants To Marry a Multi-Millionaire?* Those programs were all created with much bigger budgets than the one Shayla had to work with. Every penny counted on a GoGo Girls production. The company was small and relatively new, and it was still struggling, despite their successes. It was one of Shayla's responsibilities to make sure their production looked as smooth and appealing as the other matchmaking programs had. With less money to spend, meeting the competition required some serious creative thinking on her part.

Besides paying for the bulk of the shooting, which would be done at the studio and the hotel, she had to figure out how to cheaply film the group dates and, eventually, the evenings when Camilla paired off with the finalists in the competition. D.C. was a great backdrop: elegant, classy, and highly recognizable to the viewing audience as the nation's capital city, so she could use that to her advantage. Shay planned a picnic at the Mall and a tour of the Washington Monument, as well as a helicopter tour for a couple of lucky contestants. She wouldn't know who Camilla would be partnered with for the more intimate dates until Wednesday, after the lottery, so there were some aspects of each outing that she couldn't possibly prearrange, but all in all she'd gotten a good bit of scheduling done by the time her sister arrived to go out with her to lunch.

"I know you said to call from the security desk, Shay, but the guard recognized me from the Victoria's Secret ad, and he told me to go right in," Deanna explained when she appeared at Shay's office door at twelve-thirty.

"Fine," Shayla answered, rising and reaching for the jacket draped over the back of her seat in one quick motion. She hoped no one had seen Deanna come in, since she had neglected to mention her family connection to the singer before.

"I wanted to see where you worked, anyway," Dee said, standing in the doorway and looking down the corridor, obviously hoping Shayla would offer her a tour.

"This is it, the inner sanctum. It's not much, but it's mine," Shay said, intentionally misunderstanding Dee's meaning. "Let's blow this two-bit popcorn joint." She had absolutely no intention of bringing Dee within fifty feet of Camilla, nor did she want to run into any of the men who were spending most of the day on the studio set. The contestants' fascination with stars, as a breed, had been amply demonstrated over the past few weeks. She didn't want to watch them drool all over Deanna the way they did over Cami. It was bad enough that they treated the woman they said they wanted to marry as if she were a piece of meat; she didn't think she could keep from losing her temper if they treated her sister the same way. Absolutely nothing good could come out of these people discovering that her sister was a famous singer, which was why she'd never told anyone connected to the program that Deanna Jones was her sister.

She set a brisk pace as she led Dee down the hall, back toward the front entrance, but she should have known her luck wouldn't hold that long. Ten feet from the security desk, in sight of the exit to the parking lot, they ran into both of her bosses, who were also heading out to lunch. Marsha James, Shay's immediate superior, was dressed in her usual hippy-throwback style. At five foot eleven, she was a mountain of madras cotton. Lita Tolliver, so slim and petite that she looked almost like a child beside her partner, was dressed impeccably, as always, in the latest classic style. She looked like a slightly updated, black Jackie O.

Both women recognized Deanna immediately, and they stopped when they saw her, with a big show of recognizing the celebrity in their midst. "Oh my God, is that really you? Deanna Jones!"

There was no way Shay could pretend she hadn't seen them. "Hi, Marsha, Lita," she said as the three women waited expectantly. "This is Deanna, my sister. Dee, I'd like to introduce you to Lita Tolliver and Marsha James, the producers of *Lady's Choice.*"

"It's a pleasure," Lita said, pumping Dee's hand enthusiastically. "We've been following your career," she continued.

"I loved your latest release. You are one of the few women musicians who is really making a statement with your stuff," Marsha said.

Shayla admired her sister's accomplishments, but the compliment still seemed a little overblown to her. Dee hadn't invented any time-saving devices or exposed any white-collar criminals; she sang songs and danced. She did her job, and she did it well, but calling her work impressive was a bit much.

"Thank you," Deanna said graciously. "That's always nice to hear."

"Well, we've got to get going," Shayla exclaimed, eager to escape work and to regain the sense of well-being she felt earlier at the prospect of spending her lunch hour continuing to develop a closer relationship with her older sister. Had it been only that morning that she had felt so optimistic about their future? It seemed so much longer.

A nice intimate lunch was just what she needed to bring it all back, Shayla told herself. The feeling of contentment, of affection, would come rushing back when she was alone with Dee. At the moment, all she felt toward her sibling was a slight annoyance as she accepted the empty compliments of the two women who, until this very moment, Shayla had always held in the highest regard. Dee seemed to accept the producers' flowery compliments at face value, while Shay couldn't help but notice they were using the same patronizing tone they usually reserved for those whom they considered clueless but useful—such as their contact with the network and the other executives from AAT.

If Shay hadn't known any better, she'd have thought they were considering offering her sister a job. But they already had their star. Maybe, she thought, they were looking ahead to the sequel. They always said that if this program was successful, they might follow it up with some variation on the same theme. Just last week they'd told her they were seriously considering pitching *Marry a Top Male Model!* next.

From: Marsha James
To: Shayla Tennison
Bc: Lita Tolliver
Cc:
Subject: The dates are in.

Shayla,

The dating schedule is set for the week:

Monday: Jordan, Lance, Michael, and James

Wednesday: Claude, Jared, Chris, Julian

Friday: Steve, Anton, Luther, Charlie

P.S. About Michael Grant. Don't worry about it. He may be a little paranoid, but it doesn't mean he's wrong. And I think we can all agree, security is a problem on the set. If he wants to keep an eye out, let him—it may reduce our liability.

Chapter 4

That afternoon Shay was called to the writers' room. She was needed to intercede, the intern told her, in an argument between the show's three-person writing staff. There wasn't much original writing done on *Lady's Choice,* since the host of the program was given only some basic guidelines for his spiel, and their star and her twelve supporting players were supposed to just "be themselves." The men were given some advice concerning how they might want to present themselves, but generally there was little creative writing required in the filming of this kind of television. It might look and feel like a soap opera, but it was, for the most part, real life. The show was subject to the strange impulses of the star and the contestants, and the producers' only protection was the fact that the show was taped and they could edit the footage they filmed to achieve the effect they wanted when events didn't go as expected. The writers on this show were called upon to write press releases more than anything else. Every once in a while, though, they were given an assignment. Today, it seemed, was one of those times.

Shayla followed Felicia, the intern, into the staff writers' office to find two of the three writers sitting on opposite sides of the round conference table glaring at each other. Brenda, their only woman writer, was a forty-two-year-old mother of one, with hazel eyes hidden behind horn-rimmed glasses and a compact body swathed in baggy jeans and an oversize sweatshirt. Lazar, a short, squat, balding man, wore his usual professorial suit and bow tie.

"What's the problem?" she asked, although Felicia had given her a quick description of the dispute as they rushed down the hall.

"This quiz is going to be a joke, that's the problem," Lazar said, waving a sheet of paper at her.

"No, *he's* the problem," Brenda growled.

"Where's Dominic?" Shay asked. It was always easier to speak to all three writers together, since the odd number tended to solve problems for her. Dominic was as smooth and easy-going as his two cowriters were stiff and contentious. Because of the differences in their personalities, the writing staff formed shifting alliances, and the two-against-one formations that resulted meant that Shay was rarely forced to make a final decision—her job was to comfort the staff member who had been outvoted. Although it didn't always work, it was her preferred method for dealing with this trio. In order to use it, however, she needed the three of them in the same room. First things first.

"Dominic?" she asked again when neither answered her.

"Who knows? He's taken off again," Lazar answered in a disgusted tone she was very familiar with. The writing staff didn't much like one another, but they were forced to spend a lot of time together, so they generally maintained a sort of a guarded truce. It wasn't exactly ideal, but it was all she had to work with. Apparently this time, her usual method for dealing with a crisis situation was not going to be an option.

Shay sighed. "Okay. So, what specifically is the problem with this quiz?" she asked Lazar.

"Oh, good." Brenda snorted. "I can't wait to hear this."

The older man ignored her. "The quiz is moronic," he answered. "These questions are just stupid."

"Of course it's moronic. We're talking about men with the IQ of gnats," his cowriter interjected.

"They're not that bad, Brenda," he answered. "You're trying to make them look even more idiotic than they are."

"Impossible," their only female writer said.

"Let's see it," Shay answered. She couldn't believe she was being forced to mediate this spat. The assignment was to write thirty or forty questions for the guys to answer in order to win a date with Cami. How hard could it be?

"Oh my God," she said as she read. "'Who was the president of the U.S. during the Civil War?'"

"It's a trick question," Brenda said. "There were two presidents, sort of."

"Look at question three," Lazar urged gleefully.

Shayla had just finished reading number two on the list: *Place these five cities in geographic order from east to west: Chicago, Denver, Houston, Los Angeles, and New Orleans.* She read the third question aloud: "'What are the five food groups?'"

"She originally suggested asking them what carbohydrates are," Lazar said with a wry smile.

"Well, all these guys keep talking about carbing up," Brenda defended herself. "I figure they might have a chance of answering that one without straining themselves too much."

"Brenda, what are you trying to do here?" Shayla asked.

"What we were asked to do. Write a quiz for the men to take to win a date with our actress."

"The quiz is supposed to be fun—it's not supposed to be a complete joke," Shayla pointed out.

"I know that, and believe me, this is no joke, girlfriend. I researched this. I did. I called some of my friends, regular folks, and I brainstormed with them. I am not kidding—they did not know who our sixteenth president was. When asked about Lincoln, they knew he freed the slaves but not which year. Lincoln freed the slaves, that was it. The extent of their knowledge. At least the question, 'Who was the president during the Civil War?' was slightly more subtle than 'Which president freed the slaves?' I thought about trying modern questions, but they didn't know the name of a single member of the senate or the house. Forget about any foreign heads of state. They had no idea what the name of the new president of Iraq was, and we're at war with the country. They couldn't name the head of the U.N., honey."

"Well, maybe we should stay away from politics," Shay offered.

"Ha!" was Brenda's monosyllabic answer.

"I already suggested that," Lazar said, shaking his head.

"When I say I did my research, Shay, I mean it. I *tried* to write some questions about popular culture. Aside from sports trivia, which is not my area, they didn't know a damn thing. I knew as much as they did, or almost as much. I mean, even I know the Red Sox won the series last year. It's pretty pitiful when people who actually watch sports don't know any more than I do. And besides, we have a jock on the show. It won't look good if we ask a lot of questions that only he can answer."

"What about movies, TV, music? Those are things that all

the men have the same chance at answering. And they all talk about celebrities."

"I had a little more luck with music, but I don't even own a CD player, and Lazar and Dominic only listen to jazz. If you want music questions, you're going to have to get someone else to write them. Even if I looked up the questions on the Web, I wouldn't know which ones were fair and which ones weren't. Besides, in the course of my little survey, I discovered that some people knew song titles, some knew the names of the artists, some knew the awards, but no one seemed to know about all three. Hell, they couldn't name the author of a song written in this millennium. No one knew which movie won best picture last year. Or the title of a single book written by Toni Morrison. I swear, girl, the questions I gave you are the only kinds of questions the average brother is capable of answering."

Shayla could see she wasn't going to be able to change the woman's mind. Brenda was done. She moved on to Lazar. "What were your questions?" she asked.

"Well, um, here's one. How about, 'Name three songs that were in the top ten during the last year'?"

"The men don't have to answer all the questions correctly. We just need a winner. We've got to be able to come up with better questions than these. They're grown men, not children. What about offering multiple-choice answers?"

"Dominic suggested that," Lazar answered. "But Brenda says that won't work, either."

"It won't help. They don't know anything," Brenda said stubbornly. "I swear. Ask them."

After the last experiment, Shay wasn't willing to put it to a test. "What do you care, Brenda?" she asked. "It's not like anyone will blame the people who wrote the questions if the guys can't answer them."

"The bosses will," Brenda answered with assurance. "And what about the audience?"

Shayla hadn't thought of that, but it was true. The producers might make fun of the beefcakes behind their backs, but to their faces, they treated them with a combination of motherly solicitousness and professional courtesy. It took on the appearance of respect, at least. Neither Marsha nor Lita would want the contestants to be made to look ridiculous. "Okay, so…now what?"

"You thought we were just being difficult, didn't you?" Brenda said. "We're not doing it on purpose. This really is a problem."

Dominic chose that moment to appear in the doorway. As tall and skinny as a high school basketball player, he wore a brightly colored African dashiki. "I've got it," he said.

"You do?" Shay said, relieved. "Wonderful. What do we do?"

"I've been wandering around the studio, listening to the cast and the crew. I've made some notes. This is what people are talking about: One, Janet Jackson's boob popping out during the Super Bowl last year. That seems to fall under the heading of 'fashion.' Two, there's some controversy about whether clothes should be bought on-line or in the store. Television advertising and TiVo are popular topics, and computers—laptops versus desktops was being hotly debated by the lighting guys. Cell phones, including whether it's worth having/maintaining a land line and how not to go over one's minutes. The Net is still a popular topic. However, the main question seems to be whether its faster to get on-line with a cable connection or not. Dial-up is definitely out."

"Okay," Shay interrupted. "This is all very interesting, but how does this help us?"

But Brenda and Lazar seemed to be well ahead of her. "Okay, so then TiVo versus on demand…that could be a question."

"How?" Shay asked.

"You know," Brenda said.

"Which service charges extra for first-run movies?" Lazar threw out.

"Good," Brenda agreed. "On demand, right?"

"You got it," Lazar answered, smiling. The three writers were already tapping away on their laptops, so Shayla decided that the crisis had resolved itself. She couldn't help but be grateful, since she had had no idea what to tell them. They seemed to have forgotten her as they fired questions and answers at one another, so she escaped, closing the door quietly behind her as she left.

A young woman she recognized from the studio's make-up department, whose name she couldn't quite recall, was walking down the hall toward her as Shayla started to head back to her office. She couldn't resist stopping the woman and asking, "Do you happen to know who our sixteenth president was?"

The girl paused, thought for a moment, flipped her braids over her shoulder, causing the shells that were threaded through the thick brown strands to click against one another, and then shrugged.

"Abraham Lincoln?" Shayla prompted her.

"I got a C in history," the other woman answered, unembarrassed, and walked on.

"Please tell me I didn't sound like a complete idiot," Jordan said as the minor-league pitcher threw himself down onto the couch next to Lance, the veterinarian. Michael looked up from the book he was reading, surprised by the athlete's subdued tone of voice. Jordan Freeman was one of the most self-confident members of their brotherhood. He was tall, with the slim muscular build that one expected on a professional baseball player, and he had a face that the female crew members seemed to find extremely appealing. Lance, on the other hand, was a quiet, wiry, little man who barely reached five foot eleven inches, whom the female crew members barely glanced at. In her heels, Camilla Lyons towered over him.

"It wasn't that bad," Lance tried to reassure Jordan, but he didn't sound completely convincing. Lance Vernon was by far the nicest guy Michael had ever come across. The veterinarian didn't have a competitive bone in his body, and it looked like he was about to prove the old adage that nice guys finish last. Camilla didn't seem to notice him in the crowd, and he wasn't about to push his way forward to try and get her attention like the others did. Michael had a sneaking suspicion that Lance would be the first man eliminated from the contest, if only because Camilla didn't know him any better now than she had a week ago when they'd been officially introduced. Lance had barely spoken to the actress.

Jordan, in contrast, had already caught Camilla's attention. As a minor celeb in his own right and with golden good looks that had earned him some of the same kind of attention Camilla's exotic beauty had gotten her, they had already found a good bit of common ground. Clearly, however, he wasn't feeling great about his latest attempt to win her heart. "I can't believe I did that," he lamented, covering his eyes as if to erase the memory. "I can't sing. What was I thinking?" As a minor-league star—though one with little chance, after six years, of making it to the majors—he was one of the few contestants who rarely displayed his insecurities to the cameras.

"I think she thought it was sweet," Lance said soothingly.

Michael couldn't resist asking, "You sang? In public?" He couldn't believe how often these otherwise normal guys embarrassed themselves in the course of a day. It had been a week, and they still didn't seem to fully understand that they were constantly being filmed for a television show. Even now, a camera crew was arriving to tape the aftermath of Jordan's error in judgment.

"We were talking about high school and how we were both in the school plays, and she asked me what parts I had played. I told her I was never in the musicals because I'm tone deaf, and she said she didn't believe me, so I sang for her. To prove it."

"So now she knows you weren't lying," Lance said.

"Great." Jordan groaned.

"You did warn her," Michael pointed out.

"Yeah."

Some of the other guys were coming over, sensing that something newsworthy had occurred, probably because the camera crew was filming Jordan and Lance as they sat talking on the couch. That wasn't standard. Here in the hotel's VIP suite, which the *Lady's Choice* cast and crew had virtually taken over since the guys and Camilla had been lodging here, there were a number of cameras set up around the room that taped continuously, whether anything interesting was going on in the room or not. While one camera crew followed the soap star around most of the time in order to tape all interaction between Camilla and the guys, another concentrated on the twelve contestants, as individuals and in groups, at times when they weren't actually in the actress's presence but were talking about her or competing for her or doing anything else that might make for good television.

Michael went back to his book. Julian Lester was one of the men who was approaching; the computer programmer was a jerk. He was obsessed with weight lifting and all things related to bodybuilding. His vanity about his body aside, he was also full of himself because he'd made a lot of money de-

signing computer software. He and James Hardy, the investment banker, were two peas in a pod. Michael suspected they
gravitated toward each other because they were both as mean
as snakes. They both had a tendency to tear others down to
make themselves feel superior, and as much as Michael
wanted out of this contest, he hoped that Camilla would eliminate these guys first; so no one else, including him, would
have to spend any more time with them. Unfortunately,
Camilla seemed to enjoy Julian's sarcastic barbs and James's
man-of-the-world pose.

The other young men who joined Jordan and Lance in the
central seating area—Luther, Steve, and Anton—were a group
of young men who had been friends since grade school; they
worked together in a tire store in Detroit and had all applied
together to become contestants. They were not only supportive of one another, but of all the other contestants as well.
Luther, younger than the other two by one year and the
youngest of the contestants at twenty-five, had fallen completely in love with Camilla at first sight. His friends were not
quite as smitten, but they also had good hearts and high hopes
for their chances with the actress. They were a very high-
spirited trio, and Michael would have enjoyed having a beer
with them under different circumstances. They reminded him
of some of the young men who had served under him when
he was in the Marines—optimistic and idealistic and completely loyal to one another. Together they could hold their
own against James and Julian, so he ignored all of them. As
always, as his fellow contestants competed for "face time" in
front of the cameras by flexing their muscles and otherwise
acting like buffoons, he tried to fade into the background.

Michael sat with his nose in his book, knowing everyone
watching would assume he was listening. Actually, he was

mentally reviewing the day's schedule for lapses in the security protocol he'd suggested to Marsha James. There had been at least three breaches he'd seen or heard about. While he considered the best method for convincing the show's lackadaisical producers to heed his professional advice, he did listen with half an ear to the other men's conversation. He couldn't help hearing their chatter—they were less than three feet away, and they were getting louder every minute. Nerves were frayed. The first of three group dates was rumored to be scheduled for this evening, and two more were going to be filmed in the next day or so.

Each of the guys was determined to impress Camilla during these strange four-on-one dates. They were all excited about finally having a chance to spend time with their goddess in a romantic setting and worried that they would be upstaged by one of the other contestants during the group date. Currently, everyone was awaiting the announcement of the names of the chosen four. It didn't help that the men all knew one or two of their number was going to be eliminated during the next twenty-four hours. It all only added to the tension.

Michael had his own anxieties. He would not have minded being eliminated from the show, but he did mind having his advice ignored. Letting Camilla go off in the bushes at the botanical gardens with Jordan, or pose on the diving board at the hotel pool, which was open to any and all of the hotel's guests, was tempting fate. The woman acted like she didn't have a care in the world. The TV crew just watched through their cameras, barely paying any attention to her antics, while she exposed herself to anyone and everyone who might want to hurt her. He had warned Marsha that their star was vulnerable enough when she was exposed to the ever-changing, largely unsupervised crew during the filming; they didn't need to let outsiders have access to the actress as well. It was growing more and more difficult for Michael to keep from yelling at these fools as he watched Camilla prance around, not seeming to realize how vulnerable she was. However, he had to content himself with complaining to Shayla Tennison, who had the sense to listen to him most of the time and recognized the wisdom of enforcing his commands, though she resented him for issuing them.

She didn't know who he was, of course. His cover was all the authority he had, and he couldn't tell her the truth and blow it. She didn't appear to know anything about the threats to Camilla Lyons, so she had to think he was some kind of control freak and maybe paranoid as well. But there was nothing he could do about any of that. As long as she followed his suggestions concerning the soap opera star's safety, her opinion of him didn't matter.

"What about you, Mike?" Steve asked him, leaning over and pushing the book down into his lap in order to get his attention.

He realized he'd lost track of the conversation—something about being chosen first or last, he thought. "What about me what?" Michael responded, keeping his tone even and friendly despite his total disinterest in joining the inane conversation.

"Do you want to go on the first date or the second?" Lance chimed in helpfully.

"I don't care," he answered honestly. When he looked around at his competitions' disbelieving faces, he added, "There are advantages and disadvantages either way."

"Ha!" Anton exclaimed. "Told ya."

"We all knew that," Julian said. "But which one do *you* think is better?"

"It depends," Michael answered. "Usually I like to do my

research before I walk into an unfamiliar situation, so generally I'd say I'd rather wait and see what happens on the first date before I go out with Camilla."

"Yeah," Lance said, prompting him to go on.

"On the other hand, you don't want to overthink a situation like this one. When it comes to women, you can't really plan ahead; you're better off relying on your instincts. The information I might get concerning the first date might not be of any help on the second."

"So true," Anton agreed.

"So, which is it, first date or second date?" James pressed.

"I guess I'll leave it up to the dating gods," he answered, shrugging.

"I want to go out tonight. Waiting around here is killing me," Luther said, his impatience making him sound like a whiny child.

The cameraman in the corner was busy trying to focus on each man as he spoke, and Michael hoped he hadn't had the camera on Luther during that revealing moment. He felt for the kid. This contest was surprisingly nerve-racking. He didn't even want to win, but he still felt the rush of adrenaline every time they were in a room with Camilla or when they were questioned, tested, or just plain put on display in front of the cameras. It wasn't that he cared about the outcome of the evening, but he was a man, like any of the others; he didn't want to be humiliated on national television any more than they did. It was a paradox. He wanted out, but he didn't want to wash out. He hated not having control.

Memo

FROM THE DESK OF SHAYLA TENNISON

ATTENTION, PLEASE

Please remember that camera crews are always nearby, and we do employ hidden cameras as well, so be aware that you are at risk of being caught on film at all times, and conduct yourself accordingly.

Some tips on suggested conduct:

Opening a lady's door is recommended, though not required. It is good form for gentlemen to assist a lady into and out of the car.

Do not dominate the conversation. Be attentive to your partner's interests, likes, and dislikes.

Notice your date's appearance, but general compliments aren't as appreciated as noticing a small detail. A comment on a change in hairstyle or a pair of sunglasses will go a long way toward distinguishing sensitive, appreciative men.

The production staff will be happy to give you information about arrangements for dates, research on wine, current events, or the evening's activity, which will enable you to share intelligent conversation.

Finally: Group dates are especially complicated, and while I hesitate to suggest any particular dos, certain don'ts spring to mind. Avoid excessive drinking, and avoid any brawling, backbiting, or mashing on your date.

Chapter 5

Camilla was nervous. Shayla would have been petrified in her place, but she still couldn't believe she was actually standing in the hotel's most luxurious suite, trying to bolster the confidence of the Emmy award–winning, up-and-coming, gorgeous, young soap opera star. Worst of all, the entire scene was being recorded. It was surreal. The crew was focused on the star of the show, but Shayla knew the editors might choose to broadcast her encouraging words to the nation along with Camilla's, so she really did not want to say anything too inane.

She would have suggested turning the cameras off, but her bosses absolutely loved to catch scenes like this one on film. Cami at her most vulnerable was gold to them. When this scene appeared on television, it would be carefully edited to make it appear funnier, and more touching, than it was in real life, but the producers thought these moments were important.

Marsha and Lita thought that the audience would like Camilla more if her character's development included some insight into the flaws in her personality. They were not about to let Camilla Lyons come off as childish or too vain, though. She was the heroine of this piece.

Marsha always said that the actress was most "relatable"— the producer's favorite word—when she was at her most pathetic. Shay always felt guilty about helping to capture these moments on tape, though. She also felt very self-conscious. She knew she should have been used to it by now, but she never got used to talking to someone knowing that the conversation would be broadcast later into living rooms from coast to coast. Besides, it wasn't as if there was much she could say. Beyond assuring Camilla that she looked beautiful and that the evening ahead was going to be fun, which she had already done, she couldn't think of anything that would really help the other woman. She had never been much of a cheerleader.

"I promise, you'll be great," she said inanely.

"How do you know?" Cami asked.

"I just know. I feel it. This is the moment you've been waiting for," Shayla replied, trying her best to sound completely sincere. She was a little more convincing, she thought, when she suggested, "Cami, look in the mirror. You're going to blow them away." The woman really did look amazing. Experts had applied her make-up and done her hair so that the kinky mass was a lustrous black curtain that framed her oval face. The strapless dress she wore was a designer original by Dolce, a long fall of silk that seemed to have caught the softest pinks and most brilliant oranges and reds of the horizon at sunset. She wore amber-and-ruby jewelry at her neck and wrists, and her square shoulders rose up out of the magnificent creation, a supple, tempting display of smooth, caramel skin. Shayla would have thought that, looking as she did in that dress, Cami couldn't help but feel confident, yet the actress was obviously telling the truth when she said, "I can't believe how nervous I feel."

"You have nothing to be nervous about," Shay assured her.

"I can't believe I even care about this. I mean, it's a first date, right? They never go well."

"Wrong," Shay contradicted her, wincing as she added, "this is going to be the best first date ever." She wanted to be encouraging, but she sounded like some mindless cheerleader.

Anyway, Cami wasn't buying it. "I hope you're right, but I can't help thinking that something is going to go wrong. And it's not just me, or even the guys, it's everyone. The producers will care. The audience will care. They seriously expect me to choose one of these men as my future husband! All right, so they seem like nice guys, but still, I can't believe I'm actually going to go on a date with four of them." These were the kinds of comments that the producers were sure to edit out of the final cut. Shay didn't know if Cami was counting on that, or if she just didn't care that she'd just insulted not only her potential future spouse, and her employers, but also her entire audience. Shay fought the urge to tell the soap star that she was an adult and should behave like one, and she tried to think of something to say that wasn't quite so harsh and that might inspire Cami to stop whining and buck up. She needed words of encouragement that would boost the other woman's confidence and that would hopefully also make her sound like someone the average men and women who watched these shows could relate to. Finally, she settled on saying, "Cam, you've been dating since you were fourteen years old. You can handle this."

"Yeah, sure," Cami said. "But I wasn't on-screen. I just…I don't want to end up looking silly."

It's a little late to be thinking of that now, Shayla thought. Aloud she said, "I promise we would never let that happen. This is your show."

"Okay, yeah. I know that."

"You can do this," Shayla assured her. "You ready? They're waiting."

"I'm as ready as I'm going to be." Camilla turned away from the mirror and started toward the door. "You'll be there, right?" she asked.

"Absolutely," Shay vowed, even though she hadn't intended to hang around for the whole evening. She had planned to go home for dinner with Dee. She had only popped by the suite to brief Camilla again on the professions of the men she was going out with one more time: Lance, the vet; Jordan, the baseball player; James Hardy, the broker; and Shayla's nemesis, Michael Grant, the coast guard. She hadn't expected to find their star having an anxiety attack when she arrived. But she was willing to accompany Cami to her date if it would help. Apparently her little pep talk had been effective, anyway. By the time they reached the set, Cami seemed to have composed herself.

Although she had been surprised by Cami's meltdown, Shayla fully expected that the men who were going out to dinner with her this evening would be nervous. They knew that someone was going to be eliminated from the contest the following day, and even though any of the twelve could be rejected, it was these four gentlemen who would be spending the last few hours with the actress right before she had to choose her first victim. If they made a bad impression this evening, they could be gone in just twenty-four hours. So when Shay reached the studio set, trailing in Camilla's wake, she wasn't surprised to see that all four men looked more anxious than usual.

They were dressed, as requested, in tuxedos, and they all looked really good. Jordan and Michael stood out because of their height and athleticism. She'd have thought the clothing would detract from their bodies, but their musculature enhanced the long, clean lines of the designer suits. Lance and James also looked very handsome, though. The timid vet looked as attractive as Shayla had ever seen him. James was probably the most accustomed to wearing formal attire, and he was comfortable in the penguin suit in a way the other three men were not. It showed him off to his best advantage, and he knew it.

"Your turn will come," the host, Dan Green, was saying to the eight men who had not been selected to escort Camilla to dinner. Camilla's four lucky escorts for the evening had been chosen by lottery. Jordan, Lance, Michael, and James had been picked at random—supposedly by the computer. No one could know for sure because Marsha and Lita announced the lottery winners, and the producers might have been more proactive than advertised, but no one was about to challenge the process at this stage of the game. If, as Shayla suspected, the lottery had been rigged, she could understand why the chosen had been so honored. All, except for Lance, had already made a strong impression on Camilla. Perhaps Lance was chosen because he was the obvious exception to the rule. The producers might have planned for him to be the reject the next day. He was their least favorite contestant, chosen to provide a contrast to the other men. Although he was just as handsome and smart and really nice, he was a lot less cocky than the others. Marsha and Lita liked forceful men.

It didn't really matter. As Dan had said, all of the contestants would have their chance eventually. Which didn't make those who had been overlooked any less resentful of their luckier counterparts. The first cut was due to be made the next morning, and the eight men who weren't going out with Cami on this first date felt, at the moment, that they'd been put at a distinct disadvantage.

Dan's next comment didn't console them at all. "The rest of you can spend the evening planning what you want to say to Camilla tomorrow morning at breakfast—before the first elimination," the host said heartily. "See you then."

Steve, Luther, Anton, Jared, Claude, Charlie, Chris, and Julian all filed reluctantly off the set to be transported back to the hotel. They could commiserate with one another, which would of course be filmed, or they could try to drown their sorrows, which would also be caught on camera. Whatever they decided to do during the next four hours, the real action was going to be wherever Camilla was, as they were well aware. Still, all that could be heard from them were low grumbles. Shayla could only be glad that she wouldn't have to hear from them until the next day.

When the others were gone, the four men who were going on the group date with the actress anxiously awaited their next set of instructions. Camera two was focused on the star of the show, who stood just off the set, waiting for her cue to join her companions for the evening, while camera one focused on the show's host as he turned to face the men sweating under the studio lights in their tuxedos, each with a gift box in his hand. Lance tugged nervously at his collar, nearly dislodging his bow tie. The other three men were more collected, although the tension among them was almost palpable as well.

"Camilla?" Dan summoned the star, gesturing for her to

step forward. "Your dates for the evening." He stepped back slightly, allowing the actress to take center stage—or rather, fading back out of the picture himself.

"Hello," Cami greeted her dates, smiling graciously at the group as if she didn't have a nerve in her body. The panicky woman whom Shayla had found pacing back and forth in her hotel room twenty minutes ago had vanished and was replaced by a soigné, sophisticated version of the soap opera star. No one could have guessed that this elegant creature had been so frantic just a short time ago.

The men stepped forward to greet her, and she took her place, naturally, in the center of the group, with two contestants on either side. "For you," Jordan said, stepping closer as soon as he caught her eye and presenting her with the package he'd been holding.

"Thank you." Camilla removed the top of the box to reveal an exotic orchid corsage, its delicate, spidery petals the subtlest shades of mauve, purple, and cream. "Oh," Camilla breathed, enchanted.

"May I?" the baseball player asked, and deftly pinned the flower to her dress.

Not such a minor leaguer after all, Shayla thought, admiring the move.

When Jordan stepped back with a pleased smile, James took the opportunity to present his offering—a lovely, and very expensive, silken Hermès scarf. Camilla seemed suitably impressed, but Shay thought the gift was a little impersonal, despite its costliness. The broker had to have brought the item with him, since he would not have had the chance to buy anything like it since he'd arrived in Maryland—which meant he bought it before he ever even met Cami. While it was the kind of thing most women would appreciate, the giving of it was a little too calculated, in Shayla's view. Camilla seemed happy with the gift, though, as she placed the beautiful length of silk back in the box and stood looking about for some place to put it. James didn't seem to notice her dilemma but just stood beside her, brimming with self-satisfaction as a crew member came and took the box from her. Shayla wondered, not for the first time, how a gentleman of Hardy's obvious intelligence could have failed to learn during the course of his career what an unattractive trait vanity was.

Cami turned to the two men standing on her other side, but Lance didn't seem to realize she was waiting for him to speak until Michael gave him a little nudge. "Oh, mmm," he stammered as he met the woman's expectant gaze. "I, yes, um, thought you might like…" His voice trailed off as he held his box out to her with both hands, like a small boy giving a gift to his mother. Camilla left the box in his hands as she opened it and lifted out the scroll within. When she unrolled it, she found a beautifully rendered etching of the actress. Shayla had not even known that Lance was an artist. He hadn't included drawing as one of his hobbies in any of the fact sheets he'd had to fill out in order to get this part. If she had had a talent like that, she would definitely have said something, but the self-effacing veterinarian did not, apparently, feel that it was a skill worth mentioning. Shay disagreed. The pen-and-ink sketch of Cami's expressive face caught not only the light in her sparkling eyes and the perfect shape of her curved lips, but the beauty of the emotion behind the smile. It was incredible. Cami was taken aback for a moment, but she thanked him, automatically, before rolling the sketch up again and placing it gently back in the box that he was still holding for her.

After that, Michael's simple gift of Godiva chocolates seemed anticlimactic. Shay loved chocolate, but the candy seemed so impersonal after the portrait that Lance had drawn. In fact, James's and Jordan's gifts didn't seem very impressive anymore, either. James's scarf, though pricey and quite lovely, lacked the feeling that Lance's gift evoked. Jordan's orchid was gorgeous, but impractical. It soon became clear that Cami couldn't wear her wrap with it pinned to her décolletage because the white lace shawl she had planned to wear over her bare shoulders would crush the delicate bloom. She chose to leave her wrap behind, and—with a man on each arm to keep her warm—she followed Dan Green out to the limo that awaited the group in front of the studio.

"Tonight you'll all be dining at the Chartwell Grille Restaurant in the Churchill Hotel, which is a fabulous five-star establishment that has been catering to Washington's elite for over one hundred years," Dan told them when they were all gathered about the car.

"Ninety-nine years, actually," Shay whispered under her breath.

"Remember, this is supposed to be fun," he warned the guys. "So everyone play nice and have a good time." He stepped back, and they all got into the car where the camera crew was already waiting for them.

Shayla climbed into the front seat. Thankfully, an opaque glass partition separated the chauffeur from the passenger compartment, so she didn't feel as if she was actually a part of this five-wheeled date. She was just going along to ensure that the event went smoothly. Her job was to make sure that all the arrangements had been made for the filming of the dinner party and to take care of any detail that had been forgotten or overlooked. Although she had organized all this, chosen their destination, and prepared the menu, she was barely supposed to have any contact with the odd assortment of people who sat on the other side of the dark glass behind her head. She had planned their evening, but watching them, speaking to them, helping them in any way, were not listed among her duties. She couldn't help observing them as they got out of the car, though.

After the camera crew, Michael emerged first, then Lance. Shay congratulated herself, again, for requesting that the men wear tuxedos. They looked fantastic. Jordan followed the other two men after a moment, looking annoyed. When James emerged from the limo with his arm around Cami, it wasn't hard to guess the reason for the baseball player's miffed expression. But the soap star didn't stay within the broker's grasp for very long. She slipped away from him gracefully, winding up between Lance and Michael and leaving Jordan and James flanking the threesome as they walked to the entrance to the restaurant. Lance said something that made her smile at him, and he bowed his head in that shy way of his. Shayla thought again that if he were only a little more forceful, maybe Cami would notice that he was handsome and sweet and that he really liked her. Then again, maybe if she couldn't see what a great guy he was, she didn't deserve him.

Shayla followed the two groups—the cameraman and his assistant, and Camilla and her dates—into the restaurant. She couldn't hear what they were saying, but their body language spoke volumes. Camilla was obviously interested in Jordan. Her eyes went to him more often than to the other three combined, and she turned her whole body toward him when they talked. Shay knew her bosses were betting that Jordan was going to be one of the final contestants, perhaps even the winner, and from Cami's behavior, she thought they might just be right, but she didn't think it was a match made in heaven.

Jordan was cute, and he was a pretty good guy, but he was a little too full of himself for her.

While the group waited to be seated, Shay went to find the maître d' to make sure that the dinner arrangements were in place. When she returned, she took a last look toward the dinner table to see if everything was in order. The group was seated, drinking cocktails, and all of them were laughing and talking. Shay watched them for a moment. Cami was seated in the center of a banquette, with two men on either side. James and Jordan were on either side of her, and she sat tilted toward Jordan and away from James. Shay thought the actress was also attracted to Michael Grant, because she gave him her full attention whenever he spoke. Since Lance barely spoke at all, Cami hardly looked his way. Her reaction to James, though, was the easiest of all to read. Not only did she lean away from him in her seat, but when he said anything, her expression became impassive, almost blank, and her responses were very brief.

Shay caught the cameraman's eye, and he gave her a nod. It was clear that they were set. There was no need for her to stay. Still, she decided to play it safe. She went to sit at the bar and get a drink so she could keep an eye on the foursome. She ate some hors d'oeuvres while the group from *Lady's Choice* ate a four-course meal. She was careful to keep it down to one drink an hour, because she had to drive home tonight. She was going to be tired as it was.

Dinner seemed to take an inordinately long time, and Shay heaved a sigh of relief when the group ordered dessert and coffee. It was almost over. Shay ordered a coffee, too. She couldn't have said why she followed Cami into the women's room a few minutes later. It wasn't as if she had known there was anything wrong with her, and she didn't need to use the bathroom. But when she entered the restroom, she was very glad she'd decided to check on Cami, because the actress was very upset. In fact, she was seething. James had apparently put his foot in it.

"He said you don't need to act to be on a soap," Cami reported, furious.

"You must have misunderstood him," Shayla said in disbelief. James Hardy was a pompous, arrogant blowhard, but she couldn't imagine he would be so stupid as to actually insult Camilla Lyons—who had won one daytime Emmy award and had been nominated for another—by making fun of her profession.

"He *said* soap actors don't get their jobs based on acting talent," Cami bit out. "How do you misinterpret that? It's pretty straightforward."

So, apparently, he was that stupid. "He obviously doesn't have a clue about soaps, or talent," Shay replied.

"I know, I just…I guess I thought there was some reason that he was here. Something that he saw in me that made him want to get to know me. I mean, why else would a guy like that do this? He's got money, he's successful, powerful. He doesn't have to come on a show like this in order to meet a woman."

"He obviously agreed to be on the show because he wanted to meet you," Shay answered.

"Why?" Cami asked bitterly.

Shayla didn't know what to tell her. She didn't understand James Hardy any more than the other woman did. There was no conceivable way to defend him. Finally she admitted, "I don't know. Why don't you ask him?"

"Maybe I will," the actress replied with one last look in the mirror. This time, though, what she saw there seemed to boost her self-confidence. She appeared to Shayla to straighten, grow taller and more self-assured, right in front of her eyes. "Maybe I will." She turned and swept out of the bathroom in a swirl of peach silk.

Shayla followed more slowly. As she made her way back to the bar, she replayed the conversation in her mind. She didn't think anyone could have called her inspiring, but at least there hadn't been any cameras in the room. She tried to be a team player, but she was glad that no one had filmed that revealing little scene. The cast of *Lady's Choice* didn't seem to have a problem with exposing their flaws and foibles to the world at large, but Shay didn't like seeing them make fools of themselves on camera all the time. She preferred to think that they preserved a modicum of their dignity, and she preferred to think it even if she was just fooling herself. When she watched the tape later, she thought that Camilla Lyons had actually displayed admirable restraint in that bathroom lounge. Shay would have wanted to scratch James's eyes out if he'd spoken to her the way he spoke to the soap star.

Most of the conversation at the dinner table was unremarkable, and while the group was waiting for their dessert and coffee, Cami had launched into her by-now-familiar litany of complaints about working on a soap opera. "Nobody believes it, but it's a hard job. You guys have seen a little of what it's like—waiting around for the technicians, make-up, cameras, all the technical stuff."

"I wish I got paid for just sitting around waiting for other people to work," James quipped, then grinned at his own joke; but no one smiled back at him.

"Don't be an idiot, James," Michael said, annoyed. Cami gave him a grateful look, which he didn't notice. He wasn't in tune with every move the actress made, like Jordan and Lance were. It wasn't that he was unobservant, like James. It was just that he was more interested in scoping out the other diners in the restaurant. Shayla was reminded of their conversation earlier in the week when he told her that he felt trapped in the hotel, with only the other contestants to talk to and with no news of the outside world. In this setting, his restlessness showed.

"People say acting on a soap isn't real acting," Cami said, with a pointed glance in James's direction. "But look at the actors who got their start working on daytime television. It's not a good training ground because it's easy. Soap operas have all the same elements that theater and movies have. It's a tough schedule, five days a week, dawn to dusk. And it's not just six months or so, like a film. It's year in and year out."

"*Lady's Choice* must be easy for you, then, compared to working on a soap opera," Lance said to Cami.

"It's different," Camilla answered him. "I get to be myself. I don't have to get into character or say lines I don't believe in." Turning to James, she added, "I love my work, but it isn't easy."

"Look on the bright side. Since it drives you so crazy, you won't be upset when they force you out in ten years," he said jovially.

"What?"

"Don't women generally get pushed out of the acting business when they hit forty or so?"

Camilla visibly bristled, but she kept her temper under control. "That may have been true a few years ago, but nowadays, more lead roles are being written for women over thirty."

Jordan's attempt to defend Cami lacked that subtlety. "I think it's really great that older women can be considered sex symbols now," he said. It wasn't much of a comeback, but at least he had tried.

Michael, who had been uncharacteristically silent throughout the exchange, finally waded in. "Isn't Tamara Mills in the cast of your show?" he asked. "How do you like working with her?"

"Yes, she is," Camilla said. "She's an amazing actress. She won the Oscar for her role in *Woman on the Edge of the World*." Turning to James, the soap star added, "She's in her fifties, I think."

James had apparently reached that state of intoxication where he thought that everything he said was funny. There was no other explanation for why he would offer, as his opinion, "Women on the edge, that's the perfect description of these older actresses, especially the ones who can't do anything if it's not in a script—look at Liz Taylor. How many times will she have to get divorced before she realizes that she is a complete failure at everything except making films?"

Camilla confronted him directly. "James, Ms. Mills is a great actress and a grandmother who's been married to the same man for twenty-six years. I don't know if you've had too much to drink, or what, but I really don't think you have any right to insult her, or me."

That seemed to penetrate, somewhat, and when Lance changed the subject to D.C. and how he hoped to see more of it, James followed his lead along with everyone else. But the stockbroker had not yet finished annoying Camilla for the evening. When she went to the restroom to repair her make-up after dinner, he followed her, catching up with her before she reached the ladies' room.

"Wait, Camilla," he said. "I'm sorry." She turned to face him, and he continued, "I didn't mean to offend you. You were right, I had a little too much to drink."

"Fine, thanks, I appreciate that," she said sincerely.

"Don't hold it against me, okay?"

"Okay," she promised, softening and giving him a smile.

Unfortunately, he lost what little ground he'd regained when he tried to kiss her at the end of the evening. Watching the video, Shay was appalled.

Memo

FROM THE DESK OF SHAYLA TENNISON

ATTENTION: TO ALL MEMBERS OF THE CREW
AND STAFF

As you know, we plan to leave it to Camilla's discretion to choose the level of physical intimacy she wants to explore with these men. However, I'd like to take this opportunity to remind everyone that it must be *her* decision! If you see anything, through the camera, that looks like sexual harassment or anything else that might be considered coercive, or nonconsensual, do not remain "in the background" as usual. Although you are supposed to be as inconspicuous as possible, this is the exception to the rule.

Chapter 6

On Tuesday morning when she arrived at work, there was a voice mail message for Shayla from Marsha. Her bosses wanted her to meet them in Lita's office as soon as possible. The message sent a chill down her spine, and she mentally reviewed her behavior the night before, but she couldn't think of anything she'd done wrong. A thought struck her: She had told Cami that James didn't have a clue during that talk in the bathroom the night before, during the date. But how would her bosses have found out? They did occasionally use hidden cameras to catch the contestants off guard, but they could not have set one up in the restaurant bathroom without Shay's knowledge, could they?

Shay decided she couldn't worry about it. Even if they had, somehow, found out that she implied James was a jerk, it hadn't been her fault. He was the one who acted like an idiot. She'd done all she could to repair the damage he'd done. Nevertheless, as she called Lita's extension to be sure that the producers were in the office and expecting her, she replayed the events of the previous evening in her mind, over and over, wondering what they might have seen on the tapes, or heard about, that would cause the producers to call her on the carpet. So she hadn't defended James, so what? She had never understood why he'd been chosen as a contestant in the first place. He was nasty and obnoxious, and there was no way in hell that he was going to win this contest. Of course, her bosses were closer to his age than to hers and Camilla's. They had explained that they chose him because he was established and successful. Stable, they called it. They honestly believed that Cami might choose him because he offered her security.

Shay was still wondering if it was the age difference that made them so blind or if maybe they saw something in him that she didn't when Lita answered the phone.

"Hello?" she said.

"It's Shayla. You wanted to see me?"

"We have something to ask you," the producer said briefly. "Can you come to my office?"

There was only one acceptable answer. "Of course." She walked briskly through the maze of hallways, past the doors that led to the set. When she reached Lita's office, she tapped once, then let herself in. She had always had a good working relationship with both Marsha and Lita, since she'd been hired to assist them in producing a documentary four years ago. She'd been with them through all of the projects they'd produced since. She'd been surprised when she heard they wanted to pitch a reality show—especially a matchmaking show—but once the project had been approved by the network, she'd fallen right in line with her bosses' plans, as always.

When she entered the office, the two women who ran GoGo Girls Productions were seated side by side on the plush couch in the small, comfortable seating area across the room from Lita's massive, paper-strewn desk. The duo couldn't have looked less like partners if they tried; Lita, as usual, could have stepped off of a magazine cover with her classic, timeless outfit and flawlessly made-up face, while Marsha was the image of the contemporary ethnic African American woman, with her flowing, brilliantly colored tunic over purple satin pants and shoulder-length dreds. The split skirt of Marsha's bright red-and-blue flower-print dress covered her legs and feet, which were tucked under her backside on the sofa, her sensible, low-heeled pumps clearly visible on the floor through the glass tabletop. Lita, in contrast, sat with her long legs crossed, impeccably dressed in a black linen skirt suit, one strappy Manolo Blahnik–shod foot tapping in the air, ticking off the seconds.

They didn't rise as she came in but just smiled and gestured for her to take one of the matching chairs that faced them across the wide glass-topped coffee table.

"We think we might be able to help Camilla in making her decision tonight," Lita said.

Shayla realized she should have expected this. "You do?" she asked.

"Yes, and we think you should be with us. To talk to her."

"Me?" She didn't want to be a part of this, Shay realized. She wished she was anywhere but here.

"You've developed a relationship with her. You're probably closer to her than anyone else here. We think she'd listen to you," Marsha chimed in.

"But I—"

"You do consider yourself a friend, don't you?" Lita asked.

"I, um, like Cami, but I don't think…I mean, I just don't think she's so…difficult to understand."

"Exactly," Marsha said, looking triumphantly at her partner. "You understand her, and she understands you."

Shay had no one to blame but herself. She'd been so pleased with herself. So quick to jump in and try to smooth things over. Ms. Fix It, that was her. And look where it got her. Right smack in the middle of these two strong women and the object of their machinations.

"I'm not really comfortable with, um, us, telling Cami who she should keep on the show."

"Don't worry about that," Lita said. "We've got it all figured out. It's not like she knows any of these men yet. They're strangers to her. Since we interviewed all of them and chose them, we probably know them better than she does. And we've been watching her carefully. We're just going to give her the benefit of our vision. A sort of wide-screen view; she may be too close to see."

So much for reality television, Shay thought. "I don't think you need me—" she started to protest.

"We think it will be easier to explain with you there," Marsha said. She was usually pretty sensitive, but Shay could tell by her tone that, on this occasion, her boss was in producer mode. She didn't want to hear about anyone's feelings or doubts, not even those of her favorite assistant producer.

"So do you think we should go to her, or should we have her come here?" Lita asked.

"She's on her way in to the studio, anyway," Shay told her. "She was going to go over the blocking for tonight with Dan."

"Perfect," Marsha crowed. "We'll just have her meet with us here, then. You can bring her by when they're finished with her on the set."

There was nothing left to say. Shay knew when she'd been outmaneuvered, and this was definitely one of those times.

She brought Cami back to the office an hour later, as instructed. Marsha and Lita were waiting with a complete tea service, including finger sandwiches and a steaming pot of freshly brewed Constant Comment.

"Camilla, you look great," Marsha greeted the soap star. "I'm so glad the seventies look is back in style." Cami was wearing a flared flower-print skirt, a light green satin top, and strappy gold sandals that made her look about sixteen years old.

"Me, too," she confided to the other woman.

Lita busied herself with the tea and didn't join in the conversation. She made it a rule never to discuss clothing with her partner in the room. She said it was a painful subject. She was dressed impeccably, as always in a classic skirt suit. It looked like something Jackie O would have worn. Shay thought it might be Chanel.

"Wait until you see what I'm wearing tonight," Cami said gleefully.

Shayla didn't think she meant to be insensitive when she mentioned the expensive designer dress that had been provided for her by GoGo Girls, but the designer original had taken a healthy chunk out of the weekly budget.

Lita changed the subject. "Would you like some tea?"

"Thanks," Cami said, settling herself in one of the chairs facing the couch where Lita sat pouring aromatic liquid into delicate china cups.

"Sit down, make yourself comfortable, Shayla," Marsha urged as she sat on the couch next to her partner.

"Tea?"

"Thank you."

They all settled in with their tea cups and doll-sized dishes. Then the meeting began in earnest.

"So, Camilla, we asked Shayla to bring you to see us today to discuss tonight's elimination ceremony," Lita opened.

"Oh?" Cami stared at the two women with wide, questioning eyes. Shay recognized the expression. Cami called it her dumb-blonde look. Marsha and Lita hadn't seen that footage, apparently.

"We thought you might find our input helpful," Marsha said in a maternal tone.

"Hmm," Cami purred.

Lita seemed to take the noncommital sound as an invitation to share her thoughts. All of them. "We've been watching you interact with the men, and we have noticed that you seem to have more chemistry with some than with others."

"That's only to be expected, of course," Marsha interjected.

"They are all, of course, in love with you, which could make tonight's ceremony a bit hard on you. Marsha and I want to make this as easy on you as we can."

"Thank you," Cami said, but it was as if the other woman hadn't even heard her.

"We can't tell you who to choose, of course. We would never try to influence your decision. But we realized that you might be nervous about hurting the feelings of one or two of the contestants who are a little…um…"

"Sensitive?" Marsha supplied.

"Like—" Cami started.

Lita was on a roll. "That's it. Sensitive. More than the others."

As Lita barreled on, Shayla wondered why her bosses had bothered to ask her to attend this meeting, since they obviously didn't have any intention of letting anyone else speak. Not even Cami.

"We thought we should maybe mention that all of these men knew what they were getting into when they agreed to appear on the program. They read through all of the papers and understood the terms of the arrangement. Each of them."

"I'm—" Cami tried again.

"Don't tell us who you're thinking about rejecting," Lita said, forcing a smile. "We probably shouldn't know that. We just thought we could give you our opinion, since we probably have a better view of the big picture than you do. Where's that list, Marsh?"

"Right here."

"So, let's go through them, one at a time, and we'll tell you what we think, shall we?" She finally paused and took a breath. She stared intently at Cami, as if she was waiting for some kind of signal, and when the actress remained silent, she asked, "Is that okay?"

"Sure," Cami answered. "I'm very interested in your opinion."

"So, we thought the three boys from Detroit have been a lot of fun. They're a little young and wild, but that's probably fun for you, isn't it? And I suspect you'll enjoy spending more time with them."

"I'm sure," Cami agreed.

"You definitely have chemistry with Jordan and Julian and James. We've all seen the sparks flying between you and those three. It's unmistakable."

"Really? Sparks?" Cami asked.

"Definitely. So that's six off the list, narrowing it down, and we're left with…whom? Let me see."

"Well, Michael and Jared seem nice. They're quiet, but they both seem to have a good sense of humor. I think we can cross anyone who makes you laugh off the list," Marsha chimed in.

"That's an idea," Cami said. She appeared somewhat over-whelmed by Lita's barrage, which, for all Shayla knew, might have been exactly what the older woman intended. It was more likely, though, that Lita just couldn't wait to get to the point she was trying to make. She hated to pull her punches. In fact, she was frighteningly direct. This was probably the closest she had ever, or would ever, come to anything that even approached tact.

"Claude…hmm," Lita said, tapping her chin. Shayla already knew that she was rooting for Claude and was actually hoping he would win, and she guessed Cami could see right through Lita's transparent attempt to act as if she wasn't sure about him. "He's an amazing cook, according to his reviews," she said finally. "How could you possibly let him leave without tasting one of his dishes?" Lita said musingly. "That leaves just three to choose from. Charlie, Chris, and Lance."

"Mmm-hmm," Cami murmured, just watching the other woman at this point with a bemused expression on her face.

"So, I guess these three have the least to offer you. Not that they aren't charming, lovely men. We didn't choose anyone for you that we wouldn't be interested in dating ourselves. But there's one thing that we couldn't have known, in advance, and that was whether there would be any chemistry between you. All three of them have been sort of hanging back. They almost seem like they're afraid to talk to you. I suspect these three are the least likely to win the contest, don't you, Marsh?"

"True, true. And they're so sweet and sensitive. I'd hate to get their hopes up just to have to break their hearts next week, wouldn't you?" she asked Cami.

"I guess so," Cami said, obviously surprised at finally being asked for her opinion.

"You never know what could happen with Charlie, though," Lita said suddenly, as if the thought had just that moment occurred to her. "Once the crowd thins out a little, he might not be so shy. It's unusual for a man that good-looking to be shy, isn't it? You two make a stunning couple." She slapped the list she'd been reading from down on the table in front of her with a flourish.

"So?" Marsha said. "That's that. I think this went very well." She gave a self-satisfied nod and smiled happily at Cami and Shay. They smiled back at her.

"That's all we wanted to say, Camilla," Lita finished up. "We hope it was of some help to you." She rose to her feet, signaling that the meeting was over.

Cami took the hint and stood up as well. "Oh. Thank you." She looked dazed, like a deer caught in the headlights, but Shay didn't know whether that was because the producers had so clearly indicated that they expected her to eliminate Chris and Lance that night, or because of the abrupt end to the meeting. She couldn't very well ask, so she started to lead the way to the door, with Cami behind her and Lita and Marsha bringing up the rear.

"You should have plenty of time to prepare for tonight, dear," Lita said to her star as Shay opened the door for her. "Shayla will be stopping by later this afternoon if you need anything."

"Okay," Cami said. "Thanks." When the door closed behind them, with Marsha and Lita on the other side, Cami smiled conspiratorially at Shay and said, "Phew. She has great breath control, doesn't she?"

Shay chuckled. "It's only one of her talents." She admired her bosses, but it was unnerving to see them through someone else's eyes. She was pretty sure Cami didn't have quite as high an opinion of the ladies as she did.

"I've got to get dressed," Cami said. "I'll see you later, right?"

"Absolutely," Shay promised. Shay had an appointment

with Jan, one of the sound guys, so she brought Cami out to the car and driver and went back into the studio to find him in the sound booth. He wasn't there. He was in one of the editing booths when she found him, watching some footage of the date from the night before. Shay had no desire to see James making a fool of himself again, so they went into the editing room next door to talk.

He was trying to explain the difficulties involved in miking twelve men at once and then trying to keep track of who was talking to whom, when they heard a commotion coming from the general direction of the set. She couldn't decipher the shouts, but the tone of the indistinct babble of raised voices was urgent, alarming, and even without knowing what exactly was being shouted, it was enough to make her heart race. Shay ran toward the sound without thinking, the techie right beside her. When they arrived, they found the crew and the cast scrambling together to try and help a man who appeared to be hanging precariously from a tall ladder that had been set up so he could work on the spotlights twenty feet above their heads.

It looked as if the man who was dangling from the ladder was hurt and might fall at any moment. People kept calling out to him, "Hold on!" and "Help is on the way!" and in minutes, he was being brought down, and then laid on the floor. Michael Grant took charge, quickly assessing him while the assistant lighting director called an ambulance.

"He's conscious, and he knows where he is," Michael said, and the other man relayed the information to the emergency medical personnel over the phone. "He's not burned, nothing seems to be broken."

"They'll be here soon," Jan reported as he hung up the phone.

The lighting director and the rest of the crew didn't seem

to mind following Michael Grant's orders as activity on the set slowly, but surely, was restored to its normal rhythm. By the time the EMTs had left with their passenger strapped into the back of their truck, most everyone had already gotten back to work. The cast had gone back to the hotel to have a drink or two or three, in an attempt to recover from the shock of seeing a man nearly fall to his death in front of them. Shayla felt as shaky as some of the other crew members looked, but she tried not to give that away as she made a show of getting back to business as usual.

Mishaps like this weren't uncommon, but, even when there were no injuries, dealing with accidents at a worksite was one of the most complicated parts of Shayla's job. She had to make sure that every detail was documented to protect the company. It was also her responsibility to make sure anyone involved in an accident at work was taken care of. It was understood that she would try to prevent any unnecessary delays in production. There was a mountain of paperwork involved, of course. In this case, she not only had to report the failure of the equipment and its cause, but she also had to monitor the health and recovery of the man who was hurt. Luckily, the last was not too difficult; the man was back at work the next day.

Unfortunately, she wasn't able to carry out the rest of her duties so easily. First, the crew couldn't seem to figure out what had caused the electrical cord to burn. The lighting director and some of the technicians tried to explain it to her, but they didn't appear to be completely clear on what had happened themselves.

"The electrical cords for those spotlights are coiled around those black metal rods. John was trying to replace a broken spot. For some reason when he plugged in the new light, it sparked and almost caught fire," Jan said.

"For some reason? What do you mean?"

"We don't know what, specifically, caused the spark. It might have been a short, but we've never had that happen before."

Then no one, including Jonathan himself, could remember how he'd been chosen to go up and repair the spotlight. It had been broken for a while. There had been no rush to repair it. The studio had row upon row of emergency procedures in place. It was only when Michael asked her why Jonathan was assigned to repair that light at that particular time that Shayla began to think that the accident might not have been an accident. She continued to try and find out what had happened on the set that morning, but she soon hit a dead end. Shayla felt there was definitely something strange about the whole thing, but she didn't know what else she could do about it. She called Marsha with a suggestion: The insurance company was equipped to investigate accidents, perhaps they could look into it. Her boss didn't think it would be a good idea to raise any questions about the safety of the set in that quarter, so Shayla let it drop. No one else seemed to be concerned. The technicians, who were responsible for the equipment, didn't think there was anything to worry about. She followed their lead.

Michael had just about decided that GoGo Girls had wasted their money hiring 24/7 Security. Camilla Lyons was not in any imminent danger. He could find no sign that she was in any kind of danger at all. The accident on the set made him wonder, but there was no evidence that it was caused by foul play. The soap opera star was not even in the vicinity, so if the faulty electrical cord was meant, somehow, to scare or harm her, it was not a very well-planned attempt. Unless, of course, the perpetrator had not been counting on a repair of the spotlight at that particular time. However, he'd had the spot and the cord checked out, having snuck it out to Darren in the parking lot within two hours of the incident.

It had been the first time he'd risked meeting his partner since he'd embarked on this assignment, because Darren's vehicle was pretty distinctive, and it was pretty hard for him to get his wheelchair in and out of the van without attracting attention.

"It's good to see you," he said, savoring the normalcy of the moment—talking to a friend in a parking lot, ordinary people leading ordinary lives scurrying around in his peripheral vision. "Hey, pard, how's the good life treatin' you?" Darren teased.

"Boring," Michael answered. He was sick of the sight of both the hotel and the studio, which were the only two places he was allowed to go. He'd been out with the *Lady's Choice* crew a couple of times, but those occasions hadn't provided any relief because there was always a camera in his face during those outings. "I cannot wait to get out of here." His partner already knew that he'd found nothing at GoGo Girls to make him think the "stalker" they'd been hired to find posed an ongoing threat.

"I told you, you've got to take it easy," Darren advised. It was a familiar refrain. He was a Southerner through and through and was convinced Michael was going to kill himself with work.

"Relax and enjoy it."

"How can I relax in this fishbowl?" Michael asked, even though he knew his complaints would fall on deaf ears. He'd been reporting to Darren regularly, and the man was convinced he just didn't recognize how good he had it.

"What difference does it make, anyway? It's not like you've got a life to get back to," Darren taunted. Michael's mind flashed to Shayla Tennison, the assistant producer whom, if he wasn't on the job, he might possibly have enjoyed relaxing with.

"Thanks a lot," Michael said, giving up on eliciting any sympathy from his friend and partner and turning back toward the studio. "Call me."

"I'll be in touch," Darren drawled as he wheeled himself onto the platform that would lift him up into the van.

He had already called to report that the electronics expert who had examined the device said it didn't appear to have been tampered with. He would also, he said, put a call in to the show's producers to tell them their security company was on the job.

"Great," Michael said. "I was hoping your next contact with them would be to pull me off this case."

He'd adjusted pretty well to the strange life he was leading, reliving his fraternity days and occasionally dating a beautiful woman who happened to be a TV star, but Michael chafed at how slowly this investigation was going. He had never liked this part of the job—sitting around, being patient, waiting for the next lead. He preferred to actively look for the truth, barging into the middle of a situation and turning over rocks to find the information he needed. He hated waiting for the bad guy to make a mistake, to expose himself. Darren said he lacked finesse.

Darren lectured him daily. "This is the best job you've ever had or ever gonna have. They set you up in a nice hotel, all expenses paid, and all you have to do is try and make time with a beautiful woman. What are you bitchin' about?" was his stock response.

It was useless for Michael to tell him he'd had already gotten to know Camilla Lyons as well as he wanted to, and there wasn't any point in mentioning that Shayla Tennison was still a mystery to him—one that he was more than tempted to try and unravel. Darren would just say he should go for the big fish, toss the little one back.

The fishing analogy made him think of his one real conversation he had had with the production assistant. Michael usually didn't mind doing undercover work, but in this case his false identity foreclosed any opportunity he might have had to get close to this woman. It wasn't as if this was the first time he'd ever been attracted to a client. He was no Sam Spade, but when a man spent 24/7 investigating the bad guys or guarding the good ones, the only place he could meet anyone was on the job. Sex had never interfered with his work before, though. He had dated clients and once even hooked up with a woman he'd been investigating—until he found out that she was, indeed, embezzling money from the company she worked for. But he couldn't very well ask Shayla out when he was supposed to be trying to seduce Camilla Lyons on national television. In this case, his cover was killing his chances of ever getting a date. And that was a real shame, because Shayla Tennison was someone he would have liked to get to know.

Memo

FROM THE DESK OF SHAYLA TENNISON

Gentlemen,

I wanted to remind you of the procedure for the elimination ceremonies. If you are not invited to stay on the show, after the elimination round is over you'll be taken back to the hotel where you'll pack your things and leave. But remember, there are no losers on *Lady's Choice*.

When you leave, you'll be returning to the real world, and a man who has accepted rejection gracefully is going to find himself more respected with the viewing audience—especially those viewers who have been rooting for him to succeed—not to mention his friends and family.

We try to make the elimination ceremonies as painless as possible, but we know how difficult it must be to face this trial each week. During the ceremony, remember that all of you are WINNERS! And you will be perceived that way by the people who watch the show at home if you can accept your dismissal with aplomb.

I can virtually guarantee that handling the elimination ceremony gracefully will make those of you who go home very popular with our female fans.

Yours,

Shayla Tennison

Chapter 7

That Tuesday evening, they were sending the first two men home. Camilla Lyons would be announcing which two of the twelve she had chosen to eliminate from the competition. This first round of rejections was going to be an important scene in their series, and it was Shayla's job to prepare the soap opera star for her part. She was not looking forward to the task. She wasn't particularly worried about Cami's ability to dump a guy, as she was sure their star had had plenty of practice. It was just that, on a reality show, the whole process had to be drawn out as much as possible in order to build tension. This was done for the gratification of their audience.

It seemed unnecessarily cruel to Shayla to prolong the torture just so they could get some good film footage. But, as Marsha had pointed out in their meeting earlier, the contestants knew what they were in for when they signed up for this gig. Still, filming the men as they were being rejected was, as far as Shayla was concerned, the most horrifying aspect of producing a reality show by far.

Her only consolation was that at least her prep session with Cami would not appear on television. She had to prepare Cami to play her part in a certain way and to say the right things to the right people, and there was no way the producers would want the viewers to know how much they influenced their star's decisions concerning which men got to stay and which men were sent packing.

"Afternoon, Cami," Shayla said as she entered the actress's hotel suite. She was conscious, as always, that everything she said was being recorded—even though the broadcast would only include Camilla; she would be completely off camera. They would edit out her part of the conversation and only include Camilla's responses, and only parts of those. The hundreds and hundreds of hours that were taped during this production would be reduced to only about fifteen hours in the final cut.

"All right, so tell me, how do I let these guys down easy?" the actress demanded.

"We've actually been working on that," she answered, pulling a small sheaf of papers from her tote bag. "We've got some suggestions."

It was the first time that Shayla had ever brought Cami a script, so she wasn't surprised when the actress asked, "What's that?"

"A few phrases that the writers jotted down for you, to help you with the shoot tonight. We thought you might find them useful. The first couple of pages are just for the guys who are being eliminated. The other four are things you might want to say to the men who are remaining."

"'I wish I could have gotten to know you better, Lance,'"

Cami read off of the first page. "'I'm sure you're a great guy, and there's a woman out there who's perfect for you.'"

"The script isn't in order. You'll be saying the lines on the first two pages after you talk to the guys who are staying. That's the way to look at this, not that you're rejecting these two, but that you're choosing the rest."

Cami flipped through the rest of the sheaf of papers, spotted a line, and smiled. "You want me to tell Jordan he's sexy?"

"Not if it will make you uncomfortable."

"Nah, it's okay. It reminds me of some of the dialogue from the soap, though. I mean, it doesn't sound like me."

"Change anything you want," Shay told her. "Nothing is written in stone."

"How about this? 'I'm sure you're a great cook. I am looking forward to tasting one of your dishes," Cami read aloud. "You want me to actually say this to Claude? I've never even talked to him about his restaurant. And what about this part, where I tell him that I'm worried that he might be a little too intense for me. Is he intense?"

"Definitely." Shayla found the restaurateur to be a little self-absorbed. But Lita, like a lot of other women, thought that having a man cook for you was incredibly romantic.

"So what do you think of those first couple of pages? Do you like them? Lita and Marsha had the writers come up with them. As you can see, they've prepared some specific dialogue just in case you choose to eliminate Lance and Christopher. We know it isn't going to be easy for you to do this, and we want you to know we're on your side. But we also want to soften the blow as much as possible for the men who are leaving."

"I feel bad for them, but I had to choose someone. It's nothing personal."

"I know, don't worry."

"Shay, do you think I made the right choices?"

"Sure," she said as convincingly as she could. She didn't have any particular opinion about which men Cami should eliminate; Marsha and Lita had been very clear about who they wanted gone. Shayla had remained quiet as Lita had steered Cami toward choosing the two men the producers had decided she should eliminate—it was a little late now for her to say anything. Lance, the veterinarian, and Chris, the school teacher, had been doomed since the day they met Camilla Lyons. When the producers introduced Camilla to the contestants, they'd instantly noted which ones seemed to lack any chemistry with their star. They'd also chosen the men whom they hoped Cami would seriously consider marrying five minutes later. As far as they were concerned, barring any big surprises, they'd mapped out the entire trajectory of the series before the first day of filming. Marsha was sure the actress would end up marrying the sexy baseball player, while Lita was rooting for Claude Foster, the restaurateur.

"Is there anything else I need to know?" Cami asked.

"Like what?"

"You've gotten to know these guys better than I have. What are these two like? How are they going to take the rejection?"

"Lance is a good man." Shayla was going to be sorry to see the veterinarian go. He was probably the nicest guy in the group. "He's very sweet. I'm sure you won't have any problem with him. Chris is a little trickier. He's quiet. I don't know what he'll say, but I doubt he'd say anything nasty to you or anything. He'll just want to get out of there is my guess."

"Lance, he's the quiet one from last night, right? I might be sorry about kicking him off the show. He stood up for me when James said all that stuff about women actors."

I wouldn't mind seeing James get kicked off the show,

Shayla thought, but she didn't say it out loud. Lita thought he was a good prospect.

Luckily, Cami didn't seem to expect an answer to her question. "I'd better memorize this."

"Fine. I'll leave you alone."

Shayla knew that none of this conversation would ever appear on the TV screen. While the audience might suspect that they were being manipulated, the show's producers were much too clever to reveal to them exactly how much of the seemingly natural behavior of the cast that they saw on their television sets was actually planned, and delivered, through the intervention of professional writers, a director, and crew members like Shayla herself. They would never expose the inner workings of the show to that extent.

She headed back to her office to handle the next item on her agenda, but she was stopped on the way by one of the cameramen who was on his way out to lunch. She knew there was a problem as he stopped in midstride when he saw her.

"Shayla, it might be a good idea for you to check on the set," Paul said.

"Why?" she asked suspiciously. The crew was a group of jokers, and they weren't above setting her up for a laugh.

"The guys are melting down."

"Oh." She was tempted to pretend she hadn't seen him and just continue on toward her office.

Paul must have seen her reluctance to deal with this crisis, because he added, "I wouldn't've said anything, but nobody else is gonna do anything about this until it gets all blown out of proportion, except you."

"Thanks," Shayla said, turning around to go to the set. Paul was right. Most of the staff and crew tended to ignore the cast of this show until and unless they were doing something eminently filmworthy. There had already been two drunken incidents—besides James's display on the group date—and one shove out by the pool, all of which could have resulted in injuries. Luckily, no blood had been spilled. Although the rest of the production company seemed to think these juvenile outbursts might be good for the show's numbers, Shayla just didn't believe that any good could possibly come of allowing the contestants to become violent with one another.

When she reached the set, she took in the situation at a glance. Paul hadn't been exaggerating when he suggested that tempers were rising. The tension was palpable.

"There's no way she's going to eliminate Jordan," Julian said to Luther. Of course he would be the one fanning the fire, Shay thought. It was just his style.

"Good," Luther responded angrily. "He's a nice guy."

"Sure he is," Julian said in that superior tone that made Shayla feel like slapping him. "I'm sure he spent the whole night last night telling Cami what a great guy you are, too."

"Shut up, Julian."

Three of the contestants were not a part of the fray. Claude, the laid-back restaurateur, the incredibly handsome Charlie Thompson, and Chris Davis, the school teacher, hadn't gotten caught up in the river of testosterone that flowed so freely around the other contestants. They were probably just as anxious as their counterparts, but they were all three, for different reasons, unlikely to add their voices to the din. Claude Foster was extremely self-assured. From his attitude, it was clear that he'd always been very successful with women, and he appeared completely oblivious to the fact that his situation here was unique. He didn't seem to be getting the hang of being the pursuer rather than the pursued. Charlie Thompson was gorgeous but brainless. Moreover, he was clearly aware of his limitations, and he didn't even try to maneuver like Julian or try to impress the actress like James, or even to talk to her like Lance and Luther. He had been out of his depth from the moment he arrived, and he stood around, looking pretty but doing nothing more. Chris Davis was intelligent and good-looking and was willing to make the effort, but he was socially inept. He couldn't flirt at all. When he tried, it was almost painful to watch. Where Claude had too much self-confidence, Chris had none.

Julian took great pleasure in baiting Chris and Charlie, but since they were out of range at the moment, he'd set his sites on Luther, which was apparently very amusing to James.

"It's a good thing you're making all these new friends here," Julian quipped. "At least when you get sent home, this experience won't have been a total waste of time."

Steve and Anton, Luther's buddies from Detroit, would have stepped in even before this latest diss, but Lance and the carpenter, Jared Appleton, were keeping them in check. Jared was the oldest contestant, and his quiet fatherly manner seemed to have a positive effect on the younger men in general. With Lance, now, he tried to calm the rest of his competitors, but his words fell on deaf ears where Julian was concerned.

"Come on, man, let's just sit down and take it easy. Ignore him; he's just trying to get you worked up so you'll get kicked off the show."

"I don't need to do anything to get him kicked off, Gramps," Julian replied. "He's already gone. You'll see."

"What makes you think any of us give a damn about your opinion, Julian?" Jared asked.

"You may not think much of it, but look at him. He's frothing at the mouth," Julian answered.

Luther had reached the end of his tether. "Julian, you've got your head so far up your ass, you could probably remove your own tonsils," the younger man said childishly. Julian just smiled nastily, making Luther's temperature rise even more.

Shay knew this outbreak of hostility was the natural result of the pressure the men were under. The boys were feeling very vulnerable as they awaited Camilla's decision. They had to find some way to assuage their anxiety; blowing up at one another was a release. Unfortunately, it wouldn't make it any less nerve-racking for anyone for these guys to fight among themselves. She looked around for someone who could break this up before Julian could incite the others any further, but the cameramen didn't feel it was their job to monitor the cast's behavior, the lighting director was too busy with lighting angles to notice that these men were people with real feelings and emotions, and the director was the worst when it came to stuff like this. It was true that, generally, the director on a program like this didn't so much direct as edit. He was the man who told the crew where to place the lights and cameras before important or complicated scenes, and he co-ordinated the crew's technical work, but he didn't interact much with the cast. Even so, he could have used his authority to settle the men down, but he didn't even seem to have realized that a fight was brewing right in front of him.

Frankly, Shayla felt the man her bosses had chosen to direct this project was the wrong man for the job. He was way too self-involved to work well in this tense atmosphere. His only concern seemed to be whether Camilla Lyons looked good. Like Paul, the cameraman who had asked her to step in before he left on his midmorning break, all he had to do was pay a little bit of attention to what was going on in front of the cameras in order to prevent a lot of damage, but he had never taken on that kind of role in the production. While it wasn't his job to tell the actors what to do or say, the least he could have done was film the scene, possibly separating the combatants at the same time. But apparently that hadn't occurred to him or to anyone else. In fact, no one in the room seemed the slightest bit interested in the drama that was unfolding on the set.

If they had noticed, they probably would have encouraged it, Shay thought, annoyed, as she stepped toward the group.

Before she could say anything or even make her presence known, Michael was suddenly between her and the men. His back to her, he whistled sharply to get the others' attention. "Hey! Guys! The cameras are rolling. You want your families and friends to see you acting like this on television?" His words had the intended effect on at least one of the men. Luther looked mortified. The rest of his audience, however, continued right on as if they hadn't heard him.

It was the second time in two days under a week that Michael Grant had taken charge of the set, and once again, Shayla found she didn't mind. She didn't know if it was because her judgment had become impaired or because he had worn her down, and, at the moment, she didn't care. He was handling the situation perfectly, and no one seemed to question his authority. She didn't think she could do any better. Luther had joined Steve, Anton, and Jared on one side of the couch, and Lance and Jordan were talking on the other while Chris, Charlie, and Claude still stood to the side of the set, almost out of the view of the cameras. Julian and James were still seated in the center of the stage, but they were silent. The two of them were friendly only when they united against the others. Otherwise, they were no more friendly with each other than they were with anyone else.

Camilla's arrival was heralded by the arrival of the second camera crew, which ratcheted the excitement up another level. Camera two and its operator were to wait on the set to follow the men who were rejected tonight back to their hotel so they could be filmed while they packed to go home. Just thinking of it made Shay feel ashamed. If the producers had never manipulated the cast in order to make them look foolish or exposed their fears and insecurities and then broadcast their most embarrassing moments to the world at large, Shayla thought they would still have a lot to answer for, because the success of *Lady's Choice* depended on how well the producers exploited the humiliation that they were about to subject these men to.

Shayla's stomach was full of knots as Dan began his explanation of the procedure for the first round of eliminations. She had been dreading this moment. Now that it had arrived, it was even worse than she had imagined. This evening's ceremony was going to be degrading for most of the people in this room. Not only were two men about to suffer a brutal public rejection, but ten others would be forced to wait, helplessly, to find out if they had been the ones who were chosen for this treatment.

"Gentlemen," Dan began. "As you are aware, two of you will be leaving tonight." He gestured for Cami to join him in the center of the stage. "Camilla, welcome back."

Cami moved to his side and smiled, first at him and then at the men who were scattered about the large room, still loosely gathered in the small groups they had formed before she had arrived: James and Julian, drawn together by their mutual antagonism toward the others; and their opposites, Luther, Steve, Anton, and Jared, who had formed a team of sorts in which each rooted for the others as well as for himself;

Chris, Claude, and Charlie whose sole connection was their shared confusion at the situation in which they had found themselves; and finally Jordan and Lance, the only two men who were certain of their fate, stood with Michael, the only one who didn't really care.

Most of them managed to smile back at Camilla, despite the pressure they were under. At that moment, Shay forgot her distaste for Julian and the arrogant James, her distrust of the jock, Jordan, and her resentment toward Michael. Her heart went out to all of them, and she felt ashamed that she had played any part in arranging to film their public humiliation.

She couldn't believe she had actually chosen to be a part of this. She found it incredible, now that she was here, that she could have carefully considered her choices, and then blithely decided to remain with GoGo Girls Productions after she was told they were going to create this inane reality show. She had gone against her instincts, ignored the little voice that told her she should walk away, and this was the result. She had helped to set up the scene they were going to shoot tonight, as well as countless others. There was no other way to put it—the future of this television program, and by extension her own career, would be determined by how dramatically these men reacted to being rejected and by how well that pain was captured on film.

Caught up in her own thoughts, she missed the first few lines of Camilla's speech. "I have really enjoyed meeting each and every one of you," the actress was saying when Shayla finally began to listen.

The men were all nodding, listening, silent. The room was quiet. Only Shayla, Camilla, and the director knew which two men were going to be eliminated, so everyone else was waiting expectantly to find out who she was going to choose.

All eyes were on the soap opera star, and she knew it. Luther was biting his lip he was so nervous, but Cami was fine. She didn't display any of the nervousness that she had shown when she was preparing for the previous night's date. Instead, she seemed to shine under the spotlights, her skin aglow, her eyes bright.

She called the first man. "Luther?" He approached her slowly, and when he reached her, she kissed his cheek. "Luther, I am looking forward to getting to know you better. I'd like to invite you to stay." The boy looked as if he couldn't believe his ears.

Luther's relieved sigh was audible, and the huge grin that spread across his face left no doubt as to his feelings. "I'd love to," he answered joyfully.

She repeated the speech, almost word for word, to Steve and Anton, Luther's buddies. Claude and Michael and Jared followed. The writers had talked to Camilla about the order in which the sequence should go. They suggested that she speak to six of the men, half of the pool, before gently rejecting the seventh. When Cami called Lance up to speak to her, with the half-dozen men who were remaining on the show lined up behind her for now, Shay wanted to duck out of the room. She didn't think she could bear to watch.

"Lance," Camilla said softly, wetting her lips.

Lance approached manfully, as certain as Shayla that he was about to be rejected by this dazzling creature, and stood tall before her. She took his hand. "Lance," she repeated.

"Yes, Camilla," he replied.

"I feel like we could be very good friends. I've really enjoyed talking with you."

"I'm glad we met," he said sincerely.

"And I'd like to get to know you better," she continued.

Shayla's breath caught in her throat. That wasn't the line the writers had written for her. Cami was supposed to say something like, "I wish we'd had the opportunity to get to know each other better." Shay waited for her to correct herself, to add a "but" or to explain, but instead, Cami just smiled at the shocked man facing her and waited for the implications of what she'd just said to sink in. Lance's expression reflected his confusion, then comprehension dawned. "I hope you'll stay with us."

Although any man could choose to leave during one of these ceremonies, it was clear that Lance never even considered it. He smiled almost as broadly as young Luther had and lifted her hand to kiss it. "I'd be honored," he said.

Shay couldn't believe her ears or her eyes. This wasn't what her bosses had planned. This wasn't what anyone had predicted. This was a total surprise. And she was very, very glad that it had happened. Camilla Lyons had just restored her faith in this television program. If she could derive this much pleasure from watching the scene she had just watched, then maybe producing *Lady's Choice* wasn't such a terrible sin after all. Maybe there was a good reason for the popularity of these television programs.

Of course, Camilla invited Jordan to stay, which left only James, Chris, Charlie, and Julian as candidates for rejection. Only two of them would remain at the end of the evening, and now even Shay didn't know who those two might be. She held her breath, along with everyone else, while Cami looked from one man to the next. Finally, she said, "Charlie."

When she arrived home that night and told Dee what had transpired, her sister was unimpressed. "So, she got rid of Julian instead of Lance? Good for her," was her response.

"Julian is obviously a snake, and we all knew she would never choose that guy Chris. He never does anything."

"Yeah," Shay repeated, still pleased beyond all measure at this strange and surprisingly satisfying turn of events. Julian was gone. And Lance wasn't. Camilla Lyons had not buckled under to the producers. "Good for her."

Memo
FROM THE DESK OF LITA TOLLIVER
TO: Marsha James, Shayla Tennison
Guys,
On a television show like ours, it's important to have an array of attractive and diverse gentlemen who will satisfy the vicarious desire of our diverse viewers. We have to recognize that rejecting any of our wonderful contestants will be difficult, but it is also important to keep in mind that this series will be aired on television. Our viewers range from age ten to fifty, and we need to be sensitive to their tastes and try to maintain as diverse a group of contestants as possible for the next four to six weeks.

Contestants who are cute and cuddly but who are retiring, shy, or introverted are less likely to appeal to the audience, no matter how sweet and sensitive they may seem on closer acquaintance. Denzel Washington as the heartbreaker in *Mo' Better Blues* is a more exciting romantic contestant than Denzel Washington as John Q, heroic as that character was. Tough Clint, suave Cary, or even bumbling Hugh Grant are more attractive than funny man Eddie Murphy or muscle-bound Ving Rhames or even supersmart Woody Allen.

Lita

Chapter 8

The morning after the first round of eliminations was full of
surprises. The camera crew reported to Shay the next morning
that after the ceremony, the guys went back to the hotel. They
said their good-byes to Chris and Julian, and then most of them
went to their rooms. Steve, Anton, and Luther, the youngest
members of the cast, drowned their sorrows in the bar, but they,
too, were subdued after the events of the evening. Apparently,
however, the guys were in a celebratory mood this morning.

They had all gathered at the hotel pool and were swimming, laughing, talking, and generally having a good time.
Shay thought she knew why they were feeling so carefree. It
was relief. The first round of eliminations was over, and they
had survived.

She knew exactly how they felt. Her own relief at finding
she could still feel some satisfaction in her work made her feel
like throwing a party herself. By lunchtime, the impromptu

gathering by the hotel pool had brought not only the remaining male contestants together, but also Camilla, Dan, and a couple of the younger members of the hotel's staff who had been adopted by the cast members during their weeks there as confidants, mascots, and allies.

At twelve-thirty, Marsha called Shay and told her to postpone the quiz until later and arrange a buffet lunch. The producers of *Lady's Choice* encouraged the cast to drink whenever they got the urge, since a large group of drunken bachelors made for some pretty good slapstick comedy routines. There had been a couple of alcohol-induced incidents early on in the production, such as the time that a couple of the guys had performed a strip tease in the hotel's lounge. That episode had come to an end when Steve had fallen off a tabletop onto his cohorts; luckily, the only ill effects suffered by those involved were a few minor scrapes and bruises. Since then, although the men were never very far from a bar, there hadn't been any serious problems with them drinking.

"Let them have a few hours of fun. They'll be back at work soon enough," her boss told her.

Shayla didn't think it would take much to turn the poolside revelry into a full-scale party. "How much fun?" she asked.

"As much as they want," Marsha answered. "Someone might as well have a good time today." She sounded depressed.

"What's wrong, Marsh?"

"Last night," she said baldly. "That was a mess."

"It wasn't that bad. She still got rid of Chris. She just decided to reject Julian instead of Lance. I've got to say, I think Lance was a much better choice."

"Oh my God," Marsha exclaimed. "Have you not seen the footage? Julian is funny. He's sharp. He's quick. Lance just sits there like a lump."

"Julian was a snake," Shay argued. She had felt a smidgen of sympathy for the guy for about a second and a half during the taping last night, but that fellow feeling had all disappeared with the morning sun. "The show is better off without him. It's got to be."

"There are no guarantees. Our best shot is keeping the funny guys, the ones with an attitude. Lance Vernon is not a good bet."

"Hey, you never know. Still waters run deep, they say."

"They? They who? Are 'they' gonna keep on watching the show when he's sitting in a corner reading a book?"

"That was Chris," Shay corrected her. "Reading the book."

"All right, okay," she conceded. "All I'm saying is she better not plan on doing that again. Lance doesn't fit in."

"Neither does Charlie. Or Claude. They're not making witty repartee."

"I already said you might be right," Marsha snapped. "Only time will tell. But Cami really does need to listen to us. We know what we're talking about," she added in a less strident tone.

"I'm sure you do," Shay said in her most soothing voice.

"Talk to her, will you?" Marsha requested. "Explain that the show needs guys like Julian and James to keep things interesting. A room full of lightweights like Lance and Jordan and the viewers are just going to tune out."

"I've got it, boss." Shayla had no intention of telling Cami she had made a mistake. She'd have been lying if she said it. Marsha could think what she wanted.

When she arrived at the hotel to organize the buffet—and to check on how Cami was doing after her ordeal the night before—she found the party in full swing. The star was there along with the rest of the cast, looking just as happy and carefree as they did. They were a beautiful group, physically quite amazing, from Jordan's athletic body to Charlie's model-perfect face. And they were happy. That was obvious. They were all smiles, white teeth shining in the sun, bright eyed. It was a pleasure, Shay thought, just to watch them play.

"Look at Lance," Jordan said to Anton. "He's been sitting there like that for the last fifteen minutes.

"Hey, Lance, are you planning to eat that toast or are you trying to figure out some way to absorb it through your skin?" Jordan yelled at the veterinarian, who looked down at the toast in his hand as if he hadn't even known it was there.

He placed it back on the plate and shrugged. "It's cold," he said.

"That's what happens when you stand there holding it for fifteen minutes," Jared shouted.

Their teasing wasn't malicious. "He's been smiling like that all day," Anton said, grinning. "I think his face is stuck." Jordan and Jared both laughed at his joke, but there wasn't anything even vaguely nasty about it. They were just happy. Like Lance.

"I can't help it," Lance admitted, embarrassed. "I thought I was out of here. Last night. I feel like I just won the lottery."

"You haven't won anything yet," warned Jordan, the ultimate competitor.

"You'd better watch your back, Jay," Anton suggested. "You never know what could happen."

"I know that no nerdy little pet doctor is gonna steal my woman," Jordan boasted.

"Maybe she likes men with big…brains," Luther said before he and Steve slid into the pool and swam over to stand by their homeboy, Anton.

"You better hope not," Jared called out, taking Jordan's side against the threesome. "You three will be seriously screwed."

"Look who's talking," Anton retorted. It was clearly just a lot of male posturing, and everyone knew it. They were soon laughing and horsing around in the water.

Shay laughed, too. Her own relief at finding she could still derive some satisfaction in her work made her feel like throwing a party herself. She had a few reservations, but she wasn't worried that helping to crank up this party posed any real danger to anyone. It was already a little over the top, though. Lance was still walking around in a bit of a daze, and Claude had taken over for the cook who had brought an assortment of steaks and an upscale brazier out to the buffet table, but Luther and Jordan had ended up in a diving competition, which had split the other men up into cheering sections. Steve and Anton were, of course, rooting for Luther. Charlie, who had gravitated toward the baseball player from the beginning and who had displayed none of the expected resentment toward the athlete when Cami's preference for him became clear, was clearly on Jordan's side.

Luther was the underdog in the competition, smaller and less honed and sleek than his six-foot-seven-inch competitor, but Jared and Michael refrained from rooting for the underdog. He already had plenty of very loud support from his homeboys. Michael was completely neutral, and quite professional. He and Jared split their comments, positive and negative, between both men equally. James was glued to Cami's side, of course, and he kept trying to distract her from the show the divers were putting on.

Finally, probably to annoy him more than for any other reason, Cami offered to give a kiss to the winner of the contest, and both Luther and Jordan began to compete in earnest. They had been challenging each other to more and more complicated daring feats, from simple backward dives, to single somersaults, and now each tried to outdo the other with attempts at doubles, and even, from Jordan, an attempt at a pike. The acrobatics grew less graceful and more dangerous each time the men climbed onto the diving board, until finally Shay asked Cami to place a limit on the number of dives that each could do.

With Cami, Michael, and Jared as judges, Jordan was pronounced the winner. He shook hands with Luther, who acknowledged the loss with good grace and then walked toward Cami, who was lounging in a pool chair in a white cotton one-piece that looked soft and feathery against her café au lait skin.

"Dry yourself off first," she ordered as he approached. He grabbed a towel and rubbed it briefly over his chest before throwing it away. She sat up, alarmed. "I don't want to get wet," she warned.

"Why not?" Jordan teased as he drew within a couple of feet. "You're dressed for a swim." He shook his head like a dog, sending droplets of water flying, some of them on to Cami, who jumped.

"I'm just working on my tan. The water's too cold," she retorted, holding out her hand to ward him off.

He caught her hand and pulled her to her feet. "You're wrong. The water feels good," he said, sweeping her into his arms and bending her back almost to the ground as he took the promised kiss dramatically, playing to the camera. "Almost as good as you," he added when he finally lifted his mouth from hers. He started to lower his head again, but she punched him in the arm.

"One kiss, I said."

"Sorry," Jordan said, feigning embarrassment as he helped her to straighten up.

"Ho ho." James laughed hollowly. "Tell me what I can do to earn a kiss, sweetheart."

"I don't know," Cami said coldly. "Be inventive. Like these guys." Her smile took in not only Jordan, but Luther and the boys behind him as well.

"How about a little game?" James asked. "You can make the rules."

"I don't think so," she answered, starting around the pool toward the buffet table.

"Come on, sweetheart, we all deserve a chance," he said, trying to take her arm as she walked past him.

"Then why don't you dive in?" she said, casually elbowing him in the side, hard enough to throw him off balance and send him directly into the pool.

Michael couldn't believe his eyes. And he couldn't help laughing along with the others, even as he moved to fish James out of the pool. The movement toward the sputtering man was automatic, but he regretted it as soon as James refused to take his outstretched hand. The broker, wearing his Tommy Hilfiger shorts and shirt, propelled himself to the shallow end and walked slowly up the stairs and out of the pool. The long khaki shorts and striped oversized shirt now clung to his frame, dripping wet, causing a puddle to form beneath his feet.

"I'm sorry," Cami said. "I didn't mean to push you in."

He glanced meaningfully at the cameras, and stated, "I think we've got a tape that contradicts that statement."

"What I meant was, it wasn't planned. It was just instinctive. You were holding on to my arm, the pool was right behind you, I didn't think, I just…reacted," Cami tried to explain.

"And yet you still had the presence of mind to make a little joke," he said, sneering. "I believe it was something like, 'Go ahead, dive in.' I didn't realize you were quite so clever."

"You've made that clear, you twit," Michael said under his

breath. Jared, who was standing just behind him, chuckled, but he quickly covered his mouth and cleared his throat when James glared at him. The broker stomped off, presumably to change into dry clothes.

Everyone, except Camilla, had trouble keeping a straight face until he was gone. She looked mortified even after he left. Michael thought James deserved what he got. Others obviously agreed. They gathered around the soap star, trying to help her see the humor in the situation.

Michael took advantage of their preoccupation with Camilla to weave his way through the deck chairs and umbrella-shaded tables to Shayla Tennison's side. She had arrived with their lunch and then had taken up a position at an umbrella table halfway between the door to the hotel lobby and the buffet table, where she could monitor their activities—and waylay any hotel guests who might come out to use the pool. As he'd suggested to her bosses after the first time the *Lady's Choice* cast had taken over the swimming pool, she had arranged with the hotel manager to close the pool to the other guests for the few hours that Camilla would be out on the pool deck. She'd been guarding the door and surreptitiously watching the high jinks by the poolside ever since. He had been watching her while she pretended not to be watching him and the others. He had been especially amused by her shocked expression when Camilla pushed James into the pool. Her mouth had dropped right down to her chin, and then she'd hidden her face in the book she was pretending to read so that no one would see her smile.

She didn't even notice when he reached her side, so busy was she with trying to hear what Camilla's harem was saying to her.

"Don't feel bad," Jordan said. "He shouldn't have grabbed your arm like that."

"I wish I'd done it," Luther chimed in.

Their remarks didn't seem to be making Camilla feel any better, but Jared did get a wry smile when he teased, "Remind me never to make you angry."

Shayla looked up and saw Michael. She blanched. "What's up? Can I help you with something?" she asked.

"I saw you sitting over here, and I just thought I'd come say hi," Michael lied. He wished he could tell her who he really was and ask her out to dinner.

"Hello," she replied. "So…"

"So, yeah," he said, though he didn't know exactly what he was agreeing to. *Say something nice to her,* a little voice in his head prompted. "That was a good lunch you brought."

"Um, thanks."

He was not impressing her. Her attention was starting to drift back to Camilla Lyons and her entourage. "Shayla?"

"Hmm?" she murmured, distracted.

Luther was clowning around by the side of the pool, re-enacting James's humiliation. He threw himself backward into the water, making a big splash. Everyone laughed. Shayla smiled.

"Stop it, guys. I really feel bad," Camilla said, but she was holding back a smile herself.

"Our star should probably get inside the hotel."

That got Ms. Tennison's attention. "What? Why?"

"People are watching," he said, pointing at the hotel lobby door. There was a small crowd gathering on the other side of the glass-paned doors, looking out at the pool. "I think one of her fans may have recognized her."

"Damn," Shayla said under her breath. "It's the middle of a weekday. I figured no one would be here to see her."

"It's a little hard to miss her," he commented.

A woman as beautiful as Camilla Lyons did stand out, especially in the white swimsuit that she was barely wearing.

"How do we get her past them?" Shayla mused aloud.

"I noticed there's a service entrance over in that corner. That's where they brought the food out. Maybe we could ask one of the servers to let us in that way."

"Us?" Shayla said.

"I thought we weren't supposed to be talking to strangers if we could avoid it," he remarked. "But if you want us to walk through that lobby…"

"No, you're right. We'll all go through the kitchen. Let me just get someone to let us in," she replied, and hurried away toward one of the waiters in his white coat. He saw her coming and started to hurriedly clear one of the buffet tables. Michael smiled. That was what she got for being known in the hotel as a good tipper.

He started toward the camera crew and other cast members, intending to get them moving toward the hotel. He kept one eye on Shayla as she tried to get the busboy's attention, waiting for her to signal him that they could go ahead and implement his plan, but she appeared to be having some trouble getting the kitchen helper to stop and speak to her. Michael was about to switch direction and go help her negotiate when the chef from the hotel interceded, apparently asking if he could assist her. A moment later, she looked over at Michael, nodded, and gave him the thumbs-up. Then she froze, looking beyond him toward the lobby doors, her smile slipping.

He assumed the fans inside must have decided to come out, and he started to say, "We've got to go," to Camilla and the gang as he turned to gauge how eager the autograph hounds might be. They followed his gaze toward the door, but no rabid fans were approaching; there was only a woman standing on the pool deck—a beautiful, vaguely familiar girl in fashionably ripped blue jeans and a skimpy cotton tank top with a bright sunburst tie-dyed on it.

"It's Deanna Jones," Steve said, awstruck. Michael guessed the hotel manager must have allowed the woman to come out here because she was a celebrity, like Camilla. No one else had come through the doors. The rest of the gawkers were probably still being held inside by the hotel staff. He still wanted Camilla out of sight. The pool was surrounded by a high fence, and he didn't think anyone could get to her with nine men fawning over her, cameras focused on her every moment, and himself standing watch—not to mention Shayla, who, he was sure, wouldn't let anyone harm a hair on her perfectly coiffed head—but in his line of work, he lived by the motto, "Better safe than sorry."

Instinctively he continued trying to get his charges moving toward safety inside the hotel as his mind traveled back from the sight of Ms. Jones to the frozen expression on Shayla's face as she stared at the pop star. She had not looked as if she was happy to see the singer. She had appeared to be surprised, and confused, and not at all thrilled.

"It looks like some of the hotel guests spotted Camilla from the lobby. We're going to go into the building through the service entrance over there." He pointed in the direction he wanted them to go, and everyone started to gather up their sunglasses and suntan lotion.

"Come on, guys," he urged the closest member of the camera crew, who didn't seem to know whether to follow his orders or not. "Our fearless leader wants us to head inside." The cameraman, Paul, craned his head until he saw Shayla, who was walking, not toward either the cast and crew of *Lady's Choice* or the service entrance of the hotel, but toward

Ms. Jones and the entrance to the hotel lobby. Paul started in her direction, but Michael stopped him. "Not that way. Through that door." When the other man still hesitated, he offered, "I'm just telling you what she told me." That seemed to settle the matter, and in under a minute, the whole rowdy crew, including Camilla, her harem, and the camera crew, were going through the service door to the freight elevator.

He had taken one last look at Shayla before he followed everyone in and had seen her talking animatedly with Deanna Jones, her hands on her hips. Once Steve had named the young pop singer, Michael recognized her, but he realized now that it wasn't the pictures he'd seen of her on the tabloid covers that had made her look familiar when he'd first seen her. It was her resemblance to Shayla that evoked the sensation that he knew her from somewhere. The two women were remarkably similar. Deanna cultivated a trendy but glamorous *look* suitable for a successful pop artist, and her hair and clothes were always in the latest risqué style; but beneath the straightened blond locks and the leather and buckles designed to draw attention to her curvaceous body, she had the same chocolatey skin, dark oval eyes, high cheekbones, and bow-shaped lips that Shayla Tennison hid behind her small square glasses, long braids, and simple pantsuits.

They were related. They had to be.

Once Michael had accompanied the *Lady's Choice* people off the elevator, he quickly slipped away and headed back down to the first floor to see if he could find Shayla and her companion and get an explanation for the scene he'd witnessed by the pool. They were still out there, completely engrossed in a quiet, but clearly intense, discussion, seemingly unaware of the small group of disappointed guests who milled around the pool hoping to catch another glimpse of Camilla

Lyons. One or two of the soap opera star's fans appeared to be Deanna Jones admirers as well, and they were watching the two women, waiting for a break in the conversation to approach the popular singer.

Michael didn't plan to wait until someone in the crowd gathered the courage to interrupt them. He strode right up to the two of them and broke into the conversation. "Shayla? If you and your…friend want to have a private conversation, you may want to come with me." He inclined his head toward two teenagers hovering nearby, which had the intended effect of focusing their attention fully on him and his suggestion.

"Okay," Shayla said grudgingly. Deanna Jones nodded in agreement, and the two women turned to follow him away.

He had explored every inch of the hotel during the last two weeks, and he knew just where he was going to take them. He would have loved to bring them back to his room, but he knew Shayla would never go for it. She did follow meekly as he led them through the lobby, past the bar, and into the small sunroom where the hotel set up a buffet breakfast for the guests every morning. The sun-drenched room was always deserted during the rest of the day.

"Here we are," he said. "Now, how about you introduce me, Shayla?"

"Fine. Michael Grant, this is Deanna Jones, who was just leaving," she said pointedly.

Deanna ignored her. "Nice to meet you, Michael. I've heard a lot about you."

"Really?" he said, pleased at the thought that Shayla had been talking about him outside of the office.

"No. She always says that," Shayla said, disgusted. "It's her idea of a joke."

He knew from the tone of her voice, that they were sisters.

Only siblings spoke about each other with that particular mix of contempt and resignation. His little sister was the only person in the world who could get away with speaking to him that way. Lily was stationed in San Diego. Seeing these two together reminded him that he hadn't talked to Lily in about three weeks. They usually talked every couple of weeks, just to check in. Although they weren't particularly tight, at a guess he'd say that they were closer than these two women were. They were not happy with each other.

He remembered Shayla saying a week or so before that she was in a good mood because her sister had visited her. So perhaps the antagonism between them was not the norm—maybe it was just a glitch.

From: Michael Grant
To: Lita Tolliver
Bc:
Cc: Marsha James
Subject: Security

Ladies,

Today's incident at the pool was the perfect illustration of the dangers that you face in allowing Camilla Lyons and the entire cast to wander at will around the hotel, the set, and the studio without stronger security measures in place. Please see the addendum to the initial Readiness Report submitted to you by 24/7 before filming began. The need for (1) a larger security staff, (2) detailed protocols to vet visitors and locations and to escort nonemployees on site, and (3) a centralized authority to coordinate security measures is paramount to the safety of your personnel.

M.

Chapter 9

The next morning, when Shayla arrived at work, there was a message on her voice mail from Lita asking her to drop by her office as soon as she had a free minute. In the past four years, Shayla had often worked with Lita or Marsha in their office, popping her head in to brief her bosses on developments, spending the evening working with them, or just stopping by to chat. None of those visits to the inner sanctum had ever been accompanied by the feelings of fear or uncertainty that dogged her footsteps as she made her way there now. It was the second time in two days that she'd been summoned to the inner sanctum, and she dreaded what would happen when she arrived. She could only pray that this wasn't going to become a habit. She couldn't take the stress.

"Hey, girl," Marsha greeted her cheerfully, which would have put Shayla at ease if it hadn't been for Lita's tense, expectant air and slightly strained smile.

"Hello," she said somewhat nervously, trying to reconcile the mismatched pair's contrasting facial expressions as she took her seat.

Usually it was Lita who was the more confident of the two, barreling about the AAT offices and leaving panic and confusion in her wake as she issued orders without any regard for the effect her instructions might have upon the staff. She expected the people who worked for her to obey her without question or comment. Marsha's style was less commanding; she treated every employee of the company as an equal and as a consummate professional, although she, too, expected the highest degree of commitment from those she hired to work for her. Neither woman could have achieved the success they had without the other, but together they had reached every goal they had set for themselves and their production company, culminating in their current project: a network television show that rivaled the programs produced by much bigger companies for broadcast television.

GoGo Girls could have taken advantage of the loose restrictions placed on cable television production to appeal to the baser elements of their TV audience by adding more frequent and more explicit sex scenes to *Lady's Choice* than those shown on *Millionaire* or *The Bachelor*. On a cable channel, there weren't a lot of rules about a show's content like there were on broadcast television, which made creating a *real* reality program a very tempting endeavor for women like Marsha James and Lita Tolliver, whose previous productions consisted of groundbreaking documentaries on subjects such as black women's health; Rebecca Jackson, one of the founders of the Shaker sect; and women in prison. *Lady's Choice,* unlike the reality shows on the major networks, could have featured sexually explicit scenes or anything else the producers thought would sell to the audience. However, Shayla had always believed her bosses had more class than most other members of their profession. They would never stoop to pandering to the audience to sell their work.

At the moment, the production assistant wasn't certain that her evaluation of her bosses' ethics was on track. Lita wouldn't look straight at her, and there was a pinched look about her elegant nose and mouth that Shayla had never seen before. It made her anxious enough to wish that whatever the producers wanted from her they would just tell her already. Although she'd only been in the office for a minute or two, Lita's nervousness had already communicated itself to her. She didn't think she could take any more.

"Shayla, we've got a favor to ask you," Marsha said just then.

"Yes?" Shay asked, bracing herself for the worst. If they asked her to leave or to demonstrate a more respectful attitude toward the show, she didn't know what she would do.

"Why didn't you ever tell us your sister was a singer?"

"What?" she asked. "Why? Because…it…never came up, I guess. Why? What is this about?" She was lost. What did Dee have to do with anything?

"When we saw you here with Deanna Jones Monday, and then found out you were related to her, we realized that we'd been presented with a very interesting opportunity."

"What kind of opportunity?" Shayla asked with the ominous feeling that she wasn't going to like their answer.

"We were curious about what she's planning to do next," Marsha asked.

"Next?" Shayla felt completely at sea. Lita and Marsha were looking at her as if the answer to their odd question was crucial to them. "What do you mean?"

"Well, if she'd be interested, we were wondering if she would consider appearing on the show?" Marsha looked as pleased with herself as if she'd just come up with the cure for cancer.

"The show? This show?" Shay repeated, feeling as if she was stuttering. *They wanted to talk about Dee. Not the previous night. Not her attitude. She wasn't in trouble. Quite the opposite.*

She had read them wrong. Lita wasn't nervous or afraid—at least not about asking her for this favor—she was excited. They were completely thrilled about taking advantage of this unexpected chance to add another celebrity to the cast of their TV show. "Yes, do you think Dee would like to be on *Lady's Choice?* We think she'd be a great addition to the cast."

"But…but…" Shayla was actually stuttering. She couldn't quite get a handle on what was going on here. This was about her sister? Slowly, her bosses' odd behavior was beginning to make sense. They wanted Dee to appear on *her* television show, and they wanted Shayla to ask her. It made perfect sense, from their point of view. Deanna Jones was a celebrity; she might not have the star quality of a soap opera actress, but she had a similar fan base. And with her came the added bonus of bringing in even more viewers from the lower end of the all-important eighteen-to-forty-four-year-old age range. A pop artist was sure to get the attention of the twentysomethings.

With understanding came a familiar, sinking sensation that she hadn't felt in years. "You want me to ask Dee?" It wasn't really a question. "That was the favor you wanted?"

"Yes," Lita answered. Marsha was nodding, a wide grin on her face. "We figured she'd be more likely to agree if you asked her."

"You want her to…what? To date these guys?"

"Some of them, yeah. We think she should come on about halfway through the contest, when the first five or six men have been eliminated. By then our audience will know our girl and her boys and will have their favorites. Suddenly, another woman appears. No one will expect it. The men will have someone else to fight over, and Camilla's territory will be threatened. It will add tension to the show."

"You seriously want Dee to compete against Camilla?" Shay asked.

"Sure. They're both ambitious. No one gets far in the entertainment business without being driven. I think your sister might really like the competition. And it will inspire Camilla to be more assertive about staking her claim on the men," Lita said.

"Any man she doesn't want to lose, anyway," Marsha elaborated. "Sometimes it seems like Camilla isn't that interested in starting a relationship with any of these men, not seriously. If her attitude doesn't change, the show might suffer. A little healthy competition could inspire her to show some feeling, for one of these guys."

"So Dee would be brought in to make her jealous?"

"I don't know if Camilla would get jealous; that might be a little too strong, but I suspect she wouldn't just sit around and let someone else steal the show out from under her," Lita explained.

"Who would?" Shay said under her breath.

"What?" Marsha asked.

"Nothing."

"So, how about it, honey?" Lita asked, sounding almost like her old self. There was a diffident note to her voice that was new, but all in all, Shayla thought she had gotten over her initial embarrassment at having to ask her assistant for a favor, now that it was done. She wasn't having any trouble meeting Shay's eyes anymore. It was Shayla who didn't want to make eye contact now. She was appalled. Not by the suggestion—it made perfect sense, now that they'd mentioned it, to provide Camilla Lyons with a foil like Deanna Jones midway through the competition—but by the idea of having her sister here, a guest star on her show. She started to say yes; she opened her mouth to say it, but she couldn't do it.

She didn't want Dee here, she realized. Her house was one thing, but having Deanna at work all day every day was something else again. It was hard enough to manage all the inflated egos on the show as it was, without throwing her beautiful, talented sister into the mix. On top of the havoc this could wreak on the set, she didn't know how it would affect her burgeoning relationship with her sister. She was enjoying this time alone with Dee. She was excited about the possibilities that seemed to be opening up to them. They were slowly but surely getting reacquainted with each other, and it felt really good. Working together would almost certainly complicate things. If Dee appeared on the show as one of the stars, their reunion would have to take place with everyone watching.

"I'll ask," she said slowly, not at all sure that she could do what they asked, but she owed it to them to try.

"That's fine," Marsha said. "We really appreciate this."

"We never would have thought of inviting a rock star. We were looking for another soap actress, but someone like Deanna Jones would add a whole new element to the show. If it hadn't been for you bringing her here…well, we think it was amazing timing, you inviting your sister. What I'm trying to say is thank you," Lita said graciously.

"Um, thanks," Shay mumbled.

After agonizing for an hour, Shay bit the bullet and called home. Dee had said she was just going to be hanging around the house today, so she spoke into the answering machine until her sister picked up the receiver.

"Hey, sis," Dee greeted her. "What's up?"

"I had a very interesting talk with my bosses today."

"Oh yeah? Did they give you a raise?"

"No, but they had a very interesting idea about the show."

"Yeah?" she prompted. "What was it?"

"Well, it involves you, actually."

"Me?"

"Yes. I thought about waiting until I got home to ask you this, but…" Shay had decided it was better to talk about her bosses' proposition over the phone. This was business, and she felt better discussing it in her office, where she felt less like Deanna Jones's less-glamorous little sister and more like Shayla Tennison, assistant producer. It was weird enough to be mixing her work and her home life and family without adding the element of doing it in her own home. She didn't want to ask Dee to come into the office to talk, because she was afraid that Dee might pick up on her mixed emotions about this if they were face-to-face.

"I hate waiting. Go ahead," Dee prompted.

Shay took a deep breath. "I feel sort of funny talking to you about this like this, but they asked me if you might want to guest star on *Lady's Choice?*" Shayla asked unceremoniously.

"Guest star?" she echoed. "You mean, be on the show?"

"Uh-huh."

"They want me to be on your TV show?"

"Uh-huh." Shay couldn't seem to manage to form more complete sentences.

"Why?" Dee asked.

"Well, uh, they liked you…and they thought it would be good for the program. It would be a surprise for the viewers, and it would add more tension to the competition."

"Really." Her sister sounded flattered. That was a good sign.

Assuming Shay actually wanted her to agree to do this, which she wasn't sure she did. "Yes, and…there are a number of other reasons, thoughts that went into this decision. You know, the producers are always thinking of ways to spice things up. Throwing you into the thick of things would be good television."

"It would?"

Shay wasn't sure Dee had taken it in. "Dee?" she queried.

"Yes, I'm just thinking. I mean, I didn't expect this."

"No, of course not." Shay was still in shock, and she'd had a little time to get used to the idea.

"You know, just think about it. I don't need an answer right this minute."

"Um, okay," Dee answered, sounding distracted.

"I'll talk to you later, okay?" Shay said.

"Okay."

"If you think of any questions or anything, you can call me. Or just ask me when I get home tonight," she suggested.

"Fine," Dee said. "I'll talk to you tonight."

She didn't have a lot of time to think about what her sister would decide to do since it was, as usual, a very hectic day. She took a break at lunch, though, and went out. She hid herself at a little hole in the wall that was only a ten-minute drive from the office where the crab cakes were served with a rémoulade sauce that had a nice bite, and they served a decent white wine by the glass. Shay felt slightly more relaxed after that little respite, and she returned to the office ready to face whatever new challenges were in store.

Memo:
From: Marsha
To: Shayla
Revised dating schedule:
Wednesday: Jared, Claude, Charlie
Friday: Steve, Anton, Luther

Chapter 10

That night when Shay got home from work, Dee was waiting for her with a question: "Are you having an affair I don't know about?" Dee asked.

"Huh?"

"Someone keeps calling and hanging up when I answer."

"That happens all the time. It's probably one of those computers calling, trying to sell me something."

"Maybe, but I thought I heard someone breathing."

"That's creepy," Shay said with a shudder.

"So you're sure you're not secretly involved with some guy you're afraid I wouldn't approve of?" Dee teased.

"Me? I couldn't keep any secrets from you—you know that." They laughed, but it was true that they talked about everything these days, or almost everything. There were a few topics that were out of bounds, such as Leon, Dee's last record deal, and Shay's love life, which were all subjects that tended to lead to sisterly sniping, but they talked about the past and the future and their ambitions, and especially about the popularity of reality programs, a phenomenon that continued to confound Shay and seemed to fascinate Dee. Yet she couldn't bring herself to talk to her sister about the offer her bosses had made to her to be on the show. She told Dee about the accident on the set and about all of the day-to-day workings of the dating game that had taken over her life. But she couldn't seem to tell her sister what she thought of the possibility that Dee might join the cast of *Lady's Choice*. Dee talked, and she listened, but that was the extent of it. She didn't seem to be capable of doing anything more.

"I think I want to be on the show," Dee said the next morning as they were eating their breakfast cereal.

"Really?" Shay asked. She had a sinking feeling that this decision was going to haunt her forever. "You know it's a real commitment—you can't just leave. Once you sign the contract, you're in. For the duration."

"I know that, Shay. I've been signing contracts and not walking away from them for over ten years. I do know what's involved."

"Okay, okay. I just thought I should mention it because the producers are my bosses, you know. If you decide you don't like this gig, you could get me fired."

"I'm aware of that." Dee was exasperated. "I'm not going to flake out on you, Shay. I haven't done anything like that since I was eighteen years old. I'm completely grown up now. An actual adult. A professional. You don't have to worry that I'll embarrass you."

Shay couldn't help thinking that having Dee on *Lady's Choice* would not be good for her. It wasn't that she thought that Dee would purposely, or even consciously, do anything that reflected poorly on her sister. She was afraid that Dee would just be her usual self, and that would drive her crazy. She was usually a very rational, unemotional, professional woman. She didn't snipe at her coworkers or dump her personal problems on them; she was the voice of reason in any interoffice dispute, and she was always calm, cool, and collected. But Dee pressed all her buttons. She behaved differently when Dee was around. And she didn't know if she could handle that at work, where she had put a lot of effort into being perceived a certain way—as a problem solver, the go-to girl, solid, reliable, and dedicated.

She wasn't really worried that Dee would flake out. She was worried that she herself would.

"I guess you should set up a meeting with the producers," Dee said, oblivious to Shay's rising panic.

"I'll do that," she said, and was surprised to find that she didn't even sound anxious about agreeing to make The Call. She couldn't believe she had managed to speak as if arranging for her sister to come and work with her was just another insignificant task on her daily to-do list. How could she tell Marsha and Lita that Dee had accepted their invitation to appear as a guest star on the show as if it was fine and dandy, as if her whole world hadn't just been turned completely upside down?

When Shayla went to brief Cami on her next two dates, Shay was treated to the first of the negative ramifications of her sister's decision to join the cast of *Lady's Choice*. The star of the show was having her make-up applied by Lynette, the young woman who hadn't known that Abe Lincoln was the sixteenth president of the United States. The process seemed to have Cami's full attention, because she didn't respond to Shay's greeting.

"Are you ready for this?" Shay asked.

Cami ignored her. "Maybe my eyebrows need to be shaped a little?" she said to the cosmetician.

It was only when Shayla asked, "Cami? It's the big day. How are you feeling?" and she still didn't answer, that Shayla realized she must have done something to offend the actress. It was so completely out of character for Cami to subject her to the silent treatment that it took Shay a moment to grasp that that was what was happening.

Generally, when Camilla Lyons wasn't happy, everyone within earshot knew the reason. She actually seemed to enjoy making noisy dramatic scenes. Shay's relationship with the actress had suffered from these minor disruptions before, but this was different. She had never seen this side of the soap star, and this quiet anger seemed more real than her previous outbursts somehow. Shayla did not have the time, however, to explore a new facet of Camilla Lyons's personality. The day's schedule was already full. Shayla decided to confront the problem, whatever it was, head-on. "What's wrong?" she asked.

"I thought we were friends," Cami said accusingly.

"We are," Shay answered, surprised. "What is this about, Cami?"

"Your sister."

"My—? What?" Shayla was dumbfounded. Deanna hadn't even officially been added to the cast yet. How in the world had Camilla found out about it already?

"Lita told me she's going to be on the show."

Well, that explained that. Shayla wondered what Lita could have been thinking. The producer should have known that Camilla would not react well to the news that another woman had been added to the cast.

There was nothing she could do about that now. It was done,

and she was stuck with the result of Lita's handiwork. "That's right," Shay admitted. "But we're still friends. Of course."

"A real friend would have told me, not gone sneaking around getting her sister on my show."

Shayla didn't think it would help to explain that asking Deanna to appear on *Lady's Choice* had not been her idea. "It just happened. I was planning to tell you and introduce you to Dee. I think you'll like her."

"I might like her, but she won't like me. Women never do."

"I like you, so what does that make me? A man?"

That got a little smile. But it vanished almost immediately. "You're different," Cami said sullenly. "At least I thought you were."

"I'm no different from anyone else," Shay replied. "I like you because you're funny and smart, and you can be a sweetheart when you're not being a total idiot. And Dee will like you, too."

Somewhat mollified, Cami nodded. "If you say so," she said doubtfully.

"It'll be fun," Shay lied. "You'll see."

"And don't think I'm going to forget that crack about being an idiot," the other woman warned.

"Me? I would never say anything like that," Shay retorted, leaning over to wrap her arms around Cami's shoulders for a moment, until the make-up woman nudged her with her hip. "You must have heard wrong," she said as she stepped back out of the woman's way.

"I heard you just fine," Cami insisted as the cosmetician put the finishing touches to her face. "And I've got it on tape. So watch your back, sister, because I don't take these insults lightly. I'll make you eat those words."

"I'm shaking in my pumps," Shay said lightly.

"That's good," Cami said, but she was talking to the make-up woman, who was carefully examining her work. "Thank you." Lynette picked up her bag full of magic ingredients from the counter and left.

Shayla waited for the door to close behind her before she said, "Cami, you've got two more group dates coming up, so things are about to really heat up. You know the guys a little better now, so the next two dates will be different. You have to be more assertive about getting to know them. You know, talk to each man individually. The first elimination was interesting, but it was just based on your first impressions of the guys. Next time, you're going to be getting rid of someone you know, someone who has invested something in having a relationship with you, not just some guy you talked to for a few minutes."

"I know," Cami said. "I'm nervous about it. I am starting to like all of the guys. I wish I didn't have to hurt any of them." The way she said the line made Shayla feel that that was just what it was, a line. It sounded rehearsed. Shay liked Cami, but the soap star was a little hard-hearted. Which was why she'd been chosen to star in this reality show. Marsha and Lita knew perfectly well that Camilla never intended to marry any of these guys. It didn't worry them. Most of the men who had starred in similar shows—*The Bachelor, Ordinary Joe*—had not ended up marrying the women who won. The *Millionaire*'s well-publicized breakup with his chosen bride had been followed by a string of similar failures. None of the men who starred in these matchmaking contests had chosen well. The relationships just didn't seem to last. On the other hand, the women did tend to stick with the mates they had chosen.

Camilla didn't think she was like those women. She had more in common with the reality show bachelors, and her producers agreed with her. If Cami was still concerned about hurting the feelings of any of her admirers as she left for her date that evening, she hid it very well. She seemed more excited than nervous about the prospect of spending the evening with the guys. They didn't seem to mind her high spirits; instead they seemed to share them, so Shay decided not to waste her time worrying about it. How Cami treated these men was her own concern—it was none of Shay's business, really. She already had enough to take care of.

Preparations for the second date went, in some ways, more smoothly than the first. There was no lottery this time; the lucky fellows were simply chosen by the producers. The men who accompanied Camilla to dinner this time had an advantage over the first group in that they'd been through some stuff with Cami, and everyone was more comfortable together. Her escorts were Jared, Claude, and Charlie, which left Luther, Steve, and Anton awaiting their turn to spend time with the object of their desires. Shayla wasn't sure which group needed baby-sitting more. The three men Cami was dating that evening were very different from the first batch. The evening was going to have a very different dynamic from her date with Jordan, Michael, Lance, and James. Charlie wasn't the sharpest crayon in the box, but Jared's wisdom and intelligence balanced that out. Claude was arrogant, but he was not nearly as bad as James, and he didn't seem like the grabby type. He talked almost exclusively about cooking and his restaurant. Shay didn't think Cami would need rescuing from anyone in this group.

Shay castigated herself for putting Group Two down, even if it was only in her mind, and turned her thoughts to Group Three. They were a spirited bunch under the best of circumstances. She suspected that, given that they might well be feeling neglected this evening, it would be a likely time for them to show their true colors.

Since Cami was not as nervous this time as she had been on her first date, Shay decided she had better keep an eye—and possibly a leash—on the three young men. They were planning to hang around in the hotel that evening, as usual, which meant they would probably end up in the bar. Jordan would probably join them since he usually spent the evenings with the group. It was harder to predict whether Lance Vernon or Michael Grant would be there with them. Those two were usually a good influence on the other four, so she hoped they would show.

She no longer found Michael quite so annoying. He might be domineering and hard to control, but he was also responsible, and he'd been very helpful on a number of occasions. And he had been instrumental the day Dee showed up in the hotel without warning. If he hadn't whisked the two of them out of sight, she didn't know what might have happened. For that alone she was willing to forgive quite a few of his faults. Regardless, however, of how useful he might be, she couldn't very well ask him or Lance to chaperone the others. That was her job.

Shay suddenly had a brilliant idea. She'd organize a group activity for the bachelors. They could all be required to participate. That way Luther, Steve, and Anton would not have time to work themselves into a tizzy over what Cami was doing on her date, and Michael and Lance could assist her in keeping a lid on the younger, rowdier men. The only disadvantage to the plan was that James would have to be included, and she could have done without seeing him. But it was a small price to pay in order to keep Steve, Anton, Luther, and Jordan from acting out.

She ended up arranging an unofficial pool tournament in the hotel's recreation room and managed to get special permission for the men to drink beer in there. The contestants had a lot of nervous energy, and Shay wasn't sure she would be able to keep them in control, but she didn't think they could get too crazy in that atmosphere.

"I am going to take you out," Luther said to Jordan the minute he had a pool cue in his hand.

"Give it your best shot," Jordan challenged with a confident smile.

Uh oh, Shay thought. He looked way too sure of himself. She had a feeling he was going to be good at this game. She hadn't really thought about that. Luther had accepted his loss manfully after the diving contest, but if Jordan beat him again tonight, he might not be able to handle a second defeat.

"I'm playing Jordan," Michael interjected. "It's me and Lance against Jordan and James. You and Steve and Anton can play Trips."

"Sounds good," Luther agreed.

"Let's keep this friendly, gentlemen," James said.

As the bachelors started to play, Shay congratulated herself for coming up with this idea. The guys were mellow, their mood congenial. For a couple of minutes, the only sound in the room was the gentle clicking of the cues against the balls and the balls against each other.

"I call the one ball in the corner pocket," Lance murmured.

A moment later, Michael whistled softly between his teeth. "Nice shot."

"Damn, Lance. What are you? A pool shark?" Jordan exclaimed petulantly.

"I've played a lot," Lance said simply. "Thirteen in the side." He made the shot and made a small satisfied noise.

"Are you planning to leave anything for me to do, partner?" Michael asked, impressed.

Lance just smiled. "Ten ball off the thirteen, into the corner."

"He's never gonna make that," Jordan said, then grimaced as the veterinarian sank the ball.

"How the hell did you do that?"

"You have your game, I have mine," Lance said happily, surveying the table for his next shot.

"Lance is going to run the table," Luther reported gleefully to his companions.

The three men had been listening and glancing over at the other pool table since the play had started.

"I want to watch," Anton said childishly.

"Hey, ref," Steve called to Shay, who was sitting quietly at the side of the room, near the door. "We're gonna take a break and watch Lance mop the floor with Jordan and James."

"Fine," Shayla agreed. She didn't think any harm could come of it. She hadn't counted on James's spleen.

"You knew, didn't you?" he accused Michael. "When you made up the teams, you knew how good he was."

Michael looked offended. "I just chose partners at random."

"Then let's change partners," James suggested. "No one else has played yet, so it doesn't make any difference to the score."

Lance studiously ignored the whole exchange.

"Sure," Michael said coolly. "Fine with me. Lance?"

"Yeah, okay."

Shayla had to hand it to him. If Michael was the slightest bit annoyed with the broker, it didn't show. She didn't think she could have been so unaffected by the insult. James was truly an ass. Shay could easily imagine what James would have said if Michael had suggested he be partnered with Lance before the broker had actually seen the veterinarian play. He would have thrown a fit. Michael had taken Lance as a partner because he knew no one else would want him. They called him a nerd and treated him as if every day that he was on the show was his last. They liked him, because he was an easy man to talk to and was a good guy, but no one thought he was any competition for them, and they didn't mind letting him know it. Shayla was getting a kick out of seeing him top them for once.

As they stood around watching him clear the table, Luther wondered aloud, "Can you picture Claude at an intimate dinner? Poor Camilla."

"Poor Jared," Anton said. "That has got to be one boring date."

Luther was still trying to imagine the conversation between Claude and Camilla. "This fish is very nice, but…I would not prepare it like this. I would grill it on a very hot grill with some basil and a little white wine," he mimicked the restaurateur.

"At least Charlie and Jared will look good in comparison," Steve said.

"She's stuck with all three of them, though. How good can they look?"

"I've seen some of these shows, man. *The Bachelor* and stuff. They go off on these group dates, but they don't all have to stay together. Sometimes the bachelor ends up in a corner or at a bar with one girl, and they talk. Sometimes they do more than talk." Apparently Anton had done some research before he'd arrived.

"Is that what happened on your date, Michael?"

"On our date? We were too nervous to try and get Camilla alone. Wouldn't you say, Lance? We pretty much stuck together."

"I didn't," James said, smirking. "I talked to her alone."

Steve let out a harsh bark of laughter. "You sneaky old bastard. You cornered her and then you just talked to her?"

"Well," James drawled, feigning embarrassment. "I only

meant to try and speak to her alone. But she looked so beautiful, I kissed her."

"So that's why you got pushed in the pool," Anton said. "That wasn't the first time you grabbed her."

The other men looked at James suspiciously, and the mood in the room suddenly shifted. "I did not grab her; I was just offering her my arm," James defended himself.

Lance stepped in. "Next," he said quietly. While the others were talking, he had cleared the table. They looked from him to the one white ball in the middle of the table, and Jordan smiled.

"Damn, man. You *are* a shark."

"I break."

A chorus of groans and protests arose at his announcement. Steve, Anton, and Luther insisted that they wanted to play partners, with Michael making a forth. Michael bowed out, ceding his place to Jordan, who was happy to continue his rivalry with Luther.

"Now I'm going to finish what Lance started," Luther boasted.

"Fat chance," Jordan retorted.

Michael joined James and Lance in a threesome at the other table, and then stood back as Lance took over the table. James sat glumly watching, but Michael just seemed amused at Lance's transformation. Shayla was pleased with herself. This had all worked out very nicely.

After a while, she realized Michael was staring in her direction. It was a strange feeling, as if she'd been pinned to the spot where she sat. Shay could feel his eyes on her, even when she turned away. She didn't like it. Unfortunately, there wasn't a thing she could do about it. Someone had to make sure that other hotel guests were guided gently, but firmly, away from the scene they were shooting, and the camera crew sucked at it, as she'd discovered early on in this production. They tended to sort of hide behind their cameras, pretending they just weren't there whenever difficulties arose that didn't have any direct bearing on their lighting, focusing, or filming. Since those first days of production, Shay had spent an inordinate amount of time watching various doors in this hotel.

She could do her watchdog act on the other side of the door, she realized suddenly. Then she'd be out of this room and away from that gaze. She tried to slip outside without attracting any attention and thought she had succeeded, but Shay had been standing at her new post outside the recreation room for only a couple of minutes when Michael came through the door. "What's going on?" she asked him as he approached, thinking that she was needed inside.

"Nothing. I just wanted to see where you had disappeared to," he answered. "You didn't get very far."

"No, I just wanted to stretch my legs a little," she said, wondering as she did so why she was bothering to explain herself to him. He had no right to question her. What did he think he was, her bodyguard? Somewhere along the line, she must have given him the mistaken impression that she appreciated his interference in her work, and while Shay could admit she had been moderately grateful for his assistance on one or two occasions, she didn't need his help.

This was the perfect opportunity to correct any misconceptions that he might have. "You don't need to concern yourself with what I do," she said firmly. "The only person you need to worry about is Camilla Lyons."

"I know that, I know. Just sit around looking pretty, right?"

Shay hadn't meant to insult him. "You should do what you came here to do," she suggested.

"How do you think I'm doing?" he asked.

"What?"

"Do you think she likes me?"

"I don't know, I—" she answered, flustered.

"You don't know? You two are friends, aren't you?"

"Yes, well, in a way," Shay mumbled, not sure how she should answer that.

"Does she ever talk to you about us? Who does she like best?" he asked.

"I don't think she's decided," Shay retorted. "Anyway, I thought you didn't care about winning."

"I wouldn't turn her down. She is beautiful, intelligent, sexy, famous. I'm not counting on anything, but I wouldn't be averse to winning."

"Well, good luck, Michael." She was surprised to find that she was a little disappointed that Michael was turning out to be more like the rest of the boys than she had thought.

"But she's not really my type," he said.

"Right," she said sarcastically. "She's beautiful, rich, talented. Who would want a woman like that?"

"She's a little high-maintenance for me. I prefer the girl-next-door type."

"The what?"

"You know, nice, sweet, easy to talk to. Like you."

"Like who?" she said in disbelief.

"You," he insisted. "Half these guys have a crush on you. I swear."

"Sure they do," Shay said sarcastically.

"I'm serious," he insisted. "Just watch the tapes if you don't believe me."

"Oh, I do. Believe you. I'm sure these guys are falling hard. In fact, I was worried that something like this might happen. Thanks for telling me."

She made him laugh. And she didn't have any idea how adorable she was. He'd have bet nine guys out of ten would choose Shayla Tennison over Camilla Lyons any day. He couldn't resist leaning over and kissing her, right on the lips.

She pushed him away. "Are you crazy? What do you think you're doing?"

"Proving my point," he said. She really didn't have a clue. "For a smart woman, you're a little slow on the uptake."

It was a backhanded compliment, at best. Shayla looked annoyed. "You're supposed to be falling in love with Camilla Lyons."

"I already told you, I'm not that interested," he said.

"I thought you still wanted to win," she retorted.

"I do."

"Well you've got an odd way of showing it."

"Hmm, I guess that's true." She was looking at him as if he'd lost his mind. He looked back at her, quizzically, and she turned and went back into the recreation room. He followed right behind her, but once inside, she turned to the right, back to her seat at the bar so he couldn't follow her. Michael continued straight into the room toward the other men to see how the pool tournament was coming. Lance, as he would have guessed, was way ahead of everyone else.

As they headed up to their rooms later that evening, the guys started speculating about how the second group date was going. The subject had not been far from their minds, so when the conversation began, it was as if it had started in the middle.

"Those guys don't have a chance in hell of making it with my woman," Jordan said.

"Your woman? Ha! You blew your chance, buddy. All three of you did," Luther said, looking from Jordan to Michael, then glaring at James. "And that group she's out with tonight is no competition. She's probably bored stiff with those losers. On our date, we're going to dance, yo," Luther said. "Me and my boys are going to show Camilla a good time."

Memo
FROM THE DESK OF LITA TOLLIVER
TO: Marsha James, Shayla Tennison
Marsh,

The first small group date went okay I think, but these next two group dates are absolutely *crucial!!!* The boys are not really rising to the challenge. We need all of these guys to start showing us who they really are and what they're doing here. Adding Dee to the lineup should spice things up. I want to make her debut a really exciting event—use it to create a lot of tension and give the show a shot in the arm! Let's do some brainstorming later, okay?

Lita

Chapter 11

The second date yielded spicier results than the first had. Shay, watching the videotape the next day, was sure the producers would be pleased. Cami had kissed Charlie Thompson for no apparent reason except perhaps his incredible good looks. They had barely talked, though. Claude, as Luther predicted, discussed food preparation all night, and Cami was visibly bored. But her interaction with Jared led to some unexpected and satisfying scenes. The older man was a carpenter—good with his hands, as he liked to say to the younger guys. If Cami hadn't been interested in finding out exactly what that meant prior to the group date, she certainly was now. Jared was charming on their date. He picked up the slack the other two men left, and he drew her out in their conversation. Then, when they were alone—as Anton had told the others, the producers did arrange for the contestants to spend some time alone with the star during the evening—Jared was so funny and sweet and irresistible that Cami kissed him, too. Unlike the kiss she shared with Charlie, however, this one was a sizzler. Or at least Shayla thought it sure looked like it when she viewed the tape.

When they got back from the restaurant where they had dinner, the men had gone into the hotel lounge for a nightcap, where they found Luther, Steve, Anton, and Jordan waiting up for them, expecting to be told that the date had been a dud. Since both Charlie and Jared had had such good luck with Camilla, they were unable to issue the report that their eager audience was waiting to hear. Charlie was soon outmaneuvered, revealing that the evening had afforded him some alone time with their goddess, and he told them what had transpired during the interlude. Jared would probably have been more discreet, but once Charlie let the cat out of the bag, he told the truth about his encounter with Camilla, too. Luther, Steve, and Anton were torn between feelings of disappointment and hope that they would all be as lucky on their date.

The producers had decided to wait to hold the next elimination until after the third date, giving each of the men the chance for some time alone with their star before she made the decision. "In the interim," Marsha told Shay, "we don't want to create a lull. The pace of the show has been good. That pool scene was great, and the second date had some nice moments, but it's time to raise the stakes, pit the guys against one another and see who comes out on top."

Shayla knew they wanted to keep the pressure on the contestants so they could capture any angst the bachelors might feel. "If we can get these guys to talk about their hopes and their fears for their futures, I think that could lead to some interesting scenes," Lita confirmed. "I think it's time for that quiz we postponed."

"Sure," Shay agreed. "The writers nearly declared war over it; we might as well use it after all that fuss."

"And the viewers can root for their favorites," Marsha added.

Shayla proposed to the director that the contest be held on the set, with the look and feel of a game show. He loved the idea, and she started to set it up, visiting the property department to have them make up the backdrops and scoreboards, and then checking on bringing in a studio audience. When she went to speak with the editors about the best way to shoot the scene, she was told Dee had decided to visit the set.

"Deanna? She's here?" Shay hadn't expected to see Dee at work yet, and she didn't feel prepared to face her in this setting, but she set off to find her, telling herself that this little visit had to go better than Dee's last unexpected appearance. After all, it couldn't be any worse.

She discovered her sister in an editing booth, watching the first cut of the date with Group Two, Charlie, Jared, and Claude. Dee thought it was hilarious, if her loud laughter and running commentary were any indication. "He's savoring the bouquet, sipping, swishing, is he going to swallow? Yes, he actually drinks the wine!" She broke into applause. The editors who were showing her the tape seemed to find her as amusing as the film footage itself. "Good for you, Claude. I knew you could do it. Oh my God, he's talking about the *nose,* now. Yes, yes, that's it, her eyes are about to glaze over. And…Jared swoops in to save the day. Again. What a man! He may be as old as the hills, but he's still cooler than Chef Claude the Clayfoot. What is that man's problem? He's paying more attention to his pork chops than he is to her. On the other hand, maybe he's the smart one. Look at her, all 'Oh, Jared, you're so funny,' and, 'Jared, you're such an interesting man.' She's obviously just leading him on. She's not really attracted to him. She likes the looks of the other one, Mr. Tall, Dark, and Handsome. Look, she's sneaking another peek. And there's the hair toss. Jared, don't be fooled, buddy. All that vivacious chatter, the sparkling eyes, the husky laughter. It's not for you. She's putting on a show. Look, see, she did it again. She doesn't want you, she wants the man who doesn't speak. It doesn't make any difference to her if he's as dumb as a rock. He is getting the coy come-hither looks, not you. Don't you see it, man? Run. Run while you can still get away. Don't get caught in her net. But it's too late. She's got him just where she wants him. He's fallen for her act."

"Dee," Shay interrupted finally when it became clear that her sister could go on with the play-by-play forever.

"Shay, hey, have you seen this? It's good stuff."

"Yeah, I've seen it. That's my job, remember? That's why I come here every day. What's your excuse?"

"Do I need an excuse?" Dee asked. "I'm going to be working here soon myself. I thought I'd come on down, give it a look. I know I'm not welcome at the hotel. But I might as well get familiar with the layout here in the studio, right?"

"The layout? That shouldn't take long. It's not too complicated."

"No, it's pretty straightforward. I think it's going to be fun filming the show here."

"Great. So now you know that, I think it's time for you to head on home."

"What's your problem, Shay?"

"My problem is that you're not supposed to be watching film footage. You're not even supposed to be here until you actually start working. You're going to appear on this show next week, and meanwhile, you are supposed to stay away. I told you that yesterday, remember?"

"Why, though?" Dee asked.

"Come on." Shay accompanied her out of the editing room and down the hall a bit so the men inside the booth couldn't overhear their conversation. "You know why. You're going to be competing against Camilla, and we want it to be a fair fight."

"She's already got home-court advantage. She's been here longer. Plus, these guys have already spent time with her. If you want to make this fair, you should be helping me, not getting in the way. Whose side are you on, anyway?"

"I'm not on anyone's side."

Dee's face fell. "Oh. I didn't realize that. I thought, as my sister, you'd be rooting for me."

"For you to what? Ignore the rules? Do whatever you want?"

"Well, yeah," Dee said, recovering her smile. "That would be great."

She was hopeless. Shay decided to switch tactics. "Come on, Dee, you're better than this. You don't need to cheat. I told you, you aren't supposed to meet the guys until you're formally introduced, but after that, they'll be dropping like flies. You don't have to do this. All you have to do is be your usual, sweet, charming self, and the guys will love you."

"It can't hurt to get a jump start on the competition."

"You and Camilla have a lot in common. You could be friends. When you costar with her on the show, you might want to work together instead of against each other. There are more than enough men to go around."

"Shay, you are completely missing the point. There's only one way to win, if you really want to win. That fair-fight stuff is for suckers."

"What do you have against Cami, anyway?" Shayla asked. She had been avoiding this conversation since the moment it had become clear that Dee nursed some kind of grudge against the actress. It was better to know what she was up against, now that they were going to be sharing the stage and the screen.

"It's no big thang. That girl has no class. I met her a few years ago at an after-party, the Emmy's maybe, and she was into the guy I was with."

Shay made some sympathetic noises and waited for Dee to continue telling her story, but her sister did not go on. "And…" she prompted.

"And what?"

"What happened?" Shay asked.

"Nothing. That was it."

"That was it. She was flirting with your date?"

"You make it sound like that's okay. I used to have to practically put on a burka when your boyfriends came to the house, but you think it's fine that she was all over my date?"

"I never made you—" Shay started, then gave up. "Okay, listen. This doesn't sound like much of a reason to hate someone."

"I don't hate her. I just think she's skanky. I can't wait to kick her butt."

"Fine," Shay said. Her bosses would love this. She knew it was useless to try to get Deanna to play by the rules. She would just have to keep an eye on her. And in situations like this, she would have to play the bad guy. "Time to go," she ordered.

"I don't wanna," Dee said, trying to be cute.

"Too bad. You've seen the set and met some of the crew. Now you've got to go home." She felt like Dee's mother, not her little sister. But that wasn't a new sensation. Deanna had acted like an immature brat before. She just hadn't done it in front of Shayla's coworkers. She escorted Deanna as far as her office, picked up her messages, and went back to the set to talk to the crew about the setup for that afternoon's fun and games.

She thought Dee had left the studio, but later found out she had never even left the building. Deanna had gone up to the business offices for a little while, "to hammer out the remaining details of her contract," she told Shay at home that evening. She had come back down to leave just as the guys were being brought in for the quiz and stopped to introduce herself. Shay learned from Claude that Deanna was there, when he came to the set without the other bachelors after the drivers had dropped them all off in front of the AAT building. The other nine men were, as he had intimated, all still in the lobby chatting with Dee when Shay came to investigate the holdup.

"Oh, here you all are," she said, keeping her tone light and avoiding looking directly at her sister.

"Sorry," Dee said unapologetically. "Were you waiting?"

"Yes, well, we do have a TV show to make," Shay answered, hoping she didn't sound as annoyed as she felt. She didn't need to worry, as it turned out. The bachelors were so excited about meeting yet another famous, beautiful woman, they didn't pick up on her caustic tone at all.

"Deanna Jones is your sister," Steve said, obviously awestruck. "Why didn't you tell us?" Shayla wasn't sure how to answer him. She didn't know whether Dee had already told them she'd be appearing on *Lady's Choice* with them. If her sister had had the good sense to keep her mouth shut for a change, she didn't want to be the one to divulge the secret.

"It was a surprise," Dee answered for her, getting Shay off the hook. "And there are more to come, boys. This woman has hidden depths." She winked at Shay.

Dee's innocent act didn't fool Shay for a minute. She knew perfectly well that wherever the guys were going, and whether they were late or not, they were not supposed to be talking to Dee. Not until she was formally introduced to them on the show. However, Shay didn't have time to discuss the breach in protocol right then. She needed to break up this pleasant interlude before Cami arrived and saw the men clustered around her soon-to-be rival. She could not have the actress walk in on this scene.

"You're late; you'd better get to the set, gentlemen," she told them.

"Oh, right," Jared said immediately, and turned to Dee to say good-bye. The others followed his lead, and one by one they headed down the hall.

The last to leave was Steve, who was obviously having trouble pulling himself away from the singer. "See you later, Deanna Jones," he said finally, reluctantly following the others.

The quiz went pretty well. The only surprise was the winner. Anton, the quietest of the three young men from Detroit, won. He took to the game-show format as if it was the most natural thing in the world, not displaying a moment's hesitation or uncertainty in his answers. His self-confidence paid off. He answered all but three of the questions correctly and easily outstripped everyone else's scores, winning the first one-on-one date with Camilla. Luther and Steve gave less-than-stellar performances, but—as had been the trio's way throughout the production—they cheered for their more astute pal and seemed to feel as if his triumph was the same as their own. If neither of them could win the date, they'd rather Anton did than anyone else.

James was able to answer only two of his questions correctly. Predictably, he wasn't nearly as good a sport as Luther or Steve, or any of the other men for that matter. Claude tied the broker, answering two food-related questions correctly, and he appeared completely unconcerned about his poor showing. His lackadaisical attitude was shared by Charlie

Thompson, who was the only contestant who didn't get a single answer right. It didn't seem to faze him that his score at the end of the game was a big fat zero. Shay couldn't decide whether it was a lack of intelligence or just his easygoing personality that made him so unconcerned about losing. Lance and Jordan were neck and neck through the whole game—with Jordan displaying a comprehensive knowledge of sports trivia, and Lance answering all of the mathematics and literature questions. Michael and Jared were right behind them, getting the same right answers to a lot of questions, but not as quickly as Anton or Lance.

The third and final group date took place that Saturday. As it turned out, however, Camilla's date with the boys from Detroit was not the roller-coaster ride that Luther had hoped it would be. This time, Shay didn't chaperone either the date or the guys who stayed behind. She needed a break from baby-sitting. She did have to watch the tapes, though. Though the editors would not do the final edits until Cami had chosen the man of her dreams, it was Shay's job to vet the film in the interim and give the producers an account of the promising parts and give them either transcripts or copies of the best scenes that had been taped each day. The first date had not provided a lot of exciting footage. The best material that night had been the complaining of the men left behind, although the electricity between Cami and Jordan had been tantalizing, and James's surprising behavior had provided a few minutes of juicy film footage. The second date was more successful. Camilla seemed to get along well with Jared, and her interest in Charlie had been unmistakable.

On the third date, as Luther had promised, the group went dancing. The boys from Detroit were a fun group, young and wild and not easily embarrassed. Their personalities complemented one another. Luther, though one year younger, was the acknowledged leader on this venture, because he was the one who was obsessed with Camilla Lyons, but it seemed from the stories they told about their lives and exploits that they each had their leadership roles. Anton owned the business where they all worked, which was a very successful auto shop with more than one branch in the Detroit area. He was the responsible one in the trio. It was Steve who usually led the other two into trouble. Where Anton was tall, slim, and self-controlled, he was short and a bit rounder than the other two, in both face and body. Steve and Anton were twenty-six, but he sported a goatee that made him look a bit older.

Cami got up on the dance floor with all three men, together and individually. The boys could all move, and she had a great time with them. The group drank and danced for hours, and on this date, no ugly incidents marred their enjoyment of the evening; but Luther's age did show a bit, especially after he had a little too much to drink. When Cami was dancing with Steve for the second time, he left the table saying he needed air.

To the cameraman who followed him out of the club, he admitted, "I'm not worried about Anton. He wasn't even sure he wanted to do this, and he isn't even sure he wants to marry her, or anyone else, yet. He's not sure he's ready to settle down, especially with someone who's got this great career. I mean, he thinks it's great that she's got this amazing job, but it would mean he might have to put his own work on hold or something, and he's not sure he wants to do that. That's the thing about Anton. He thinks about everything. He's like that, you know. He doesn't just do stuff, like me or Steve—he always has to think it out first. This whole trip wasn't his idea. We talked him into it because we wanted to do it together. We're tight like that. But he never even watched her soap opera until after he got chosen to do the show. He researched Camilla Lyons and found out she went to college and studied romance languages and had a family that lived in the Midwest and all that, so he decided he would come with us. I respect that. He wasn't all gaga over meeting her, though.

"Steve's not like him at all. All he had to do was see a picture of Camilla and he was in. He was like, 'I wanna do this because she's hot, and rich, and beautiful.' He doesn't care about her as a person like I do. He just wants to stay on the show and date her. He'd marry Camilla in a minute, though, if she wanted to, because, like, who would say no to *that*. Except maybe Anton. Anyway, Steve's just into having a good time. He might fall in love with her, but he will probably just want to fool around, and I already feel like we have a connection with her. He won't care about that, though. He's a good friend, but he doesn't think about stuff like that. My feelings, her feelings, are not that important.

"Ever since I met Camilla, it's been amazing actually talking to her and flirting, and the dancing tonight and everything. She is so perfect for me. I just hope…I think she feels me, but I bet she's a little worried because she's a couple of years older than I am. Not a lot, and I know plenty of people where the girl is a little older, but women don't like that. They want the man to be older, or at least the same age. So, maybe that's going to be a problem for her. But since I'm on the show and she didn't get rid of me right away, I think I've got a shot. She can get to know me and see it doesn't matter. Steve's her age, and I'm better with her than he is."

Having unburdened himself, Luther was ready to go back into the club. When he went inside, he was visibly pleased to see Steve sitting at the table while Camilla danced with Anton. "She just danced one song with you?" he asked.

"Your insecurity is showing," his buddy teased.

"Hey, I know I'm next, man. I've got nothing to be insecure about. I was just chillin' out because I didn't want to drink too much. Now I'm ready for another round."

"I'm just messing with you, man. Don't worry about it. Drink up." Steve got the waitress's attention, and they shook hands.

Luther ordered drinks, his high spirits recovered. They sank again when Anton came back to the table alone. "Where's Camilla?"

"Bathroom, I think. She said to tell you she'd be right back."

"Me?" Luther asked, smiling.

"Yeah, just you. She said don't tell Steve nothin'."

"Very funny." Luther tried to settle back into his seat, but a second later he was hunched over the table again, grilling Anton about her whereabouts. "Which way did she go?"

"What, are you gonna go stake out the women's room?"

"Why'd the other cameraman go with her then? They never followed us into the bathroom."

"Just finish your drink and stay cool. She'll be back."

When she returned, Luther jumped up from the table immediately. "Wanna dance?"

"Sure," Camilla agreed.

Once on the dance floor, Luther was happy again. He danced close, and she didn't do anything to discourage it, which appeared to be enough to reassure him that she was open to talking about their relationship. "We're good together," he said. "Are you having fun?"

"Absolutely," Camilla replied.

"With all of us, or with me?" he asked.

"Both," she answered promptly. "This has been a great date."

"I'm glad," he said. "I'm looking forward to getting to know you better. I've really enjoyed spending a little time alone together tonight."

"Yeah, me, too."

"I can't wait until we spend a whole evening together, just the two of us."

"Uh-huh."

Luther didn't know that, between her dances with Anton and with him, she'd taken a break at the bar and talked about how she didn't quite know how to deal with the trio. "They're so close to one another, it's hard to imagine going out with any one of them," she had said. "I wouldn't want to get in between them. They've been friends since they were five or six years old. They're all sweet, and I like each one of them, but they go together. I wouldn't want to break up the set."

Shay, watching the tape later, winced when she heard that little tidbit. Up until that moment, she would have given each of them an even chance at winning this competition. Each of the boys got to dance and talk to her alone, and she kissed all three—the first two while Luther was outside, talking to the cameras. Steve gave her a hug and a kiss at the end of their second dance. Anton she offered a kiss to when the music ended, saying, "I don't want to play favorites." Luther missed seeing both of these events, since he was outside at the time. Shay didn't think he'd have been quite so happy about his own kiss if he'd known that he was actually the last to get one at the very end of the night.

When they arrived back at the hotel, the other two men said good-bye and went inside, but Luther lingered a while with her, clearly unwilling to bring the date to an end. "That *was* a really great time," he said cheerfully. "I thought."

"Definitely," she responded.

"Better than your other dates, from the sound of it," he pressed.

"It was a lot of fun. I'm tired, though," she answered.

"Not me."

Shay guessed, watching the tape, that Camilla finally kissed him as much to get rid of him as anything else. She couldn't just push past him into the hotel. It would have been cruel. Instead, she said, "Good night," and reached up to give him a kiss. Luther was thrilled and deepened the kiss until she pulled away, gently, saying, "I should go."

"Of course," he agreed immediately, stepping back. "I'll see you tomorrow." He watched her walk into the hotel, away from him, with a goofy smile on his face, then went up to the room he shared with Steve and Anton and told his friends about it.

They didn't tell him they'd kissed her, too. They just congratulated him and urged him to go to bed.

Memo

FROM THE DESK OF SHAYLA TENNISON
ATTENTION: ALL DEPARTMENT HEADS

As you all know, security is important in a production like this one. Only the public relations department and the producers are authorized to give anyone not employed by this production any information about filming. We cannot have leaks! It is everyone's responsibility to make sure that what happens on the set and on location is kept under wraps.

Relatives of the cast and crew should be treated like any other members of the public. They can wait to see the show until it is broadcast, just like anyone else. This includes my sister, Deanna Jones. This order applies to everyone on the set. Anyone caught releasing information without authorization from the producers or public relations will be summarily fired.

Chapter 12

The truth came out the next day, of course. Shay grabbed a danish for breakfast in the lounge and checked up on the boys on her way to see Cami that morning. The second round of eliminations was scheduled for that night, and she wanted to make sure no one was freaking out. Last time, Luther had been on tenterhooks, but after his date the night before, he was feeling pretty confident about his chances of being asked to stay on the show. He, Steve, and Anton were all feeling good, drinking mimosas, and talking about Anton's upcoming date with Camilla.

James made the mistake of commenting about the size of Steve's breakfast. "Carbing up?" he asked sardonically.

"What's that supposed to mean?" Steve responded belligerently.

"Nothing, really. I just wondered if you ate like that every morning?"

"Why are you so interested in my diet?" Steve asked.

"Diet?" James said, smirking at him.

"Funny," Steve replied, annoyed. "You aren't exactly the man to beat in the body department, James. Not on this show. There are a lot of guys who make you look like the desk jockey you are."

James's smile slipped a little. "Maybe I'm not a professional athlete, but I take care of myself."

"I know you do. What are you, forty-five? Forty-six?"

"I'm thirty-eight," James said angrily.

Steve had hit a nerve. Cami, grabbing a danish from the buffet for her breakfast, hid a smile.

Steve shook his head ruefully. "Whoa, thirty-eight? And you've got a good job and muscle tone and the teeth. So why are you still single, anyway? Is there something we don't know about you?"

"Not at all. As you just pointed out, I'm successful in business, and in life. I've just been waiting to meet the right woman. Now that I have, I may have ten years on you—"

"Twelve," Steve interjected smugly.

"But I'll still bet she'll choose me over you, dough boy."

Steve moved toward him menacingly, but his friends were able to move between the two men and divert him.

"Come on," Luther said as if nothing had happened.

"Sit down," Anton said forcefully. "Don't let that idiot get to you."

"Fine," Steve replied, grumbling under his breath as he walked to the table his friends had chosen. "'Do you always eat that much for breakfast?' Yes, I do, dickwad."

"Give it a rest," Anton advised. "We're supposed to be having fun here, not losing it in front of the cameras. People back home are going to see this, remember?"

"I know, I know," Steve said, subsiding.

After that little tussle, Steve was on edge for the rest of the morning, and by noon, when Dee showed up at the hotel, he was primed for trouble. He slipped away with her, out of sight of the cameras, before the crew even knew she was there. Shayla didn't find out about any of this until a couple of hours later when she arrived at the hotel to give the boys a pep talk before they went up to get ready for the evening's festivities. They were supposed to meet her in the lounge after lunch, but only Anton, Luther, Lance, and Jared were there when she arrived. When she told them they had to wait for the others, Luther took her aside and whispered that he thought he saw her sister right before Steve disappeared. He didn't want to draw attention to the situation by searching for his friend himself, but he was worried about what Steve was doing to his chances with Camilla. "I want to win," he said. "But not that way."

Shay found the two of them drinking and flirting in a booth at one of the hotel's bars, which was empty on a weekday at two in the afternoon. "Dee!" she exclaimed, exasperated.

"What!" Dee responded, sounding equally frustrated.

"Come out of there, and go home. You're going to be appearing on the show next week. Can't you wait that long?"

"I want to get to know all of these guys as well as I can," Dee answered, smiling at Steve, who didn't seem to notice that she'd just admitted she intended to carry on with the other bachelors just as she had been with him.

Shay decided to appeal to her practical side. "There will be only eight men left by the time you join the cast," she reminded her.

"So?"

"So, two of these guys will be gone by then."

"Are you, by any chance, suggesting that I'd be wasting my time by talking to two of these gentlemen?" Dee asked.

Steve looked disappointed when Shayla answered honestly, "I don't see the point, since you can't see them once they've been eliminated from *Lady's Choice.*"

"Nuh-uh," her sister corrected her gleefully. "I can. Camilla can't, but I had my agent take that clause out of my contract. I can see these guys whenever I want to, no matter what happens on the show."

Steve shot Shay a triumphant look and wrapped a beefy arm around Dee's slim shoulders. "I thought you were on our side, boss," he said to Shay. "But now it looks like your sister's a better sport than you are."

Shay didn't think Dee's attitude had anything to do with good sportsmanship. "You'd better get back to the others, Steve, before they notice you're missing."

Unfortunately, James had already missed him and had come looking. He spotted the three of them as they emerged from the lounge. "So this is where you've been hiding. Well, well, well."

He couldn't wait to drop the bomb on the other guys, and of course he had to do it in front of the cameras. "Guess who Camilla's going to get rid of next," he taunted the younger man.

"Shut up," Steve ordered.

Luther arranged himself by his friend's side. "Leave him alone, James. He didn't do anything to you."

"You might not be so eager to defend him when you hear what he did with Camilla last night when you weren't looking," James said.

"Wha-at?" Luther asked, confused. "What's he talking about, Steve?"

"One of the crew members told me you weren't the only one to get some lip action, bud. Your friends were in there."

Luther looked at Steve questioningly. "It was nothing," his friend assured him. "We were just fooling around, you saw."

"I didn't see you kiss her."

"You kissed her, too."

"*And* Anton?" Luther spluttered. "When?"

"Last night while they were dancing," James reported. "I didn't think they told you. You were in much too good a mood today to have any idea that your friends were trying to screw you."

Jared stepped in at that point. "James, that's enough."

"Enough what? Honesty? It's not like he won't find out eventually, anyway. This way at least he knows who his real friends are—or aren't."

"I hope you're not including yourself in that category," Michael said.

Jared broke up the conclave, planting himself between Luther and Steve and the older man and saying to James, "I think you'd better go. You made your point—now leave these boys alone."

"No. Why?" the broker protested. "You can't tell me what to do."

"Come on," Lance suggested. "Before someone else says something they shouldn't." James didn't seem inclined to take either man's advice, but the veterinarian didn't give him much of a choice. He led him away, saying, "James, you've done enough damage."

Shay waited a moment to make sure the argument wasn't going to start up again, then left for Cami's room. Marsha and Lita had come up with a new ploy to influence their bachelorette's decision in the second round of eliminations that evening. They hadn't included Shay in their plans this time, but they had given her a video to show Cami this afternoon before the ceremony, and she was sure that it contained some kind of message from them about which man she should reject. Apparently, it was top secret. She was supposed to let Cami watch it, stay in the room, and then take the tape back to the studio as soon as she was done.

She had been curious about the precautions they'd taken, but she'd never have guessed at the lengths they'd gone to if she hadn't seen it herself. They had combed through a number of transcripts, looking for certain scenes and dialogue, and then had the editors create a kind of retrospective that showed the men Marsha and Lita liked most in their best light. Shayla watched their little docudrama in wonder. It was not hard for them to find scenes in which the bachelors said flattering things about Cami, but she imagined it was a little difficult to create the section of the tape that they spliced together so that it looked as if Lance, Jared, and the boys from Detroit—all their least favorite contestants—said uncomplimentary-sounding things about her.

The last two minutes of tape was a montage of Lita and Marsha's favorite bachelors interacting with the star of the show. The producers hadn't had any trouble finding great moments between Jordan and Camilla, but it was harder to make James and Claude look as if they were clicking with the actress—though her bosses did their very best. Shay's favorite part was the bit where Michael was shown, in all his glory, judging the swimmers as they competed in their diving contest. Although he looked great in his swim trunks, they chose to focus on his thoughtful expression and the way the other men deferred to his judgment when he gave them coaching tips; finally, then focused on his protective behavior toward Camilla when he brought over an umbrella to shield her from the sun.

Although it was a nice montage, and Marsha—Shay was certain it *was* Marsha's handiwork—was careful to get in a shot or two that displayed all the rippling muscles to their best advantage, the most amazing part was the footage of Charlie Thompson. No one could deny that he was a painfully beautiful man, but seen through Marsha's eyes, the computer salesman looked like a god. His portion of the tape bordered on the erotic. In it, he stripped poolside; rubbed lotion onto Camilla's calves; stretched out on a lounger; and fell asleep in the sun, at which point one of the camera crew had taken a long slow panning shot of his body from head to toe. Marsha wasn't foolish enough, or perhaps able, to include any footage of him conversing with anyone, but the visuals she included made him look sizzling hot.

Shay showed the tape to Cami, as instructed, who seemed suitably impressed by all of the images, and even asked, "This show is gonna be hot."

"Some parts more than others, I'm thinking," Shay said, and left the actress pondering her decision. After she closed the door behind herself, she leaned back against it and released the laughter that had bubbled up inside as she watched her bosses' masterwork unfold. To her, the collection of pretty pictures and half-truths was a transparent effort to influence the soap star's decision; but it was different for Cami, who had no way of knowing how much of what she was shown was false or how many of the implications were misleading.

Camilla didn't spend any time just hanging out with the guys, and she didn't get to see the hours of film that were taped, some showcasing the boys at their best, some giving the impression that they were complete morons. They drank and fought and sniped at each other, and they talked about Camilla, and most of it was not footage that Shay would have wanted her mother to see. On the other hand, as a group, they were romantic and hopeful and human. With some judicious editing, they would all have moments on the show when they were quite adorable. She suspected that when they left *Lady's Choice,* they'd have more than a few fans waiting for them.

At the second round of eliminations that evening, Dan Green played the part of host with his usual bonhomie. "Welcome back, gentlemen." His role for the evening was to lend authority to the ceremony, but his only tools were his deep voice and calm manner. Like the rest of the cast and crew on the reality show, his job was to react to events rather than to try and set any particular tone. The appeal of *Lady's Choice* lay in capturing authentic moments and capitalizing on them. These elimination rounds would be the climax of each episode, and as such, they were vitally important to the production.

"Camilla has an envelope for each of you," Dan announced. "Nine of them are invitations to spend time with the lady. The tenth contains a good-bye for the man who is going home tonight." Some of the bachelors nodded, some smiled at him, and a couple of them grimaced. The men stood in a loosely formed row, quietly waiting for the announcer to turn the floor over to Camilla.

Anton was probably the most nervous. Since he'd won the trivia quiz, he would automatically be the first to have a one-on-one date with the soap star, but that was contingent upon his not being rejected here tonight. According to the rules of this contest, as Dan explained again now, any one of the bachelors could be asked to leave at any time. So, even though Anton had won the competition, it didn't necessarily mean that he would not be eliminated. The guys had all talked about it. Shay had seen the tape. Luther and Steve had made a pact with each other—if Anton was rejected, they would go home with him. Everyone agreed that it would be a shame if he was deprived of the fruit of his victory in the trivia contest. It wasn't necessary to have seen that tape, however, to know that Anton was very anxious. He looked as though he were going to fly out of his skin.

He jumped when Camilla called his name first. He walked toward her slowly, searching her face. He seemed to be holding his breath. "Anton," she said again when he reached her; she handed him his envelope. All ten envelopes displayed a single name, and nothing else. Anton's hands visibly shook as he opened his envelope. The smile that spread across his face told everyone watching he had not been rejected yet. "You are invited to give me a tour of your favorite museum," he read aloud. "Thank you."

"You're welcome." Camilla was smiling, too. She gave him a kiss on the cheek and let him take her hands in his. "You want to stay, then?" she asked.

"Absolutely," he stated. "If you didn't know that, then I'm doing something wrong."

"No, you're not," she said. "I have to ask, that's the rule."

"You don't need to bother," he said. "I could never leave you."

"I'm glad to hear it," Camilla replied, laughing. "I'll try to make sure you don't change your mind."

"That's my line," he quipped. Now that he'd actually gotten his invitation to stay, he was able to make jokes with the show's star again. Of the three younger men from Detroit, he was the calmest, and probably the brightest, Shay thought. But he was relatively quiet. Not like Charlie or Claude, who were so self-involved they didn't seem to realize what was going on around them half the time, but because, like Lance, he was more of an introvert than the other contestants. Most of the men were outgoing, charming, likable guys who had always been successful with the ladies. One could call them players.

Anton and Lance, while just as charming and likable, could not, by any stretch of the imagination, be mistaken for players. They were nice, intelligent, good-looking guys and were far from shy, but compared to their rival bachelors, they seemed like geeks.

Camilla gave Jordan his envelope next. He opened it with none of the nervousness that Anton had displayed. He clearly expected it to contain an invitation to remain on the program. Camilla did not disappoint him. She had asked him to stay, and his challenge was to take her sailing. He accepted it, gave her a kiss on the cheek, and joined Anton a bit behind her and to the left. The two men shook hands, and murmured quietly to each other as she called the next contestant forward. Both Luther and Steve were soon aligned with their friends behind her, as were Michael and Jared. Only Claude, Charlie, Lance, and James remained for her to choose from. The ceremony had gone without a hitch, Shay was pleased to note, although the tension slowly rose as the pool of possible rejects dwindled. James was probably the person she would have recommended that Cami eliminate in this round, and she would definitely have wanted to keep Lance around and gotten to know him better, but that had not been the advice the star had received from her producers. Marsha and Lita, still hard at work behind the scenes trying to manipulate the outcome of this ceremony, were determined that Lance should be the one to go. Lita had a crush on Claude because of his profession, and Marsha thought Charlie's good looks alone made him a viable contender, but Shayla wasn't sure why they were so set on keeping James around. He was obnoxious. Then again, they had always said that he and Cami would have been the most likely to meet and pair up in the *real world*.

James was a well-groomed, wealthy, successful, New York

banker. He was the type of guy who always appeared at theater openings and charity balls with a runway model or TV star on his arm. Marsha and Lita had definitely been told about the embarrassing scene he'd created during the first group date, and Shay knew they must have been aware of the sullen, childish behavior he'd often indulged in since then, but they seemed intent on ignoring it and on influencing Cami to overlook it as well. From the actress's noncommittal response to the carefully edited videotape she'd viewed that afternoon, Shay could only assume that Cami was not averse to their hints that she eliminate Lance tonight and invite James to stay, but if this had been Shay's decision, it would have been a simple one: Lance was a sweetheart and James didn't hold a candle to him.

When Charlie read his challenge, Shayla gasped. "You're invited to cook me dinner," he read. He looked back over his shoulder at Claude, who looked as stunned as Shayla felt. That invitation had clearly been meant for the chef. The producers had chosen a large variety of events and activities for the couples to enjoy on their one-on-one dates, but this one—cooking dinner—could only have been intended for Claude. Luther had been invited on a helicopter ride, Jared to an open-air market, Michael to the Vietnam War Memorial, and Steve had been challenged to show her the ropes at a rock-climbing place.

Only two envelopes remained. If Shayla remembered correctly, the only two invitations that remained were to take Cami on a tour bus around Washington and a shopping trip at the mall. Cami looked down at the last two envelopes in her hand and then back up at Lance, Claude, and James. She had not been told which order to give the invitations out to, nor which man to invite to which event. Like the final decision concerning whom to reject, the producers had left those choices up to her. Shayla felt she'd given the cards out in the order of her preference for these men, excepting possibly Anton, who had already won the next date when he won the trivia quiz. Shayla could have been wrong, but Cami had more than hinted that that was her plan. The actress had not, however, intimated to anyone that she planned to reject Claude. Maybe she just wanted to do something else with him, Shayla thought as she waited for the star of the show to call on the next man.

"Lance," Cami announced once Charlie had rejoined the contestants who had already been invited to stay. The veterinarian stepped forward tentatively. "This is for you," she said, handing him an envelope. Shay almost let out a cheer.

"Thank you," Lance said with a relieved smile. "I'm very happy to stay," he forestalled her question. "You don't even need to ask. Thank you." He hugged her.

"You're welcome," Camilla said, smiling at him.

The smile faded away instantly as she looked at the two remaining bachelors. James shifted uncomfortably but held his head up high. Claude looked confused. He didn't meet her gaze until she said, "I'm sorry I won't be getting to know you better, Claude." Then he stared straight at her, stunned.

"This invitation is for you, James. Will you stay?" Cami asked. He didn't hesitate but came forward immediately and took the envelope from her outstretched hand. He kissed her cheek and gave her a quick hug as the others had, but her attention, like that of all the other bachelors, was focused on Claude.

The chef came toward her slowly and stopped about a foot away, speechless. "I'm glad I met you, but…I didn't feel we really connected. I'm really sorry," she tried to explain. He recovered himself enough to give her a quick hug, and then he walked around her toward the door.

There was a car and a camera crew waiting outside to take him back to the hotel to pack up his things.

Meanwhile, Camilla and the men who were left gathered in a small circle, relieved that the ordeal was over. "I'm glad you're all staying," Cami said.

"We are, too," the men answered. Someone said, "Of course," and everyone laughed.

Cami's good mood lasted approximately ten minutes, at which point she spotted Deanna, who was watching the filming from a corner of the room, behind the lights and cameras, where it was unlikely she'd be seen. Dee realized she'd been spotted and disappeared through the door before the camera crew caught her where she wasn't supposed to be, but Cami called Shay over and told her she'd seen her sister. "How long was she standing there watching?" she asked.

"I didn't even know she was here," Shay said. When Cami looked at her dubiously, she added, "I swear."

"She isn't supposed to be on the set. She's not even allowed to meet these guys until she's on the show," Cami whined.

"I know, Cami. I'm sorry. I'll just make sure she's gone."

Shay flew. She didn't know where exactly Dee might have gone, but she was pretty sure she hadn't gone home. That would just be too sensible of her.

Her suspicions were confirmed when Shay reached her office. Dee was sitting at her desk, waiting for her. "What do you think you're doing, Dee?" she asked. "You know you could have been seen. In fact, Cami did see you."

"Who cares if she saw me? What's she gonna do about it? Besides complain to you, I mean."

"She could get your contract cancelled. You agreed not to meet these guys, remember? No contact."

"It wasn't that strict. The contract just said when I would meet them. It didn't say I couldn't talk to them before that if I just happened to meet them."

"Just happened to? Here, at the studio, on a night when you know there's going to be an elimination? You're planning to tell the lawyers that that was just a coincidence?"

"What lawyers? Cami's not going to call a lawyer," Dee said confidently. "She'd look like she was jealous of me, or nervous, and that's not her style. She wants to seem cool and in control. You know. Like you." Shay was taken aback by the comparison, but only for a second. Long enough for Dee to find a hole in her theory. "No one is going to call a lawyer, Shay, because everyone except Ms. Thang is hoping I'll win this thing."

"Not everyone," Shay muttered.

"Not you, I know. You're on her side. But everybody else likes me better than that stuck-up stick figure. You saw those guys when they met me. They loved me."

"They don't even know you. And besides, it's just not true. Some of these guys really like Camilla; they're not *all* in it because she's a celebrity." Shay was thinking of Lance and Jared and Luther, who were all clearly infatuated with the soap opera star, perhaps even falling in love with her.

"You really are on her side, aren't you?" her sister asked. She sounded disappointed, and she looked hurt. Shay felt a twinge of guilt because she had been thinking of herself, too, not just the men. "Of course not—I'm not on her side. I'm not on anyone's side. There's just one show, and we're all in it together."

"We can't all win," Dee stated.

"Yes, actually, you can. We can. Cami can end up with Mr. Right, and you can weave your spell around one of the other guys, and the show can get good ratings. That way everyone ends up happy."

"She wants Jordan, though. And I'm going to get him."

"This is ridiculous. I'm not going to stand here arguing with you, I have a television show to produce."

"Well, get to it then, sis. I'm not stopping you."

"Yes, you are. When you come into the studio and onto the set and disrupt filming, you are stopping me from doing my job. What's with you? Why can't you just wait until next week? Then you'll be able to hang out here and in the hotel all you want."

"I'm going to win this, Shay, whether you help me or not."

"It's not a matter of my helping you or hindering you. I have a job to do, and part of that job is making sure that no one cheats. You can't just show up on the set uninvited. How many times do I have to tell you this?" Shay asked, frustrated.

"As many as you want, I guess," Dee answered.

When Shay finally got rid of Dee and went back to the set, Cami was getting ready to be driven home. She'd cheered up a little, but she still gave Shayla a nasty look as she asked, "Did you get rid of her?"

"Of course," Shay replied, trying to sound reassuring.

Camilla didn't appear to be buying it. "I know she's your sister, but you've got to make her stay away."

Shay tried. She really did. But Dee was shameless. No matter how many times Shay told her sister to stay away from the studio, she kept showing up over the next few days. She wasn't supposed to come anywhere near the set until it was time to film the episodes in which she was to appear as a guest, but, then, she had never really been good at obeying the rules.

That was another difference between them. Shayla had always pretty much done what she was told.

The men loved Dee's illicit visits, especially the boys from Detroit, who were fans of her music. Cami, on the other hand, was not thrilled. Shayla agreed with the actress that her sister's behavior was unprofessional, but there was little she could do besides lecture Deanna, and that didn't seem to have any effect at all. Shay appealed to Marsha to mention to Dee that she wasn't authorized to enter the studio prior to the start of her contract, but the producer was pleased that Dee was so eager to appear on the show that she couldn't seem to wait.

"What harm does it do?" she asked.

Shayla was tempted to tell the bosses that Deanna was playing dirty, trying to get a jump on the competition by flirting with the contestants, but in the end she kept her mouth shut. It wasn't her job to police the sets. If the guards couldn't, or wouldn't, keep her sister out of the studio, Shay wasn't going to be able to stop her. She had too much work to do; she didn't have the time to play watchdog. Shay had tried reasoning with Dee, appealing to her sense of fair play; and she even threatened to disqualify her from the competition, but Dee refused to cooperate. She took pleasure in figuring out how to get around the restrictions that her contract imposed on her, and she was good at it. She was never caught on tape—she only spoke to the men when the cameras were focused on someone, or something, else. She hung around at the fringes of the set, and, like an exotic flower, the men were drawn to her.

Not only the cast but the crew also liked her. A large part of her attraction for the technicians and office staff was that it annoyed Cami to see that Dee was so popular, but when

Shay pointed that out to Dee, she just said, "So what?" She didn't waste any energy worrying about why she was welcome on the set—she just took advantage of the fact that she was. She might even have gotten some added satisfaction from knowing that her presence in the studio was tolerated solely because it upset the star of the show. Dee had always been ultracompetitive.

Whatever Dee's motivation for hanging around, the worst aspect of it for Shay was its effect on the men. Steve, in particular, was completely besotted with her. The tire salesman acted almost as nutty about her as Luther did about Cami.

Memo

FROM THE DESK OF SHAYLA TENNISON

Gentlemen,

I would like to address the worries that some of you have expressed to me concerning the next elimination. I know some of you feel others have been given an unfair advantage. However, I am pleased to announce that there will be no elimination round until after everyone has had the opportunity to spend some time alone with Camilla.

The producers wanted to give each contestant the chance to speak with Camilla, at least once, and so those who have not yet gone out with the star will definitely be going out on a date with her this week. Invitations will be delivered to your rooms.

Speaking of the elimination ceremony, I want to state, once again, that there are no losers on *Lady's Choice*. It has been my pleasure to work with everyone on this production, and Camilla and the crew of *Lady's Choice* have all stated that this cast has the kind of unusual energy and enthusiasm that will help to make *Lady's Choice* a hit.

Good luck to you all.

Yours,

Shayla Tennison

Chapter 13

There was only going to be one contestant rejected during the next week, because the producers had planned that, at this juncture in the show, their star would have dates with each of the contestants before rejecting anyone else. Strangely, the pressure felt by Cami and the guys was even more intense than it had been during the first couple of weeks, when she was eliminating the men at a faster rate. It made sense, though, when Shay thought about it, because now instead of just rejecting strangers, Cami was eliminating men whom she had chosen to keep around during the previous rounds, people she had decided, at some point, that she wanted to get to know.

Since the boys each felt they had some kind of burgeoning relationship with the soap opera star, the atmosphere among the bachelors was more strained now that their number was down to nine. Over the next few days, Cami went on her tour of the Air and Space Museum with Anton, then dinner alone with Charlie Thompson. She had invited him to cook for her, which he did, but despite the possibilities for romance, the evening was uneventful. He served her steak, which he grilled, along with some asparagus, at Shay's suggestion. Marsha—who'd been hoping that sparks might finally fly between the gorgeous couple during the intimate dinner—began to clue in to the fact that Cami probably wasn't going to choose the handsome but not very clever computer salesman as her future husband.

On Tuesday Cami visited the Vietnam War Memorial with Michael, where they walked and talked about his time in the army and about the father whom she had never met because he died in that conflict. She had protested the first Gulf War, she admitted to him, and he told her that that was her right. The reason he fought in the war, he said, was because he believed in democracy. That included her right to protest. Their political conversation was followed that evening by another night of dancing, this time with Cami and all of the bachelors together. There Cami was put to the test, because she had to divide her attention between all of her escorts, but she rose to the challenge very well and managed to keep anyone from feeling slighted or neglected.

Shay arranged a couple more group dates, including a trip to the National Archives with four of the guys: Jared and the three from Detroit. Cami seemed to prefer talking to Jared, which made the younger guys, especially Luther, very nervous; but Luther didn't get nearly as upset by that as he did when she went on a shopping spree with Jordan, Michael, Lance, and Charlie and came back chattering about what fun they had. James, too, was upset, because he was supposed to take her shopping at the mall on her date with him.

Shay felt a twinge of satisfaction when she realized James

was feeling insecure. Although that hadn't been her intention when she arranged the group date, she wasn't exactly unhappy about this unexpected development, especially when he chose to confront her about it. "Did you plan this?" he asked her belligerently.

"If you mean did I handle the arrangements for the outing, then yes," she answered without apology. "That is my job." There was nothing he could say to that, but from then on he behaved coldly toward her, which was just fine with Shayla. The more she saw of the stockbroker, the more she disliked him. Cami, though, seemed to enjoy her second shopping trip just as much as the first, possibly because James went all out, arranging a romantic luncheon in the trendiest shop in the mall. After that, James's fears were put to rest, but Luther's insecurities were heightened. Cami's date with Jordan was just too much for the boy. The suave baseball player took her for a moonlight sail, and Luther was so jealous that he started pacing around the room, unable to sit still for a minute.

"This is a joke," he said. "He doesn't really care about her. She can't end up with him."

Steve and Anton tried to reason with him. "You're taking her on a date tomorrow," Anton said. "Just wait."

"A helicopter is way cooler than a boat. You are so going to blow sailing out of the water," Steve quipped.

Luther didn't appreciate the pun. "I have to tell her now before he gets her alone and does a number on her."

"She's a big girl, Luther, she can take care of herself," Steve replied. "Don't freak out, man. Stay cool."

"You can't let her see that you're so worried about this," Anton said. "You have to show her that you're the better man, and you can't do that by running after them and trying to stop her from dating him."

"By tomorrow it may be too late," he said. "I've got to say something before she gets sucked in by him."

Lance and Michael added their voices to Steve and Anton's. "What are you going to say to her?" Lance asked.

"If you bad-mouth him, it's not going to make you look good," Michael added.

"You can beat him," Anton said. "But not if you act crazy."

Luther was beyond hearing a word they said. "I'm going to go after her." It took him approximately ten minutes after Jordan and Cami left, to work himself up enough to follow them. The camera crew was right on his heels as he jogged out of the lounge. A taxi was just dropping off a fare as Luther exited the revolving doors, and he jumped into the cab as the driver unloaded the suitcases from the trunk of the car. The cameraman followed him.

"I know she can handle him—I'm not worried about that. But he really wants to win. I mean, he really wants it. He'll say whatever she wants to hear, whether it's true or not." He lapsed into a gloomy silence, and the cameraman filmed him sitting in silence for the rest of the ride. Luther jumped out of the taxi at the Happy Harbor Marina and headed for the pier. The man filming him couldn't maneuver as well with his camera equipment, but he caught up with Luther as he stood on the dock, silhouetted against the sunset, staring disconsolately after the yacht that had already left the dock and was sailing away toward the setting sun.

It was great footage, which the editors cut up and interspersed with the opening minutes of the film of Cami's date with Jordan. The baseball player was quite at home on the boat, which was actually manned by a professional captain and crew, leaving him free to hold hands and steal the occasional kiss from Cami. She seemed mesmerized. She couldn't stop looking at him, and he couldn't stop touching her. As the sun set and the sky darkened to a deep azure, they kissed, and then they kissed some more. Even Shay thought this would be great television. Their dialogue wasn't bad, either. Jordan Freeman had come prepared and was as smooth as silk. "I watched your soap before I came here, and I've been wanting to tell you that you are really talented. The scene where your son was put in jail for arson, where you proved he couldn't have done it, was incredible."

"Thank you," Cami said. "I didn't think you'd like that kind of show."

"I usually watch thrillers, mysteries, or maybe action-adventure, but that part of your show was as good as anything I've seen on the big screen. It was tight. Suspenseful."

"That was what we were hoping for," she responded with a wide, pleased smile. "There's a large crossover audience these days for the soaps. More men are watching them, and we try to provide entertainment for that demographic."

"It's the same in baseball," Jordan said. "People thought for a long time that women didn't buy tickets, especially to minor league games, but now they've done some research and found that women and girls are fans. Almost as much as boys."

They were so wrapped up in each other they barely noticed that there had been any trouble with the engine. The threat couldn't penetrate the haze that surrounded them. By the end of the evening, they were in love. At least, that was how it appeared. Both Jordan and Cami were reluctant to say good-night. It took a while for them to pull themselves away from each other, but in the end, both had the good sense not to go to bed together on their first date on national television. They said good-night at the door to Cami's hotel room and went their separate ways.

Luther was subdued on his date with Camilla the following day. His mad rush to the marina seemed to have taken the edge off of his anxiety. Watching the tape, Shayla thought that Camilla was getting to see a much more attractive side of him than she had on the night of their group date, when he'd acted so young and needy. That afternoon he'd been much mellower and seemed more mature. The helicopter ride was a first for both of them, and they enjoyed it and each other's company. It didn't lead to the kind of intimacy Cami had shared with Jordan, however, and Shayla thought it was pretty clear that the soap star wasn't even close to feeling for him what Luther felt for her. Whether the young tire salesman got that was anybody's guess. He wasn't talking.

When Anton and Steve tried to find out how the date went, all he would say was that it was fine. "I think Camilla had a good time," he added, when they pressed him for more details, and they left it at that.

Camilla's date with Lance was the really big surprise of the week. She joked, while she was getting ready to go out, that she had saved the best for last, but no one believed it. The guys figured Lance was the last one she dated because she'd forgotten all about him. Lance, as usual, didn't complain. He didn't even bother to speculate—at least not in view of the cameras. By tacit accord, all the contestants joined him in the lounge while he waited to be summoned on Saturday afternoon. No one seemed able to think of anything to say to him, though.

"Have you spoken to Shayla about the tour?" Michael finally asked Lance.

"Yes, she helped me to make some plans," Lance said happily. The other bachelors avoided eye contact, obviously convinced that he didn't stand a chance at impressing Cami no matter what he had arranged to do on their date.

"Wish me luck," he said when the limo driver came to fetch him.

There was a chorus of male voices calling, "Bye, Lance," and "Later," and "Have fun," as he strode to the door, but the moment he was gone, everyone dropped their forced cheerful expressions, and even Luther couldn't seem to help but feel sorry for him. "I can't believe he has to do a tour the day after I took her up in a helicopter," he said, shaking his head.

"That's tough luck," Jared agreed.

"He made it a lot longer than he thought he would," Steve said pityingly, once he was sure the veterinarian was out of earshot.

"A month," Anton confirmed. "He thought he was outta here the first week."

"Two rounds of rejections, that's something to be proud of," Luther added. "And at least he got to go on a date with her."

"Right before tomorrow's elimination round," James commented. "I'd say this was more of a formality than a date, wouldn't you?" he said to the room in general. Everyone ignored him.

Shayla thought the editors did a clever job of editing the tape of the guys commiserating while Lance toured around the D.C. sites with Camilla. Shay had helped Lance to arrange a distinctive tour of the city, with some unusual stops along the way. So on the film, while the other men were saying good-bye, he and Camilla were greeting each other. Though he was nervous, he was also happy to be with her, and his good spirits seemed to be catching. On tape, while they were shaking their heads, the two of them were sitting in the limousine and he was telling her that, for the next part of the tour, they were going to take a double-decker bus but that they would take the limo to the first stop if that was all right with her. "I thought this would be more comfortable," he said, opening the small refrigerator and pulling out a bottle of Piper Heidsieck champagne.

"Where are we going?" she asked as he poured.

"Mount Vernon," he answered. "George Washington's home. It's about forty-five minutes from here."

While the other bachelors predicted the worst, he was showing her around the well-preserved grounds of the first president's mansion in Virginia.

With his slim build and nondescript style, Lance might look as if he was the least suited of the bachelors to play Camilla's escort, but when he offered her his hand into the tour bus, he suddenly appeared seven feet tall. It was not his stature, but his bearing. He was a gentleman, not a condescending sexist pig like James or a player like Jordan. When he held out his hand, it was clearly a gesture for her benefit, not to make himself feel big or for an excuse to touch her— it was obviously automatic for Lance to treat his date like a lady. The only thing more endearing than the gesture itself was his smile when she allowed him to take her hand.

He was the only contestant under six feet tall, but he was only a shade under. He sometimes looked tiny in comparison to the other contestants, but once alone with Cami, they didn't look like such an odd match at all. In fact, they seemed to fit together, in a way. They looked like an ordinary couple, perhaps slightly more attractive than most, and they talked to each other like two people on a first date, about where they grew up and the books and people that influenced them. They were alone on the top of the bus, the sun casting the last long golden rays of the afternoon across the white marble of D.C.'s public buildings and monuments and verdant grass. The two of them glowed as they talked together, and then laughed together at the zoo, the last stop on Lance's tour. It was as though the cameras weren't even there. Unlike the other contestants, Lance seemed more focused on the woman he was with than on the impression he was making, and it was a very appealing quality.

Watching the tape of their date later, Shayla thought that everyone was counting him out of the game way too soon.

Camilla Lyons had received a couple more letters from her stalker over the past couple of weeks, but there had been no sign that he was going to do anything more than admire her from afar. Michael thought that it might be safe to let his guard down a little. After the incident at the hotel pool, thanks in part to Shayla Tennison's report about the crowd of gawkers who had gathered and the way she had to sneak Camilla out of there, the producers of *Lady's Choice* had finally started to take his advice about security. The guards who worked at the front desk of the studio, and especially those who patrolled at night, had all received more and better instruction in the proper protocols. The hotel staff hadn't required much from the production company, just a daily briefing on Camilla's schedule and a list of people who had been cleared to work with her.

There was no evidence that the accident on the set had been anything more than that—a simple accident. This latest incident, on the sailboat, hardly seemed to be connected to the reality program at all. It would have been nearly impossible to arrange, since Camilla Lyons's dates weren't planned in any particular order. She chose when and whom she would see each day and then told Shayla, who made the arrangements. Rarely did the producers or anyone else on the show know what their star would be doing or where she'd be going more than twenty-four hours ahead of time. As far as he could tell, Camilla herself didn't plan that far ahead. There was no way for anyone to arrange for the engine to fail at precisely the time it had—there wasn't enough advance notice that Jordan was going to have his dinner date on that boat on that night.

Still, Michael was tempted to tell Shayla the truth. He wanted to warn her to be on the lookout for the stalker, just in case. He didn't think Shayla was in any real danger, but she spent most of her day taking care of a woman whom some psycho had fixated upon, and it was possible she might inadvertently put herself in harm's way. If she knew what was going on, there was a better chance that she could handle the creep in the unlikely event that he did make an appearance in Camilla's vicinity. Michael was there to look after both women if necessary, and he was confident that he would succeed, but he wasn't comfortable with the situation. He had feelings for Shayla, and there was absolutely no reason to hide them from her—except for his cover. He was supposed to be interested in marrying Camilla—that was why he was here. Or at least, that was what Shayla believed.

He really wanted to set her straight. He could just imagine the look on Shayla's face as he told her that he wasn't interested in Camilla Lyons at all. He'd like to see how she'd react if he told her he couldn't stop thinking about that kiss—and about doing it again. He was dying to argue with her some more, just to annoy her and to make her eyes spark with that flame she tried so hard to hide, and then he wanted to convince her that she was indeed beautiful—just as he had told her. He knew she had not believed him. It would be a pleasure to work on changing her mind. It was one argument he was sure he couldn't lose.

When he met with Lita the following Saturday night, he told her that it would be a good idea to bring Shayla Tennison in on the secret.

"I thought you said there was no reason to think the problem tonight had anything to do with the letters?" Lita said.

"I don't think it did. But if I could have talked to Shayla, it would have been much easier to find that out. She makes the arrangements for Camilla's travel to and from these dates and for most of the other elements of the dates themselves. She's the best source of information about these details, and we could save a lot of time if we coordinated our efforts."

"It hasn't been necessary up to now, though, has it?" Lita asked reasonably. "So what's changed?"

"I just feel that for her own safety, as well as Camilla's, she should really be told that there may be someone out there who is watching her."

"I'm sorry, I still don't think it's a good idea," the woman argued. "I'm not sure what she'd think about us including a bodyguard as a contestant on the show."

"It's not her decision to make. It's yours."

"I know that," Lita responded. "I still think it was the right decision. I just…I'm not comfortable having to justify it to our assistant producer."

"You had a responsibility to protect Camilla Lyons, and you did what you had to do. I can't imagine that Shayla—Ms. Tennison—could argue with that."

"You don't know her, Michael. She almost left the company when we told her we wanted to produce *Lady's Choice*. I didn't want to let her go then, and I definitely don't want to lose her now. We do not have time to find a replacement, even if we wanted one, which we don't. I'm sorry, but if we tell her that you didn't audition for the show because you aren't really a contestant but just a security consultant that we hired to protect Camilla Lyons, she will not be happy. She might even quit."

"Shayla is dedicated to you and to GoGo Girls. She basically lives for this company and her work."

"I'm telling you, she almost resigned over this show. I don't want to take the chance that this time she might actually do it. I'm sorry." Lita rose from the chair behind her massive desk. Michael recognized the move as a signal that the meeting was over. "We're going to have to continue with things the way they are. It's been fine so far."

Michael could see that he wasn't going to change her mind. He had persuaded her, and Marsha, to take the measures he requested to secure Camilla's safety, and that, it seemed, was as far as he was going to get with these ladies. It appeared that he'd never be able to change their minds about telling Shayla the truth about his appearance on the show. He could tell her himself, of course, but that would be going directly against their wishes, and in his business, the client—even when wrong—was always right.

As he left, he did issue one final warning. "You might want to keep Deanna Jones off the set until you're ready to start filming her."

Lita seemed thrown off by the change of subject, but she recovered herself quickly. "Oh? Why?"

"You don't seem to want to lose Shayla," he answered simply.

"Shayla doesn't care if her sister pops by to see her occasionally," Lita said a little too casually.

"You said yourself that she likes everyone to follow the rules. Even you."

"Deanna's not doing anything she shouldn't. Technically, there's no rule against her visiting the offices or the set."

"I'm pretty sure that Shayla does not care about technicalities."

All through the previous week, Deanna Jones had been

popping up in the hotel and in the studio, using her sister as her excuse for these visits. This week, she showed up at the National Archives as well, just when half the cast of *Lady's Choice* happened to be visiting. Unlike Michael, who had been told that she was going to guest star on the show, the other men didn't know yet, and they found her interest in them flattering. Although Jared hadn't been particularly interested in Deanna, she appealed to the younger men, especially Steve. Michael could appreciate why they felt drawn to her, especially since Camilla was forced to keep them all on tenterhooks until the final show. If she could have, he suspected the actress would have told the men more of what she thought about each of them, but the format of the television program demanded that she didn't give away too much of what she felt or thought too soon, even if she wanted to put their minds to rest. She couldn't choose just one man at this stage; she had agreed to follow the rules of the game.

Deanna Jones, on the other hand, let each man think he was the one she would choose, if she was forced to choose between them, from the moment she met him. She didn't say so, exactly, she just had a way of looking at a guy that made him feel like he was the smartest, best-looking, funniest person she'd ever met. Michael didn't know if it came naturally or if she'd cultivated the talent, but it was powerful, and he understood why the boys found it impossible to ignore. She had even tried to get him alone, but it hadn't been hard to outmaneuver her. She was young, eager, and entirely without scruples. He might even have been tempted to respond to her flirting if he hadn't met Shayla first. He much preferred the younger sister, however.

"Shayla's a stickler for the rules, like you said," he told Lita now. "When Deanna shows up and starts flirting with the boys, it bugs her."

"Well, you might be right about that. I'll think about it," Lita said.

Michael doubted that either of the producers would actually do anything about Deanna Jones's impromptu visits, so when he later saw Shayla in the hotel when she came by to check that all the arrangements had been made for that evening's elimination ceremony, he asked, "Does your sister plan to stop by today?"

She looked surprised at the question and seemed a little nervous. "Dee? I don't think so. Why?"

"It just seems as though she keeps turning up."

"Yes, well, uh," she stammered, "I know. That's not going to go on, though. Dee is, um, just a fan of the show, you know. And she's on vacation here and doesn't know a lot of people, so she…she's at loose ends…and she doesn't know her way around the city…" Her voice trailed off as she came to the end of her list of excuses, and she shrugged.

He was tempted to say that it sure looked as if she knew her way around to him, but Shayla looked so uncomfortable he decided he'd teased her enough. "I see," he said instead.

"Mmm," Shayla murmured. She headed toward the elevator bank.

He followed her. "I've got a younger sister."

"Dee's not younger," she said quickly.

"Lily is stationed in San Diego."

"She's in the army?"

"Swabbies."

"Huh?"

"Navy. Flight school."

"Wow. And you're not worried?"

"About what?"

"About what could happen to her? What if she had to go to Iraq or something?"

"She's tough. And she's smart. She'll be fine."

She looked at him in surprise. "What?" he asked.

"You don't strike me as the type of big brother who would let his sister join up."

"Let her? Like I could stop her." He could imagine what Lily would have said, and done to him, if he'd tried. "Once my sister makes up her mind about what she wants, you'd better get out of her way." He was willing to guess Shayla was just as stubborn. He knew she was strong-willed—he'd seen her at work.

The elevator arrived, and he followed her on. She pressed the button for the top floor where Camilla's room was located, then looked at him curiously. He leaned toward her and pressed the button for his floor. As the elevator doors closed, she faced it and asked, "So I was right? You would have stopped her if you could."

It was his turn to look surprised. "No, why? I'm proud of her."

"Sure, of course." She backpedaled quickly, looking up at the lights over the door.

But Michael wasn't about to let it pass. He waited until she looked back at him, caught her eye, then asked, "Why do you think I wouldn't want her to serve her country?"

"I didn't. I don't. I mean—"

"What?" he asked, stepping closer to her, forcing her to step back and to crane her neck to look up at him. "What did you mean?"

"I just thought you'd…be worried about her getting hurt or something. I…you—"

"I what?" he pressed.

She took another small step back, away from him, and came up against the elevator wall. "You're always so concerned about Camilla's safety. I thought…about your own sister…you might be even more…" she said, nervously licking her lips.

"Overprotective?" he asked, smiling. He had her cornered. There was nothing she could do, no way she could avoid answering the question.

She didn't smile back. She was trapped, and she knew it. "Paranoid," she snapped, going on the offensive. "You drive everyone nuts with this security stuff, and I'm the one who has to deal with it."

"Sorry," he said softly. "I was just trying to help."

She had been about to lash out at him, let him know what a pain in the neck he had been, but his quiet apology had completely derailed her—just as he'd intended. "I don't know what to say to that," she admitted.

He could almost see her mind working as she tried to decide whether to yell at him some more or just let it go. She looked confused and a little bit frustrated. He had her just where he wanted her. Off balance. And they were almost at his floor. "Shayla," he said, even more softly, "I want to kiss you again."

She looked alarmed. "Don't," she ordered.

"I've got to." He barely recognized his own voice as it emerged from deep down in his throat.

"No, you don't," she said, trying to push past him.

He trapped her in the corner, with an arm on each side of her head. A sound that was not quite words came from his throat in a deep rumble, almost a growl. "I do."

"You can't," she said. "In about one second, those doors are going to open up behind you, and…"

He waited.

"And I'm…" she began again.

He stood still, his body taut with the effort of not quite touching her, electrical energy coursing through him and across the inch of space between them and back. Michael realized Shayla had never finished her last sentence. "You're what?" he asked. "Gonna throw me off the show?"

"No," she said sadly. "But you're going to lose," she warned. "Camilla will find out."

"Is that all you're worried about?" he asked. Shayla shook her head. "What else?" She didn't answer. He took that as a sign that she had come to the end of her list of objections. Happily, it wasn't a long list. He lowered his head.

"Someone's going to see," she said.

The elevator doors opened behind him, but Michael was beyond caring. He kissed her gently, just at the corner of her mouth, and felt a soft whoosh as she let out all her breath, as if she'd been hit in the solar plexus. He knew just how she felt. He was having a little trouble breathing himself. "Just one more," he promised himself out loud. Her arms twined around his neck, and his laced around her back as their lips met, but he had only a moment to enjoy the taste of her before he heard someone coming down the hallway. "Damn," he cursed against her lips. He forced himself to straighten up and release her.

She leaned back against the wall of the elevator, looking slightly dazed as he backed away. He gave her a quick, apologetic smile as the couple he had heard coming reached the door of the elevator; then he turned and stepped through the doors before they could enter. He had to clear his throat before he could say, "I'll talk to you later." Then he walked away without looking back as the elevator door silently closed behind him.

At the elimination that night, Camilla chose to say good-bye to Charlie Thompson. The man wasn't surprised, and he didn't try to pretend that he was. He reacted just as he had to everything else during his stint on *Lady's Choice*—without much emotion or many words. His quiet good-bye provided little in the way of drama, and it didn't make him any more relatable, Marsha said to Michael when they talked about the next day's agenda later that night.

"It was just as well that he left now, because if he'd been among the final contestants and this was all we got from him, it would have been a waste of perfectly good film."

As far as Michael was concerned, the whole program was not much more than that, but he kept that thought to himself and just murmured, "Mmm-hmm."

Marsha gave him a sharp look. "I know you don't really care about the show's success, but you've got to get a little more invested in it. We're getting down in the numbers now, and there's not a lot we can do to help you stay on the show." Once again, Michael held his tongue, though he'd have liked to tell her that she was right and he could care less about being kicked off the program. "There's no telling what kind of repercussions there would be if anyone found out why you're really here," she continued. "You're going to need to put some effort into winning this thing. Not the final round, of course, but up till then, we need you near her, in case anything happens. If Camilla rejects you, it would be impossible to explain your staying on the set."

Everything she said was true, much to his regret. "I know," Michael reluctantly agreed.

"So you'll try a little harder?" she asked.

"Sure," he answered. "I'll do my best."

"I know you can do it," Marsha said in encouragement, reverting to her hippy-dippy-sisterwoman-sixties-throwback persona. "You're such a handsome man. So forceful, and so charming, when you want to be," she gushed.

"Thanks," he replied. He knew now that Marsha couldn't be nearly as ditzy as she pretended to be. She was a successful businesswoman in a tough industry, which meant that she had to be as professional and as manipulative as her partner Lita—otherwise she never could have gotten to where she was. The earth-mother image was a clever camouflage the television producer used in order to get what she wanted without having to directly confront the people under her command. It worked for her. It was less disconcerting to be reprimanded, much less praised, by Marsha than by her partner.

"I think Camilla is intrigued by you since your date. That little kiss on the cheek at the end was a good move. It got her wondering why you didn't go for it, like all the others. I know I seem to be suggesting that you be more aggressive, but you should also trust your own instincts. They're perfect."

He found it much more palatable to receive advice from this smiling, friendly woman than her alter ego, the woman who had just told him that he wasn't doing a good enough job and that she expected better in the future.

"Of course, it's hard to say what she'll do. We haven't had any luck predicting who she'll reject," she said sourly.

Michael knew that both Lita and Marsha had expended both time and effort to keep Julian and Claude on the program, and he had to admit he thought it was funny, but he didn't have to tell her any of that. "Mmm-hmm," he mumbled again. Marsha looked at him suspiciously, but she didn't bother to expand on her earlier lecture, thank goodness.

Michael left her alone and headed back to the show, trying to figure out how to keep his promise to do his best to win Camilla Lyons's heart. At least he wouldn't have any trouble figuring out what the effort should look like. All he had to do was imagine that Camilla was Shayla. If he could do that, he was sure his pursuit of the soap star would look real. The irony of the situation was not lost on him. In order to stay close to the woman he cared about, he had to pretend to make love to someone else.

There were less than four weeks left in the shooting schedule. He had to take advantage of his proximity to Shayla during that time. He doubted she would see him after she learned who he was unless he'd already gotten to her. He'd done his best to get her attention. And he thought he'd been pretty successful so far. He was going to spend every free moment that he had left on this assignment trying to get close to her—or as close as he could without blowing his cover.

If he couldn't tell her the truth about what he did, or why he was there, he could at least show her who he was, lay the groundwork for a real relationship once this job was over. The closer they got now, the harder it would be for her to walk away when she found out who he really was.

Memo

FROM THE DESK OF SHAYLA TENNISON

ATTENTION, PLEASE

The schedule for this week is very complicated:

Monday: dinner with Jordan Freeman

Tuesday: dinner with Michael Grant

Wednesday: lunch with Jared, dinner with Anton

Thursday: dinner with James

Friday: dinner with Luther

Saturday: lunch with Steve, dinner with Lance

Chapter 14

That week, Shayla had eight dates to arrange. After a month of this, she'd have thought it would get easier, but she felt just as much pressure to make the evenings special now as she had when she made the phone call arranging the first dinner date. At least she didn't actually have to go out with eight guys in six days. She felt for Cami. The actress seemed to thrive under the pressure, but it was a very tight schedule. She had dinner with Jordan on Monday, which ran late, and with Michael on Tuesday, which didn't. Shay watched the tape reluctantly, only because it was part of her job; at the end, she was relieved when he agreed to go straight home after dinner when Cami told him she was tired.

"He was a really good sport about it," Cami said to Shay on Wednesday morning. "I was tired after staying out with Jordan so late, and I needed the sleep before today's marathon." She was scheduled to have lunch with Jared, and dinner with Anton. She had chosen to double up with them in the middle of the week, because both men were pretty easygoing. "I'm going out with James tomorrow night, and I think I'm going to need to rest up for that one. He, um, lacks self-control."

That was putting it mildly, Shay thought, thinking back to the first group date. "It's probably not a bad idea to take a little break before dealing with him," she agreed, then worried that that sounded like a criticism, which, of course, it was.

"He's a little intense," Cami agreed, but she was smiling. "It's the suit and tie," she said. "I don't think men were meant to work in that hubbub on Wall Street." She clearly didn't see James the way that Shay did.

Cami did notice Luther was a little on edge, though. She wanted time to recuperate from the evening with James before she saw Luther on Friday night, too. She decided to take it easy during the day on both days and was still exhausted by Saturday because, as she had predicted, she had to work at regaining ground with both men after making them wait.

She did manage to make both men feel better, though. "James was actually fine as soon as we were alone together," she reported to Shay on Friday afternoon. "I just hope Luther is okay tonight. He's been acting pretty moody all week."

As it turned out, Luther required some reassurance before he could relax and enjoy the evening. "Friday night is date night," she said when he asked why she hadn't wanted to see him earlier in the week. That seemed to satisfy him.

On Saturday she had lunch with Steve and dinner with Lance, both of whom were charming and amusing during their time with her. Steve was on his best behavior, for reasons that were not explained until later that night. After Lance left for his date with the soap star, he told the guys, "Someone told

me that Camilla said she hadn't really gotten to talk to me seriously, because I was always clowning around."

When Shay saw the bull session on tape on Sunday morning, she recognized the statement. Camilla had said it, almost
word for word, on Saturday morning as she was dressing for
the date with Steve. And the cameras had been rolling. But
no one could have seen that tape but the editors. Shay had been
the only one in the room with Cami at the time.

Shay looked up at the editor who was showing her the
footage and asked, "Was my sister here last night when you
were editing this?"

The expression on his face gave him away. "She likes to
watch," the balding little man said in his defense.

"Great," Shay said. "You know she's not allowed to be in
here, right?" she asked. It was a rhetorical question. She had
informed him, along with everyone else on the crew, that
Deanna Jones was persona non grata in the hotel, on the set,
or anywhere in the studio, no matter what Deanna said. But
she had known it probably wouldn't work.

Shay had given up trying to control the rumors that Deanna
was being considered as a possible guest star on the show. The
producers were trying to keep it as secret as possible, even
going to the extent of drawing up bogus contracts, identical
to Dee's, for two other television stars.

"You cannot let her in here, Herb. You know how important it is that we don't have information leaking out about the
show until it's on the air." On a matchmaking show, it was
crucial that the public didn't know who was going to win
until the very last episode. Otherwise, people wouldn't tune
in to watch the program. It was the suspense that kept them
coming back.

"I'm sorry," he said penitently. Shayla couldn't bring

herself to fire him, as she should have done. She knew how hard it was to say no to her big sister. Deanna was inexorable, like a tornado, a force of nature.

She also had a very big mouth. Shay knew that it had to have been Dee who told Steve what Cami had said about him. She confronted Dee later that morning when she went home to help her pack her stuff. Even though she was only guest starring on the show, the producers had decided that she should move into the hotel with the rest of the cast of *Lady's Choice* while she was appearing on the show.

"When did you see Steve?" she asked.

"I didn't," Dee answered.

"When did you talk to him then?" Shay persisted. "I know you told him what Cami said about him. He told the rest of the guys last night."

"He did?"

"Yes, he did, so just tell me, Dee. What have you done?"

"I called him up," her sister confessed.

"You called him and told him what Cami said? Just like that?"

"Yeah. Why? You said I couldn't go to the hotel anymore until I moved in. You never said I couldn't talk to anyone on the phone."

Shay had to ask. "Weren't you at all worried about helping him? I mean, you told him just what to do to make him look good to Camilla."

"Yeah," Dee said, smiling. "Now she likes him, and he likes me even better. I love those love triangles, don't you?"

She was incorrigible, but Shay admired her chutzpah. "You really are sure that you're going to win, aren't you?"

"I can't lose," Dee said. "That's why I agreed to be on the show. I can steal all of Camilla's boyfriends, and no one can blame me. It's the perfect setup."

It might have seemed like a win-win situation to Deanna, but her sister was not in the same position that Shay was. She had to actually deal with the men who Dee and Cami were busy treating like prizes at a ring toss.

Everywhere she turned that day, the tension was escalating. Only Jordan was calm, since, after his second successful date—at the end of which he and Cami had again pulled themselves away from each other regretfully—he was absolutely convinced that he was going to be Cami's choice in the end. And his attitude only exacerbated the situation. As Dee's television debut approached, however, the other bachelors were not happy. James walked around growling at everyone, and the boys from Detroit kept quarreling. All of the men were on tenterhooks, except perhaps Michael, who never seemed to lose his cool, and Jared, whose philosophy didn't permit worrying about a situation that was completely out of his control. Lance looked incredibly sad but resigned to his fate. The men didn't know that that evening's elimination had been cancelled in favor of Dee's introduction.

Unfortunately, however, Cami did. "They're all going to give her credit for postponing the elimination, and she had nothing to do with it."

"Yes, well, um…" Shay said helplessly. She couldn't argue with Cami's logic. Not that it was irrefutable, because it wasn't—the men would be fools to think that Dee had anything to do with their reprieve, and it was unlikely they would thank her. Far from logical, Cami wasn't even making sense. She had had as little to do with the boys' reprieve as Dee did. It had been the producers' bright idea to postpone the forth round of eliminations, and Camilla Lyons had nothing to do with that decision. The shooting schedule had been changed, not because of any one person or any one event, but because the addition of a guest star to the program hadn't been anticipated by anyone, hadn't ever been thought of until Shay happened to make a lunch date with her sister, and it required certain changes to the logistics of producing the television series. Dee's big moment finally arrived, and she spent the morning of the day of her television debut at a salon, having her short hair dyed and unbraided, set and then rebraided in a softer shape and style. Her bangs were twisted into short delicate threads that just brushed the arch of her eyebrows, and an intricate network of cornrows fanned out from her temple in a series of graduated vees that looked like artwork against her golden skin. The pattern rose like a wave to the top of her head where her hair was released from the fine braids to flow silkily down over her neck in a fall of soft black curls. It was really beautiful, and the ultrafeminine hairstyle was complemented by a form-fitting electric-blue satin sheath provided by the show. From head to toe she looked like a girl, she said to Shay, pleased.

"You look gorgeous," her sister agreed.

"Camilla's going to die," Dee said.

Shay suspected that Dee wasn't far off. The soap star was not going to be happy about Dee's transformation.

Cami was prepared to compete with the leather-clad bad girl that Dee had always cultivated as her public image, but this elegant, beautifully dressed, and perfectly coiffed woman was going to knock the soap opera star on her butt. Although Dee always accused Shay of being on the actress's side, Shay was sort of looking forward to seeing Cami's reaction to her sister's new look.

She wasn't disappointed. When the contestants had been assembled in the studio and Cami had taken her place center stage, Dan announced, "Tonight we will not be eliminating any of our contestants." There was a relieved murmur from the bachelors, but the whispers died quickly as the show's host went on. "Instead we have a special guest visiting us this evening."

Dee came out from the editing booth where she'd been hiding, followed by a camera crew that caught the sway of her hips, the smile on her face, and the twinkle in her eye as she made her surprise appearance. "Deanna Jones, ladies and gentlemen. Singer, songwriter, and star." The stunned silence that met this surprising announcement was all the producers could have hoped for—and more.

"May I introduce our remaining contestants, Ms. Jones?" he asked. Dee nodded graciously, and he began. "I'll start with the gentleman on the far left. Jordan Freeman, a triple-A baseball player who currently holds the minor league record for double plays this season."

Dee gave the athlete a little wave, which he began to return, until he saw Cami glaring at him. He dropped his hand back to his side.

After introducing the rest of the contestants, Dan explained, "I should warn you all that, now that Ms. Jones has joined us, the rules have changed. Any of the contestants can still leave whenever they choose, including during the elimination ceremonies, but there is one new choice each contestant can make; when invited to stay, they can not only choose to stay or leave, but also to propose to Deanna Jones. If anyone decides to pursue that option, then just speak up, and we'll give you a chance to ask the lady if she agrees."

After the first couple of weeks, it had become part of Michael's routine to stop by Marsha's office after the elimination ceremonies. The night that Deanna Jones joined the cast of *Lady's Choice* was no exception. But the producers had a surprise waiting for him when he arrived that night. It was another letter from Camilla's devoted fan, but with a new twist. *No other woman will ever come between us, my love. Just as no other man can take your heart from me. Send me another sign, and I'll take care of her.* He had signed it, *Hers,* as usual.

"Did you send a copy to the police?" he asked.

"Of course," Marsha said.

"As usual," her partner confirmed. It was clear that the producers were not particularly alarmed by the contents of the note, but Michael had a bad feeling about it.

"Did anyone read it?" he asked sardonically. His gut told him this was a serious departure from the sender's previous communiqués. They were all only a couple of lines long, like this one, and in them he always raved about his love for Camilla and how he was the only one who truly understood her, but Michael was sure there was something different in this one. It sounded even more psychotic than usual.

"Did you show it to my partner?" he asked.

"No, not yet. We thought we'd send it over tomorrow," Lita said. "We knew we'd be seeing you tonight."

Michael went to the phone on her desk and dialed Darren's cell number.

He had never agreed with the producers, or the police, that the person sending these notes was a complete stranger—and the timing of this note seemed to confirm it. It had been delivered two hours before the announcement was made that Deanna Jones was going to guest star on the show. "Hey, Darren, Camilla's received another note from her secret admirer, and I've got a feeling our friend is about to do something new."

Marsha was starting to pick up on some of Michael's nervousness. "Why?" she asked. "What's different about this one?"

Michael couldn't answer her while he briefed Darren and faxed the note to the office. "I'll have the original sent over by messenger tomorrow."

Although all the other notes had mentioned that Camilla had sent him signs of her love, this was the first time one of his love letters ever contained an overt threat against anyone; they had barely contained any mention of the male contestants on *Lady's Choice,* for example—which was the main reason the police hadn't thought he posed any real danger to the soap opera star. Their expert had analyzed the early messages and offered the opinion that this loony thought Camilla was starring in *Lady's Choice* in order to communicate her love to him. The author of these scary little missives was glad that she'd chosen to star on the show. He didn't feel threatened by the competition, the police psychologist said. He believed the television program was her way of letting him know that she returned his feelings.

When Michael hung up with his partner, he tried to explain his concerns to their client. "This note contains a direct threat against Deanna Jones," he said.

"But I thought Camilla was the one he—" Marsha started to say when Lita cut her off.

"'I'll take care of her,'" the other woman said disparagingly. "This guy's a loser, and this is just another pitiful attempt to get Camilla's attention."

"Maybe," he agreed. "But do you really want to take that chance?"

Apparently they did, because Lita refused to treat this new note any differently from any of the others. Even Marsha wasn't sure she agreed that the threat was escalating. "We appreciate your concern, but we're sure you can handle this," Lita said. "Just tell us if you need anything."

Michael knew if he told her what he needed, she'd just tell him he was overreacting, because what he needed was to tell everyone what was going on so that they could be on their guard. That was not what the client wanted to hear. They were not about to broadcast to the world that there had been a series of threats against the star of their show, and they were sure as hell not about to let him do it. And that was what he really needed to do—tell people who he really was so they would listen to him. He also needed to put another man or two on Camilla, 24/7, and he needed to find some way to keep an eye on Deanna Jones now, too. He needed his partner to find out who these notes were coming from and how they were getting delivered, because he was sure it was someone connected with Camilla Lyons or the show. Unfortunately, he knew none of that was going to happen, because he was the only one who was really alarmed about this situation.

What he really needed was for the clients to take this threat as seriously as he did.

Memo
FROM THE DESK OF LITA TOLLIVER
TO: Marsha James
Marsh,
Adding Deanna Jones to the show was a stroke of genius! She is bringing just what we needed, an edge, a level of competition, that is cranking up the excitement and suspense 100%! I can't wait to see what she'll do next, and if I can't wait, the audience probably won't be able to, either. This is just the kick in the pants Camilla needed. She's going to have to start to commit, be more aggressive, and get in there. She's been coasting, but no more! Did you see her face during Deanna's debut? It was priceless. I can't wait to see what she'll do when we tell her about the bracelets!

   Lita

P.S. What do you think we should do about Michael and this note business? He thinks this threat could be the real thing!

Chapter 15

The night after Dee joined the show, the producers decided the entire cast, including their new guest, would all go out dancing together. They had some other surprises in store for everyone as well, which they told Shay about during their weekly Monday morning meeting.

"Camilla and Deanna will each get three of these ID bracelets, which they will then give to the man they'd like to date this week," Marsha explained. "Camilla's are gold and Dee's are silver, which should create a nice effect on camera."

"Three each?" Shay said. "I don't understand. There are eight men left."

"We know," Lita said, smirking.

"So two of the guys aren't going out with either woman?" Shayla asked, still trying to comprehend her bosses' master plan.

"Yes, they will. They just won't know it," Marsha interjected. "They won't be told until after Camilla and Deanna make their choices, but they will have dates on Saturday, before the elimination Sunday night."

"It will be interesting to see what the rejects do, don't you think?" Lita asked.

"No, I don't," Shayla said, annoyed at both Lita's choice of words and her pleasure at the thought of coming up with a new torture for these men. "Don't you think throwing Dee into this mix is enough for one week?"

"Not really, no," Lita said. "We're offering them a bonus they never expected—they've got a new girl. I think it's only fair that we take something away to make up for it."

"Lita, stop. You sound like a total bitch, and you promised when we agreed to become partners that you'd stop doing that," Marsha said to her partner. Turning to Shay, she tried to explain, "That is *not* why we're doing this. This show is about drama, which means conflict makes the characters. That's how we get to know them. When these guys have to choose, when the girls have to choose, when people are rejected, that's when we see who these people are. It's important to see how they react when only six bracelets are available. All eight men will have to think carefully before they reject any offer they're given."

Lita was nodding in agreement. "That's right," she said.

Marsha hadn't finished. "And this evens the playing field for your sister. They'll all be too nervous about not being chosen to turn down an invite from her, even if they want to in order to show their loyalty to Camilla." She winked at her, but Shay was not appeased. Marsha might not know it yet, but she had miscalculated when she tried to appeal to Shay's sympathy for Dee. Shay didn't have any. Dee deserved whatever she got, as far as she was concerned. It was the boys' feelings that concerned her. This manipulative little ploy was designed to make them even more insecure than usual.

"Why push it?" she asked. "They'll be nervous enough as it is. If you want to develop their characters, why not give them the chance to turn Deanna down and show Camilla how they feel about her?"

"You're missing the point," Lita said, shaking her head. "If they care about Camilla at all, they shouldn't be considering a date with your sister. This is a test, and I have a funny feeling they're all going to fail."

"That's because you're setting them up to fail," Shayla commented.

"I disagree," Marsha said. "With both of you. Shayla, we're giving them a choice. They don't have to take it. They could always just rise above the competition. I'm betting that at least one of these guys will do it. He won't betray Camilla."

"So when this is all over and Cami has to choose one of these men over all the rest, what do you think will happen? Who do you think she'll choose once you've made all these men look bad?" Shay asked.

"I haven't got a clue," Lita answered. "That's the fun part."

"*I* think that the guys who do well tonight will have a good chance at winning. This contest is going to demonstrate that they've got character, Shayla," Marsha said. "That's why we do stuff like this. To give the contestants a chance to show what they're really made of."

Bull, Shayla thought. *You're not doing this for them. You're doing this to create conflict, so people won't tune out on your precious TV show. You're hoping they'll try to kill one another.* But she didn't share these depressing thoughts with the other two women. It was obvious that there was no point in arguing with them.

The next evening, Dan played host at the dance party, and Shayla went along, just in case anything went wrong. When they were given their gold and silver bracelets, Cami and Dee didn't hesitate for a moment. Cami got to Jordan before Dee could get anywhere near him and gave him a bracelet right away. Dee asked Michael out, then approached Jordan and started flirting with him. Cami was not pleased. She quickly broke up that tête-à-tête.

Dee wasn't concerned. She cornered Shay, off camera, and told her sister, "I'll get around to the baseball player in my own sweet time, and she can't stop me. I just wanted to see what she'd do if she saw me poaching on her property. She's so easy."

"Are you saying you only flirted with him so she'd be jealous?"

"Yup. Just yankin' her chain, Shay. She's already got Jordan. She doesn't have time to worry about me and him. She should be thinking strategy. If I were her, I'd be giving my bracelets to the guys who are on the fence. She's got Lance, Luther, probably James, all tied up, too. That leaves Jared, Steve, and Anton. I've got a pretty good chance at getting them if she doesn't start paying attention."

"*That's* why you picked Michael? Because you don't think he's as into Cami as some of the other men are?" Shay asked, a little shocked at her sister's callousness. Not that she had expected Dee's appearance on *Lady's Choice* to showcase the better aspects of her sister's nature, but she hadn't expected her to actually kick off her stint on the show with such a marked display of heartlessness. When Dee immediately gave Michael an ID bracelet, it had reminded her of Dee's reaction when she first saw Michael on the first night of her visit, when they watched the premier episode together. Dee had made it clear then that she thought he looked good. Shay thought tonight she was attracted to him. Instead, it turned out, she was just trying to win. "That's the only reason you chose him?" Shay asked, confounded.

"Yup. He's definitely up for grabs. She should have been concentrating on him more, but she just kept him on the back burner. She didn't figure on having any competition. She just thought she could turn it on later, snap her fingers, and he'd be hers. Now she's got me to deal with."

"Dee, be careful. These men aren't just toys for you two to play with," Shay warned, but her sister just smiled and shook her head and went off to join Cami, who was standing with the boys from Detroit. Cami saw her approaching and gave Steve an ID bracelet next. Dee looked back at Shayla and winked, then abruptly changed direction to bear down on Jared.

"Would you accept this?" she asked him with a coy smile.

"Um, sure," he said after a moment's hesitation. If Shay knew her sister, Dee would not be discouraged by his lack of enthusiasm. Instead, she'd take it as a challenge.

Cami also took time out of the hunt to speak to Shayla. While Dee was busy choosing her final victim, she motioned Shay over to the bar with a surreptitious hand gesture, eyes glued on Dee as she mingled with the men. "I don't know who else to choose," she admitted when Shay joined her by the bar. "I've only got one bracelet left. I think Luther's too far gone to go for another woman, but what about Anton? Or maybe James? She's circling them like a vulture."

"I can't advise you," Shay replied, incredibly glad at the moment that she couldn't.

"I don't think James will go for her. She's too cheap for him. Sorry. I know she's your sister, but—"

"Don't worry about hurting *my* feelings," Shay started to say, feeling sorry for the men the two women were treating like cuts of meat at the deli counter.

Cami cut her off. "You're right. I didn't think of that. James has a thick skin. He's older, and I can explain. Anton's a young man, and he's a worrier. He may take it badly if I don't choose him. It could push him right into her arms."

That wasn't what she had meant, but Shay didn't bother to voice the protest that rose to her lips. She didn't think Cami would hear her, anyway. She was too caught up in this ridiculous competition to even realize what she looked like.

Shay couldn't help wincing as she admitted, "I knew choosing Steve would make her mad. I saw the way he was looking at her, and I just know she talked to him before tonight, probably tried to get her claws into him." Shay just stared at her, amazed that this woman, whom she had thought she had come to know pretty well over the last month, was capable of such petty vindictive behavior. She was proud of it. Worse, how could she have registered Dee's subtle reaction to her choice and failed to notice that Luther was crushed?

Cami didn't seem to expect Shayla to say anything. She left her standing there and made her way toward Anton. But she was too late. Dee had just given him her silver bracelet, and he had just accepted. Although he didn't look exactly overjoyed that she had chosen him, Anton was much more grateful than Jared had been, and when he glanced around and saw Cami's stunned expression, he actually looked as if he was glad for a moment. It was all over very quickly. Cami didn't even take a beat. In a second she was at Luther's side. His relief when she offered him a gold identification bracelet was the only vaguely redeeming moment of the evening. He was so patently pleased at being chosen by the woman he so clearly adored that even Cami couldn't fail to notice. "I'm sorry it took me so long," she said.

"I'm honored," he replied, and, being Luther, he kissed her hand.

"That's sweet," she said with genuine affection. "It was so hard to choose just three of you to ask. I really like all of you. But you and Jordan and Steve have all made me feel like I did the right thing." His expression darkened slightly when she mentioned the other two men, but he was able to smile and assure her with such sincerity that she had indeed made the right choice that she seemed completely convinced. The sentiment might have been touching if it hadn't been tarnished by the triumphant look that Cami then cast in Dee's direction, but Shay was glad that she had at least given the younger man some slight encouragement.

Perhaps it would have been kinder to let him down now than to let him go on hoping, but Shay found it was impossible not to root for each of these men each time they faced the chance that they would be rejected by the object of their desire. It was pitiful, really, but she couldn't help but get caught up in Luther's ill-fated obsession. Even though she kept on thinking that it would be a disaster if he actually won the competition and married the soap opera star, she was happy for him every time he managed to snatch a victory like this from the jaws of defeat.

At the end of the night, Dan Green appeared again to make a couple more announcements. Most weren't exactly ground-breaking. He told the men they would have their identification bracelets engraved with their names, and he also explained they would be going out to dinner in the order they were chosen. But the final item of business was a shock to everyone but Shay. "The producers," he reported, "would like me to pass along a message to the ladies. They cancelled last night's elimination in honor of Deanna's debut. Tonight, they will intervene again, this time on behalf of the two unhappy fellows who thought that they were not going to get to go on a date this week."

Lance had been the object of many sympathetic looks and heartfelt commiseration since he had become the odd man out earlier, and even James had received a "That's too bad," from one or two of his competitors. Both Cami and Dee had also spent some time consoling the two men and told them how badly they felt that they were limited to only three dates each. So everyone was thrown for a loop by Dan's little bomb, and they waited with bated breath for his next revelation. They didn't have long to wait.

"James and Lance, the producers have decided that you will each have a champagne brunch with the woman of your choice next Saturday morning, before Sunday's elimination round."

After the show, Shay went home to her empty house and tried not to worry about what was going to happen the next morning at work. With Dee gone, she was alone for the first time in weeks. It was blissfully quiet in her cozy little house. As much as she loved her sister, it was a relief to be able to unplug the phone, light some candles, and soak for an hour in a scented bath undisturbed. She could enjoy her solitude in the privacy of her own home. Unfortunately, however, she just couldn't seem to relax. She was worried about how Cami would greet her in the morning. The soap star had not looked happy about how things had gone at the party that evening. Dee, on the other hand, had been in seventh heaven. And Shay couldn't help but think that that couldn't last.

Apparently Cami seemed to have forgotten that she'd ever worried about whether Shay's loyalties might be for her sister. On Wednesday, when Shay visited Cami to brief her on her date for the evening at one of Washington, D.C.'s, finest restaurants, she also planned to give a short speech she had prepared that was designed to convince the actress that she was going to remain as impartial as possible during the coming weeks. But Cami talked about the previous night without the slightest circumspection. To Shay's surprise, it wasn't Michael that Cami regretted losing most. She was upset that Dee would be brunching with Lance, even if by default.

"Of course I'm glad that James chose me, but…the only reason that I didn't pick Lance was because I knew she would never ask him." Shayla was not buying it. Cami hadn't been thinking of Lance—she'd been thinking of herself. If she'd given a single thought to how the veterinarian might have felt, that thought was probably that Lance would never choose Dee over her. Lance was in love with her, and she knew it.

When Cami whined, "I didn't think I had to worry about him," it was the first thing she'd said that morning that rang true. "He's not her type at all," the soap star went on. "And I really like him. Now she's going to act as if she wanted to go out with him when she didn't, and I do."

Shay hoped Cami was telling the truth about her feelings for Lance. If it was true, the star of the show would have plenty of opportunities to prove it. But not this week. This week, she was going out with three other men, the first of whom was Jordan. At least, Shay thought, there really seemed to be something between those two. A little part of her actually thought that they should end up together. While Shay's thoughts had drifted to Cami's date with Jordan, the actress was still going on about Dee and Lance. "I want him to know I care about him, for real, not like her," she said childishly.

This selfish, self-centered woman was not the Camilla Lyons Shay had thought that she knew. Shay definitely did not approve of Cami's treatment of the guys, but what surprised her even more was her assumption that Shay was on her side. Either Cami was the world's greatest actress, or she was completely convinced that Shay was rooting for her over her own sister. Shay hadn't expected that. She decided to give the little speech she'd prepared after all, even though Cami obviously didn't need any reassurance about where her loyalties lay. Shay couldn't leave the room without letting the soap star know that she wasn't planning to take sides.

"I'm not going to get pulled into this thing between you and Dee," she started.

"I don't expect you to," Cami said airily.

"That doesn't mean I don't want both of you to be happy," Shay explained. "I just can't…be in the middle."

"Of course not."

That seemed to take care of that, so Shay briefed her on the night ahead with Jordan. She left Cami planning what she would wear that evening and headed for Dee's room. She had to tell her sister about the dinner date she'd arranged for her and Michael Grant.

It was strange arranging a date between Deanna and the man who had kissed her—twice now. Shay felt guilty that she hadn't told Dee what had happened between Michael and herself, but she couldn't figure out how to make it right. The cameras were rolling as she told Dee about the restaurant where Shay had arranged for her to dine that evening, which meant she couldn't say anything about Michael, anyway. And even if the camera crew hadn't been recording every word, Dee didn't give her a chance to say anything, anyway. She was still talking about the night before, which she saw as a very successful beginning. Dee had every intention of making a splash on *Lady's Choice* and had no compunction about admitting it to the viewing public.

"Tonight I see Michael Grant, then Jared, and then Anton on Friday night, right?"

"Yes," Shay confirmed.

"I have a feeling I'm going to have a great week, don't you? They seem like really good guys. I'm glad they all accepted my invitation. I haven't asked a man out in a long time, and I was a little nervous, but they were all so sweet. I think I'm really going to enjoy getting to know each of them." Dee was going to be really good at this, that much was obvious. Shay was impressed with the ease with which her sister slipped into her role. She couldn't have done it. Not that she would have wanted to.

"Jordan's gorgeous, and Luther looks like a sweetie, and I'm sure Steve is a lot of fun, but I think I got the pick of the litter," she boasted with just the right mix of pride and humility. The audience was going to love her, Shay thought. And even she had to admit, Dee had chosen her dates well.

Shay almost felt sorry for Cami. Almost. But she had a feeling that Cami was more than capable of looking out for herself.

Memo
FROM THE DESK OF SHAYLA TENNISON

Dating schedule:

	Camilla	Dee
Tuesday:	Jordan	Michael
Wednesday:	Steve	Jared
Friday:	Luther	Anton
Saturday:	James	Lance

Chapter 16

Shay hadn't planned to go along on Dee's first date with Michael, but the restaurant manager called at the last minute to say that the private room that had been promised was not available. Smoothing over mix-ups like this one had become second nature to Shay at that point, so when she couldn't reach the man on the telephone, she drove over, confident that she could get in and out before Dee and Michael got there. She had an hour before they were supposed to arrive at the restaurant, which was plenty of time to convince the restaurant manager that making an accommodation for *Lady's Choice* was like getting free prime-time television advertising. That always seemed to work.

The restaurant was lovely. The decor was elegant, all gold and white and crystalline. The tables, with their gorgeous settings, glowed in the low light. She could picture the romantic meal, background music tinkling, champagne bubbles in the tall crystal flutes. Shay rushed the manager through the meeting, because she didn't want to see the couple together if she could avoid it, and she was in and out of the establishment in a half hour, well before the contingent from *Lady's Choice* was due to arrive. She had already seen enough of Michael and Cami flirting with each other. She didn't need to see him turning the charm on with her sister now. Not that she had any reason to object. Just because he had kissed her a couple of times and said he wanted her did not give her any claim on him. He was free to do whatever he wanted with whomever he wanted. She just didn't want to watch. She went home, to bed.

Shay didn't watch much of the footage of the tape the next morning, either—she saw just enough to know that Dee had a very good time. Michael was attentive and charming. Dee was lively and charming. They made a gorgeous couple. That was more than she needed to know. She told the editor to summarize and hit the highlights for the daily report to the boss, then she moved on to Camilla's tape. She had just finished viewing the first few minutes of Camilla's date with Jordan, which looked as if it was going to be hot, when the editor's phone rang.

He picked it up, and said, "Ralph, here." After a moment he held the phone out to her.

"For me?" she asked. No one ever called her here. Usually anyone who called when she was out of the office in the morning just left her a message on her voice mail.

"Marsha," he told her. He looked a bit nervous, which would have been perfectly normal if it had been Lita on the line, but Marsha was a pussycat, or at least that was what the crew thought. They bought her earth-mother act hook, line, and sinker.

"Hello?" Shay said into the receiver. "What's up, Marsh?"

"Shay? There's been an accident, honey," Marsha answered. "It's…it's your sister."

"Dee? What are you talking about? Is she okay?"

"She's…she's hurt. They're taking her to the hospital now."

"The hospital? What happened?"

"We don't know exactly. The hotel is investigating. We can talk about that later. You've got to get going."

"Yeah. Yes. I'm going."

Shay hated hospitals, and Bethune Hospital was just as intimidating and off-putting as hospitals always were. This visit was even scarier than usual because she was anxious about Dee. She didn't have any real information, just that her sister was hurt, and she felt panic well up inside as she passed through the doors. She hated not knowing what had happened, but she was almost more afraid to find out. At the information desk, she asked the bored-looking nurse-type person, "Deanna Jones was brought here a little while ago. Can you tell me where to find her? I'm her sister."

The woman consulted a computer screen and told her, "Take a seat. Someone will be out to talk with you in a moment."

Twenty minutes later, Shay was still waiting, her stomach in knots that felt as if they were doubling in size with every few seconds that passed, when Michael Grant walked into the room. Without thinking, she walked straight into his arms. They closed around her. "How is she?" he asked.

"I don't know. No one has told me anything, and I don't even know what happened. How did she get hurt? Did they tell you? I tried calling the office and the hotel, but all I've been able to do is leave messages, and no one's called me back."

He led her over to a chair and sat her down, then took a seat next to her. "She got an electric shock from the light switch in her hotel room."

Shay stared. "That's all, a little shock?" She nearly laughed out loud. "I can't believe this. I've been sitting here imagining all kinds of disasters and she's in there because she got a little shock from the light switch?"

"Not so little," he said gently. The impulse to laugh died, and warning bells started to ring again somewhere inside her. His serious expression and the tone of his voice telegraphed bad news. "It was big enough to start a fire and set off the fire alarm, which is why they found her so quickly."

"Found her? In a fire? I don't understand. How could a light switch…" Shay's voice trailed off. Another freak accident. So soon. Something was wrong here.

"She was unconscious, but breathing. They told me at the hotel. The paramedics were confident that she would be okay, once they got her here."

"Oh my God," Shay breathed. "How could this happen? I mean what? What else did you find out?"

"That's about it," he answered. "Light switch, shock, ambulance, hospital. Now you know as much as I do."

They waited together another five minutes before a doctor appeared in the doorway and called Shay's name. They rushed over to him, together, to get his report.

"Your sister is responding well to treatment. We're confident that she will be just fine with a little rest and care."

"What happened to her?" Shay asked. When the doctor stared at her without comprehension, she clarified her question. "I mean, what are her injuries? Is she badly hurt?"

"No, no," he assured her. "She hasn't regained consciousness, but we think she will. She's got a bump on the head, a burn on her hand, a few scrapes and bruises, but she was lucky. Taking that kind of a jolt could have ended up much worse. You can come see her now."

Dee was asleep, or what looked like sleep. "You can talk to her," the nurse said.

Shay approached the bed slowly. "Dee?" She didn't look too bad. Her make-up was gone, and the hospital sheet did nothing for her complexion, but at first glance, Shay could barely tell Dee had even been in an accident. As Shay examined her more closely, though, she saw that there were some signs. There was a large bandage on her hand and arm, and it looked as if she was going to have a black eye in a couple of hours. Otherwise she might have been asleep—except that no one could sleep here. There was a constant hum from the hallway and buzzing from various machines, not to mention the voices of doctors, nurses, and patients as they did their work.

"Dee? I'm here."

"We'll be moving her in a little bit. If she wakes up, press that button there," the nurse said as she started to leave.

"Can she hear me?"

"You never know," the woman said, smiling encouragingly. "It's always good to talk to them. To let them know you're here."

She left, and the room felt different somehow, as if her busy, competent, bustling had filled it up. Without her, Shay couldn't move, or even think. She just stood there, staring down at her sister helplessly, feeling as if she ought to do something. "I have to call my parents," she whispered, feeling strangely guilty at the thought of telling them about what had happened.

Michael nodded. "Yeah, go on." His strong presence at her side was comforting, though she knew he shouldn't have been there. He was a virtual stranger. She barely knew him. And what she did know about him didn't make any sense. He was a contestant from a dating show that she was supposed to be in charge of. He was a bachelor from San Diego and he was also the man who worried about every tiny little detail of the production. Open doors and windows, seating arrangements in cars. Apparently, he wasn't so crazy after all. Someone had ended up hurt, just as he'd predicted.

She should have told him to go, that he didn't belong there. Instead, she drew in a deep breath and told her parents that their other daughter had been injured and that she was with her in the hospital, waiting for her to wake up. They took the news as well as could be expected, and she promised to call them as soon as she learned anything else. When she clicked the phone closed, she was crying silently.

"She'll be all right, you'll see," Michael said, stroking her arm. It sounded as if he really cared. She suddenly remembered that he'd been out on a date with Dee the night before. She remembered how perfect they had looked together. Shay couldn't believe that the pang of bitterness she suddenly felt could be jealousy. It was impossible. She was standing four feet away from her sister's hospital bed; it would be stupid to be envious of her sister at this moment, when Dee was lying there, unconscious. She was supposed to feel sorry for her, sad, worried. Even her irrational fear that there was something strange about this accident wasn't completely out of place. But it was crazy to be wondering about whether Michael was here out of concern for Dee or for some other reason. He was here, and he was large and comforting, and that should have been the end of it. It wasn't, though.

"You'd better go," she forced herself to say.

"I'm not leaving here," he answered, much to her relief.

Shay didn't want to be alone. She was afraid that she would lose it. Her sister was lying in a hospital bed, unconscious, and she didn't understand why this had happened, or even, really, what had happened.

Michael found her a chair and brought it over by the bed; then he went to stand on the other side. They both looked down at Dee; then she asked, "They talked to you at the hotel? What did they say caused…this?"

"They didn't know yet. They were going to look into it."

"Why did they tell you?" she wondered aloud.

"I was there," he said. She thought she understood. He was always there. Whenever anything went wrong, before anything went wrong, Michael Grant seemed to be everywhere, watching, commenting, interfering. It might bother her, but no one else seemed to mind. They didn't question why he was always popping up in the strangest places, suggesting solutions for problems that hadn't even arisen. Even her bosses accepted it. His first day on the set, he'd talked to everyone. He spoke to the gaffers, the electricians, the cameramen. In the beginning, Shay thought it was just natural curiosity because he'd never been on a television set before. But it wasn't long before it had become annoying. And then, she had started to get used to him. She even liked him. A little.

Maybe that was because he had started flirting with her. And then he'd kissed her. That had been unexpected. To be honest, though, he might have been sending out some signals. The day that Dee had arrived, she remembered, she had decided to try and mellow out toward him, and they had a nice conversation. Then he'd been so helpful that day at the pool. Thinking back on it now, she realized he might have taken her attitude toward him as encouragement. She had to admit, she hadn't exactly *dis*couraged him. At least, not the way she probably should have. She'd known that after the kiss in the elevator.

After that, she would have thought he'd avoid her. Especially now that her sister had joined the cast of the show. Now that he had seen that Dee was interested in him and that he'd flirted with Dee and taken her out to dinner and kissed *her,* it seemed more than likely that he would give up on her very ordinary, very bossy, and very annoying little sister. But here he was, seemingly as concerned about her as he was about Deanna Jones.

She didn't have a clue what to say to him about that. She didn't even know what to tell herself. The voices in her head were clamoring that it was wrong to depend upon him. He shouldn't be here; he was supposed to be back on the set, or in the hotel, or somewhere. She couldn't, at this precise moment, remember the schedule, but he was definitely meant to be somewhere else. He was supposed to be concentrating on competing against a group of other men for the attention of a talented, beautiful TV star.

Despite all that, and no matter how foolish she kept telling herself it was to feel this way, she was glad he was with her. And that seemed wrong, too, somehow.

For this latest meeting with his clients, Michael should have been prepared to bring them up-to-date on what he'd found out about Deanna Jones's accident. He'd discovered a number of interesting facts about the incident—the most important of which was that it wasn't an accident at all. Someone had rigged the pop singer's light switch to explode. Darren was working on finding out who had had access to the room—going through the hotel's security videos to compile a list of the people who'd had access, and then checking that list to find someone who didn't fit. He also had his own man, Joshua—whose freak accident had first alerted 24/7 to the possible existence of a saboteur on the program—keeping an eye on Camilla Lyons, in order to keep her safe.

Unfortunately, Michael found he couldn't seem to focus on these rather important details. He couldn't concentrate on anything except how he was going to convince Marsha James and Lita Tolliver to use Shayla as Dee's replacement on *Lady's Choice*. It was wrong to be so focused on that one item on his agenda, but it had come to him, just that afternoon, and he hadn't been able to stop thinking about it since. He had suddenly been granted an opportunity to tell Shayla the truth about himself and to continue to be around her, and that was something he dreaded. If he could remain a cast member on the show and she was forced to work with him, he might be able to undo some of the damage he'd done by lying to her since the day they met. It was a long shot, but if he could pull this off, he'd at least get the chance to try and persuade her that his interest in her was real and not just some crazy side effect to competing on this dating game show.

"Hey, Michael," Marsha greeted him when he came into the office. Lita just nodded at the chair facing her desk, indicating that he should sit down.

"How are you?" the motherly one of the pair asked him solicitously. She'd been feeling very guilty about not listening to him more when he'd warned them that something more serious might happen soon. Lita remained as brusque and businesslike as always, just as if nothing had disrupted her precious program at all. Michael knew he didn't have time to spend resenting her attitude. Especially since he planned to use her thoughtlessness to his advantage.

"I'm fine," he answered soothingly. But he couldn't resist adding, "I'm just doing the job you hired me to do."

Lita wasn't fazed by his pointed remark. She lacked her

partner's heart. Marsha would at least hear him out, he was sure, and would probably be persuaded. But Lita was a different story.

"The police are useless," she announced now. "They barely tell us anything and say that there's not much they can do—unless we want someone stationed outside of Camilla's room, which we don't. What good would that do?" she wanted to know.

"You did see a cop at the hospital before you left, though, right?" Marsha said anxiously.

"Of course," he assured her. "I wouldn't be here if she wasn't protected. I've got my own man on her and on Camilla, too. But…" He prepared to make his pitch. "I need to do more in order to make sure they're safe. I'm going to need cooperation from your staff in order to make sure nothing else happens."

"Of course," Marsha said, at the same time that Lita said, "How can you do that without letting them know that you're a bodyguard? We can't reveal that now. It would look like the show was rigged." Marsha nodded.

"That's true," he agreed. "But if I'm dating the assistant producer, I would have access to anywhere she would," he answered. "And I'd have a good reason to be anywhere she was."

"The assistant producer?" Lita said. "You mean Shayla Tennison?"

"Yeah," Michael answered. "That's her. She pretty much runs the day-to-day production, doesn't she? So if I was working with her…" He let his voice trail off, gave them a moment to let the idea sink in.

"Our Shay?" Marsha echoed. "What are you saying?"

"You could replace Dee. Shay is her sister. They look a lot alike. She'd be a great contrast to Camilla Lyons, and she's your production assistant; she could help me find whoever is behind this. It's got to be someone on the inside. His information is just too perfect."

"Let me get this straight—" Marsha started to say.

"I'm not sure she'd agree," Lita began at the same time. "Shayla wasn't exactly gung ho about making this production in the first place, and I don't think her opinion has changed much since then. She thinks these dating shows are sexist." The woman rolled her eyes, making her opinion of Shayla's reservations very apparent.

"You can't make her do it, of course," Michael agreed. "I just thought it might be a simple way to solve our problem. There's no reason for anyone to be suspicious, because she's Dee's sister."

"Instead of two celebrities, we'd have a TV star against… against…what would you call her, a professional woman?" Marsha said. She sounded intrigued.

"She's the girl next door," Michael answered. "It's a natural."

"It may be a little too much like that *Ordinary Joe* show," Lita said doubtfully.

"Shayla is not ordinary," Marsha said, before Michael could. "I think it just might work. If we can convince Shay."

They spent a little while working on the details, then tried to decide when would be the best time to speak with Shayla.

"She's probably at the hospital," Marsha said. "We can't really bother her there."

"Why not?" Lita asked.

"Because it's not a real smart move to call someone away from the bedside of a sick relative when you want to ask them for a favor." The acerbic tone of her voice was apparently lost on her partner, who shrugged.

"The ICU nurse agreed to call me if there was any change in Dee's condition," Michael volunteered. "If I hear from them, I'll get in touch. Meanwhile, I would give her a call and see if she's planning to come in to work tomorrow." Lita reached for the phone. "Not now."

"Tonight," Marsha explained patiently. "Or tomorrow morning, Lita. That will be soon enough. We've already lost a good bit of time, since we're going to have to reshoot the last two shows. This is going to cut into the budget. Let's see what we can do about that."

Michael went back to the hotel. He found the other contestants in the lounge, as he expected. They'd been sitting there most of the morning, gleaning what news they could from the camera crew and the hotel staff. He told them he'd been in his room all morning since he'd seen Dee loaded into the ambulance, but he knew they sensed the lie. Luckily, they were pretty good guys and didn't say anything that would have looked questionable on camera. He told them what he could, and they broke up into smaller groups. Steve, Anton, and Luther went for a swim at the hotel pool. Jordan and James said they were going to have lunch in the bar, and Jared and Lance said they were going to their rooms.

"I'm going up, too," Michael said. Pretending to go back to his room would satisfy the cameramen, and he could see that Lance was worried.

Apparently, Jared had seen that Lance was upset, too. "I'm going to get a book and read, because I'm old and I could use a break from drinking with these young guys," he said. "What's your excuse for hiding out in your room?" he asked Lance as they walked toward the elevators.

"I'm concerned about Camilla," the younger man said. "The buzz is this wasn't an accident, and if this was about the show, then maybe…I don't know…whoever did this could hurt her."

Jared was shaking his head. "Nothing's going to happen to the Goddess, son. Not with us around. She's going to be just fine. You leave the worrying to the police. They know how to do their job."

"Yeah," Michael agreed. He almost told them there was a cop guarding Dee right that moment, then remembered these men weren't his coworkers—they just felt that way because he had spent so much time with them over the last few weeks. "I'm sure Camilla and Deanna Jones are being protected."

"I just wish there were something I could do," Lance said. The elevator arrived, but none of them got in.

"Go baby-sit that gang out by the pool," Jared suggested. "I'd do it, but I can't tell them anything. Steve told me I reminded them of their fifth-grade shop teacher."

Michael grinned. The older man reminded him of his uncle, Doc, his father's older, very distinguished brother. There was something about courteous, older southern black men that made younger guys feel like they had to prove themselves—sometimes in the most obnoxious ways.

"What makes you think they'll listen to me?" Lance asked.

"They'll listen," Jared said, looking to Michael to confirm the fact. He smiled.

"But…" Lance protested half-heartedly.

"Shayla probably isn't going to be able to check on them today, and it would be too bad if she had to come back to another warning from the hotel, or worse."

Michael had to hand it to the man—he was good at this. A lot like Uncle Doc, actually.

"Okay." Lance headed off toward the pool, slowly but determinedly.

"Go," Jared said to Michael, pressing the elevator button again. "Do whatever it is you do."

"I—" Michael started, ready to tell the usual lies to maintain his cover. But Jared just waved him off. "Bye." He took his usual back way out of the hotel to the rental car he kept in the parking lot.

He called Darren on his way to the hospital and got a quick update on the progress his partner had made in his investigation. There was no news. The search through the hotel's video wasn't complete, and the police report hadn't come in yet.

"I'll be at the hospital," Michael reported. "You can reach me on my cell."

"Did you tell her yet?" Darren asked. Michael knew he was asking if he had told Shayla about his real identity and about the plan he'd come up with for catching the psycho who had put her sister in the hospital.

"Not yet. But the producers agreed, so it should be soon. I'd just rather not have to add to her problems. I hope Deanna wakes up soon."

His wish was granted. His cell phone rang while he was on his way to Bethune Hospital. The singer had awakened, and there didn't seem to be any permanent damage. Her burns would take time to heal, and she was going to be in pain, but with time, the doctors thought she'd make a complete recovery. Michael turned around and went back to the hotel. He wouldn't bother Shayla now. He'd be talking to her soon enough.

Memo
From: Marsha
To: Everyone
Deanna Jones is going to be all right! The producers appreciate your expressions of concern, and we will keep you updated on her progress. The doctors tell us she will make a full recovery, thank goodness. Her family requests that we stop sending flowers, so please honor their wishes.
Marsha James

Chapter 17

Mom and Dad arrived a couple of hours after Dee woke up. Shay was so happy to see them and to turn over to them the job of talking to the doctors and worrying about Dee and comforting her. She felt overwhelmed and on the verge of tears, and just having her parents in the room was a huge relief. Mom had been a nurse for thirty-five years, so she instantly took charge. Dad gave Shay a big hug, which she could have stayed in forever. Then he hovered near Dee's bed, afraid he'd hurt her if he touched her but seemingly unable to move more than a foot or two away.

"Deanna, honey, everything is going to be all right. You'll see," Mama said, over and over. The litany seemed to help, and so did all the other little things she did—rearranging pillows and straightening the sheets and giving Dee water. In a half hour, the patient was sleeping comfortably, and the knot in Shay's stomach had shrunk to the size of a walnut.

Mom also took care of finding out everything they needed to know from the doctors and nurses—how long Dee was going to be in the hospital, what they would be doing for her and why, and what her outpatient treatment was going to consist of. Dad, meanwhile, put in a couple of calls to the police. As he was a retired police officer, they were willing to talk to him, although they didn't have much information to share yet, they said. Still, it was a start. It was more than Shay could have done.

She took them to her home eventually. Dee had taken over her guest bedroom during her visit, so even though she had moved to the hotel in order to appear on the show, Shay had to straighten up the clothes and other belongings her sister had left behind before they could settle in. Once she had done that, she left them alone in order to check whether she had any food in the refrigerator. Luckily, since Dee had come to visit, she'd gotten better about at least keeping staples in the house. Her father suggested they have a light dinner, and they settled on an omelette and some home fried potatoes.

They were tired from the flight. After dinner, they watched a little television, then went to bed. It was only nine o'clock, and even though she was exhausted, Shay didn't want to try to sleep yet. She was afraid if she went to bed this early, she'd wake up in the middle of the night. Then she'd be alone, and the house quiet, and she wouldn't have anyone to talk to. She checked her messages and left one for Marsha saying she would talk to her in the morning. She wandered around aimlessly and tried to read and watch TV, but nothing held her attention for long. Her mind was going a mile a minute, around and around, and always ended up in the same place: wondering how this could have happened.

She finally went to bed around eleven o'clock, and although her dreams were a bit disturbing, at least she didn't awaken until her alarm clock went off in the morning. She and her parents had breakfast, and then they talked about the day ahead. "I should go into the office sometime today," she explained. "I just dropped everything yesterday. And I didn't talk to anyone. I should go just to make sure they can find the schedule and understand it."

"That's fine," her mother said. "Why don't you go this morning? Visiting hours aren't until eleven, and your father and I want to do a little grocery shopping and pick up a night-gown for Deanna."

"I can get the groceries, Mom," Shay argued. But Trina Tennison was determined to do the shopping herself.

"I like to do it," she said. "Just give your father directions to the market, and we're good."

Shay promised to meet them at the hospital later and reluctantly said good-bye. When she got to the office, she found that everyone seemed to have picked up the slack for her—nothing important had been left undone. She was told that the boys had been very bored since they hadn't been given anything to do, and the footage that had been filmed wasn't very interesting. Camilla had stayed in the previous evening, but she seemed fine. The editors said there wasn't any good footage for her to watch, just some stuff that might be good for filler in the end. Of course, the bachelors were all talking about what had happened to Dee, and they didn't know if she was going to even be on the show in the end. Her guest appearance had been exciting but short-lived. No one knew what the producers planned to do now that she couldn't continue in her role.

Shayla didn't really care what her bosses were planning to do about the hole Dee's accident had created in the show's roster. Compared with the pain Dee was suffering and what her parents were going through—and the fear she herself felt when she thought of her sister lying helpless in that hospital bed—Marsha and Lita's concern about how to handle the unexpected development was the last thing Shay needed to worry about. *I'll just check in with them,* she thought, promising herself she would not get dragged into their problems. She called them from her office before leaving for the hospital.

"Oh, you're back," Marsha said when her secretary put the call through to her.

"I just wanted to make sure everything was okay here," Shay explained. "I am planning to go back to the hospital, though. My parents are here helping out, and I'm going to meet them."

"That sounds fine," Marsha said sympathetically. "You take all the time you need. We'll take care of everything here." Just when Shay was beginning to feel she wasn't needed and to wonder if she was really that expendable, her boss added, "We've got some ideas about what we want to do with the show, but we can wait a day or two until you're ready to come back."

Shay couldn't resist asking, "What kinds of ideas?" She didn't think they could replace Dee at this point, but so much had been planned around her sister's guest appearance, she didn't imagine that they'd been able to make any adjustments this quickly.

"It's not something we have to discuss this minute. You go, take the rest of the day off. We've got everything under control until tomorrow, or the next day even. Then when you're ready, we'll bring you up to speed."

"All right, then," Shay said reluctantly.

"Call us later and tell us how Dee's doing, okay?" Marsha asked.

"Definitely. Bye."

After she hung up the phone, Shay looked around the office, made a couple of notes for the staff and the crew about items she thought they might be handling that afternoon, and she left for the hospital.

There was nothing much to do there, though. Her mother was taking care of everything, and her father was at loose ends, which had gotten him to thinking again about the incident that had brought them there. Shay didn't have any answers to his questions, and soon she, too, was wondering what the police were doing about it. The police seemed just as stumped as they had the day before, and they did not appear to be particularly worried about it. They had a man posted at the hospital; a nice young uniformed officer who she and her family had met and liked but who wasn't involved in the investigation itself.

By the end of the day, she'd decided she would probably go back to work in the morning, and she called Marsha to tell her. She got Lita on the line, who was flatteringly thrilled by the news that Shay was returning to the office so quickly.

"I didn't want to pressure you," the older woman said. "But we need you. It's wonderful that your sister is doing so well. Thank God."

Shay spent another quiet evening with her parents, amazed that there wasn't anything about them to indicate that their lives, and her life, had been touched by something so horrible just a day before. It was a mild spring evening, and the golden green leaves of the trees swayed outside her window. The world just went on, as though nothing had happened. People went to work, bought groceries, talked as they made dinner. They didn't know. The news that Deanna Jones had been taken to the hospital had been reported on AAT news and possibly to some other small outlets, but since there hadn't been any information released about the particulars, it hadn't made much of a stir. Shay couldn't decide how she felt about that. She knew Dee hated it when her celebrity caused people to invade her privacy, but she also appreciated her fans' interest. She maintained a Web site to keep them informed about her professional life and even about some of her personal stuff. Somehow Shay didn't think her sister would want her fans to imagine her lying helpless and bruised in that hospital bed, though, so she guessed it was better that there hadn't been a big fuss made about the incident that put her there. Dee had already asked Shay what the producers were going to do now that she wouldn't be able to appear on *Lady's Choice,* and she was surprised when Shay said she didn't know because she'd only been in the office for an hour or so that morning.

The next day Shay went into the office, intending to stay all day. Dee's question had been the push she needed to get back to work. As soon as she had gone through her mail and her messages, she made her way to Marsha's office. The producers were expecting her. "How is Deanna?" Lita asked.

"She's doing better, thanks," Shay answered. "The burns on her hands will take a little while to heal, but she's going to be fine."

"And how are your parents?"

"Good, thank you."

It was nice of them to ask about her personal life, but Shay really wanted to know what they planned to do about the production. She would have thought they'd be going crazy with the unexpected disappearance of their guest star. It had to have thrown them for a loop, not to mention the havoc that had been created with the budget and the shooting schedule. This was the third day in a row without any dates to film, but they seemed fine. More than fine. They seemed excited.

"Shayla, we have something to tell you," Marsha said.

"What?" she prompted when Marsha looked at Lita, who just stared back at her.

"It's about Michael Grant." That was a surprise. Shay hadn't realized that anything could have happened to him during the past thirty-six hours. "He's not like the other contestants."

She could have told them that. In fact, she had told them exactly that. "So?" she asked.

"He's a security consultant. We hired him to be a bodyguard for Camilla because we received some letters for her from some nutty fan who thinks he's in love with her."

"Oh my God," Shay exclaimed. She didn't know which part of that revelation was more shocking. That Camilla was the object of a fan's obsession wasn't that surprising, but that they hadn't told her about it was…harder to comprehend. That Michael Grant was something other than a normal bachelor—if there was such a thing—was even more difficult to digest. "A fan? That's…that's wild. And Michael is…"

"He's working undercover as a contestant on the show. Not that he wasn't a perfectly good one. I mean, he was perfect for the part. Good-looking, smart, successful. He had just as good a chance at winning as anyone. He's a private investigator from right here in D.C., and he's working on our case."

"He is?" She was flabbergasted. "Really?" *Why the heck did he kiss me, then?* Shay thought. She didn't say it aloud, though. She needed more information so she could figure this all out. A lot more. "Our case being…?"

"An investigation of who sent those letters. And why."

Shay's mind leapt from place to place. That was why he'd

always seemed so nosy, so assertive. He'd been doing his job. And that was also why he'd been so helpful. He was working. All the time she thought he was attracted to Camilla, he'd just been putting on an act. Maybe kissing her had just been part of his cover. Had he been trying to get Shayla on his side just so that she, as the assistant producer, would let him get away with breaking the rules she was supposed to make sure that all the contestants followed?

All that charm and the flirting and the dates she had had to arrange and then watch on film—had it all just been a lie?

Shay knew she probably should have been happy to have so many questions answered—the mystery was solved. She should at least have been relieved to know that she didn't have to be jealous of his relationship with Cami. It was only now, knowing that his pursuit of the actress had all been just a part of his cover story, that Shay could finally even admit that she had been a little jealous. She had thought that, at best, he'd been pursuing two women at the same time. At worst, she had told herself, he was using her somehow.

"What about Dee?" she asked. Was her sister just another part of his job or had he genuinely been interested? "Was that why this happened to her? Was the attack on her connected?" Even before her bosses answered her, she knew that the answer to her question was yes. It was only logical. If there was someone on the set who was obsessed with Cami, someone watching her and writing her letters and thinking that that was love, then that person also had to be the one who hurt Dee. There couldn't be two different people lurking and creeping about the hotel and the stars of *Lady's Choice*. It was not possible.

Michael Grant agreed with her. He arrived a few minutes later and confirmed it.

"We received a letter from Camilla's stalker that contained a reference to Dee," he said. Her bosses, however, weren't as sure. "Deanna has whacko fans, too, doesn't she? Maybe this was someone who was after her before she ever came here?"

Shay was still trying to make sense of all she'd been told, but she wasn't buying that argument.

"You're kidding, right?" She looked from Marsha to Lita accusingly, and asked them and Michael, "Why didn't you tell me? I had a right to know. And Dee did, too."

"We did tell your sister," Marsha replied immediately. "We asked her not to tell you because we were afraid you would… worry." She looked away guiltily.

"She wasn't. She didn't. This happens all the time, she said," Lita continued. "None of us thought that anything would happen. I mean, even the police said that these guys rarely do anything. They just like to write letters."

"Rarely?" she queried.

"That's why we took precautions, put Michael on the show. We didn't want to take any chances," Marsha said in their defense. Shay glared at Michael. He had not shared the producers' optimism. That was clear from everything he'd done since he'd been here. He'd been busy running around, trying to watch over Camilla, complaining about their lax security. He had known the danger was real. "What else could we do?" Marsha asked.

"You could have told me," Shay said again, frustrated with all of them.

"I'm sorry," Michael said.

It wasn't enough. "I quit," she said firmly.

"You can't!" Lita cried.

"We need you," Marsha said. "Your help."

"What?" She couldn't believe them. Any of them. All she

wanted was to leave this insanity behind her and go sit with her sister and her parents and get on with her life. "My help? You want my help? You put my sister in danger and didn't even tell me, and now you're asking me to keep on working for you? Are you serious?"

"Yes," Marsha said. "We are. We're sorry we didn't tell you. We should have. But that's in the past. We can't finish this project without you."

"Did you really think I'd say yes?" Shay asked in disbelief.

"I want you to help me catch the guy who did this." Michael jumped in. "By taking your sister's place on the show."

"You've got to be kidding me."

"Shayla, we've put too much work into this project. GoGo Girls is done if we don't deliver," Lita said.

"I don't care," Shay lied.

"We've got to replace Deanna Jones right away. We've got to start shooting again. And we can't revamp everything at this point. The publicity, the film we made, it's all geared toward introducing a rival at this stage. We already lost two days; we can't afford to lose any more time." Lita's impassioned plea was filled with more emotion than Shay had ever heard from her, but it failed to move her. Someone had tried to kill her sister. These women didn't even have any right to say Dee's name, let alone complain about how the incident had hurt their precious television program.

"Just think about it," Marsha said, tears in her eyes. Shay wondered coldly if those tears were for her, GoGo Girls, or for the woman herself. "Don't say no now. You're upset. It's perfectly understandable, but…please, give us a chance to make this right."

"No," Shay said, and turned on her heel and left.

She didn't even stop at her office on her way out of the

building. She headed straight for the hospital. She was furious with them. All of them. She had thought Marsha was her friend. She had believed that Lita valued her, too, at least as an employee, if not more. And Michael. She had turned to him, in her sister's hospital room, and he had been lying to her. His very presence there had been a lie. He'd been working. She had leaned on him and he let her, and all the time he had been trying to figure out how to use her to do his job.

When she got to the hospital, she checked on Dee and her mother, and then whispered to her father that she needed to talk to him. She told him about the threats against Camilla, and the bodyguard, and the last letter with its mention of Dee, and her bosses' latest crazy plan. She expected him to be as outraged as she was, to jump out of his seat and go looking for the man who had rigged an explosive charge to explode when his daughter flicked a light switch. She thought he would feel the same way she did.

Instead, he said, "Shayla, those women may be right."

"What?" She couldn't believe her ears.

"We, the police, can't do much in situations like this one. We have to wait for the guy to actually do something."

"But there are stalking laws…"

"They don't work. Maybe if it's your ex, or your boss harassing you, or some nut who walks right up to the lady and tells her what he's doing, but a guy like this…it's hard to even prove they did it if they don't confess. And that's if you can find them. This man who's been stalking your TV friend, they may never figure out who he is."

"Can't they…I don't know, get his fingerprints off the letters or something?"

"They didn't get any at the crime scene, the hotel room. He may be too smart. Or maybe he's just lucky. But either way, the police haven't got anything on him. I'm not even sure they're going after the stalker for the bombing. They never mentioned it to me, and I think they read me the whole file."

"Why wouldn't they, though?" Shay asked.

"Where's the evidence?" he answered.

"But—"

"It's common sense, I know. We both know it's got to be the same guy. But that's not how it works on the job. They can't just assume anything. They have to prove it."

"And you don't think they will?" she asked, deflated.

"I don't think they can," he answered. "There may not be any other way to catch this guy. He didn't come out to get Camilla; he only did it to hurt another woman, a woman he thought was a threat to her. He may not surface again unless you take Deanna's place."

Shay couldn't believe he was suggesting that she should act as bait for a trap. "I don't know," she confessed. "It would be…so…this all feels so unreal."

"You don't have to do this, honey," her dad said, putting his arm around her shoulders. "It's up to you. But it sounds like that Mike guy is right. You're the only one who can."

She was her father's daughter. Of course she had to agree.

There was a long debate between herself, Marsha, and Lita about how they would handle the switch on the show. They considered using the footage they'd shot of Dee and then having Shay step in right where she'd left off—after her first date with Michael—and telling the audience Dee had been incapacitated and that Shay would go on in her place. The producers said telling the audience about Dee would create sympathy for Shay's character, but Shay wasn't comfortable about using her relationship with Dee that way. Finally, everyone agreed that Shay would come on the show as herself, the assistant producer. It would be known that she had been involved with the program from the beginning but had no idea that she would ever be in front of the cameras. She would be introduced as a real woman, as opposed to the fantasy, Camilla Lyons.

Shay insisted on a few conditions that her bosses hadn't expected. She didn't plan to reject anyone, and she was determined not to publically choose any of the men, either. To her, picking and choosing from among the bachelors was just the opposite side of the same coin, and she didn't want to humiliate anyone on national television. It was decided that at Shay's debut, Camilla would ask all but one of the men to go out with her, and Shay would go on a date with him. Lita had lobbied for having Camilla choose only four of the men, thus splitting the guys in half between herself and her rival again, but Shay couldn't imagine dating four of the guys this first week. She needed time to adjust, she told them.

As she moved her belongings into the hotel, Shay tried to remember what had made her decide that working on *Lady's Choice* was a good career move, and couldn't. Her sister in the hospital, her attacker on the loose, the competition with Cami, her bosses' crazy idea that she appear on the show— Shay couldn't her get mind around all of it. And then there was Michael. The man was a private investigator. He was working undercover. What had she said to him? What had he said? Something about how he originally suspected it might be a hoax, and that she might be in on it.

At least it couldn't get any worse than this. Dee was safe with Dad guarding her, and Camilla was safe with Michael guarding her, and now Camilla wouldn't feel threatened by Dee anymore. Camilla could get down to seriously considering which of the men she was dating might actually be husband material. She didn't seem to mind that Shay was replacing Dee. She welcomed her to the show, on camera, and seemed to really mean it.

"Are you all right?" she asked, when the cameras were turned off. "I didn't want to say anything before, but…I know this has got to be hard for you." Since Dee's debut on *Lady's Choice*, Cami had turned into someone that Shay didn't recognize, but now her friend seemed to be back.

"I think so," Shay said. "Thanks, Cami."

"Hey, I may not have liked your sister much, but I didn't want anything like this to happen to her. Or to you or your family."

"I know," Shay assured her. "Dee is going to be fine. Thanks for asking."

Memo

From: Marsha

To: All contestants

We are pleased to announce that Shayla Tennison will be joining the cast, pitching in while her sister is recovering. There will be some slight changes to the format, but the rules will remain essentially the same. Any contestant who wishes to may leave the program or may choose to try to make a match with either Camilla or Shayla Tennison.

We will reshoot Sunday night's episode, but as when Deanna debuted, the elimination round will be cancelled this week, and the bracelet dates are also cancelled. Camilla will choose four men to go out with this week, and Shayla will date the remaining four contestants. Next week, the elimination ceremonies will resume.

Chapter 18

That Sunday night, the elimination round was cancelled for Shay's first appearance, just as it had been when Dee debuted on the show. This time, Cami had to choose all but one of the guys to go out with, leaving that one man for her rival to date. Shay was worried that she might not choose James, but, much to her relief, the stockbroker was one of her first choices, after Jordan and Michael, which left the boys from Detroit, as well as Jared and Lance. Cami had spent a long time trying to make her decision that day, and even as late as the ride over to the studio from the hotel, she said she still hadn't made up her mind. To Shay's surprise, and she suspected to everyone else's as well, the actress chose Lance next. Shay liked to think that Camilla had learned from her mistake the week before not to take him for granted.

It was even more of a shock when Cami chose Steve and Anton next, before Luther, and then stood, seemingly torn between the youngest contestant and the oldest, Jared. It was somehow hard to believe she might choose Jared over the younger man. Shay had assumed he would be the one who wasn't picked. The carpenter had always been the odd man out in the group, and over the weeks, he had never seemed to grow any closer to the actress. It was only when they were out together, away from the others, that he and Cami had ever really seemed to click, and even then, no sparks had flown. But, looking from him to Luther, Shay had to admit he'd make a better match for the soap star than Luther would. He was a good guy, steady and solid as a rock, but it was just so improbable that a twenty-five-year-old tire salesman from Detroit could end up marrying a woman like Camilla Lyons, no matter how devoted he was. If Luther had been a more mature twenty-five, perhaps it would not have seemed he and Cami were so ill suited to each other, but although he was clearly in love with her, it didn't seem as if that was enough. He was impetuous, hot-headed, and jealous, and those character flaws kept getting the better of him.

As the seconds ticked by and everyone waited for Cami's decision, it became more and more clear that the lady was not going to make the obvious choice. Finally, she said softly, "Jared, will you stay?"

Jared, like those called before him, crossed the stage to give her a hug and a kiss on the cheek, and said, "I will."

Luther looked devastated. He hadn't been expecting this, and he was completely unprepared for the blow. He walked across to Cami and stopped in front of her, at a loss for words.

"I'm sorry," she said. "I think this is the right thing to do. I think you should try having a date with someone else, see how it goes."

It was probably true, but it was hard to watch him

struggle to accept her decision. He looked as if he was going to choke on it.

Shay didn't know how Cami could stand to stay in her room all day. The soap star spent her days running around working, too. But Cami didn't seem to feel guilty about lounging around watching TV or reading on a weekday. To Shay, it felt wrong, as if she was goofing off. And getting ready for her nightly dates just didn't take her that long. She could spend only so long picking an outfit or putting on make-up, and her braids were wash-and-wear. By her second day at the "Honeymoon Hotel," as the show's staff had dubbed the place, Shay had to get out of her suite. Although she had visited the lounge frequently during the last month to find the guys and talk to them about their dates with Cami, it felt different walking in there without her PalmPilot in her hand.

The boys all greeted her with waves and smiles as she walked slowly toward the group that was gathered in the central seating area, in their usual groupings. Jordan and James weren't there—they usually spent the morning working out in the gym; Anton, Steve, and Luther took up the couch and small table that dominated the small central area; Jared sat to one side, reading; and Michael and Lance stood chatting nearby. Now that she knew about Michael, Shay recognized his watchful, wary pose. He was alert and ready, keeping his eye on all the doors. He noticed right away when she entered the room, but she had almost reached the group before the others saw her. "Hey, Shayla, good to see you," Steve said, moving over so that she could sit beside him on the couch.

She sat in a big, comfortable armchair instead. "This is good," she said, smiling.

"This is different," Steve commented.

"What?" she asked suspiciously.

"Having you come to us. Cami never hangs out in here."

"Well, you can understand that, right? I mean, you guys do get a little overly competitive when she's around. She couldn't exactly relax with you, could she?" she asked sensibly.

"We'd be good, I swear," Luther said, crossing his heart.

"Uh-huh," she said skeptically.

"We're being good now. With you. Doesn't that mean anything?" Steve asked.

"I'm not Cami. You aren't all fighting over me," she pointed out.

"Yes, we are," Anton countered. "We're just a little more civilized when you're around for some reason. You don't make us feel so...self-conscious. Talking to you is easy, like talking to a friend."

Steve, always the clown, added, "But we still think you're hot."

"Sure you do," Shay said sarcastically.

Lance, always the gentleman, summed up all their compliments into one, all-encompassing statement of fact. "It's true. We like you a lot."

"You're a sweetheart," Jared threw in.

Michael was silent, but he nodded his agreement when she glanced in his direction.

Shay sighed. It was to be expected that they would treat her differently now that she represented their last chance of not being rejected on national television, but she'd have thought that they would realize after all this time that she didn't believe in this kind of matchmaking. They weren't likely to go on treating her the same, now that they were all supposed to date her, but they should have known better than to start paying her ridiculous compliments, trying to flirt with her. Men were all so predictable. She didn't know how they ever managed to take over the world.

"Guys, are you seriously going to try and convince me that you've suddenly fallen out of love with Camilla and in love with me?" she asked.

"There's nothing sudden about it," Michael said quietly. "We always liked you." It was the others' turn to nod. But Steve, as usual, couldn't let it just go at that. He had to get in the last word. "We didn't fall out of love with Camilla. We love you both." That got a smile out of Shayla and ended that debate.

After that, though, the boys kept on trying to prove the point. They flattered her constantly, at breakfast, lunch, and dinner. She received roses, daisies, tulips, and lots of flowers she couldn't name, as well as chocolates and other treats on a regular basis. They continued to do it, even after she told them all she didn't want any more gifts. Now she understood why Cami spent so much time working out. Between the candies and the pastries and the four-course dinners she ate on her dates, it became clear to her these guys had decided that the way to a woman's heart was through her stomach. With nothing much else to do, she ate the fattening gifts and meals, until her life seemed to revolve around food. And men.

Michael was even more persistent than the rest of them. On Friday, the day she was supposed to go on her date with Luther, he actually came to visit her in her room. It was almost as if he was jealous, Shay thought, but she quickly banished the notion that he might have any extracurricular interest in her at all. She was determined not to let herself forget why she had agreed to appear on *Lady's Choice* in the first place. She was here to catch a crazy man. That was all.

There was a motion sensor on the camera in her room, so

she suggested they take a walk in the hope that he had come with news about Dee's attacker.

"Thanks," she said as she closed the door behind her. "I know it would all be edited out of the show, but I thought it might be better not to talk about Dee in front of the camera, just in case *he's* watching," she said, looking at Michael to see if he approved.

"Good thinking," he said.

"I don't know how you can stand having Big Brother watching you all the time, anyway," she added.

"Wrong reality show," Michael said in answer to the Big Brother reference.

"I was thinking of the novel," she said. "By Orwell."

"Sure you were," he teased, and she laughed. "You're beautiful when you laugh, you know that?"

Shay had had enough of the constant flirting. "Give it a break, will you?" she begged. "There is no camera crew here. That's why I wanted to get out of the room, remember. We can forget about all that for now. Until they find us, anyway."

"It has nothing to do with the show," he said. "You're beautiful with or without the cameras rolling."

She was about to tell him again to cut it out, when they reached the elevator, he stopped to press the button, while she continued down the hall toward the stairs. "It's only three floors," she said. She had no intention of riding in that little box with him again, especially now that he was intent upon wooing her.

He followed her without protest, but said, "I don't have anything new to report on the case. I just wanted to see you."

"Why? What's with you?" she asked. "Do you feel some need to stay in character or something?"

"No," he answered. "I'm not playing a role now. You know

all about me, and why I'm really here. So you know I was never interested in marrying Camilla."

"Then why keep flirting with me?" she asked, annoyed. She didn't need this kind of distraction right now. She had to focus all her attention on catching the bastard who tried to blow up her sister.

"I'm not flirting," he answered, bringing her thoughts back to the present. "It's the truth—you are beautiful."

"That's enough of that," Shay said drily. "What is it with you guys? Why are you all acting like this?"

"Um, well now, let me take a wild guess.... Maybe we'd like to get to know you a little better, now that we have the chance."

"All of a sudden?" she asked skeptically.

"It's the best offer I've had all month," Michael said. When she grimaced, he shook his head at her reproachfully. "Why are you so surprised? We've spent as much time with you as with Camilla. Maybe more." He sounded sincere, but Shay was having trouble swallowing this. It didn't make any sense. She was no prize. Her dubious expression, rather than discouraging him from continuing along this track, seemed to spur him on. "You were here with us through all of this. And you helped us. Look what you did for Lance, helping him arrange that tour. And all the other stuff you did..."

"That was my job," she pointed out.

"It was," he acknowledged. "But you didn't have to be nearly as nice about it as you were. You actually listened. You were the voice of reason when the guys were going nuts. You were our lifeline. Maybe you don't know how much we appreciated that, but I told you a long time ago that the guys were always saying good things about you, remember? It was true."

Shay remembered he'd tried to sell her this nonsense once

before. It had been the night that he kissed her for the first time. She had tried to block out the memory, but it came back now, just as if she'd recorded the entire conversation. He had said then that the boys were half in love with her and she should watch the tape if she didn't believe him. She hadn't believed him, and she hadn't bothered to watch the tapes. "It was true then, and it still is now. No one else gave a rat's ass about us. You did."

"Uh-huh," she said wonderingly. She couldn't figure out why he was so intent on this.

"Face it, kid. We like you," he said.

"Right," she replied sarcastically. "Now it all makes sense. I'm the world's greatest assistant producer, so all the guys want to marry me instead of a TV star."

"Is that so hard to believe? You've got more going for you than Camilla Lyons, star or not."

She could handle the you've-got-a-beautiful-smile line—barely—but this kind of talk was dangerous. It wasn't flowery or fake. She was tempted to believe it. "Well, I win, then, I'm sure," she quipped, playing it down.

"Maybe these guys were foolish to look for a wife on a reality show, but they're not stupid. Or blind. They can see what kind of woman you are."

"Really? Because last week I was pretty invisible," she retorted.

"You were never invisible. They just didn't have any reason to say anything to you," he countered.

"They *said* they were all in love with Camilla," Shay said with a wry smile.

"Not me," he protested. "And you know it." He sounded serious, which made her very nervous. But she'd agreed to this walk and to this talk, so she was stuck with him for the moment.

Shay tried to make another joke. "You're all the same. Camilla, me, it doesn't matter. You all just want to prove on TV what big studs you are."

"Not me," he said again, stopping her with a hand on her arm as she reached for the door into the lobby. When she looked up at him, he said, "I don't have anything to prove." He let go of her arm and opened the stairwell door but stopped her as she tried to step through. He stepped out into the lobby, checking it out automatically; then he ushered her out.

There was something comforting about having him around, now that she knew he was a professional bodyguard, but that didn't make her any more inclined to trust him. He had been using her before, maybe he still was.

It wasn't worth arguing about. She decided to change the subject instead. "At least I know Luther's not going to start in," she said. "Unlike the rest of you, he really is in love with Cami."

"You're right. You don't have to worry about him," Michael agreed. "But that still leaves the rest of us. And we're not going to stop, because we were all halfway in love with you already, before you even came on the show."

"Don't be ridiculous," she snapped, speeding up as they approached the lounge. She couldn't believe she was actually looking forward to seeing a camera crew, but she had a feeling she'd feel safer with the cameras as a buffer. They would serve as a reminder of what they were all doing here.

"You'll see," he said confidently.

"Don't be so sure," she warned, hoping to wipe that cocky smile off his face.

"It's eight to one," he said with assurance. "We've got the odds on our side."

* * *

That night, on his date with Shay, Luther told her he was leaving the show. They came back from the date early, and he announced it to the rest of the cast at the hotel.

"I don't think I've got any chance with Camilla, and it's just too hard to see her with other people," he said. "It's not healthy."

"Don't make any rash decisions," Jared advised.

"Luther, give it a chance," Anton suggested.

"No," he said. "It's no use. I know she's not falling in love with me."

"But, Luth," Steve started to protest, but he fell silent at a look from his friend.

"I told Shayla," Luther said to both Steve and Anton, whom he had warned beforehand as it turned out. "I didn't want her to think it had anything to do with her. She's not to blame for any of this."

"You're really leaving?" Anton asked.

"Yup. I'm going home," Luther announced. "I've got to go pack."

Anton and Steve exchanged looks. "We're going, too," they proclaimed.

"We came together," Anton said as Luther started to protest. "We should leave together."

"It wouldn't be the same here without you, Luther," Steve added. "You were the one who got us here."

"Aren't you going to say good-bye to Camilla?" Anton asked.

"I can't," Luther answered.

Michael didn't think anything like this had ever happened on one of these programs before. It felt…real. He wondered what the producers were going to do about the strange twist their show had taken—losing three contestants in one night, and all of their own accord. They hadn't been eliminated by the star—they had chosen to leave. His guess was that Lita and Marsha would figure out some way to capitalize on this unexpected turn of events. The cameraman had followed Luther in, so it was on film.

Whatever happened with the rest of *Lady's Choice,* at least these three boys were going to leave Baltimore with their dignity intact. He hoped he would be doing the same thing. Appearing on *Lady's Choice* had been a risk, both personally and professionally. He had known, from the beginning, that there was a good chance he would be rejected by a national celebrity on television. Worse than that, it was possible he might be so recognizable after competing on the show that he could never safely do any undercover work again. Those were the dangers he had known about. There was no way he could have foreseen falling in love in front of millions of viewers.

His relationship with Shayla had stalled out. She was still miles away from accepting his transformation from coast guard to security consultant. She was willing to talk to him about the case, which he had taken advantage of in order to speak with her out of sight of the cameras for a few minutes here and there, but she had made it clear that she wasn't interested in talking about anything else with him. It wasn't just the lies he had told, or the fact that those lies might have contributed to her sister's situation, that had placed him in hot water. It was more than that. He couldn't convince Shayla he was serious.

If he could have gotten her away from work, it might have been easier. The reality show did not help his cause. Even though she knew now that he'd never been interested in Camilla, it didn't make her any more receptive to him than to any of the others. Shayla didn't think any guy would choose her over Camilla Lyons, and that included him. He couldn't convince her that she was more attractive to him than Camilla could ever be. She was sexier than her sex-kitten sister, Deanna, even if she wasn't famous or wild enough to dye her hair six different colors at once. She was herself, and that made her more appealing than designer dresses or ripped jeans ever could. He didn't know how he was going to get through the wall she'd erected around herself. As long as she insisted on seeing herself as somehow the lesser choice, there was nothing he, or anyone, could do. She didn't believe that she could compete with Camilla, and the bachelors' attention just frustrated and annoyed her because she didn't believe a word of it.

While she wasn't interested in romance, she was friendly, and the atmosphere in the hotel and the studio had changed since she arrived. Deanna Jones and Camilla had been like oil and water, and the animosity between them had infected the show. Shayla and Camilla were more like girlfriends than rivals. It was obvious that they got along. Camilla had her moments, when she was jealous of the way her guys spoke to Shayla, but she was able to rise above it.

Luther, Steve, and Anton's departure on Friday night could have left a blight on the rest of the cast, but on Saturday, the remaining five men and the two women went out together on a group date and had a great time. They danced and drank and shouted at one another over the music, and it felt as if they were all old friends, just enjoying the party. Shayla and Camilla were at the center of the action, of course, and the men revolved around them. Even with the odd number to deal with, they formed into couples, and then reformed, and all without any of the rancor that had arisen during the first few group dates whenever Cami had chosen to spend time with one of the men over another. Maybe it was because less than half the original contestants remained on the show, but Michael didn't think that was the reason for the changed atmosphere. It was Shayla. Somehow, she made her rival look good.

Michael didn't know if it was because Camilla had been lonely before or had needed a friend to talk to in order to handle the stress of her role, but since Shayla had been on the show, Camilla appeared more attractive than she ever had before. She treated the bachelors with consideration and with a new respect. The effect of a kinder, gentler Camilla on the men of *Lady's Choice* could only be described as electric. The guys had been infatuated with the TV star who flirted with them and teased them and put them to the test, but they really liked the new Camilla Lyons.

The producers, meanwhile, just loved these new developments—almost as much as they had loved the catfights between Camilla and Deanna. They were convinced that the change in their star would make her even more popular with the audience when the show aired, and they took full credit for her transformation. But it was Shayla who had caused it, Michael was sure. She was a good influence on all of them, not just Camilla. He didn't know what it was about her that made everyone in the cast behave, but it had improved the tone of the television show to the point where he wasn't nearly as embarrassed that his little sister would see him on it. Of course, he was opening himself up to a much bigger humiliation with Shay than he ever had with Camilla. He hadn't cared if Camilla rejected him—no matter how many people were watching. With Shayla it was different. He had fallen for her, and he was pretty sure that that was going to be obvious to the entire viewing audience. Even if Shay couldn't seem to see it.

He was frustrated. Usually he would have gotten to work, but he was trapped here. Darren was trying to get the police to run all the fingerprints taken from Deanna's room after the explosion, but they were stalling. It was a hotel room, they said. And the scene had been a mess. The police department didn't generally run fingerprints until they had more evidence, and in this case, they had nothing.

Michael normally would have been on it, but he was constrained by his role on *Lady's Choice* from making any kind of an effort to force the police to spend the time and money necessary, and Darren's style was a lot more laid back than his own. His partner said he was working on it when they talked. So far he had apparently called a buddy in the crime scene lab and an old friend from the arson squad, but neither had the juice to affect department policy. He was currently going another route, talking to a guy he knew at the FBI. Michael wanted to be out there, throwing his weight around, getting things moving, but he couldn't. He was stuck.

Camilla,
*Those other men are not worthy of a woman like you. I
would never be tempted to turn from you. No woman
will ever come between us, my love, just as no other man
can take your heart from me.*

*I will never let anyone hurt you. I will get rid of her
for you, like the other one.*

Hers

Chapter 19

A few weeks ago, if Shay had been asked if she and Camilla Lyons could ever be friends, she would have said it was impossible. But spending time with the actress, both on camera and off, she actually had come to like the woman. They were back where they had been a month ago, before Dee had moved into her apartment, when Shay felt as though she understood Camilla and could empathize with her. They spent most of their time talking about the boys, as might have been expected, but Cami had really opened up to her as she tried to figure out what she should do next. There were five contestants remaining on the program—James, Jared, Michael, Lance, and Jordan. Cami genuinely liked all of them, but she wasn't sure if she could love any of them. Jordan, she said, was the easiest to be with. Lance made her feel really good. She admired Michael, Jared, and James and thought they were all men she could imagine dating seriously.

"I don't know how to decide between them," she told Shay

on Saturday. The next elimination was to be held the following night, and she was at a complete loss as to who she should reject. "I need help," she confided. "I don't want to hurt any of them." She had said the same thing about a month ago, after Dee's debut, but Shay had not believed she meant it then. She did now.

Shay had been Cami's adviser and confidant almost since the project had begun, but as the show wound to a close, she didn't feel comfortable giving Cami advice about something as important as whom she should marry. They weren't talking about dating anymore. This was a serious decision, with serious implications. The choices Cami was about to make were major and could have major repercussions.

To Shay, though, there was one very obvious choice to be made. She was tempted just to tell Cami straight out that she thought she should dump James, but she didn't, because apparently the actress saw something in the man that Shay couldn't. She couldn't completely discount Cami's instincts. James did not seem, to her, to be a very nice guy, but people fell in love with jerks all the time, and married them, and presumably lived happily ever after with them. It was always possible that the reason that he had survived all the cuts up until now was that he and Cami were meant to be together.

They talked until late into the night about all five men and about how Cami felt about her chances for a future with each of them, but she didn't seem to come any closer to making a decision. So Shay was surprised the next night when she rejected James with hardly any hesitation at all. "I have come to care about you," she told him at the elimination. "I just don't think we have a future together. Our careers are very different, and I think we both love what we do too much to give any of it up for the other person." She explained to the other four afterward, "I had to choose someone, and I felt I had more of a real connection with each of you."

"We're glad we're here," Jordan said simply, and there was a chorus of agreement from the other men.

"Me, too." Camilla's relief at completing the ceremony was evident. "Let's go home," she suggested.

She had dates with all four of the remaining contestants—Jordan, Jared, Michael, and Lance—that week. So did Shay. Her dates were less serious than Cami's. She was just a placeholder for these guys until they got to see Cami, and she knew it. Michael kept trying to convince her that he didn't feel that way, but she didn't believe a word of it. He was different, it was true. He hadn't waited until she was a contestant to start playing games with her. But she didn't trust his motives. And so she couldn't believe him.

Every morning she met Cami in her room for a postmortem of the night before, which is how Shay found out that Jordan was a great kisser, since Shay hadn't let him kiss her; that Michael was a gentleman, which struck her as funny; that Jared really was good with his hands, about which Camilla said she was not about to go into detail; and that Lance was sweet and funny and he might truly love her, which Shay already knew.

Shay didn't have that much to report. She enjoyed dining out with the boys, and they were charming and attentive, but she knew they would rather be with Cami than with her. Her last date that week was with Michael, on Friday night. He was always so much more insistent than any of the others that it was she, and not Cami, that he was most interested in dating.

"Don't try to sweet-talk me, Michael. I'm a lost cause," she said. She had seen videotape of his dates with Cami, had seen him hold out her chair and laugh with her and kiss her good-night. Although she hadn't watched the whole video of his date with Dee, she imagined that it had followed the same basic format. She reminded him that, as assistant producer of the show, she knew all about his dates with Cami, in every detail, and that she wasn't interested in being his second choice. Since their date was filmed from beginning to end, he couldn't very well say that he had dated Camilla only in order to hide the fact that he was working as her bodyguard, so he was left with no argument.

"I had a really good time tonight," he said on the drive back to the hotel.

"Oh, really?" she responded drily.

"Yes," he said definitely. "I did. How about you?"

She had actually had fun. "The food was good," she said, smiling.

"Very good," he agreed. "I may not be the connoisseur Claude was, but I do my best."

She laughed, and came back with "I suppose you're going to take credit for the quality of the meal?" He nodded. "Remember, I used to be the one who arranged these dates for you guys. I know you had nothing to do with the restaurant selection."

"Oh, but I put in the request for your favorite spot," he retorted. "Where I grew up, it was understood that if a boy bought you dinner, you owed him."

"What neighborhood was this? Neanderthal?"

"Nearby."

"And what happens if the girl buys dinner?"

"Then he owes her," he said promptly. "And he has to do whatever she wants him to." He raised an eyebrow. "Is there anything you'd like me to do for you?"

"Anything?" she teased, feeling safe in baiting him with the cameras rolling just a foot and a half away.

"Your wish is my desire," he said, his voice a deep rumble in his throat.

"How do I know that?" she asked. "I don't even know you." Shay was only half joking.

"You will," he promised. He leaned toward her, turned his face toward the camera, and whispered, "Hey, can you hear me?"

"What?" the camerawoman asked. "I can't hear you."

"Good," he said to her in his normal speaking voice. Turning his head in Shayla's direction, he whispered, "You're stuck here with me in this fishbowl." Raising his voice for the camera, he added, "I'm not giving up on you, Shayla." He kissed her cheek, but before she could object, he sat back on his side of the car seat.

Shay didn't think it was her place to tell Cami that one in her stable of men had switched horses, but it wasn't long before the soap star heard about what he'd been doing. To her surprise, Cami didn't seem at all upset. "I heard he's been making it pretty clear he's interested in you. What do *you* think of him?" she asked Shay. "Are you interested?"

"Me? I think…he's…I don't know." She took a deep breath. "He's okay, I guess."

"Oh my God, what are we, in high school? Do you like him or not?"

"Cami, I don't think I'm his type," she said with a wry smile.

"Why?" Cami asked. "I mean, what makes you think that?"

"Because *you're* his type," Shay said, embarrassed at how insecure she sounded but absolutely sure she was right.

"Apparently not," the actress replied.

Shay had permission from her bosses to visit the hospital whenever she wanted in order to check on Dee's progress. Ten days after she'd been admitted, the doctors started talking about letting Dee go home. Shay was happy for her, of course, but afraid that that meant her parents would leave her alone with Deanna, and she didn't think she was quite ready for that. There were a lot of things they hadn't talked about—such as what was happening on *Lady's Choice*. It hadn't seemed appropriate to bring up a subject that might be touchy while the woman was flat on her back in a hospital bed. So she had never asked her sister how she felt about being replaced.

Shay might not have wanted to appear on the show, but Dee had. Shay didn't want to blather on about what she was missing until she knew, for sure, that her sister didn't feel cheated or—worse—betrayed. Shay had certainly not meant to hurt her by agreeing to take her place. She only wanted to catch the man who hurt Dee, and if there had been any way she could have done that without joining the cast of the television show she was producing, she would have. She had never harbored any wish to appear in front of the television camera. It was only because Michael and her father had assured her that this plan was the only one that would bring the stalker out into the open that she had agreed to appear on the program, and only that hope kept her going through all this craziness.

She didn't like being at the center of so much drama. It wasn't her style. It would have suited Deanna to a tee, she knew, but Shay couldn't help feeling that her presence on *Lady's Choice* was the punch line of a very bad joke. When she'd been producing the series, she'd wondered what in the world she was doing on that set, but it was even worse now that she was a member of the cast. If Dee came home now, to her house, she'd be shuttling between the show and the sick bed, and it could be extremely awkward if Dee resented Shay working on the program.

She wanted Dee out of the hospital as soon as possible, but it meant she would need to convince her mother to stay in Baltimore to help her take care of Dee, at least until they finished filming the last episode of the show, or else she needed her mom to take Dee home to Detroit with her. Either way, while they waited to find out when Deanna was going to be released, Shay had to bring up work and the question of whether her parents could continue to help out.

"Mom, you know that I have to continue living at the hotel until the show wraps up, right?" she asked.

As she always did, whenever the subject of the reality show came up, her mother voiced her surprise that anyone would want to be involved in it, let alone her daughter. "I just don't understand why these shows keep getting made. Does anyone really think it's a good idea to look for a husband or a wife on television?"

"Well, you know, Mom, it's not easy to find someone these days," Shay told her jokingly. She agreed with Trina completely, but she'd spent so much time with the bachelors that she'd actually heard all the reasons a person would choose to be on a matchmaking reality show.

"That's nothing new. It's always been hard to find someone you really care about. You don't think doing it with these crazy rules makes it easier, do you?" They hadn't told her mother the details about why Shay was replacing Dee on the show, just that she was going to stand in for her sister because it was important to the show and to the police in catching Cami's stalker. Her mom didn't know that she was bait. But she did know that Shay had absolutely no interest in finding a husband on *Lady's Choice.*

"Me, Mama? No, I don't. I'd just as soon meet someone the old-fashioned way and get to know them without the whole world watching."

"Those men on that show, and the girls, too, they're making a big mistake. Anyone who would even be on one of those TV shows must be missing a little something upstairs. All these reality shows these days are insane. I don't know why anyone watches them."

"They're very popular," Shay said, the perfunctory effort to justify the show's existence the only effort she planned to put into defending the project.

"I think that woman on your show is probably not a very attractive person. She's got all that money and a good job, and she has to go on television with all those boys to find a husband? There's something wrong with her."

Cami, Shay would defend. "No, she's okay. Maybe it wasn't the best idea to decide to find a husband this way, but there's nothing wrong with her. She just thought it was time to settle down, and she figured she could probably meet a good guy this way. The producers would weed out all the strange men and the players, and she'd end up with a group of nice guys to choose from—and then they'd get to know her and see if they could love her, in a fun, romantic way. It will make a good story to tell her grandchildren, you have to admit."

"You know her, honey, I don't, but I'm willing to bet she's got psychological problems. And these boys are exactly the worst ones for her, because they think it's fine to fall in love on TV, too. They're as crazy as she is. More. At least she gets to be in charge. They're just subjecting themselves to the worst kind of exploitation, where they are locked up in that hotel and followed around by cameras and have to date her with everyone watching."

"Okay, Mom, at least these guys are willing to put themselves out there. They're not bad guys. They just want to meet someone they think they can love. And they do it in front of everybody to show they're serious about making a commitment. That's not easy to find these days."

"Shayla, that woman is fooling around on each and every one of those men. She knows it, and they know it. The whole country will know it when they watch that show. So why do those men think she'll be faithful to them once the TV cameras aren't watching? And what do you think they're going to be doing? If they think it's okay for her to play the field, don't you think they're going to do the same?"

"I'm not sure that's fair," Shay said. She had thought she was judgmental about Cami and her boys, but she had nothing on her mother. "I work with these people. I promise you, they're not all liars and cheats. I don't think any of them are."

"I don't want to speak badly of your friends, Shayla, but if they go on television and put their private affairs out there for everyone to see, they better be ready to hear people say a lot worse than what I do about them," her mother said, unrepentant.

"Okay, Mom, I'm not going to get into a debate with you about this. It's not worth it. First of all, you may be right, for all I know. And second, I'm not on the show to find a husband, and I'm not interested in falling in love with any of these guys." Michael's face flashed in her mind's eye as she said it, and she almost started to explain to her mother that not all of the contestants on *Lady's Choice* had appeared on the television show in order to fall in love and find a wife. One was just there in order to do his job, but she realized there was no point in telling her this, since, in the eyes of the television viewing world, he would always be just another contestant. And it had nothing to do with her. "They're not interested in me, either," she assured her mother, and steered the conversation back to her original question. "The doctors are saying Dee will be coming home soon. Do you know where she wants to go?"

"Not really," Mom replied. "I assumed she would move back into your house. It's close by the hospital, and she's going to need to come back for her checkups and such."

"Yes, but Dee can't just walk out of here and back into her old life. She's going to need physical therapy and all, and I don't think she's going to be completely steady on her feet. She can barely get to the bathroom now, and that's only five feet from her bed."

"That's true. And you say you can't take a vacation from work?"

"Not right now," Shay answered.

"So I guess we'll be staying, right, Frank?" Shay's father nodded enthusiastically.

"How's it going on that show of yours?" he asked, out of politeness, Shay was sure. He didn't have any more interest than his wife did in the reality show, but he didn't think it was as incomprehensible as she did. Why run around looking for a husband or a wife if they'll bring a batch to you to choose from? was his attitude.

"It's going fine, Dad," Shay answered.

"That Michael guy?" he asked. "How's he?"

"He? There's no he. I mean, there's a group, four actually, I'm going to be dating this week, but no one I—" Suddenly she realized he was talking about the investigation, not romance.

"The bodyguard?" he clarified, just as she figured it out.

"Michael is fine, I guess," she said cagily. "He's in charge of an investigation that's not going anywhere, so he's a little antsy, maybe."

"Yeah, I hate that feeling. Waiting around for someone to make their move, so you can catch 'em at it has got to be one of the worst parts of the job. But he's holding up okay, you said. Right?"

"That's right."

"So that's good," he said.

"Uh-huh," Shay agreed.

He looked at her strangely, as if he wanted to say something, but he didn't speak.

"What?" she asked.

"Nothing."

"What, Dad? I can see it on your face. You have a question."

"I just wondered if you maybe liked this guy?"

"What?!" she said as her mother's head whipped around. "No. What in the world made you think that?" she asked.

"I don't know. Cop instinct. I can sense there's something up with you, that's all. And you get uptight every time his name comes up, so I put two and two together…"

"And came up with five," Shay said. "There's nothing up with me." *Other than being the bait in a rat trap,* Shay thought. "Or with Michael and me." She couldn't protest any more strongly. It would seem suspicious.

She needed to take a walk to stretch her legs and to get away from her parents' curious looks. "I'm going to get a soda from the machine," she said as she headed toward the door. Michael was standing in the hallway, facing the door of her sister's room, when she stepped outside. She'd almost forgotten he was there. Shay thought back over the conversation with her parents and winced as she thought of him hearing her mother's opinion on the men of reality matchmaking and her father's hunch about her feelings toward him. She prayed he'd missed all that.

If he had heard, he didn't say so. He had news of his own. "We got another letter. This time it's about you."

Memo
FROM THE DESK OF LITA TOLLIVER
TO: Marsha James, Shayla Tennison
Marsh,
This week's elimination will bring us down to the last three contestants. Are we still thinking about doing that hometown visit thing when we get down to just two? Like on *The Bachelor?* Because, if so, we'd better start making the arrangements.

    Lita

Chapter 20

Ever since The Letter had arrived, Michael went with her everywhere. Or almost everywhere. He was still on duty guarding Camilla, but he had help from the hotel staff, and as long as Cami stayed in her room—which she usually did—he felt she was pretty well covered. He preferred to watch over Shay personally, he said. So he went with her to the hospital to help her get Dee and her parents and take them to her house. She wanted to help get Dee settled in. Her parents were relatively comfortable in the house and in the neighborhood, and they had even taken the Metrorail into D.C. a couple of times to do some sightseeing. But they had only been in town for a little more than a week, so she wanted to be available to them, and to Dee, in case she needed a prescription filled or needed something from the store in order to be comfortable.

The doctors agreed to let Dee go home exactly ten days after she was admitted to the hospital. They had packed up

Dee's few belongings and were getting ready to help her out of bed when a man appeared at the door of her private room. It took Shay a moment before she recognized him.

"Leon!" Dee cried, smiling widely for a moment before she remembered that she was angry with him, and her lips drew down at the corners. "What are you doing here?" she asked.

"I came to see you," he said simply.

"Oh?" she asked, feigning surprise. "Why?"

"I heard that you were in the hospital, and since you pulled that disappearing act last month and changed your cell number and told your agent not to give out the new number, I had to come all the way here just to see if you were all right. You are, I see."

"Yeah, I'm okay," she answered, pulling the sheet up over her a little more so he couldn't see all the bandages.

He came farther into the room. "What did you do to yourself, you little idiot?" he asked.

"Hey! This was not my fault. Some crazy tried to blow me up, but it wasn't even about me. It was Camilla Lyons's stalker."

"You can't stand Camilla. What were you doing with her?" he asked.

"Evening the score," Deanna said, her dimples showing as she smiled at the thought. "She's on this reality show, *Lady's Choice,* and my sister's the assistant producer. You remember Shayla, don't you?"

"Sure, of course," Leon said. He was a tall, slim, serious man. He looked like the artist he was. He offered her his hand to shake, then moved past her to her parents, who'd been watching the exchange between their daughter and him with great interest. "Mr. and Mrs. Tennison, it's nice to see you again."

"You, too," Dad said, pumping Leon's arm up and down

with a gleam in his eye that Shay recognized from her preteen years as the one he reserved for boys he approved of.

"Hello, Leon," her mother said, looking from him to Dee with a knowing smile. "It was nice of you to come."

"Thank you, Trina."

"We'll leave you two alone," she offered, herding her husband and Shay out of the room. "You must have a lot to catch up on."

Leon's focus had moved back to Deanna, who had been slowly slipping downward in the bed ever since he'd arrived, until at this point all that could be seen of her was her gamine face. He moved toward her, the family apparently forgotten before they had even exited the room. "Let me see," he ordered, just before Mom closed the door on the scene.

"Hey, Trina," Shay's father protested.

"Let's give them a little privacy, Frank," her mother responded. "I have the feeling we're going to be seeing a lot more of him in the near future. You can act all protective and disapproving then."

Michael had been waiting outside of the room, leaning against the hallway wall. He stood patiently as Shay hesitated, clearly expecting her to come to him. She was tempted to ignore him and walk the other away, but she couldn't, so she decided she might as well ask him what he was up to.

"You let a strange man come into my sister's room," she accused him.

"I checked him against the list," he insisted. "He was on there. You should know. You gave me the names of the people on it."

"Oh, right," she said. "How did you know?"

"I've got a copy of his driver's license picture in my Black-Berry. All I had to do was look him up."

"Very high tech," she said with grudging admiration.

He smiled. "Twenty-four-seven is on the cutting edge," he replied.

When Shay and her parents reentered Dee's room, Dee and Leon looked very cozy. He was sitting on the edge of her bed. She'd emerged from beneath the sheets. And the two of them were holding hands, or at least that was what it looked like.

"So, Deanna, are you ready to go home now?" Mom asked.

"Yup," Dee said. "I'm feeling a little better, actually. I think I can manage to get dressed pretty much on my own while you and Dad get me checked out of here, okay? Maybe you can help me, Shay?"

"Sure," Shay agreed.

Getting Dee released from the clutches of the staff at Bethune Hospital was no easy task, but now the driver of the limo Shay had gotten was pulling into her driveway. The family—Dee, Trina, Frank, and Shay—and Michael and Leon all climbed out of the luxurious vehicle and headed toward the front door. There was a man waiting on the small front stoop. As they approached the tall, thin man in the black suit and sunglasses, Shay thought he looked vaguely familiar, and tried to figure out where she had seen him before. It was only when he took off the shades, though, that she realized it was Josh, the guy who had revamped the computers at GoGo Girls right before they began filming *Lady's Choice.* Suddenly it clicked. When she had ushered everyone into the house, including the computer geek cum bodyguard, she turned to Michael. "Yours?" she asked.

"Yeah, he's here for the next few weeks until we find the man we're looking for, or until the show wraps, whichever comes first," Michael answered. "He's going to keep an eye on Dee and your parents." He looked ready to argue the point. "I doubt that anything will happen. This is just a precaution."

"That's a relief," she said.

"You mean you're actually going to be reasonable about this? I had all my arguments lined up."

"You want to fight? Go ahead. I'm sure you don't need any help from me."

"No, no. I'm happy you're on board."

"Great," Shay said. "Take all the precautions you want. I don't want anything else to happen to Dee."

"I don't want anything else to happen, either. To her. Or to you."

"Let's go inside," she said. "Everyone's probably waiting."

But when they went into the house, everyone was busy getting Dee settled into her bed. They hadn't even noticed that Shay and Michael weren't with them. Nor did they seem to realize the phone was ringing. Shay answered it, listened, and hung up.

"Who was that?" Michael asked curiously.

"We have a heavy breather."

"A breather? You mean an obscene caller?" he queried.

"Yeah, I guess. He calls, listens, then hangs up," she explained.

"And you don't know who he is?"

"No," she said, looking at him as if he was crazy. "At least, I hope not. It would be weird if someone I actually knew was doing this."

"Don't you have caller ID?" he asked.

Shay knew Michael had paranoid tendencies, but she really did think he was overreacting. She'd been getting these calls for longer than she'd been assistant producer on the show. It was highly unlikely that the two things were related. "Yeah, I have it, but The Breather always comes up as either an unknown caller or a pay phone."

"And you didn't find that to be worth reporting to me? Or to your bosses at least?"

"Do you know how common this is? Every woman I know gets calls like this," she said airily. "Guys probably do, too. They just don't get freaked out about it. It's no big deal."

"Maybe not, but coming at this particular time, I wouldn't just ignore it. Did you call the phone company?"

"Of course not. What would I say? I'm getting phone calls from some creep who hangs up without talking. What could they do?"

"They could find out who's doing it, for one thing," he said. "I'm going to dial star-six-nine."

"Do you know how much that costs?" she started to object, then decided it wasn't worth the trouble of arguing with him. "Okay, it's just a buck seventy-five. Go ahead."

He hadn't waited for her to give him permission. He had already dialed and was waiting for an answer. No one picked up the phone, no matter how many times he let it ring. He called his partner on his cell phone. "Darren, check the incoming calls to this number. I just got a hang up on Shayla Tennison's phone, and she tells me it's part of a pattern." He listened for a moment, then added, "I would check incoming calls to Camilla, Dee, and Shay's rooms at the hotel."

Her father joined them by the living-room couch where the phone was located. "I noticed that she's been getting a number of hang ups, but I figured someone had memorized the number wrong or the line was crossed. I didn't think it meant anything."

"It doesn't, I'm sure," Shay reassured him.

He ignored her and continued speaking to Michael as if she wasn't there. "He or she always hung up as soon as I picked up the phone."

"Dad, please, I'm sure it's nothing."

"I'm not so sure," her father said. "Michael's right. The timing suggests maybe this is connected to what's going on at the show."

"Even if it is, it's not even creepy. Just annoying. If he's trying to scare me, he's failing."

"Maybe he's not trying to scare you. Maybe he's doing research."

"Huh?"

Dad explained. "It tells him where you are, and if he's been doing it regularly for a long time, it tells him when you're usually home."

"Okay, that's creepy," Shay said.

Cami wore a swirling, knee-length, black chiffon dress for this elimination round. In the limo on the way to the studio, she told Shay she liked all four men a lot and said she could see starting a real relationship with any of them. "I really can't decide," she said. "Jordan is so perfect for me, and Michael is my protector, so I can't get rid of him. So it's between Jared and Lance, I guess. Lance is by far the nicest guy I ever met, and he and Jared are just so…different from anyone I've ever dated. They're the reason I agreed to be on this show. I wanted to meet guys like them. They're so *real*. I honestly don't think they even care about my being on television. I can just be myself with both of them."

Shay didn't know what to say. She liked both men, but Lance was in love while Jared was not. It would hurt him less to be rejected. But it might be the right choice for Cami to make, especially if she was going to choose Jordan in the end. She supposed it would be kinder, under the circumstances, not to let the veterinarian continue to hope. Still, Shay couldn't help rooting for the vet to make it through the night without being eliminated from the contest. Against all the odds, he'd held on for this long. It seemed a shame to see him rejected now.

"I think they both like me for who I am. Lance likes me partly for what I do, and that's fine. I worked hard to get where I am, and I'm proud of it, but there's something different about Jared. I guess it's because he likes me in spite of what I do, not because of it."

"Oh," Shay said, her heart sinking. That kind of thinking did not bode well for Lance.

"It's just that Jared…well, he's the kind of guy who would never ask me to go out with him. Men who aren't interested in all this stardom stuff don't generally even talk to me, let alone ask me out. They think I'm…I don't know…not a woman they could relate to. I feel like, if I choose Jared, I'll find out why, maybe learn something about myself, about why that type doesn't think I'm their type. You know?"

"I think I understand, but…I think you're going to have to just accept that you may never know," Shay replied. "Who does?"

"That's true," Cami said thoughtfully.

They rode the rest of the way to the ceremony in silence. Shay didn't know what Cami was thinking about, but she herself was thinking about what the other woman had said about not knowing why someone chose you, why certain people were attracted to certain other people. If someone had told her a month ago that she would be drawn to one of the contestants on *Lady's Choice,* she would have thought they had a screw loose. She had disliked Michael then, and for good reason. He was arrogant. He refused to follow the rules. And he seemed to enjoy annoying her. Now, though, she found his self-assurance…sexy. There was no other word for it. He was overprotective, a little paranoid even, and she liked it. He made her feel feminine, almost fragile, and she liked the feeling. Even though he was bossy and domineering, which should have frustrated her, no other man had ever treated her like her safety was so important to him. Shay felt like she was so important to him. He might not really care about her as much as he seemed to, it could just have been that he was really good at his job, but there was something about the way he looked at her, the way he spoke to her, the way he kissed her, that made her feel like it was more than just work.

He wanted her. He had chosen her over Cami, and over Dee, with all their beauty and fame and talent. He kept saying he liked her better than them. As hard as it was to believe, maybe it was actually true. Shay shook herself mentally. Maybe wasn't good enough. She couldn't trust him. She had to remember that. Because she was tempted, very tempted, to forget. And she couldn't afford to let herself be pulled in to the madness. She was only pretending here, only playing a role, and so was he. They were on a reality show, but this wasn't reality. This was television.

At the ceremony Cami chose Jordan and Michael right away, then hesitated. She looked from Lance to Jared and back. "This is the hardest decision I've ever had to make," she said. "But…I have to do it. I'd really like more time with both of you, but I can ask only one to stay, so…" She paused again, looking down and swallowing hard before she raised her head and set her shoulders. "Lance, will you accept my invitation to remain here with me?"

Lance's smile made it clear what his answer was. It disappeared as he turned toward Jared. "I'm sorry," he said sincerely.

Jared grabbed him in a manly hug, then pounded his back twice with his fist. When he let him go, he was smiling at the younger man.

Obviously heartened, Lance walked up to Camilla and gave her a kiss on the cheek.

"Thank you," Lance said, his smile returning. Shay's eyes were misty as the veterinarian walked over to join Jordan and Michael. Jared approached Cami.

"I actually agreed to be on *Lady's Choice* to meet someone like you," she told him. "You challenge me. You make me feel I could be different. But, in the end, I guess I wonder if the reason I feel I could be different if I was with you is because I feel like maybe, deep down, you think I *should* be different. I wish I had more time to find out, but I don't. I have to choose right now. And this is really hard for me, but I think I have to let you go. As much as I like you, and as much as you challenge me, I'm afraid the reason I'm attracted to you is because there's a part of you that I don't think I can ever really touch. And there's a part of me that you will never understand. So, as much as I hate to do it, I have to follow my instincts and say good-bye."

"Good-bye," he replied.

As he walked away, Dan Green stepped up to her with his microphone in his hand. "We could all see how hard that was for you, but that's why the show is called *Lady's Choice,* isn't it, because it's up to you to make the tough decisions."

"I guess so, Dan," Cami answered, looking over at the three contestants who remained, Jordan, Michael, and Lance. "I think I made the right choice, though."

"I'm sure you did," Dan said. "You've got to follow your instincts when it comes to these things. You're down to just three men to choose from, and I've got to tell you, the tension is building about who the lucky guy is going to be."

Back at the hotel after the ceremony, Jordan, Lance, and Michael went to the hotel bar to get a drink. They had ridden back in a separate car from Cami and Shay, as always, and they were already into a third or fourth round of drinks by the time Shay found them in the lounge.

"Congratulations," she said to Lance. "How are you all doing?"

"We're just waiting for Jared to finish packing and come down. He said he'd be by to say good-bye," Lance said. "Would you like a drink?"

"No, thanks," Shay answered. "I had a couple with Cami before the ceremony."

"So did we," Jordan said, smiling. He grew serious as he added, "They're tough, man."

"They're the hardest part of this whole thing," Lance agreed. "For us, and for Camilla, I think. Is she okay?"

"She'll be all right," Shay said, thinking again that he had to be the sweetest man she'd ever known. She was tired, but decided to wait with them to say good-bye to Jared.

"I liked him," Jordan said regretfully as Jared walked away. The baseball player was starting to show the effects of the scotch he'd been drinking. "But I think Cam made the right choice, don't you?" he asked. "I don't think he was all the way on board with this thing. I mean, he wasn't like the rest of us. Don't get me wrong, he's a good guy, and I think he was here for the right reasons, but still, she was right—he didn't get her like we do."

"I'm beat," Lance said. "I'm gonna head up. You coming?" he asked the baseball player.

"I'm going to finish this one," Jordan said, holding up his drink.

"Night," Lance said.

"Night," Shay said, ready to go up to bed, too. But Jordan

clearly expected her and Michael to keep him company, and she figured it couldn't take him long to finish his scotch.

"My Camilla's got heart—she's not just interested in looks or money," he opined after another swallow. "She cares about what's inside. Take Lance, for example. He's not exactly a hot prospect, but he's the nicest guy of all of us." Shay couldn't help wondering if Jordan thought he himself was a hot prospect, but she kept her mouth shut, even when he added, "Too bad nice guys always finish last. Ha-ha." Jordan might be a little conceited, but he really did care about Cami, she thought, and he had good reason to believe that he might win this contest. Even Cami had said they were perfect together.

He seemed to share that opinion. "He would be a good choice, but it's sort of like she was saying about Jared—he doesn't understand where she's coming from, like I do. He's a doctor."

Shay was glad this was being recorded. It was probably the first and only time his vulnerable side had ever been caught on camera. She hadn't realized he had a vulnerable side. Marsha was right, she realized. Seeing Jordan making a fool of himself made him more attractive.

Michael didn't seem to share her newfound empathy for the man. "Yes, we know," he said. "Now finish that drink and let's get out of here."

"We care about the same things. He doesn't even work out. You don't work out, either," he said. "You look like you do, though."

"I work out sometimes," Michael said. He hauled Jordan out of his seat. "Come on, big guy. Bedtime."

Shayla was too tired, and Jordan was too drunk, to walk the three flights of stairs up to her room. Since Michael had to prop up the six-foot-three baseball player, she wasn't worried about riding in the elevator with her bodyguard. After the incident with the telephone call at her house, she was sort of glad he was with her on the ride up to the third floor. There she disembarked, leaving the two men inside the elevator, and walked down the hall to her room. She had just gotten inside when a knock on the door made her jump.

Her heart pounding a little faster than usual, despite her resolve that she would not let herself be affected by Michael's paranoia, she called out, "Who's there?"

"It's me."

Shay opened the door. "Michael, what are you doing?" she asked.

"May I come in?" he asked. "I wanted to check the room."

"No," she answered firmly. "I didn't touch any light switches, and I don't plan to, so I think I'll be safe enough for tonight."

"Okay," he said. "But I should tell you. My partner checked out the origin of that call at your house. The Breather, as you call him. And it came from this hotel."

She shivered. There were a million reasons someone might call her from this hotel, but none she could think of that would explain the caller's silence on the other end of the line. "Maybe it was someone who didn't expect to hear a man's voice answer?" she pondered aloud.

"Why not just ask for you, then?" he asked reasonably.

"Okay, it's a bit scary, but that's no reason to get carried away," she informed him. "I'm sure I'll be fine for tonight."

"I don't like this," Michael said, frowning.

"Neither do I," Shay agreed. "I am not going to let it get to me, though. If I walk around in a constant state of fear, then that psycho wins, and I'm not about to let that happen. I won't let him control me."

"All right, but…" Michael stood in the doorway, staring down at her, his expression revealing the warring emotions he felt. She knew him well enough at this point to know he was perfectly capable of forcing his way into the room in spite of her objections if he felt she was in any danger, and she appreciated the self-control it took for him to back away. "I want you to change rooms in the morning, and every day after that."

"Fine." She smiled. It sounded like a sensible plan. "I'll see you tomorrow."

"Shayla?"

"Yes?"

"This isn't a joke," he admonished.

"I didn't think it was. I was only smiling because…because I knew how hard it was for you to back off," she said.

"Okay, then." He leaned down suddenly and kissed her cheek. "Be careful."

She felt the imprint of his hard, smooth jaw on her skin. "I will," she promised, thinking that nobody else was as dangerous to her, at least not to her peace of mind. All thought of the stalker was erased. She closed the door on him and went into her room, wondering how long he would stand out there.

There was a message on his voice mail from his partner when Michael returned to his room.

"Two fingerprints from the letter matched with two from the crime scene," Darren's recorded voice announced with satisfaction. The police are going to run them, and so are the FBI."

Michael called him. "What do we know?"

"We've got a name—Peter Johnson. But he doesn't have much of a record," Darren said. "Domestic violence charge. He beat up his girlfriend. He was out of jail in one night."

"She didn't press charges?" Michael asked.

"She would have, apparently, but he never showed up for his court date. There was a warrant out for him, but he surrendered eventually. She moved out of the district as soon as she got out of the hospital. The charges were dismissed for lack of evidence. She was the only witness, of course."

"Of course. So what's his address?"

"Nothing current. But they're going to send me the photo. I'll drop off a copy to you as soon as I get it."

"Great. But meanwhile, what about getting fingerprints here, see if we can find a match?"

"You know how much that would cost?" Darren said. "And how do we get every man at GoGo Girls to give us his fingerprints?"

"We ask," Michael said.

"And you really think this guy will just agree to let us print him?"

"I know I'll be looking hard at anyone who doesn't."

"Who's going to ink these guys? And where? You want to set up a blotter at the security desk at AAT? And even if we could get everyone's prints, we don't have a lab or access to the police databank or a fingerprint expert to compare them. We can't afford to set all that up. We're not the cops, or even the marines, anymore. We're a private company. You know how complicated it is."

"Maybe your friend at the FBI could—"

"How?" Darren said reasonably. "No one's going to authorize that. The FBI wouldn't be able to use a match against the guy, even if we found one."

"So we get other evidence against him. Once we find him," Michael answered.

"No," Darren said. "We know his name, we know what he looks like. He can't be far. You're going to have to try and spot him. The police can get his fingerprints after we make a citizen's arrest."

From: Michael Grant
To: Darren Collins
Bc: Lita Tolliver
Cc: Marsha James
Subject: Security
Darren,
We've got both women covered, but in order to cover their rooms twenty-four hours a day, I need three more men. I know this will be expensive, but I have a gut feeling that this guy is nearby, and I don't want to take any chances. If he can get into either Camilla or Shayla's rooms, he can leave another little surprise package in minutes. I spoke to the producers of the show, and they're in agreement about the need for this measure. They still want us to use a high degree of discretion, of course—no sunglasses or men in black suits camped out in the hallways. They're afraid it would be caught on the camera. Do you think you can find me the men?
M.

Chapter 21

After weeks of running at the front of the pack, of knowing that he was definitely going to be the last man standing on *Lady's Choice,* and acting as if he was, without a doubt, the best possible match for Camilla Lyons, Jordan Freeman made his one big mistake. He'd managed to avoid most of the minor squabbling that the other contestants occasionally engaged in. He'd never been caught on camera displaying his insecurity or petty jealousy. But on his date with Cami that week, he choked for the first time when he shared his suspicions about Michael and Shayla with Camilla.

"He's got it bad for her," he said ruefully, shaking his head and chuckling at the same time. "I don't know if you talk to Shayla about your dates or not, but I was hanging out with them after the elimination, and if I hadn't been there...I don't know what would have happened between them."

"That's...interesting," Camilla said to him. To Shayla,

later, she made it clear that she hadn't appreciated the news bulletin. "Does he think I'm blind? Or just stupid? It's obvious that Michael is falling for you. Anyone can see it."

"Cami, I don't think—" Shay started to protest.

"Oh, don't start that again," the actress interrupted. "It's as clear as the nose on your face, as my mother used to say, and it doesn't matter how many times you say you're not his type. Maybe he's not running true to type. Maybe he's mistaken you for somebody else. Whatever. Anyway, he wants you, not me, and I'd have to be an idiot to miss the signs. What does Jordan think I am?"

"Jordan doesn't know about Michael's…" She looked over at the cameraman who was filming the conversation and decided it would be better not to say outright that Michael was working undercover, even if it would be edited out later. The stalker was among them, somewhere, and he might not know about Michael's profession. "He doesn't know that Michael has…already been honest with you about his feelings," she said to Cami. "And he has no way of knowing how you feel about him, either. It sounds like he's a little jealous."

"I hate that," Cami said.

"It was bound to happen," Shay said. "You are dating three guys at once—it's only natural for them to feel a little competitive."

"Competitive is fine. It's just that…I've had jealous boyfriends before. It's not great."

"Jordan isn't operating under typical dating conditions. He might not usually be the jealous type, but it's normal for him to be a little worried about why you're keeping Michael around. I think you have to cut him a little slack."

"You and your types. Men aren't types. They're individuals. And they can surprise you." Shay looked at her in surprise. The soap star treated men like meat half the time. Where had that insight come from? "I do really like Jordan."

"But?" Shayla asked.

"But? But nothing. I think I could fall for him. He's a good person, and he looks great, and he really seems to care for me. Plus, he's a lot like me. People told him he would never make a living as a baseball player, but he followed his dream and worked hard at it, and now he does what he loves. I just wish he hadn't said anything about Michael and you. It makes him seem…different from who I thought he was. I mean, Lance, he's a bit insecure, and I would understand if he said something, but he didn't."

"Uh-huh." Shay nodded. Lance probably hadn't said anything because, no matter what Jordan and Cami thought, it wasn't all that obvious that Michael was in love with her. He definitely seemed to like her, and he was pursuing her more actively than he was the soap star, but that didn't mean he was falling in love with her. It might just mean that he thought she was a safer bet than the highly contested star of the show.

"He never talks anyone down. Lance. He never says anything bad about anyone, except himself. He's so…nice."

"Is there something wrong with that?" Shay asked.

"No, of course not," Cami answered, but she didn't sound certain. "He may be a bit low in self-esteem, but he knows who he is, and he doesn't need to put anyone down to make himself feel better. I wish he was more sure of himself, or maybe I wish he trusted me more; but I guess, like you said, it's natural for him to be worried under the circumstances."

Cami had her date with Michael that night, and Shay didn't want to be anywhere near that, so she stayed in her room, hiding from the cameras, the sight of Cami and Michael together, and, she hoped, from the stalker.

The next morning Cami asked Shay to come up to her room for breakfast, and she reluctantly joined the actress for croissants and fresh fruit. She didn't expect Cami, while she was serving her coffee, to lean over and whisper, "I tried to let him down gently."

Shay hoped she didn't mean what she thought she did. Cami couldn't eliminate Michael—he was her bodyguard. She virtually forced the other woman into the bathroom in order to ask her, "What are you talking about?"

"I warned him to be ready at the elimination ceremony. Subtly, of course. But I think he got the message. I didn't want to blindside him. Plus, he may need to make some kind of special arrangements about security, since he won't be around to handle that stuff himself anymore."

"You're eliminating Michael?" Shay asked, stunned.

"Of course. What kind of woman do you think I am? I'm not going to stand in your way."

"You think I want you to reject him?" she said incredulously. "Why?"

"Because it's the right thing to do," Cami answered. "Come on. We can't stay in here all day."

Shay followed her out of the bathroom, saying, "We need to talk privately."

"Look, I was trying to keep it a secret until Sunday, but I can tell you are not going to cooperate, so I think we might as well do this out in the open."

"You shouldn't do it at all," Shay argued.

Cami addressed the cameras directly. "I told her I'm going to reject Michael at the next elimination."

"Cami!"

"Whether you want me to or not, it's the right thing to do," Cami said. "Solidarity, sister. If I have to throw another one back, at least it's for a good cause and to a good woman. I'll feel better knowing he will have you."

"He doesn't *have* me—I'm not a case of the mumps," Shay corrected her. "Cami, I don't think this is a good idea." How was his plan supposed to work if he wasn't there to protect her when the bad guy showed up?

"I beg to differ," Cami replied. "You two need some alone time."

"He can always quit the show."

"You know and I know that he can't do that," the actress said. Shay knew she meant that he couldn't leave because he was her bodyguard, but Cami offered another explanation to the audience. "He's not the type."

"Cami, even if you're right and he is interested in me—"

"If I'm right? If? There's no if about it. He's made it very obvious—the way he looks at you and talks to you and spends every minute hovering around you. What else could he do?"

Shay didn't know how to answer that. She found it incredible that both Cami and Jordan were so convinced that Michael was in love with her. But she couldn't talk the star of *Lady's Choice* into rethinking her decision. Cami held firm.

When Shay went home that afternoon to check on how Dee and her parents were doing, she told her sister about the soap star's crazy plan. For once, however, Dee and Cami were on the same side.

"She's right," Dee said. "He likes you. You can see it when you two are together, you know. I knew it the day you two brought me back here. I'm surprised Camilla was able to see it, but she's not wrong."

"Even if he does like me better than her—"

"Or me," Dee interjected.

"What makes you think he's interested in anything more than a…a playmate?" Shay asked. "Don't forget, he didn't sign up to be on the show because he wanted to get married, like the others. He came because it was his job."

"So you can't date someone unless you want to marry them?" Dee asked sensibly.

"No, of course not," Shay answered, flustered. "We could date. But…but…"

"But what?"

"I mean, don't you think, once all this is over and he's out in the world again, that he'll see that this was a mistake? I'm…he's…we don't fit."

"Why not? You've got a lot in common," Dee said.

"Are you nuts?" Shay asked. "I'm a television producer. I spend my days, and most nights, staring at a computer screen writing memos and making schedules. He…he's an ex-marine, a bodyguard, for God's sake. He shoots guns."

"You're both control freaks," Dee said baldly. "And I suspect he's a workaholic, too. Like you. And you make each other laugh. I've seen you."

"I don't think—" Shay started to argue.

"Stop," Dee commanded. "You think too much." She waited until she caught Shay's eye to continue. "The question isn't what you think, it's how do you feel?"

Shay found she had no answer for that question. At least none that made sense. She didn't know if she could trust Cami or Dee and their perception of Michael, and she was even less willing to trust her own mixed-up feelings about him. She wasn't at all sure if she wanted to find out if her instincts were right or if theirs were. The elimination round was coming up in two days, and she was afraid that when Cami made her choice, she would never see Michael Grant again.

She was also scared to death that her sister, and her new friend, were right about him and that he really was interested in dating her, rather than them. Shay was sure of only one thing: whether he was interested in dating her or not, he could not really be serious about her.

Michael knew his partner was not going to be happy about his elimination from the cast of *Lady's Choice*. But he hadn't expected Darren to be quite so disappointed. "Man, I didn't think she'd do this," he said when Michael called to tell him that Camilla was about to reject him on national television. "She knows you're there to protect her."

"Yup," Michael said. "But I guess that's not as important to her as keeping these other two contestants around. I think she's in love with both of them."

"Damn," his partner exclaimed. "I was hoping you were going to win."

"You're kidding, Darren. You know I wasn't even in the running."

"You were," the other man argued. "She kept you around for a long time before she even knew you were her bodyguard. They were dropping like flies, but she didn't reject you."

"I can't believe you ever thought I was going to win. What would I have done if she had chosen me? I would have had to tell her the truth. And I sure as hell couldn't marry her."

"Why not?" Darren retorted. "She's gorgeous, rich, famous. Think of the publicity. And she's got lots of TV star friends with kids to protect, and houses and cars. She would have brought in tons of business."

"I hate to have to break this to you, Darren, but I'm not planning my love life, or my marriage, around 24/7 Security," Michael said drily. "I just called so we could figure out what kind of alternative arrangements we're going to make, now that I'm not going to be allowed on the set or anywhere near the client."

"We'll think of something," Darren said. "Hey, what about sending you in to the studio as a security guard? I bet no one would recognize you dressed in that uniform...with a pair of shades, maybe. Like Superman when he becomes Clark Kent."

"I don't think so," Michael answered.

"Maybe we'll find Mr. Johnson before Sunday," Darren suggested hopefully.

"Any luck getting a current address?" Michael asked.

"Nah, that case was eight years old. He moved from that address, and no one's seen him since."

"But you're working on it."

"Yes, I'm working on it. I was able to trace him to his next job, on a loading dock. Took his former boss out for drinks and got him to think back. He worked there almost a year, but then he left, and the boss never heard from him again. He didn't have any family or friends that he could remember."

"And the police. The feds?"

"Nothing comes up under Johnson's social security number. That's pretty much as far as they check. They don't have him showing up as dead or working anywhere, according to Uncle Sam. Since there was never a prosecution, their paper trail ends with the police report, and you know they aren't going to take his old boss out for drinks. They lost track of him when he moved out of the apartment he was living in at the time."

"Great. I guess that means I just keep looking around." He said good-bye to Darren and went out for another short prowl around the hotel, as had become his habit ever since he'd received the package containing Peter Johnson's mug shot.

The picture was not very helpful. Like most mug shots, it made the subject look gray and washed out. According to the description that accompanied it, the guy had no distinguishing characteristics. Nothing about this guy stood out. He was six feet tall, about two hundred pounds, dark skinned. At the time it was taken he was twenty-two years old, wore his hair in long, reddish dreds, and his skin was the faded, cardboard color of a man who had been drinking or drugging. Michael doubted many people would recognize the guy from the photo if they saw him today.

He'd shown the picture to Marsha, Lita, and Shayla, and they were all certain that no one connected to GoGo Girls looked anything like him. They wouldn't have hired anyone who looked like that, they insisted. Darren had one of his men show the photo to the hotel's personnel department and to the security guards at the studio, but it hadn't set off any bells. Peter's appearance would be completely altered with a good hair cut, a pair of glasses, and a suit, or even a uniform. It was unlikely that the round-faced, gray-skinned boy in the mug shot bore any resemblance to his thirty-year-old self.

Michael had stared at it for hours by this point, until he was reasonably sure that he would know the guy if he saw him, but he didn't have much time to look. He kept his eyes open in the hotel, in the studio, and on the set, and once or twice he thought he caught a glimpse of someone who might have born a resemblance to their suspect; but on closer examination, it always turned out to be just another ordinary six-foot-tall, dark-skinned man. Joshua and a couple of other men who spent their days watching over Camilla and Shayla had all had similar experiences, and Michael was starting to feel as if Peter Johnson could have been anywhere. They knew he had to be someone inside of the production, but that list extended from the GoGo Girls offices to anyone who'd done any work for AAT for the last two months, and that was not a short roster by any means.

He ended up, as he always did, at the door to Shayla's room. She was with Josh, visiting her sister at her house, so he didn't have to worry about her walking in on him as he let himself in, using the card key he insisted the producers provide him with each day when Shayla moved to her new accommodation. It was probably an unnecessary precaution, but he liked to check each new room assigned to her personally, just to be sure. Whoever had rigged the light switch in Deanna's room was an accomplished electrician. Michael doubted he'd need more than a few minutes to turn one of the many electrical appliances provided by the hotel into an explosive device.

He checked the room methodically, as always, starting with the light fixtures, the radio, the clock, and the television set. When he reached the coffeemaker, he'd gone on autopilot, working by rote as he eased the plug out of the electrical outlet and followed the cord to the body of the small coffee machine. It took a moment, after he saw the electrical tape on the back, for his brain to fully register the fact that someone had been tampering with the appliance.

He called the head of hotel security first, whom he had already established a relationship with, and phrased a request for a room visit to inspect the anomaly; then he called his partner. "Who drove Shayla out to her house?" he asked as soon as Darren answered.

"Bobby," Darren said, picking up the tension in Michael's voice immediately. "Why?"

"Get on to him and tell him to make sure she stays there for a couple of hours. I'm in her hotel room now, and I think someone's rigged her coffee machine."

"Holy shit! She was moved into that room only two hours ago. How did he find out and get in there that quickly?"

"Hotel security is working on that. Darren, I need you to get someone in here who can disarm this thing. Not the cops."

"Are you kidding?" his partner asked. "We've got to call the police. Right now."

"We can't," Michael said, prepared for this argument. "The bomb squad will come marching in here like storm troopers, and we'll lose the only advantage we've got over this guy. He might even disappear."

"Do you know what will happen to us if that thing explodes in someone's face?" Darren protested. "We could go to jail. We could lose the business. We could be *sued.*"

"I don't care," Michael answered.

"You'd better care. This is not your call, Michael. We're not the cops. This is obstruction of justice."

"I know that, Darren, but I can't just let this guy go. We've got a chance to catch him. He doesn't know we've found this, and he's got to be somewhere close, waiting to see it go off. You know the police are just going to make a big mess here and scare him away."

"Michael, we can't. That's a bomb you're looking at. We have to inform the proper authorities."

He pulled out his last card. "Darren, do you want to see this guy get away?"

"You know I don't."

"And you know I'm right. If we call the bomb squad, Peter Johnson is in the wind." Thankfully, there was a knock on the door, forestalling any more debate for the moment. "Hold on, Darren."

"What? Hey!" Michael tuned out the rest of his partner's spluttering objections as he opened the door and found

Edward Fromm, the security chief, standing outside. He told Darren, "I've got hotel security here. I've got to talk to them. I'll call you right back."

"Michael, wait! I'm serious. We have to call the police. You're talking about playing with peoples' lives here." He knew his partner was right, but he hated to give up the first lead they'd had.

"Let me talk to hotel security first. Maybe they have some way to keep it quiet at least. I mean, they don't want the bomb squad running through the lobby, scaring the guests."

"I'm surprised they haven't already called for everyone to leave their rooms. No alarms?"

"Nope," Michael said. "I'll call you in five, ten at the most." He quickly closed the cell phone and ushered the hotel staffers into the room.

Ed was followed by another man Michael didn't know, a young guy in the hotel security uniform of black suit, white shirt, and headphones. His boss was a retired cop and a former master chief in the Navy, whom Michael had bonded with over coffee at four in the morning the night after Deanna's room exploded. It had been a long day and night for both men, and they'd commiserated with each other over how impossible it was to provide security in busy, active buildings like a hotel.

"It's this way, Chief," Michael said.

"I brought the video from the front lobby," he said, handing it to Michael. "It's been slow this morning, and the guards who watch the monitors said they thought only a couple of guys came in through the lobby alone in the last two hours. One was about an hour ago."

Shayla's room, like all the luxury suites, had a VCR below the television, and Michael popped the tape in. As the two men examined the coffee machine minutely but without touching it, Michael fast-forwarded through the tape. "Are you going to have to evacuate?" he asked, his eyes on the screen as a family of four appeared on the monitor, mom and dad struggling to hold on to their carry-on luggage and shepherd their kids through the revolving doors. "If you can just have this checked out without alerting everyone in the hotel, I might be able to set a trap for our guy."

"I don't know," Ed said, shaking his head. "After the last bomb? I don't think we can take any chances."

"But we don't even know for sure that this is a bomb," Michael started to argue with him, slowing the tape down to get a better look at the first lone black male to enter through the revolving door. He had to be a couple of inches under six feet, though, and Michael sped through the next half hour of videotape quickly. As he watched white guests, various bellboys, and other hotel staff, quickstep across the screen, entering and departing from the hotel lobby through the revolving door, Ed replied, "Mike, I'd better call the bomb squad. Just in case this is an incendiary."

Michael spotted the second man Ed's guys had mentioned, and put the tape on pause. "My God," he said. "I know him. That's one of the technicians from the show. John something."

"You know him?" Ed asked.

"He was in an accident on the set a few weeks ago. He was fixing an electrical cord on a ladder, and…he said it sparked. He nearly fell twenty feet." Michael tried to remember what the man had looked like, comparing it mentally to the image he had stored in his head of Peter Johnson, but he couldn't come up with a clear memory of the man's face. He hadn't really noticed what the guy looked like at the time; he'd been too busy working damage control. Since then, if Michael had even seen him, he didn't remember it. He was one of the nameless, faceless crew who worked behind the scenes on the television set. Nothing stood out about him. As he had that thought, Michael became convinced that he'd stumbled onto the right man.

"I think I've got him. Is there any way you can sit on this thing for a little while?" he asked as he dialed Darren's number on his cell phone.

"I don't know," the security chief replied nervously.

Darren picked up his phone on the second ring, already talking: "If you don't call the cops, I'm going to," he said.

Ed's voice in his other ear kept Michael from answering his partner right away. "What if this thing goes off before they get here?"

"You do what you've got to do," Michael told him. "Meanwhile, in case he's still here in the hotel, can you have your staff check the public areas? I doubt that he'd hang around, especially since Shayla isn't supposed to be back here for a while, and he has no reason to think she'll use that machine right now, but you never know with these crazies. You've got a picture of him now." Darren was still squawking in his ear about being responsible and how it was their duty to inform the authorities in a situation like this as he started for the door. "Partner, I think hotel security's going to take care of that."

"You think, or you know?" Darren asked.

Michael ignored the question. "Look, get an address on that guy John who had the accident on the set. He was here in the hotel about an hour ago, and I think he might be our stalker."

That seemed to divert Darren's attention from the need to call the cops. "What are you talking about? Who's this guy? Why do you think he's the one who—"

"Just look it up, Darren, and call me back," Michael said, hanging up and finding GoGo Girls Productions' number on his cell. He pressed a button and got the voice mail directory, asking him to dial an extension directly by hitting the star key.

He was already walking out of the hotel before he'd gotten through to Marsha James. "It's Michael. I need to know if one of the technicians is at work," he told her when she answered the phone. "And I don't want him to know I'm looking for him."

"I guess paging him is out of the question, then," she said. "Which one is it? Maybe I can call the director. I think he's on the set."

"I don't remember his last name. First is John. He was the guy involved in that accident, remember? He had to go to the hospital."

"Jonathan, right. I'll call the director—he's on the set. Hold on." He ran to his rental car as he waited for her to get back on the phone. "Yes, he's here, Michael. Jonathan. He's on the set."

"Okay, great. I'll be there in twenty minutes," he said, climbing into the car.

He was about to hang up on her when she asked, "What's this about?"

"I can't talk now," he said. "I'll explain when I see you."

"Is there anything I can do?"

"No!" he nearly yelled. "No," he said more calmly. "Just sit tight. I'll be there soon."

While Michael drove to the studio, Darren sent two men out to the apartment that Jonathan had listed as his place of residence on his W-2 form. They found, as Michael had expected, the evidence necessary for him to make a citizen's arrest. He thought there was enough there for the man to be charged with both stalking and arson. He'd been taking pictures of Camilla, obviously without her knowledge, and he had also kept thorough records of both her schedule and

Dee's, and, more recently, of Shayla's comings and goings. There were also various electrical devices, which Michael hoped would connect him with both bombs.

Apprehending him was no problem. Johnson was taken completely by surprise when Michael arrived unexpectedly at the studio and explained that he was performing a citizen's arrest. He never even had to draw his gun. The sight of the nine millimeter in its holster was enough to discourage Johnson from making any attempt to escape. He was also smart enough to keep quiet on the way to the police station, where Michael turned him over to the custody of the sergeant on duty at the front desk. A call to the detective in charge of the Deanna Jones case was enough to get the paperwork going and get Peter Johnson charged officially.

Rather than talking to Shayla, Michael spoke to Frank Tennison, who was well versed in the workings of the system and could explain what would happen to his daughter even more thoroughly than Michael could. He would have spoken to her himself, but he had to rush from meeting Darren and arranging for the release of the guys guarding Camilla and Shayla to meeting with Marsha and Lita and give them his report.

He felt a little strange about seeing Shayla at the moment, now that he was officially done with his assignment for GoGo Girls but still nominally a contestant on the program. He asked Lita and Marsha if he could just gracefully withdraw from *Lady's Choice*, but they—like everyone else at this point—knew that Camilla was going to reject him at the next elimination, and they asked him if he could just hold out, so they wouldn't have to try to explain his leaving the show.

"We'd need you to do at least one more interview," they said. "No matter what spin we put on your leaving, but this way, all you have to do is show up for the ceremony and let

Camilla Lyons do her thing. It will be so simple then to interview you on your way back to the hotel to pack, and we won't have to explain anything about your appearance on the show."

Michael thought there was a good chance this story would leak out somehow, but he was more than willing to try to avoid generating any extra publicity. He still hoped to continue doing undercover work after this assignment on *Lady's Choice* was over, and that required keeping as low a profile as possible, so he agreed to stay on as a contestant on the show with one proviso: the producers had to agree to sign an agreement not to release to the media any of the details of his story or to discuss the fact that he was a professional bodyguard. If the press found out about what he'd done, they could speculate all they wanted, but at least this way, GoGo Girls wouldn't be able to exploit the job he had done for them. It was one less worry. Unfortunately, it didn't help with the problem that had suddenly assumed prominence in his mind. How was he going to persuade Shayla to continue letting him see her?

Memo
FROM THE DESK OF LITA TOLLIVER
TO: Michael Grant
Mike,
As you know, the rules of the contest forbid unauthorized dating between contestants, and after an elimination, there is not supposed to be any more contact with the star of the show. But we did not include a similar provision in the contract regarding Shayla, so legally we can't stop you two from going wherever you want and doing whatever you want. However, Marsha and I are quite worried about your being seen together, and we would appreciate it if you would try to be very discreet about where you go together.
Lita

Chapter 22

At the elimination on Sunday night, Camilla rejected Michael as promised. Shayla had been dreading this moment, but he took it very well. He was positively beaming as he thanked Camilla and turned to Shay, which should have been her first clue that something very strange was about to happen. However, she just stood there, just off camera, awaiting her cue to come forward and join Camilla in the center of the stage, which was what she was supposed to do after the rejected suitor exited. Michael didn't walk away. Everyone watched and waited as he walked toward her and tugged her gently forward in front of the cameras.

"Michael?" she breathed, smiling nervously in the direction of the steady red light that shone from beneath the lens of the Opticam, signifying that the camera was rolling. "What are you doing?" she asked out the side of her mouth.

"One second," he answered as he directed her into position,

not on her mark beside Camilla, but in the center of the stage. Then he went down on one knee in front of her. Shayla gasped, and she didn't think she was the only one. "Shayla," he said seriously. "Will you marry me?"

She stared down at him gazing up at her; his sincerity was no longer a question in her mind. No one would do something this embarrassing if they didn't mean it. "But…" she spluttered, "I…I don't know what to say."

He grinned. "Say yes then," he suggested.

"I…I can't," she stuttered. "I barely know you. Get up," she urged.

He stood, looking disappointed but not surprised. "You do know me," he said.

"Not very well," she said. "I never would have thought you'd be the type to do something like this."

She heard Camilla's jaw snap shut behind her and realized she'd said the word *type* again. She would have said something, apologized, but her eyes were caught and held by his as he took her hand.

"Shayla, you can trust me. I promise."

"Michael, I like you. Really. But I can't give you an answer now. I can't marry a man I met less than two months ago. I'm sorry, but I have no idea what you're like away from all this. And you don't know me, either. This isn't my dress, or my shoes, or my make-up. This isn't really me."

"I know that," he said. "As long as you're willing to give me the chance to get to know you, I will settle for that."

There was a murmur from the people around them, a collective sigh of relief and approving whispers. "I'd like that, I guess," Shayla said, unable to say no to him under the circumstances and not unwilling to give his proposal a shot. She liked him. She was intrigued by him, especially now. She might as well discover whether she could love him.

"Camilla," he said, looking over Shay's shoulder at the star of the show, who stood a couple of feet behind her. "I'm going to borrow your friend here for a little while, okay?"

"Sure," Cami agreed. To Shay's ears, it sounded like a purr of satisfaction. "Take her. Talk some sense into her."

As they walked off the set, Shay thought she heard him murmur, "She's got too much sense already." But when she asked him what he said, he just shrugged and walked faster, out to the limousine that was waiting to take him back to the hotel. After he'd helped her into the car and climbed in, he closed the window between the driver's seat and the passenger area.

"I can't believe you just did that," she started. "On national television—"

He cut her off. "I didn't have a choice. I couldn't just walk out of your life, and I didn't know any other way to get you to listen to me."

"So this was just your way of making sure I couldn't say no to you?" she asked, offended.

"You can say no or whatever you want. I couldn't take the chance that I would never get to see you again. I needed to be able to keep on dating you at least."

"You asked me to marry you so we could keep on dating?" she asked, marveling at the deviousness of his plan and a little impressed by his ingenuity.

"I didn't think you'd agree to marry me, no," he admitted.

"That's…that's insane," Shay said. "You're out of your mind."

"But I wouldn't have minded if you said yes," he continued. "I'm falling in love with you, Shayla, and I need to be able to see you so I could get you to believe me, finally."

"You know what I think? I think you spent too much time with the boys," she stated. "You've started to believe the hype."

"I think that's enough talking for now," he said. "If you don't mind?" And he pulled her to him and kissed her, long and deep and hard.

His mouth and his body, felt warm and hard and familiar, and she kissed him back.

"Okay?" he asked, when he finally released her.

"Uh, sure," she answered when she managed to catch her breath. So he kissed her again, pulling her across his body, almost onto his lap, as his hands roamed from her waist to her hips and across her back. He explored the contours of her body through the silk of her designer dress, and Shay was encouraged to slip her hands under his tux, and let them wander up across his shirt to his chest.

He cupped the back of her head with one hand and his fingers tangled in her hair, pulling her head gently back until her throat was exposed to his warm, hungry mouth.

A tiny sound escaped her throat as he nuzzled the sensitive spot behind her ear, and his teeth nipped at her chin. "Michael," she murmured into his ear, and felt him shiver. "You have to pack." They had reached the hotel, and he slowly withdrew from her, setting her back up straight on her side of the seat, his breathing ragged as if he had just run a race. It took her a minute before her heart rate settled down, too.

"So when am I going to see you again?" he asked.

"I don't know. I'll have to talk to my bosses," she answered. "I don't think we have any rules for this."

"There aren't any," he said. "We're going to have to make them up as we go along. And I'm not letting those two witc—" He cleared his throat. "I'm not letting those women decide for us. I'm not on the show anymore, or the payroll, so I'm officially outside of their jurisdiction now. This is our relationship, and *we* are the only ones who get to make the rules."

"Fine," Shay said. "But I still work for GoGo Girls, and I'm still on *Lady's Choice,* so I don't think I can afford to completely ignore Marsha and Lita. I will talk to them tomorrow."

"I can't believe this," he said. "I feel like I'm back in high school. We're two mature, single, intelligent people, at the mercy of two of the most unlikely matchmakers in the world, not to mention the entire TV-viewing nation."

"And don't forget my parents," she reminded him. "And Dee."

"Great," Michael said. "I can't wait to hear her opinion on this."

"Don't worry," she reassured him. "She likes you."

"Somehow I don't think that's the recommendation you're looking for," he replied.

As the day of the final elimination grew closer, Camilla entered a dating frenzy with Lance and Jordan. The men were just as eager to spend time together as she was, so every day and night was a whirlwind of intimate lunch dates, cocktails, dinner dates, and every other kind of rendezvous they could come up with. The producers were happy to help. They said Cami's indecision made her very relatable.

The two men she was dating were so different from each other that it seemed odd, to Shay, that she would be torn between them. But, the actress confessed, she just couldn't make up her mind.

"I really like both of them. I can imagine myself back in the real world with both of them. I don't want to give either man up."

"I'm afraid you're going to have to choose" was all Shay could offer.

"I know, I know. I can't believe I've gotten myself into this," Camilla moaned. "How did this happen?"

Shay was wondering the same thing about her own love life. She had fallen for Michael Grant, and he appeared to be equally attracted to her, but she still didn't fully trust him or her own feelings. Unlike Cami, she didn't feel that spending every spare minute she had with the man was going to solve her problem. She probably would have put him off until after the show was wrapped up, if he'd let her. But he was persistent, and she couldn't keep saying no, especially since she was deeply in like, or perhaps in lust, with her bodyguard. But every dinner they shared felt a little strange to her after two months of the dating mania on *Lady's Choice*. She was constantly reminded of how they met and of how she had felt about him before she discovered he wasn't really a contestant on the program—less than a month ago.

He had always intrigued her, and his kisses had been nice, but…he was one of the boys. When he had kissed her, he had done it in secret, while he had declared in front of God and everyone that he was looking for a wife in Camilla Lyons. Then he had dated her sister. She knew now that it had all just been part of an assignment, but she had been convinced then, and it had not been all that long ago. Shay wasn't able to shake the belief that Cami or Dee would be a more suitable match for him than she was, despite the fact that the soap star wasn't interested, and her sister and Leon were a couple these days.

Shay didn't know where these feelings came from. She had had her share of failed romances, and her first boyfriend had been more interested in Dee than in her once he met her famous older sister, but she had never been particularly insecure about her own appeal before this. Maybe it was just the memory of the way it made her feel when she thought Michael might actually fall for her sister that scared her, but as long as she felt so confused about him and her feelings, she couldn't really commit to a relationship with him. She just didn't feel they had any future together, no matter what he said.

On Friday night she made her final appearance on *Lady's Choice* and then went out with him afterward to celebrate. Michael had been even more insistent than usual that they had to spend the evening together. "To commemorate your release from your bosses' clutches," he said. She suspected he had an ulterior motive, but she couldn't figure out what it could be until they were in his car on their way to dinner.

"Now neither of us is on that damn television program. We're both free to forget all about it," he said. "A sad, somewhat embarrassing, interlude in our past from which we can only be grateful we escaped unmarried."

She laughed. "You sound like you were afraid they were going to force you to actually tie the knot."

"That was the point of the whole program," he said.

"Yeah, but neither one of us was ever going to marry anyone," Shay pointed out.

"That's what I've been saying all along," Michael replied. "You're the one who keeps acting as if appearing on *Lady's Choice* meant something. It might be called a reality show, but it had nothing to do with reality."

"Okay, okay," she conceded. "Maybe I did get sucked in. A little. But so did you."

"Never," he protested.

"What about when you dated my sister?" she asked. "You seemed pretty eager to make that connection."

"Because she's *your* sister," he said in explication.

"Oh," Shay said, finally starting to understand.

"You didn't think I was really interested in Deanna, did you? I mean, I thought I had made it pretty clear that I was attracted to you by the time she came along. I only wanted to go out with her because you two were close. I figured she could put in a good word for me."

"I didn't think of that," Shay said thoughtfully. In fact, it had never occurred to her that he might date Deanna in order to get closer to her.

"I've said it before, and I'll say it again. For an intelligent, educated woman, you're not always too quick on the uptake."

"Sorry," she said. "I am a little bit backward when it comes to relationships."

"So is that what we've got here?" he asked. "A relationship?"

"I guess you could call it that," she answered.

"Good." They had reached the restaurant, and he pulled into a parking space and turned the car off. When she reached for the release button for her seat belt, he stopped her and leaned over to kiss her instead. She curled her hand around the back of his neck and kissed him back, her tongue darting into his mouth to flick the now-familiar toothpaste-and-chocolate taste of him on his teeth. He was a secret snacker, and a chocoholic, and she thought those were the cutest weaknesses that a big, strong bodyguard could have. "Do you, by any chance, sleep with a teddy bear?" she asked against his mouth. He froze. She'd only been joking, but it seemed she'd hit on another little foible.

"A moose," he said, burying his face in her neck, where she could feel the huh, huh, huh of his embarrassed laughter rather than hear it. "Boris."

She giggled, and he twisted his head to cover her lips with his own again, scraping the soft flesh of her chin with his not-so-soft razor stubble. He'd always been clean shaven on *Lady's Choice,* because, he said when she mentioned it, he had had time to shave two or three times a day. In real life, he only shaved in the morning. She had grimaced at him, but honestly she loved the feel of his stubble against her cheek.

His tongue tangled with hers, and his breath mingled with hers, and his mouth slanted over hers, and Shay basked in the warmth that spread from him to her and over her whole body. He was a great kisser. "We're going to lose our reservation," he warned.

"We'd better stop, then," she replied. "I'm hungry. I skipped lunch today." She had been nervous about filming her final scene as Camilla's rival. Dan Green had, of course, asked her if she was still getting to know Michael Grant. She'd told him yes, of course, and so he'd asked how it was going.

"It's going fine, Dan," she answered, smiling at the camera as nonchalantly as possible. "Just fine." And then she tried to look mysterious and self-confident, rather than embarrassed and confused as he pumped her for more information about the relationship.

"I'm hungry, too," Michael growled as he pulled himself away from her. "But my stomach is not the part of my body that is clamoring for attention right this minute."

After dinner he drove her back to the hotel and walked with her up to her room. They'd spent several hours, she thought, kissing in front of that door. But he hadn't come inside before tonight. "Not while you're on the show," he had said. "I've developed a phobia about hidden cameras."

Tonight, as usual, she turned to him and asked if he wanted to come in and have coffee. He stood staring down at her for a moment while she waited for him to say no, and then he nodded once.

"You would?" she asked for confirmation.

"Yes," he said. "I would. But I'm checking for those cameras."

He took the card key from her and entered the room first, which she gathered was a habit of his, as was his quick scan of the room before stepping forward to let her follow him in. The door had barely swung shut behind her when he swept her into his arms in a bear hug that nearly took her breath away. "I'm so glad that madness is finally over," he said.

"*Lady's Choice?* It's not over yet. We have the final elimination round tomorrow and editing and a follow-up show to shoot with Camilla and the man of her choice. Lita and Marsha were hinting today that they wanted to get an interview with the two of us for that, too."

"I hope you told them they could forget that idea."

"Of course," Shay answered. She led the way farther into her room, laying her purse and card key on the dresser and wondering if she should mention that she'd had the coffee-maker removed. She stood awkwardly, wondering whether he was planning to get around to touching her any time soon while he wandered about the room, apparently, as he had promised, checking for hidden cameras.

"The room's clean," he said, smiling at her as he walked back toward her. He reached out to cup her chin with his hand. "Alone at last," he quipped. He bent his head, and she raised her lips to meet his, but he didn't kiss her on the mouth. His lips feathered over her forehead, eyelids, the bridge of her nose, her cheekbones, and then slid down to the hollow beneath her ear. He nipped her earlobe, and she jumped.

"Sorry," he said.

"It didn't hurt," Shay assured him, wrapping her hands around his waist and pulling him as close as she could. From here, the only part of him she could reach was his shoulder, so she kissed that through his shirt.

"Can we get rid of this?" she asked, starting—even before he nodded—to undo the buttons, then, pushing the cotton oxford out of the way, so she could repeat the kiss on his bare skin. He was hard and smooth and—despite the rate of growth of his facial hair—not very downy, except for a little mat of curls that formed a vee across his pecs, pointing downward. She ran her fingernails across the soft dark patch, contrasting it with the smooth skin beneath her other hand as he eased her shirt off of her shoulders and let it fall atop his on the floor at their feet.

They both took their time, familiarizing themselves with the unfamiliar landscape of chest, shoulders, back, and stomach, touching and tasting each other as they sidled toward the inviting expanse of the bed. He laid her down, and the rest of their clothes followed in the way of their tops as they continued their exploration of each other's bodies, from fingertips to toes. He took a long time measuring the small of her back with his hands and the curves beneath, his eyes closed as if he was a blind man trying to learn that part of her anatomy without having the use of his eyes. She found the column of his neck just as fascinating, and she nuzzled it, licked it, and then nipped it when he, having found his way from the back of her body to her front, flicked the tip of her breast with his fingernail.

"We're really going to do this," Michael said, his eyes gleaming.

"Yup," Shay answered. "But I've got to do something in the bathroom, and you need to take care of your end, too."

"Of course." He smiled lazily down at her, and she slid off the bed and grabbed her purse on the way into the bathroom. Not that she'd been anticipating this, exactly, but she always tried to be prepared for every eventuality. She hurried into the bathroom, but on her return, wrapped in a towel, she took her time, admiring the sight of him all long, lean muscle under taut golden brown skin. He, too, let his eyes travel over her in a long slow perusal that made her feel as warm as if his hands were on her.

"Enough foreplay, woman," he said huskily. "Get back in bed."

"There's no such thing as enough," she answered, her voice containing the same rasp in her throat as she shucked the towel and stretched out next to him, against him, and ran her hand down his arm to his thigh.

He sighed happily. "We'll see if you still think that after a couple of days." He chuckled at her look of astonishment.

"I was thinking a couple of hours," she confessed.

"So there is a limit, then?" he asked. "To how long you're going to drive me crazy?"

"Who's driving who crazy?" she wanted to know as he mimicked the caress, and then let his fingers continue to roam, finding her most sensitive spots and lingering there until she was gasping at the sensations that spread through her body.

They came together finally, well within her two-hour minimum, and then he tested that limit, again and again, until they finally fell asleep in each other's arms.

Just as she was drifting off, he whispered, "I dare you to say you don't know me now."

In the morning they both woke late and had to rush to shower, dress and, in his case, get home to change, and so they didn't have much time to talk. But as he kissed her good-bye, he asked, "How about we do this again tonight?"

"I move back to my place tonight," she answered regretfully. "Of all the rooms I've stayed in, in this hotel, I think I like this one best," she said.

"So how about my place?" he asked.

"It will be my first night back at home," Shay said. "I think I should spend it with my family."

"Fine," he said. "Got space for an extra place at the dinner table?"

"I never would have pegged you as the clingy type," she teased.

"I think we've established that you're not that good at pegging my *type* at all," he countered.

At dinner that night he told her parents about how she'd turned down his marriage proposal without the slightest sign of embarrassment. Shay was mortified.

"He didn't mean it," she told them in her own defense. "He was trying to manipulate me."

"That's an unusual approach," her dad commented. "Most guys try to avoid mentioning marriage when they're trying to get a woman into bed."

"Dad!" Shay cried, laughing. "He wasn't trying to get me *into bed*—he wanted to date."

"Well, it seems to have worked," her mother said.

"I can be very persuasive," Michael said, twirling an imaginary mustache. "When I want to be."

"A lot of trouble to go to just to get a date," her father pointed out.

"He got his way; that's all he cares about," Shay taunted him.

"I hate to have to tell you this," Dee chimed in, "but that's all anyone cares about, Shay."

"That's a very cynical attitude," Leon said. "True, but cynical."

"That's reality," Dee said. "Not to be confused with reality television, which is pure fantasy."

"Shay's wrong, anyway," Michael said. "And so are you, Dee. I don't know about everyone else, but getting my way is not the only thing I cared about."

"Oh, really?" Mom asked.

"No. I really did want to marry your daughter."

"No, you didn't," Shay retorted.

"Yes, I did, I think."

"Ah, but now you have doubts," Dee teased.

"No, now I'm sure. Unfortunately, Shay still has doubts. But I'm working on it."

"Good for you," her father said.

"May I talk to you privately?" Shay requested. When he looked at her curiously, she nodded toward the front door. "Come outside."

"Uh-oh," Leon joked. "You're in trouble now, big guy."

She led the way out of the house and then spun and confronted him. "Michael, you've got to stop doing this."

"What, proposing to you? I can't. Not until you say yes."

"Was that supposed to be a proposal, because that wasn't what it felt like," Shay complained, frustrated. "Forget it, I knew this would never work."

"Why not?" he asked.

"You asked me to marry you on TV!" she yelled.

"It wasn't like I asked you on the six-o'clock news," he said. "It was *Lady's Choice.* The whole point of the show was for someone to ask someone else to marry them."

"Camilla Lyons. She's a soap opera star. Not me."

"So now we're not on TV, and I'm asking you again. Marry me."

He was serious. Suddenly Shay's anger left her. "Michael, I can't marry you. We've only known each other a couple of months, and most of that time you were pretending to be somebody else."

"When are you going to stop using that as an excuse? I'm sorry I had to lie to you, but it was my job. I'm sorry I dated Camilla Lyons and your big sister, but again, it was just work.

I was never interested in either of them, and I didn't want to lie to you."

"I'm not using anything as an excuse. I don't want to marry you because I don't think we're right for each other. We don't fit."

"I think we fit very well," he said suggestively.

"I didn't mean that," she retorted.

"So you'll sleep with me, but you won't marry me?" he asked.

"Marriage is permanent, Michael."

"And the way I feel about you isn't going to change. I love you, Shayla, and I want to marry you. How can I prove it to you?"

"You can wait," she said. "You're just going to have to wait."

"I can do that," he told her. "I'm in no hurry at all."

Epilogue

Both Lance and Jordan were planning to propose to Camilla at the final round of eliminations, and everybody knew it, including the woman herself. She was pacing around in her room like a caged animal when Shay stopped by for her daily visit.

Shayla could relate to the other woman's dilemma after Michael's unexpected marriage proposal the previous night; but Cami had had a lot of time to prepare for this, and Shay suspected, deep down, the actress knew which man she wanted.

"I can't believe I have to decide between them," Cami said as she had so often before.

"They're both great guys, Cami. Maybe you should just flip a coin," Shay suggested, trying to lighten the moment.

"Shay, this is serious," the other woman moaned. "Jordan's expecting me to say yes, and Lance is hoping I will, too. I can't accept both of them."

"No, you really can't," Shay agreed, stating the obvious.

Roberta Gayle

"So what am I supposed to do?"

"You're the only one who can make that decision, Cami. I can't even advise you on this. This is marriage you're talking about. It's permanent." It was ironic that she was saying the same thing to Cami in almost exactly the same words she'd used with Michael the night before, but for the opposite reason. He was absolutely sure he wanted to marry her, and Cami didn't seem to be sure of anything. Which suddenly seemed to be the answer to Shay's question. Michael was absolutely sure that they belonged together. He loved her, and she loved him, and it didn't matter how it happened. They had found each other.

"It's not that simple," the actress replied. "I love Lance and Jordan. They're both so amazing. I don't want to hurt anyone. I didn't expect this. I didn't really think I would fall in love on this show, and I definitely didn't think anyone would fall in love with me."

Shay knew exactly how she felt. She had never signed on to star on the show, but she and the soap opera star were in the same basic position. Neither of them believed that love, real love, was something they would find on a television show. The only difference was, Cami thought that she had while Shay still didn't believe in it.

At the elimination that night, Jordan spoke first while Lance waited out in the limousine in the parking lot for his turn. "Camilla, I love you," he began. "I believe you love me, too. And I think we were brought together here because we were meant to fall in love." At about that point, Shay believed, he forgot about the cameras, and the lights, and the sets, and his prepared speech. He continued, "I never really believed in fate, but now I do, because I found you. I never thought I would find anyone who was so perfect for me, who thought the same way I did, and felt the same way I did, and who loved me for myself. And I think the reason we're so right for each other is mainly because we both thought we would never find someone who loved us just for ourselves, not for some image we have in our head of the other person. I know you so well. I know how you feel about things, and I love to make you laugh and to talk to you and to look at you. I love everything about you. Camilla, will you marry me?"

She was crying, silently and beautifully, and Shay couldn't help thinking that at that moment, Lita and Marsha couldn't have found a more relatable star, because she felt for her. She recognized her sorrow. Shay knew, a split second before she said it, that Cami was about to say no.

"Jordan, I do care about you, but I can't marry you. I'm in love with someone else. You are a great guy, and some lucky woman is going to get the perfect man when she finds you. I'm sorry."

The baseball player was clearly stunned. He'd been expecting a different answer, and he stood there, stock-still, as her words sank in. Then he shook his head as if to clear it and looked into her eyes again. What he saw there finally convinced him that he really had been rejected.

"Well, I—" He cleared his throat. "I wish you all the happiness in the world," he said in a monotone. "Lance…Lance is great. If you had to choose someone else, I'm glad…" His voice cracked on the word *glad,* but he recovered himself quickly and continued. "He's such a nice guy."

He was escorted off the stage, and Lance was brought in through another door so that he would not know the result of the first proposal. Lita and Marsha had set up the ceremony in this way in order to drag out the tension as much as possible. They wanted to create and maintain the suspense for the show's climax.

Roberta Gayle

Lance's proposal was shorter but no less eloquent than Jordan's had been. "I love you, Camilla. I love your heart, and your mind, and your soul. Will you marry me? I promise I will always make you happy."

She hesitated for a moment and then smiled, and he knew what her answer was. "Yes," she said softly. Then louder, "Yes, I will."

While she and Lance were hugging and kissing, and while Dan was congratulating them, Shay went up to her office, dialing Michael's cell phone number as she walked.

He picked up on the second ring. "Hi, honey," he said. "This is a nice surprise. I didn't think I was going to hear from you until tomorrow."

"Hi," Shay said. "I had something I wanted to tell you, and it couldn't wait."